BLACK

IS

THE

NIGHT

ALSO AVAILABLE FROM TITAN BOOKS

BLACK

IS

THE

NIGHT

STORIES INSPIRED BY CORNELL WOOLRICH

edited by

MAXIM JAKUBOWSKI

TITAN BOOKS

BLACK IS THE NIGHT
Print edition ISBN: 9781789099997
E-book edition ISBN: 9781803360010

Published by Titan Books
A division of Titan Publishing Group Ltd 144 Southwark St, London SE1 0UP
www.titanbooks.com

First edition: October 2022
10 9 8 7 6 5 4 3 2 1

This is a work of fiction. All of the characters, organizations, and events portrayed in this novel are either products of the author's imagination or are used fictitiously. Any resemblance to actual persons, living or dead (except for satirical purposes), is entirely coincidental.

A CIP catalogue record for this title is available from the British Library.

Printed and bound in Great Britain by CPI Group (UK) Ltd, Croydon, CR0 4YY.

CONTENTS

INTRODUCTION
MAXIM JAKUBOWSKI

As an inveterate film aficionado, I had seen and thoroughly enjoyed a number of movies based on novels and short stories by the noir American writer Cornell Woolrich (1903–1968) long before I actually read any of them. But already they 'spoke' to me, full of Everyman characters racing against time, caught in the webs of fate and injustice, populated with seductive femmes fatales worth losing your heart to, peppered with nail-biting suspense, set against the background of nameless cities and hotel room windows shrouded in night and illuminated by the shimmering light of countless shady bars and dives.

Woolrich, who also wrote as George Hopley and William Irish, had a talent for turning melancholy tales of deceit and murder into something more, which is why the movies took him to heart – from the Golden Age of noir all the way to the French New Wave and later exponents.

He inspired Hitchcock's *Rear Window*, François Truffaut's *The Bride Wore Black* and *Mississippi Mermaid* (later remade in the USA as *Original Sin*), *The Leopard Man*, *Deadline at Dawn*, *Night Has a Thousand Eyes*, *If I Should Die Before I Wake*, *Phantom Lady*, *I Married a Shadow*, *I'm Dangerous Tonight*, Fassbinder's *Martha* and well over fifty further adaptations.

It was with this in mind that, in the mid 1980s when I launched my Black Box Thriller line of hardboiled classic reprints, that I inevitably turned to his books. It felt like being struck by lightning how much more powerful Woolrich's work was on the page than the way it had been diluted, however well produced, on the silver screen. He was not just a pulp writer but a poet whose sensibility still chimed strongly with the

1

modern world (and my own literary obsessions) and a storyteller with no equal even when he was churning out stories for magazines like a one-man writing factory. To this day, whenever I need reminding how powerful a mere short story can be, I always go back to reading Woolrich, whom I would place on a literary pedestal with mainstream masters of the short form like Katherine Mansfield, Chekhov, Isaac Bashevis Singer or Joseph Conrad; that is how much I rate him.

I was able to reissue four of his novels, a collection of stories and some individual tales in anthologies I edited during the course of my publishing career, and would have done more had the rights situation proven easier. Woolrich died a miserable death, almost straight out of one of his own tales, with no living relative, having during his writing life assigned rights in perpetuity to his work to an assortment of defunct magazines, Hollywood producers and publishers, complicated by the fact that, at a low point and fighting deadlines, he rejigged many of his stories under different titles and sold them illegally again to any taker! Right now much of his work is still controlled by a major bank that runs the estate without much knowledge of the literary sensibilities involved. His fascinating life has been the object of a serious biography by Francis M. Nevins Jr, *First You Dream, Then You Die*, which at times reads like a story Woolrich might have written.

But his shadow still looms mightily across much of today's varied territories of noir fiction. When I had the idea of putting together this tribute anthology of brand new stories either inspired by or in homage to Woolrich, I was amazed by the groundswell of interest from writers across not just the spectrum of mystery fiction but also in other genres and the mainstream, with authors, beyond the usual suspects, I would have never guessed at confessing to his influence and importance in their life. I was saddened to be unable to take up all the offers of those authors who wished to contribute to this volume but gladdened by their sincere interest.

As it is, we have a cornucopia of fantastic stories by award-winning authors old and new. Edgar, Anthony, Dagger winners and more; contributors from the USA, the UK, Canada, Israel, Ireland and Portugal, who have all managed to summon the phantom of Cornell Woolrich back to life in such varied ways, which I am confident the reader and that hidden mass of Woolrich fans out there throughout the world will greatly appreciate.

I would finally like to thank George Sandison, Nick Landau and Vivian Cheung at Titan Books who enthusiastically backed the project and a special nod to contributor Ana Teresa Pereira, not just one of Portugal's most award-laden writers, but also in all probability the world's number one Cornell Woolrich (and classic Hollywood movies) fan who, from her lair in Madeira, inspired me to assemble this volume.

MJ

WHY CORNELL WOOLRICH MATTERS

NEIL GAIMAN

I didn't know who Cornell Woolrich was. I picked up the book, a battered fifth-hand American paperback of *Night Has A Thousand Eyes* because I had liked the song of that name when I heard it on a Carpenters' album when I was a boy. I was in my early twenties, and I was about to fall in love. I opened the book, and I read:

Every night he walked along the river, going home. Every night, about one. You do that when you're young; walk along beside the river, looking at the water, looking at the stars. Sometimes you do that even when you're a detective, and strictly speaking, have nothing to do with stars.

Openings are hard, but that one was perfect. It reached out and took you by the hand, and told you that you were going on a journey, and that the person leading you knew what they were doing.

It was the prose as much as the plot, and the atmosphere Woolrich created, that caught me as I read: a haunting inevitability, in which fate and the fragility of life were held up for examination before ending up in the darkness. The feeling that the people in the story were trapped in it, the hope that the author cared for them as much as we did and would see them, perhaps, safely all the way to the end. The end of the book was in equal measure doomed and elegiac, and delivered on all of its promises.

I was hooked, and fascinated. It was hard to find more Woolrich to read, then. He was out of print, and I wasn't sure where to look. Soon enough I found a volume of Woolrich short stories and watched him conjure magic in tiny spaces. I understood immediately why Hitchcock would have appreciated his work, just as I loved that Hitchcock had taken the twist ending of the story he turned into *Rear Window* (our narrator was *in a wheelchair!*) and let it become the foundation that the story was built upon. And just like that, as my twenties came to an end, Woolrich came back into print. There was even a biography.

In my imagination Cornell Woolrich had been a huge bear of a man, probably bearded and brooding. It was only when I read the biography that I learned that he was slight and pale, and that life had not treated him kindly, neither in love nor in health, that he had ended his days in (appropriately enough) a wheelchair in a New York hotel lobby, glowering at the world.

The world Cornell Woolrich painted for us with his words is a world in which we will always be disappointed, always left alone, always let down; in which we can expect the worst of people, but just sometimes someone will come through; in which love leads only to betrayal and all we can expect, once our dreams are dead, is for the release of death; in which our hopes and our dreams burn brightly, but in their burning they only make the shadows darker.

Neil Gaiman

THE BLACK WINDOW
JOEL LANE

When the last film had ended,
sometimes, he'd sit in the dark
with a glass in his hand, and watch.

Himself, a thin red-haired boy
on the playing field. A shadow
that slammed him from behind,
a boot sliding down his instep
to freeze the muscle, bring numbness
and hollow pain. Breath in his ear:
How's that for a dead leg? Then tears
as he stood, unable to run away
or follow. A screen of daylight.

Fifty years later, this hotel room.
Empty bottles on the shelves
where his books had once been.
The TV, never switched off.

And sometimes, there were people:
admirers of a writer he'd forgotten,
drinking companions. He gave them
books and whiskey. They gave him
their faces to mask his ghosts.

And in the night, his dead leg
spoke to him as it blackened.
Its breath smelt of old leaves,
a lost garden, roses and briars.
On a table by the dark window,
the typewriter slept in its hood.
His leg whispered its stories.

Eventually, they cut it off.
He was dead a year later.

MISSING SISTER
JOE R. LANSDALE

When Ralph came in his mother was crying and her face had gained ten years. His father looked three inches shorter and ten pounds heavier. He appeared to have melted into his chair.

"No word?" Ralph said.

"No," said his father. "Of course not. No word or I'd tell you... Sorry, Ralph. I'm upset."

"We all are."

Ralph had never gotten along with his sister, Mae. She was always looking for attention. Now she really had it. She had been gone for three days, and things didn't look good. Today he had helped put up fliers with a photo of her on them. That's where he had been until now.

The cops had finally gotten interested in the whole thing. The first two days they said she'd come home, and now they were thinking she had run off. They weren't thinking about what else might have happened and how she might not come home ever. Or maybe they were, and just weren't saying, not wanting to upset the family.

"They've looked all over," his mother said. "They think she ran off with some man."

"She didn't," Ralph said.

"Certainly not," his father said. "She's a good girl."

This wasn't entirely true. She had taken enough drugs that if she could puke them all up from the last few years, she could fill a pharmacy. And the alcohol she'd drank. She barfed that up, she could fill the ocean, make it overflow. Add to that the fact that when he lived at home she was always prowling in his room, looking for something to steal so she could pawn or sell it to buy the pills and drink she wanted.

"Do you have any idea where she might be, Ralph?" his mother asked.

"I've thought on it, and no. Can't come up with a thing."

"When you saw her last, did she say anything?" his father said. "Was she unhappy?"

"No."

Truth was, since he had come home from university for the holidays, before she went missing, they hadn't talked much. Just something in passing. They never talked much. And then she became upset with his hobbies. She was always meddling in his business and, considering who she was and what she did, she was extremely judgmental.

Three nights back she had taken his car keys off the nightstand in the hallway. He had decided to go for a drive, as he had some things he needed to do, and then he saw his keys were missing, and immediately knew she had them. It was just like her.

When he came into his parents' garage, he found her with his car trunk open, looking through the bags he kept back there. His hobbies.

She had opened one of the bags and was looking inside. He knew what she was looking at. It wasn't something she could sell. It was what he was planning to drive out to the swamp and dispose of.

By the time Mae realized he was there, it was too late. He grabbed a hammer off the tool rack on the wall, and when she turned and started to scream, he ended it with one quick blow to her head.

He put on the gloves that were in the trunk, got a plastic bag out of there, and pulled it over her head quickly to stop the blood from leaking out. If he hadn't done that, there would have been a lot of it.

Ralph put her in the trunk with the cut-up remains of the other three. She barely fit. It was already crowded back there.

With rags from the rag box his father kept for when he worked on his car, he mopped up the blood and wiped the hammer clean and hung it back on the tool rack. He put the bloody rags in another plastic bag and placed them in the trunk, and closed it.

He pushed the garage door up and drove the car out. The Prius was nearly silent. That was one of his favorite things about that car. Its silence.

Closing the garage door quietly, he drove out to the swamp, drove off a narrow road he knew had a turnaround at the end of it, up close to the river. There was a long pier there that went twenty feet out and over a bit of the water.

When he was parked at the turnaround, he got the bags out of the back. He had already put bricks in the bags in anticipation. His sister had been unexpected. He hadn't cut her up and he didn't have weights.

Ralph walked the bags with the body parts and the rags out to the end of the pier. He brought them there one at a time and dropped them in the water. They sank. It was pretty deep there. He remembered that from fishing and swimming there, back when he was young. Back then he had hung out here and thought about his hobbies, which at that time he was yet to pursue. As a kid, at home, he had practiced by cutting up pictures of pretty models in magazines. Scissors cut paper more easily than a hacksaw cut up flesh and bone, and sinew was certainly a bitch.

He had done things with the other girls that he didn't do with his sister, and he wasn't feeling the urge to do that with her now. Mae had been killed out of necessity, not out of lust. He wasn't weird or anything. After all, she was his sister.

Thinking about what to do with Mae for a while, he finally decided to drag her down the little walking trail that was off to the side of the turnaround. He tumbled her out of the trunk and pulled her down the trail, then rolled her body into a ditch that slanted toward the river. She went down swiftly and out of sight, into the ditch, hidden by undergrowth and trees, tucked up in shadow.

He went back to the car and drove home. He opened the garage and carefully glided the car inside. He pulled the door down and looked around in there. It was all right.

He removed his gloves, knowing he'd get rid of them the next day, some place where they wouldn't be found, in case he should be suspected and looked at for DNA and such.

Inside the kitchen he drank a glass of milk and ate a sandwich. Tomorrow his parents would wonder where Mae was, and a day or so later they would panic. Even then he envisioned the fliers he would help make with her information and a photo of her on them.

But that was then, and this was now, because he had already made those fliers, and they were stapled to light poles and bulletin boards in stores, and now he was standing in the living room comforting his parents. He was not only the oldest of their children, he had become, with one swift swing of the hammer, an only child. His parents just didn't know it yet. Maybe they'd never know it for sure. If the body wasn't found, then they could think she ran off to South America somewhere and was doing fine with a mess of kids, or some such.

He decided not to think about it, not while he was with his parents. He might start smiling, and he didn't believe that was the way you were supposed to act. Yet, it was all he could do not to jump up and click his heels while his parents cried and wondered where she was.

Perhaps he would put up more fliers tomorrow, but he had to somehow find time to study. The biology test coming up at university was going to be a bitch.

A THIN SLICE OF HEAVEN

VASEEM KHAN

1

It's not that I have anything against strangers turning up at my office in the dead of night; it's just that usually they're wearing uniforms and a smirk that says one of us is about to have a good time and the chances are it isn't me.

Travis von Spee was tall, matinée idol handsome, and charged with murder.

The von told you a little something about him. I'd heard it said that it was a sign of a noble patrilineality. There's a word for you. The fact that he'd held on to those three little letters – and the Spee – suggested he couldn't quite bring himself to relinquish a last hold on the Old Country, even with a golden ticket to the promised land burning a hole in his pocket.

I wagered that Travis wasn't the name on his birth certificate.

Then again, with Hitler starting a bar-room brawl over in Europe, I didn't blame him. It wasn't a good time to be a German in L.A.

For a big man, his knock was diffident. I was used to heavy boots kicking back the door, mostly for effect. My door was never locked.

Herr Spee waited for me to usher him into a seat. Manners maketh the man, I suppose, even if you are an accused murderer.

Not that he looked like one. He looked like a tennis player, long-boned, with blue eyes, a firm chin, and the sort of slicked-back blond hair that wouldn't have looked out of place on a wooden doll.

"May I smoke?"

"Be my guest."

I watched him dig out a pack of Luckies from the pocket of his beautifully cut jacket, light one with a nickel-plated lighter held in shaky hands.

I suppose my hands would shake too, if I was facing a date with the gas chamber.

"How can I help you, Mr von Spee?"

"Travis, please."

"Sure. And you can call me Leo. And now that we're such pals, how about you explain to me what you're doing here, Travis."

"I need your help."

I waited.

"You're familiar with my case, yes?"

"Sure. I hear you brutally murdered a nineteen-year-old co-ed."

His eyes flashed. "I didn't do it. I'm being framed."

I resisted the urge to pick him up by the collar and throw him out. Not that I could. He had a good seventy pounds on me. "If that's the case, you'll have your day in court."

"I doubt it. The forces ranged against me are… Wagnerian."

Poetic. I hope he remembered to quote Nietzsche when they had him strapped to the chair with cyanide wafting around his nostrils.

"Alright. I'll play along. Who framed you?"

"James Crawford."

I tapped out a little scale on the scarred surface of my desk. Crawford. There was no need to say 'the financier'. I doubted there was a soul in the city who didn't know what Crawford did, how much he was worth, or who he'd had knee-capped for crossing him. "Why?"

"Because I'm having an affair with his wife."

I leaned back. A cry spiralled up from the street below. The lament of a drunk. You got a lot of them in this neck of the woods, especially around the witching hour. What with the depressed rents attracting a recent flood of flatfoots, the neighbourhood had really gone to the dogs.

I listened as he explained.

Three months ago, he'd met Nancy Crawford at an art gallery – he worked there as a part-time gallery assistant – while he pursued an unlikely career on the silver screen. They'd hit it off. She'd invited him back to a house in the hills, a secluded pied-à-terre her husband had bought a while back then forgotten about, the way some rich men do when they have too many toys.

Or wives.

In the normal course of things, the affair would have petered out, and young Travis would have found himself booted back out of Eden.

But Cupid had thrown a spanner in the works.

They'd fallen in love.

"I suppose the good lady Crawford bankrolled your bail?"

He gave me a sharp glance.

I took a bottle of bourbon from my desk, poured a glass. I tipped the bottle at him, but he shook his head.

"This kid you killed—sorry – *allegedly* killed – did you know her?"

He nodded. "We stepped out together before I met Nancy. She worked at the art gallery."

"And she was killed at the house where you… consorted with Mrs Crawford, correct?"

He didn't like the word 'consorted'. I'd known he wouldn't. "Yes."

"So, aside from the fact that you knew her, why does the D.A. think you did it?"

He seemed to disconnect for a moment, then, "They say they have physical evidence."

"Such as?"

"I'll find out soon."

"And your motive?"

He hesitated, and at that point the door opened and another late-night caller joined the party.

2

She was a small woman, maybe a decade older than young von Spee, but elegant in a way only the very rich can afford to be. She was nicely put together, with tawny-coloured hair in a romantic wave cut, parted down the middle. She wore expensive-looking wireframe spectacles and the clothes on her back would probably have paid a year's rent on my office, with change for dinner and a show.

Travis got to his feet and greeted her with soulful eyes. He lowered his great head and she pecked him chastely on the cheek, then the pair of them sat down, arms entwined like teenage lovers.

"Mrs Crawford, I presume?"

I knew who she was, of course, but in a town like L.A. it always paid to make the well-known think they weren't as famous as they supposed.

"Please call me Nancy, Mr Rubin."

"And you can call me Leo. Or Leonidas. My father had a sense of humour, God rest his soul."

She gave a wan smile. "I apologise for my tardiness, but Travis and I can't afford to be seen together."

"I understand."

Her eyes were the sort of blue you saw at the bottom of swimming pools. "Has Travis explained the situation?"

"He was about to tell me what motive the D.A. has ascribed to him for the murder."

She winced. The word 'murder' generated the same reaction in some rich folks as the word 'bankruptcy'.

"He didn't do it."

"That wasn't my question."

Travis stirred back to life. "They say she found out about our relationship and attempted to blackmail me. A woman scorned. I lured her to Nancy's hillside house and killed her."

"How did you get in?"

"Nancy gave me a key. The police found it in my apartment."

"Presumably you have no alibi for the time of the murder?"

He shook his head. "I was by myself. I'd been sent out of the city to pick up an item for the gallery."

"But no one can verify your whereabouts?"

"Not for the time Annie was killed."

"Motive, means, and opportunity," I muttered. "The D.A.'s holy trinity."

He said nothing.

Her hand tightened around his. I sensed her desperation. Here was a woman who hadn't expected to fall for a man like Travis von Spee. She prided herself on making sensible life choices.

Then again, she'd married James Crawford.

I sipped at my bourbon. "So... why are you *here*?"

Nancy spoke. "We want you to investigate, Mr Rubin."

I gave a faint smile. "Why me? With your dough you can afford any private dick in the city."

"Because you once helped a man called Arnold Tremaine. You helped him when no one else would. You helped him when my husband tried to destroy him."

Arnie Tremaine. A long time ago. I was a different man, then. Ten years schlepping around in shoes like mine and you learn that idealism is strictly for the birds.

"Travis couldn't have done this," she continued.

"What makes you so sure?"

"He's not a violent man." Her conviction was almost touching. I shot a glance at von Spee. How well did she really know him? What would a man do to hold on to a life of ease, bankrolled by a besotted older woman?

I thought about the last time I'd taken on James Crawford. It had cost me my job, my friends, and the life I thought I was building.

"Fifty dollars an hour plus expenses," I said. "That's double my usual rate, but I figure your husband owes me."

"That's quite acceptable… Leo."

I raised my glass. "I'll drink to that."

3

If you want to meet a dirty cop, don't go to a bar, go to church.

I'd known John Roscoe for years. Once upon a time we'd been friends, rookies on the force. The day I decided to take on James Crawford, Roscoe tried to warn me.

Needless to say, I'd had my ears on backwards.

I parked my clapped-out Packard convertible behind a black sedan that resembled a hearse, then made my way into the Church of All Saints on the corner of Highland and Fifth.

The air was a furnace. I felt like a turkey walking into an oven.

Roscoe was hunched in a pew at the rear, cigarette in hand. He'd put on weight since I'd last seen him, and hadn't shaved in what looked like a week. He reeked of sweat and a cologne so stiff it was like a crack to the jaw. Put a hotdog in his hand and he'd resemble any other bum on Wilshire Boulevard.

I slipped onto the pew and looked up at the altar, where Christ avoided my gaze, peering up at the heavens like a black man in a dark alley during a roust. An old priest shuffled around the nave, throwing disapproving glances our way.

"I think he wants you to put out that cigarette."

Roscoe grunted, then took a long deliberate draw, and launched a cloud of smoke at me.

I coughed, just to be polite, then said, "How's Arlene?"

"She left me."

"Finally saw the light, huh?"

My attempt at humour fell to the floor and scuttled off to a corner to die.

"For what it's worth: thanks for coming."

"I didn't come here to help you. I came here to warn you. Don't cross the D.A. on this one. He'll drop a building on you."

"Remind me, who's paying the D.A.'s salary these days? The city or James Crawford?"

He gave me a filthy look, then sucked on his cigarette again.

"You're here now. You might as well tell me what you know."

"He killed her. Von Spee."

"How do you *know*?"

"A little thing called evidence."

"He says Crawford framed him."

"Sure. And my old man's the King of Siam."

I took out a handkerchief and mopped my brow, then the back of my neck. "If it's as open and shut as you say, you fellas have nothing to fear from little old me."

The corners of his mouth winched up, the sort of smile you saw on a corpse with rigor mortis and a story to tell. "We have a witness at the art gallery says they've been going toe to toe for a while now. They were lovers, *were* being the operative word. But I'm guessing you knew that. Same witness swears blind he called her just an hour before she died. Moments later, she goes racing out of there like her tail was on fire."

"There's got to be more. McGregor wouldn't stick his neck out on a bunch of circumstantial hooey."

Rhett McGregor was the D.A., the sort of man who'd pick the Pope up by the ankles and shake him around a bit, just to see what fell out. He'd been a sharp prosecutor, once upon a time, before he decided he liked the high life more than he liked justice, and put up a For Rent sign outside his office.

"We found a shirt button in her hand. She tore it from her attacker when he strangled her. That was after he cracked her on the back of the head with a poker to soften her up."

"Let me guess: the button came from Travis' shirt?"

He smiled without humour. "We found the shirt in his apartment. Get this: the buttons are monogrammed. TVS. How do you like that?"

I watched the priest fiddle with the altar, wiping down Christ's feet. "How difficult would it have been for Crawford's thugs to break in to his apartment?"

He squinted at me. "Is that your angle? That Crawford did this?"

"Or paid someone to set our boy up."

"Why would he do that?"

"You know why."

He gave me a sideways look that told me he knew exactly what I meant. If the story about the two lovebirds wasn't public knowledge yet, it soon would be.

Then again, James Crawford had a great deal of clout in this city, maybe even enough to impose a sense of discretion on the free press.

For a time, at least.

4

The La Brea Art Gallery was stuck between a famous drugstore and a museum of Egyptian antiquities. The storefront was glitzy, with gold and silver trim around the windows, and all sorts of bizarre junk on display, laid out on swards of purple velvet. Art, I supposed, though you'd have to be rich, mad, or from Mars to recognise it as such.

Inside, the space was vast, with plain white walls, like a mental institution. Canvasses hung at discreet intervals, big ones, small ones, ones that made no sense. Sculptures were dotted about, on marble pedestals, interspersed with bronze statues of figures wearing less clothing than would usually be considered polite for a weekday afternoon in downtown L.A.

This wasn't the sort of place where price tags were displayed, but I could guess, judging from the pair of armed security guards lounging by the counter and hitting on the receptionist, that harried husbands didn't just walk in off the street and pick up a gewgaw for the wife's forgotten birthday.

I introduced myself and asked for a Janine Hanson.

The two guards looked me up and down as if they'd stepped in something unsavoury and it had come alive and then walked in the door behind them.

"So, fellas, I don't suppose you have anything in here by Kandinsky, specifically from his Blue Rider period? I love the way he and Franz Marc improvise colour the way musicians use tone in a piece of music."

They exchanged glances as if I'd asked them to work out the meaning of life. In Mandarin.

Hanson arrived. A tall, platinum blonde in a wide-shouldered olive dress. She could have made a killing on the impersonator circuit as a double for Jean Harlow, if Harlow hadn't died a couple of years ago.

Five minutes later, we were sitting in a spick and span office bigger than my apartment, Harlow with a cigarette jittering around in her fingers.

"He killed her alright, that Kraut son of a bitch."

For a vision of elegance, she sure knew how to cuss.

"How long were Travis and Annie together?"

"A year. He strung her along."

"He says they broke it off months ago."

"That's a filthy lie. He proposed to her back in June. She'd still be wearing his engagement ring if she hadn't thrown it in his face when she found out about Nancy Crawford."

A little detail Travis von Spee had neglected to mention.

She sucked on her cigarette. "There's something else. She made me promise not to tell anyone, but I guess it doesn't matter now." Her lower lip quivered. "She was pregnant. With Travis' child."

"Did he know about it?"

"He knew about it. She made sure he did."

"Was she blackmailing him?"

"I hate that word, don't you?"

"How about you answer the question?"

She looked at me as if I'd socked her in the kisser. "She just wanted what was owed to her. Travis made promises. And then that stuck-up bitch walks in the door and he drops Annie like it was nothing."

"He first met Nancy Crawford here, is that right?"

She nodded. "Mr Crawford is a regular here. He collects art. Spends a fortune. He was one of Annie's clients. She could charm him into buying anything. His wife never bothered to grace us with her presence. But then, one day, she just walks in out of the blue. Alone. Travis happens to be out front and offers to show her around. And that was that."

"Let's talk about the day of the murder. You told the cops Annie received a call here, from Travis. She left immediately after. That was the last time anyone saw her alive."

"Yes."

"How do you know the call was from Travis?"

"Because I heard her say his name."

"What did she say exactly?"

"I don't know. I just heard her say the name. Travis."

"So you can't be sure it was him on the other end of the line?"

"Who else would it be? Besides, they'd had a spat the day before."

"What about?"

"Nothing important. But she'd had a bellyful of him. I think she'd been threatening to go public with what she knew about him and Nancy."

"Did you tell the cops that?"

"You bet I did."

I changed tack.

"Did Annie have family in L.A.? Close friends?"

"We were her friends. As for family… She blew in from an Okie town and never looked back. The only family she ever mentioned was an aunt. A Fran Rice. She's in a nursing home in Glendale."

5

The Macon Carter Nursing Home was a stone's throw from the eastern boundary of Griffith Park, on the corner of Pacific and Vine, one of the dozens of private enterprises that had sprung up in recent years in the wake of the Old Age Assistance grants programme. By handing the cash direct to the elderly, the federal government had inadvertently provided the incentive for privately-run outfits to muscle out the public operators that had long treated their patients like cans of meat on a conveyor belt.

I flashed my PI badge at the receptionist along with a full set of gums, and was duly escorted through whitewashed corridors and out over a flag-stoned path to a walled garden where a troop of wizened shamans were sunning themselves like lizards.

Fran Rice was eighty-two years old, with thinning hair as white as snow, liver-spotted hands, and the sort of face that suggested she'd lived a life of excess. She was sat in a wheelchair staring into space.

The nurse warned me the old gal was not entirely compos mentis.

I dragged a wicker garden seat across the lawn and parked myself directly opposite her, obstructing her line of sight into whatever dimension she happened to be currently peering into.

Her face folded into a petulant frown.

Introducing myself, I explained that I was here to talk about her niece Annie Williams.

She said nothing for a while and I thought she might have drifted into sleep, with her eyes open, like they say tired horses sometimes do.

"Annie's dead."

"I know, Mrs Rice."

"Miss. Not Mrs. I never married. God never made the man who could tame me."

"My apologies, Miss—"

"Call me Franny. You're handsome."

"That's nice of you to say. Now, about Annie—"

"You're supposed to return the compliment."

Her eyes glimmered like hot stones.

I smiled. Appearances can be deceptive, and it seemed to me Franny Rice's doolally act was just that. An act.

We started talking. She told me about Annie, her only connection to the rest of her family. Annie had visited regularly, and spent hours chatting about her life.

"It was that hood from the gallery," said Franny. "He killed her. I know he did."

"The police think so," I said. "They arrested him. He's out on bail."

"Hah. The *police*. They sent an officer out here. He was all of seven years old. A runny nose and pants that didn't fit. Didn't ask me a goddamned thing. Just wanted to let me know that Annie was dead." Tears welled in her eyes.

"Well, I guess I'd like to ask you a few questions, if I may. Just to build up a picture of Annie's life in these past months. Did she mention to you that she was pregnant?"

Her head creaked up and down like a rusty derrick. "She told me. I told her to get rid of it. Nothing good could come of keeping it. But she wouldn't listen. She thought the kid was her meal ticket. Thought the father would pay through the nose."

"She blackmailed him?"

She unleashed a cackle that turned a couple of other heads. "Blackmail? Only a man would use that word. She didn't put that baby in there all by herself, Mr Handsome." Her expression became sorrowful. "I guess she underestimated him."

"Travis?"

"Travis? No, not Travis. The father."

I sat upright. "Travis *is* the father, Miss Rice."

"You're dumber than you look," she said. "Travis wasn't the father of Annie's baby."

I frowned. "But you said it was the man from the gallery."

"Yes. The other one. The older guy."

6

James Crawford's main place of residence was a white frame mansion on Lafayette Park, heralded by a gate so far from the house you needed a pair of binoculars to catch sight of the porte cochère.

A gang of hoods masquerading as security guards lounged at the gate.

They exchanged belly laughs as I wheezed my Packard up to the gate, then invited me to step out so they could frisk me like I owed them money.

By the time I was bounced up to the mansion, I felt like I'd spent an hour in a Turkish *hammam*.

Frankly, I was surprised Crawford had let me in the house, but I guess he had little to fear from me and knew it.

I was let in by a black butler named Jackson, who bade me follow him across a hall wider than a pair of football fields laid end to end, through a pair of French doors, and up a wrought-iron staircase to a carpeted landing. Along the walls were large oil canvasses of men engaged in violence throughout history: a sword-wielding Crusader, Davy Crockett at the Alamo, a soldier heading out of a trench at the Somme. I guessed Crawford saw himself as a great man of action; in some ways he was, though there'd never been anything noble about his particular crusades.

Jackson knocked on a tall wooden door, and a booming voice bade us enter.

James Crawford's study was vast, with a high ceiling painted like the Sistine Chapel, and a red carpet that stretched from edge to edge like a lake of blood. Enormous drapes had been pulled back from a window that looked out onto rolling acres in which horses gambolled and stable-hands chased them around with grooming brushes.

Antiques were dotted about, an eclectic mix that looked as if someone had raided a very expensive cupboard and then thrown the contents around the room and left them where they lay. Crawford had about as much of an eye for art as I did, but he went out of his way to convince you otherwise, and had the chequebook to buy himself a veneer of taste.

A storybook giant in a buttoned-up oriental jacket and a turban stood quietly to one side. His complexion was dark, his beard was neatly trimmed, and his demeanour suggested violence would only become an option if I made it absolutely necessary.

I resolved to not make it necessary.

James Crawford was sitting behind a mahogany desk the size of a landing field, dressed in a crisp white shirt and silk tie. His blond hair was slicked back, and his blue eyes were gazing at me with curiosity, the way a cat sizes up a mouse between its paws.

A fat cigar was held in one hand.

Crawford only smoked Partagas Habanas and made damn sure everyone knew it.

"Leo Rubin," he said, a wide grin cracking open his features. The shine on his porcelain teeth could have dazzled a blind beggar. "Abdul" – he waved his cigar at the turbaned Indian – "take a gander at our friend here. That there is righteousness personified, mister. Mark it well. It's the sort of thing that gets a man killed."

My hands balled into fists by my sides and I had to stamp down on the urge to leap across the desk.

On the surface, James Crawford was a businessman, a financier, a man who made dreams come true in the city of angels. He'd clawed his way up from the dirt, a granite-chinned personification of the American dream. The trouble is that dirt clings to you, no matter how high you climb, and, for some, it's a hard habit to break. Crawford had a hand in every dirty racket you could think of, including the dirtiest one of all: politics. Rumour had it, he'd bankrolled the crooked campaigns of more than one of the birds now sitting fat as Christmas turkeys up in City Hall.

Smoke drifted over to me, as fragrant as the perfume of a sheikh's favourite catamite. The smile on his puss gave me the itch.

"I want to talk to you about Annie Williams."

His eyes narrowed, and then he grinned. "A tragedy, what happened to that girl. I hear the guy who did it is out on bail. If the cops let me have my way, it wouldn't even get to trial."

"He didn't do it."

"Way I hear it, it's an open and shut case."

"Who told you that? Your friend McGregor?"

He smiled. "As it happens, the D.A. and I enjoyed a round of golf just the other day."

"Travis didn't do it. *You* did it."

He straightened in his chair. "I'd choose my next words carefully. You wouldn't want to say something you later regret. Not again."

"I'm guessing you don't have all of the facts. About your wife, for instance."

He frowned. "Nancy? What's she got to do with this?"

It was my turn to smile.

"Abdul. Go powder your nose."

The big man glanced between us.

Crawford reached into a drawer and laid a pearl-handled automatic onto the desk. "It's fine. Leo's as docile as a kitty kat, ain't that right?"

Abdul left the room on silken feet, closing the door behind him.

"Alright, pal. You have my attention."

"You were sleeping with Annie Williams. Nature followed its course. But when she asked you to shoulder your responsibilities, you decided she had to go. But you needed a fall guy. So you picked her German boyfriend, Travis von Spee. The perfect patsy."

He glared at me. "I never touched a hair on that girl's head."

"I guess she ended up dead in your house all by herself?"

"I haven't set foot in that place since the day I bought it." He'd stood up now and was making his way around the desk, gun in hand. "Imagine my surprise when I find out Annie's body was found there. Sure, we had a thing. But all good things come to an end. She came to see me, flapping her gums. Screwy broad. I told her it was the end of the line for us. When she turned up dead, I figured maybe some conscientious citizen decided to shut her trap once and for all."

"Conscientious citizen? You mean some thug on your payroll? Maybe the maharajah out there."

He grimaced, waving the gun at me. "The last time we met, do you remember what you said to me?"

"My memory doesn't hold up so well these days. What with your cop buddies using my head as a punch-bag every other day."

"You said I was nothing but a bum in a fancy suit. You said a man like me would never make it all the way to the end."

I smiled, a slow crooked smile that had nothing to do with humour.

"And then you slugged me. A real sucker punch. I still owe you for that."

His hand flashed out, and the butt of the automatic struck the side of my skull, toppling me to the floor in a blinding explosion of pain.

He stood over me. His manner oozed confidence and testosterone, a lethal cocktail. For a second, I thought he was actually going to do it.

And then he turned away.

"Did you know Nancy was seeing von Spee behind your back?"

He froze.

I picked myself slowly up off the floor, like a prize-fighter who realises he's taken a dive in the wrong round.

"That's right. Your wife is two-timing you with our German friend. She's the one who paid for his bail. They're in *love*."

For the longest moment, he didn't move. And then, "Nancy worships the ground I walk on. Has done from the day we met."

"You tell yourself whatever you need to, pal of mine."

"Get out. Get out before I change my mind."

"I was just leaving. It was fun catching up."

7

The problem with doing what I do is that your mind is never at rest. Little things nag away at you. You get halfway through a case and something comes along that just doesn't fit. Sometimes it's just a feeling.

I was having one of those feelings now.

James Crawford's denial shouldn't have held any water. But the hell of it was that I was beginning to think he really didn't have anything to do with Annie Williams' death.

We'd been alone in the room. He was the sort of man who would have taken great pleasure in setting out exactly how he'd got one over on me, leading me through the details of the murder, how he'd arranged it, and then pinned it on that poor sap, Travis von Spee.

But he'd denied it. Why admit the affair with Annie Williams and then not admit that he'd solved the problem himself? Murder was small change to a man like Crawford. So why the denial?

Instincts. They're like barking dogs when they get a bone between their paws. I began pulling the pieces together.

Maybe this wasn't about Annie Williams and Travis von Spee.

Who else would benefit from the girl's death?

If Travis hadn't done it, how had the button ended up in the dead girl's hands?

Who had access to his shirts? To his apartment?

Why had the killer cracked Annie on the back of the head, before strangling her? Why not just finish the job with the poker?

And why had the killing taken place at the Crawford place? If Travis were the killer, why in the world would he call her there in order to kill her? He must have known the cops would find out about his relationship with Annie and his affair with Nancy.

Motives. You never can tell what stirs beneath the surface.

A theory began forming in my mind.

I needed to make a few calls and pay a visit to the apartment complex where Travis von Spee lived.

8

Night in L.A. It's when the suckers are out in force, in the pool rooms, in the betting joints, on parquet ballroom dance floors, or out on the street looking for a moment's respite from the humdrum existence most of us call life.

Most, but not all.

The one thing I can say about *my* thirty-eight years on this earth is that it has been anything but humdrum.

Tonight was shaping up to be no different.

This time they arrived together, entering sideways through the door as if they were joined at the hip, like one of those cardboard couples you saw out front of a car sales lot. Travis von Spee's plate-sized hand engulfed Nancy's daintier mitt; hope flared in his eyes as he saw that I'd set out three tumblers of Scotch, and not the cheap kind. I could read his mind like his forehead was made of glass.

A celebration drink.

With what I had waiting in my right glove for Travis, he was going to need that drink. A knockout blow that, if he took it on the chin, would probably send him into the middle of next week.

They lowered themselves gingerly into the seats opposite and waited for me to begin.

"James Crawford didn't kill Annie Williams and he didn't set you up."

He blinked. "That can't be right."

"It's as right as right. He had an affair with Annie. She became pregnant and went to him thinking she could blackmail him. No dice. It takes a lot more than a kid in the oven to shake down James Crawford." I smiled grimly at Nancy Crawford. "But I guess you'd know all about that, wouldn't you, Mrs Crawford?"

"What do you mean?"

"I mean that your husband's tomcatting has driven you to distraction over the years. This time it was the last straw. For a reason I can't fathom, you actually love that son of a bitch. You couldn't abide the fact that he'd knocked up his little gallery girl. My guess is when she couldn't get anything out of James, she came to you, trying to play both sides." I sipped at my Scotch, eyes on her face. Not a muscle flickered. "Either way, you decided to get rid of her. But you couldn't just kill her. You knew if your husband's affair with Annie came to light the cops would be all over him like a rash. You needed a fall guy. A prize-winning donkey on which you could pin the tail. Enter young Travis here."

His eyes flared and he swept to his feet, fists balled.

"Sit down, Junior, before you hurt yourself."

I stared him out, until he gradually fell back into his seat.

"I suppose you made a few enquiries, found out a little about Annie. And then you decided to pay the gallery a visit – it's no coincidence that that was the first time you set foot in there. A couple of hours later you walked out with Travis, the guy you knew Annie had been seeing.

"Once you had him on a leash, the plan came together. You bought him a bunch of shirts with monogrammed buttons. You tore off one of those buttons and kept it aside. On the day of her death, you telephoned Annie at the gallery and told her to meet you at your house in the hills. I don't know exactly what story you gave her. Maybe you told her you'd pay her off? Perhaps you mentioned Travis too – I'm guessing that's why Annie said his name out loud on the other end of the line.

"When she got to the house, I suppose you talked for a bit, set her at ease, and then, when her back was turned, you cracked her over the head with a poker – I'm guessing you wore gloves for that part. You didn't want to risk trying to overpower her: not a frail little thing like you. And then you strangled her. It had to be strangulation because you wanted to plant the button in her hand. You had to make it look like she tore that button off in a violent struggle with Travis as he throttled her."

I sat back and drained my Scotch, then poured another.

"You don't have a shred of proof for any of that... that *nonsense*," said Nancy Crawford. Two spots of colour floated high on her cheeks.

"Proof? Well, now that's not exactly my job, lady. I'm sure when the D.A.'s office gets wind of my theory they'll find a way to dig up all the proof they need."

She flashed a cold smile. "Do you really think James will ever let it get that far? He may have his occasional dalliances, but he *loves* me. Do you understand? We made our vows, Mr Rubin. Till death do us part."

"Amen to that," I said. I turned to Travis, who had all but stopped breathing.

It took a few seconds for the shoe to drop, but Nancy Crawford finally realised she'd given herself away.

"You would have let me go to the gas chamber," he whispered.

It was a tragic comedy, in three acts, watching this mountain of a man crumbling into dust in front of little Nancy Crawford.

For an instant, naked terror reigned in her eyes.

I could have told her that Travis von Spee wouldn't harm a hair on her head. She'd been dead right about that.

He wasn't a violent man.

TWO WRONGS
BRANDON BARROWS

I stepped into the bedroom closet, shutting the door behind me and burrowing in among the hanging ranks of dresses, blouses, and skirts my wife collected like baseball cards, then shoved away, never to be seen again. When we were first married, there was space for my clothing, too, but that was years ago. It was only one of the things we fought about.

Sounds in the outer rooms of the apartment drove me into hiding. The scrape of a key in the lock, the faint creak of wood, the scuffling of a coat against the wall, the slam as Nora closed the door behind her. Any second, she would come into the bedroom, take off her coat and shoes, and put them into the closet. At least she was neat about her hoarding.

I pressed against the rear wall, trying to become invisible, though I was already hidden. My right hand, covered in a thin, blue plastic surgical glove, closed around the small, secondhand automatic in my pocket, bought under the table at an out-of-state gun show a month earlier.

My ears strained, listening for Nora's customary heels clicking on the hardwood floor of the hallway, coming towards the bedroom. There was nothing.

Damn her, I thought, feeling the sweat gathering on my forehead. It was suffocating in the closet and I was beginning to feel a little dizzy. I wanted to get this over with. I'd waited more than an hour already and my nerves were starting to fray. It was well past midnight; where could she have been this late? Nora wasn't the type to stay out nights by herself. Shopping was her only hobby and everything retail was closed hours ago.

Finally, I heard the sharp *click-click-click* of her approach. I leaned forward to peek through one of the slits in the louvered door. The overhead light flicked on and Nora came into the bedroom, her coat over one arm, her purse dangling from the other. She was making noises like she was trying not to cry. She threw the coat onto the bed and dug into the purse, coming up with a tissue, then blowing her nose.

What did she have to cry about? She got her way, didn't she? I stopped seeing Evie – for now – and I was always on my best behavior, pretending I only wanted to put things right between us and leave the past behind. For the first couple of weeks, I don't think Nora was fooled, but these last few days, it seemed like she was warming back up to me, finally buying the act. And maybe that was because part of it was true: as much as it hurt, I really hadn't tried to see Evie in more than three weeks. The last time we spoke, I told her that we couldn't see each other for a while, though not what I planned, only that this time apart was for the sake of our future together.

Just thinking about Evie made my blood pressure tick upwards. Evie was the reason I had to kill Nora, but there would be life after death. To me, Evie was life itself: warm and loving, as golden and beautiful as spring sunshine. Once, I thought Nora was all of that, but not for a long time – and without those feelings, first resentment, then hate crept in to replace them.

When we met, Nora had money and I had a job that barely paid. But it was an instantaneous thing drawing us together like magnets, and before we married we never discussed finances or raising a family, where we would live or even the things we liked besides each other. We didn't have anything in common, really, but we didn't know that at the time; even if we did, it probably wouldn't have mattered. We were in love and that was that. Love can't last when you're fundamentally incompatible, though. We learned that long after it was too late.

Now, the only thing left between us was the money – Nora's money. She would never leave me, no matter how unhappy she was. She said she loved me, and that our marriage was worth fighting for, but I'm certain her real reason was being too stubborn to ever admit making a mistake. Of course, I could leave her, but if I did I would be leaving all the money behind, too. As much as I wanted to be free of Nora, I wanted those millions. Evie deserved the high life, and besides that, it's easy to get used to never having to worry about money and much harder going back to square one.

Nora stood in the middle of the bedroom, still in her heels, dabbing at her nose with the tissue. Then she turned and moved out of my range of view. I heard the *shwuff* of the big, mission-style chair in the corner being dragged across carpet, then the *whish* of air escaping the cushion as she sat. A moment later, first one shoe, then its mate, flew across the room to bounce off the closet door, making me jump involuntarily.

What was she doing? I couldn't see and didn't dare look. Did she know I was here, just waiting for her to throw the door open so I could end our marriage? Was she sitting there, facing the closet, hoping to wait me out?

I wiped my sleeve across my sweaty forehead. I could wait, but not for long. I raised my watch; away from the light peeking through the louvers, it was too dark to see the face, but it was already midnight when Nora came home. At least ten minutes had passed since then, and it was nearly two hours' drive back to the city in the ancient, junker car I stole just for tonight. Time was getting tight.

There was a hotel where I always stayed when down in the city on business. Nora's money could have sustained us in style for the rest of our lives, but she insisted I do something with myself and wrangled me a job in a firm owned by a cousin of hers. That was one of our earliest recurring fights, but I relented for the sake of harmony, and discovered not only that the work wasn't difficult, but that I actually enjoyed it. It also gave me an excuse to travel, which was a godsend when our domestic battles started to get really bad.

After meeting my clients in the afternoon and evening, I purposely stayed out later than usual. When I returned to the hotel, I plopped myself into a chair in the lobby and feigned sleep. It wasn't long before a clerk "woke" me; I apologized profusely, acted embarrassed, and told him I better get myself to bed. I was known at the hotel and the clerk would remember the incident.

I stayed in my room maybe twenty minutes. Nobody saw me when I left via the door into the rear parking lot. It took longer than expected to find a car old enough that it could be hotwired – instructions for which I found online surprisingly easily – but if someone saw me prowling around, I probably would have been picked up before ever leaving the city, so I wasn't worried. After a long drive home, slipping into the apartment building unseen was the easiest part of my plan.

My alibi was in place, the gun in my pocket was untraceable to me, and I was careful to leave no prints on the car – but if I wasn't back at the hotel well before morning, it would all be for nothing.

A faint creak of the floor, and the *whish* of the cushion as Nora stood, pulled my attention back to the moment. I prayed that this would be it, that it would finally be over soon. My hand started to tremble, from nerves or anticipation – probably both. I tightened my grip on the automatic and pulled it from my pocket.

I heard Nora's footsteps, just whispers against the carpet, and then she came into view, divided into numerous little slices by the louvers. She stood by the bed for a moment, close enough to touch if I opened the door. I could tell from her puffy, red eyes that while I was waiting, she was sitting in her chair, silently sobbing. My whole body tensed and I strained backwards, trying to wedge myself deeper into my hiding place, afraid she would somehow see me through the louvers, just as I could see her.

Finally, Nora turned to the closet. She opened the door. A dress to my left slipped off of a hanger and slithered to the floor. Nora stooped to pick it up and from my vantage point, looking down at her, I saw her eyebrows go up. Her eyes must have gone wide when she saw my shoes peeking out of the depths of the closet. Her breath came in a sudden rasp as I lunged forward, wrapping my left arm around her neck, and dragging her into the closet with me.

Nora struggled, but I had the advantages of surprise and strength. She twisted, trying to free herself, but only managed to shift into a better position for what I already planned. My left hand came up, clamping over her mouth as I raised my right and jammed the barrel of the little automatic against her temple. Jerking my weight backwards, throwing the both of us into the smothering, insulating closeness of the dresses and skirts and blouses and coats, I squeezed the trigger. There was a subdued flash, dazzlingly bright so close to my eyes and in the confines of the closet, but the noise was barely more than a *pop* that was easily absorbed by the fabric surrounding us.

And as suddenly as it began, our relationship was over.

I stood in the closet, supporting Nora's limp weight, trying to steady myself and come to grips with the fact of what I did. I took deep breaths of the still, stifling air, trying to fill my lungs with oxygen, and realized all I was filling them with was the smell of Nora's death. A queasy feeling washed over me, but I pushed it back. There was no time for it.

I dragged Nora out of the closet, careful to avoid touching the blood trickling out of the tiny hole in her head, and over to the chair that now faced the big window looking out over the street, four floors below. I wondered what she was waiting – or watching? – for. It wasn't like her to be contemplative. It didn't matter, though. All I really cared about was the Kleenex box on the left arm of the chair and the little pile of used tissues by its foot. Nora did me one last favor and she would never even know it.

I set Nora in the chair, arranged her in a way that I thought looked natural, leaning her hips against the left corner of the seat and flopping her upper body halfway over the thick, flat armrest on the right. I placed the gun in her hand, pressing her fingers over the grip, the trigger, and wiping them across the barrel, leaving a just-visible smear on the bluing. I put the gun back into her hand, brought it up to her temple, and let it drop. The arm fell straight down and the gun flew from limp fingers, bounced once, then landed halfway under the chair. I stepped back and surveyed the scene. The out of place chair, the little pile of tissues. It was perfect. Nora, depressed and inconsolable, killed herself.

I moved to the doorway and some impulse made me take one last look back. The scene still looked real to me – maybe too real, because for an instant my heart fluttered and I felt a deep sense of sadness. Sitting slumped in that big, blocky chair, Nora looked small and fragile and I regretted what I did. Just for a second or two, though. Flashes of the past four years skipped through my mind, of all the fights, the screamed obscenities followed by hours or days of the silent treatment; the belittling comments Nora made in front of friends and business associates. Thinking of some of our worst days, it was a wonder one of us hadn't already killed the other.

And then I thought of Evie. I clung to the image of her in my mind, to my memories of her loving warmth, her kindness, and her beauty. I refused to let those thoughts slip away, to let them be pushed aside by all the terrible days and nights of the last few years. This was one last bad night and then my troubles were over.

Everything churning inside of me came crashing together and began to overwhelm me. Suddenly, I wanted to see Evie badly – so badly it hurt. I wanted to hold her in my arms, to kiss her, to feel her body against mine and tell her that soon, it would be like that forever. It would have to wait, though. Even if the idea wasn't dangerous, I needed to get back to the hotel as quickly as possible.

I made my way out of the apartment and down the back stairs, headed in the direction of the stolen car, parked several blocks away. Once at the wheel, though, my hands wouldn't obey me; instead of guiding the car towards the highway and safety, they turned it in the opposite direction, towards the neighborhood where Evie lived. It was insane, but I couldn't help myself. Everything I did was for the sake of being with Evie. I couldn't stand being this close to my goal and not seeing her just once, even if it was only for a moment, just to remind myself of why all of this was necessary.

I parked near Evie's building. I had to force myself not to run down the sidewalk. Even at nearly one in the morning, there might be someone to see and remember. I climbed the dim staircase of her building, to the door of her apartment, my heart hammering in my chest.

I never told Evie what I planned. She would have tried to stop me if I did. I only told her that we couldn't see each other for a little while, but afterwards, we would be together for the rest of our lives. I wondered, should I tell her now? Was there an explanation that she could understand? If I didn't tell her, would she somehow sense what I had done? Would she know I was responsible? She wasn't stupid. If I didn't tell her, at the very least she would always suspect.

I made up my mind. We loved each other enough that Evie would see this for what it was and accept it. She would forgive me a single night of brutality if the reward was the life we dreamed of together. We couldn't begin that life with a lie. The truth was the only way.

I put the key she gave me into the lock, opened the door, and slipped into the narrow entryway. After the darkness of the night outside and the dimly lit hallway, the brilliance of the overhead light was like being hit in the head with a hammer. But why was the light on? I couldn't understand it; it was hours past when Evie would normally be in bed and she wasn't the kind of person that would just forget to shut a light off.

"Evie?" I called softly. "It's me, Shawn." I waited, listening, but there was nothing – no answering call, no sounds from anywhere in the apartment.

"Evie? Where are you?" I stepped into the living room, as brightly lit as the foyer, and instantly jumped backwards, nearly tripping over the edge of the carpet. My head swam and I had to put a hand against the wall to steady myself as my stomach roiled. The nausea was back and this time I really thought I was going to be sick.

Evie lay sprawled on the floor, face up, eyes open, one arm doubled unnaturally beneath her body. She was wearing the lavender-colored silk robe I bought her for her birthday, the delicate fabric stained with still-drying blood.

I knew she was dead even before I saw the gun. When I did, it was like being hypnotized or drugged. Without conscious thought, I leaned down and picked it up, but already I recognized it by the crack in the walnut grip and the deep, shiny scratch on the long barrel. It was the .22 target pistol I inherited from my father when he passed the year before. I kept it on a shelf in the bathroom closet, the only place I had to store my clothing.

Tears filled my eyes and were running down my cheeks when I heard heavy, clomping footsteps behind me.

I turned, gun still in hand, and two policemen, both young and beefy, stood in the foyer, their guns drawn and aimed at me.

"See? I *told* you I heard gunshots!" a shrill, female voice from behind them said. "You boys took your sweet time getting here!"

One of the cops said something to the woman as the other addressed me, but I wasn't listening to either of them. I let the gun fall from fingers as limp as Nora's were when I staged the scene of her death. Wordlessly, I held my hands out and the nearest cop slipped cuffs around my wrists. What was the use of doing anything else? Evie was gone and nothing mattered anymore.

Damn you, Nora, I thought. I knew now why she was so late getting home and so upset when she did. I knew, too, that she wasn't just being stubborn after all.

THE HUSBAND MACHINE
TARA MOSS

June

No one pulled their blinds in this sweltering heat.

The Manhattan sun was going down, sky darkening, and one by one the little boxes in which people spent their lives lit up like television screens, windows thrown open, brows wiped, those hard-working salesmen returning home, harried secretaries escaping typewriters for lonely apartments.

Flick. Flick. Flick.

Each evening the lights came on, and her rear window portal into their private worlds began anew. In the darkness of her small apartment, she took a cool cloth and pressed it to her perspiring forehead, then gingerly placed it across her bare knees, where her nightie was pulled up to manage the stultifying heat. She adjusted herself in her chair, tapped out a cigarette, dragged a match across the wall and lit it, sucked in the smoke.

There.

Lara B. Jefferies had moved in to the building in May.

She had noticed the looks as she'd been brought in. She did not get out much – it was her condition, you see – and never could get hired for paid employment, no matter her education. She had a small set box, and like any other twenty-something-year-old girl, she watched *The Ed Sullivan Show*. But she preferred to entertain herself reading mysteries and watching the world outside.

In fact, you might say it was more than mere entertainment.

It had become a way of life for Lara. People really were fascinating creatures, and circumstances being what they were, she had come to study them. What else was there for her to do? She didn't know their names. She barely knew their voices. But night after night she became intimately acquainted with far more important details than these trifling technicalities. Having been there just a month, Lara already found that this building was as good a lab as any.

Take the ground-floor suite across the courtyard for example: there lived Mr Hearing Aid, the ageing artist. He seemed to have retired from one of the standard professions – she heard he'd been a doctor once – and his wife now tolerated his artistic dalliances, along with the rest of the building, which was forced to witness his poorly conceived sculptures as he displayed them all around the boundaries of their ground-floor patio. Lara wondered if he was trying to save money on the batteries for his hearing aid, as he often pretended not to hear his wife. Like most of the apartment dwellers here, they were well-to-do, the rooms of their suite nicely furnished, apart from the poor choice in art. This evening their apartment glowed, the pair eating a fine meal at their dining table. So far, Lara had not yet seen them exchange a word as they ate. He, hunkered over his food; her, looking up occasionally, as though about to speak and deciding against it.

Above their apartment was Mr Torso, working up even more sweat than most. Deeply tanned, he was a fine physical specimen, carefully sculpted if a tad inflated. Tonight, he was alone in his white Y-fronts, transistor radio on, dancing to a beat that floated across the courtyard to her darkened window – 'Make Love to Me' by Jo Stafford. His shaved skin glistened with perspiration, a folded towel around his neck. There was a large dumb-bell near the open window, and he took a moment to raise it up, pumping at his biceps until they bulged. *One. Two. Three…* Yes, he was a striking specimen all right, veins popping and muscles straining. Naturally, Mr Torso had his admirers, though Lara wondered if they could really compete with his boxing, or the dirty magazines he could be seen pawing over late at night, his blinds never quite fully closed. What would his various girlfriends think of the tawdry images on those pages, if they ever did look under his bed?

Pretty though he was, so far at least – such things did not last in boxing – it was just as well that Miss Lonely Heart never caught his eye. She was a kind woman, only a few years his senior, living in the apartment next to his. Tonight, she could be seen sitting at her table in a floral dress, hair done up, eating a plate of what looked like boiled potatoes, absorbed in a copy of *Reader's Digest*. Her money had been inherited, and though she was barely over thirty she was already being called 'spinster'. A woman with high standards and a meticulously kept apartment of the latest style, she'd offered to help Lara if she needed anything, and was in Lara's good books. She wasn't stuck up like so many of the others.

On the ground level, beneath kind Miss Lonely Heart, a married couple, Mr and Mrs Bland, were on the patio fanning themselves and holding iced drinks, their set box turned to face them through the glass, their living room brought outside until they retired for the evening, or the heat wave let up. They seemed happy enough and apparently childless, except for a small white dog, who had free access to the courtyard from their patio and was currently at their feet. Lara scanned upwards, past Miss Lonely Heart and her magazine, to the apartment of Mr Groom. He was a dish – trim and clean-shaven, with a curl that kept falling over his forehead. From a distance he looked a bit like Burt Lancaster in *From Here to Eternity*. In the mornings he had taken to doing push-ups before heading to work, but sadly, there was nothing to see tonight. The apartment was dark. From what she'd gleaned, it was her parents' money that saw Mr Groom and his wife living there, in this nice little uptown neighbourhood.

More than all of these, Mr Ageing Bachelor was the one to watch. His penthouse apartment was where Lara's binoculars were often trained. He was a tall and square-shouldered man, a touch heavy around the middle, and he had been handsome at some point, but was past his prime now, his tanned face seamed and sagging like a canvas bag. He was a successful businessman, self-made, she heard, and though he could still attract the odd pick up – as Lara could see from the goings on at his apartment after dark – you didn't need binoculars to see that he needed respectability now, a wife, a family. This was the next natural step. His business colleagues arrived at his flat with pregnant wives, and he left with them alone, or with a different date on his arm. Marriage material – that was what Mr Ageing Bachelor needed to find now. Someone who would make him look good. Someone befitting his status.

There was a knock on the door, and Lara put down her binoculars, rolled back from the window and swung her wheelchair around to face the door. "Come in, Betty, come in," she called out, taking the cloth off her legs and pulling down her night dress.

Betty opened the door. Backlit by the hallway lights, she cut a fashionable silhouette, all nipped waist and elegant, flared skirt. Very much the fashion plate.

"Gosh, it's so dark in here," she remarked, leaning across and flicking on a switch. The small apartment flooded with light. "What do you think?"

she asked and turned around. Betty wore a stunning dress, cut tight at her bust and waist, and flaring out around her hips, right down to the calf. Such clothes were wasted on Lara, who rarely had occasion for high fashion or Sunday Best, but she understood beauty when she saw it, and knew a bit about what was going on in the ladies' magazines. She was pretty fashionable herself, all things considered, not that she had anyone to impress but herself.

"I like it. It's a nice choice, Betty. Very Dior," she said.

Betty grinned broadly in response, showing even teeth and dimples. "I'm so pleased." It was a knock-off of course, but it did look very good. Betty did another spin, her shoulder-length blonde her bouncing. "Oh, I brought dinner."

"That's kind of you."

"It's just the fixings for chicken salad. I thought in this heat…"

Lara nodded. "Yes, that will be nice." She couldn't eat anything hot, not in this weather.

"You're not out of ice, are you?"

"Not yet. Thank you."

Betty flashed another dimpled smile, dabbed at her neck with a white handkerchief and started towards the kitchen, but stopped dead when her gaze wandered to the table next to the open window, and the pair of binoculars.

"Have you been…?"

"What of it?" Lara shot back. She looked unflinchingly at Betty, daring her to say more.

Betty did not. She averted her gaze, a frown splitting her pretty brow as she contemplated something troubling. That was the end of the conversation, for now. Betty continued towards the kitchen and soon the smells of the meal filled the small uptown apartment.

August

Yap. Yap. Yap.

Mr Hearing Aid could hear after all, it seemed, as he stormed out onto the patio lined with his creations. "I'm trying to work here. I'm trying to *create*," he complained to the small, white dog. For its part it only yapped again.

Lara took her binoculars and peered across at the apartment of Mr Ageing Bachelor. He was no longer alone. It had happened quickly. Such men were used to these things, once their minds were set upon it. He'd chosen a beautiful, shy blonde, with a lovely figure and great – working – legs, to be his wife. She spent a lot of time around the building and looked a bit like Lara, albeit without the dark hair and ever-present wheelchair. Not that anyone seemed to notice the similarities between them, what with those obvious differences. The engagement had been short, the wedding attended by all his business partners. There had been much backslapping and congratulations for landing such a pretty young wife.

Betty was now Mrs John Gordon.

Lara was certainly not jealous. Not when she showed her the sparkling solitaire or beautiful white wedding dress, and not when they settled into Mr Ageing Bachelor's apartment across the courtyard and began their married life together.

"Shut that dog up!" he shouted over the railing of his balcony, and behind him, Betty flinched and turned in alarm at her husband's raised voice. She had a bruise on her face. Lara had seen it up close, and Betty had not tried to hide it from her, though for the benefit of the rest of the building she had styled her hair differently and took to wearing heavier make-up and large Ray-Ban sunglasses. They were fashionable at least. Covering it up during work at the dress shop would be considerably more awkward, and doubtless her colleagues there were talking.

Lara watched Mr Ageing Bachelor – Mr Gordon – as he moved away from the window and stormed around the penthouse, irritated by something. Was it Betty's cooking again? Or something else? The space, though it had great views, was not really big enough for the pair, though Betty had told him that did not matter to her, she did not want to wait. Six weeks had passed since Lara turned away from their open window as he carried her across the threshold. Now she wasn't sure how much longer Betty could last, the poor woman. Lara did not envy Betty's situation, or her addition to the strange laboratory of little lit rooms across the courtyard from her apartment.

September

Lara hung up the telephone and wheeled across the bare floor to her rear window, a thick blanket across her legs.

After an unseasonably warm start to the month, the weather had finally taken a turn, cooling off. She rolled up to her open window – it was the type that unlatched and swung all the way open – and she smiled and waved at her newly married neighbours. The summer had been unusually long, but the evenings had grown cold and now her herb garden needed attention, most of it having died off. And most inconveniently, her window was stuck open. It was rattling as the wind came up, the bottom corner stuck in the twisted stalks of a barren tomato plant.

Across the darkened courtyard, Betty was pointing Lara's way, drawing attention to her predicament, about which they had just spoken on the telephone. Mr Gordon appeared to huff in response to something – Lara could almost hear him complain at the inconvenience – and then he threw on his sports coat, and walked out of the apartment, slamming the door.

Betty came right up to her window and silently exchanged looks with Lara. Yes, it was time.

Lara rolled back from the chill of her open window, mouth set, and made her way to the light switch. She turned it off, and her apartment was thrown into darkness, with only the small side table light illuminating the sparse interior. Through her window you could again see the tiny boxes that held her neighbours' lives, though many were now veiled by blinds and curtains, that sweltering heat having finally passed. She kept the transistor off, the set box off, and in time she heard heavy footsteps in the hall, and her heart sped up. There came a hard knock on the door, the knob turning slowly as Lara watched, and then there he was, tall and broad-shouldered, silhouetted by the hallway lights. Mr Ageing Bachelor, in the flesh.

"It's so dark in here?"

"My condition, it…"

"Never mind," he grumbled. "Betty says you need someone to fix your window," he said, and trundled down the three steps that led into her apartment – three steps that made it impossible for her to roll out into the hallway with her wheelchair. There were always steps, everywhere steps, preventing her from exercising what mobility she could otherwise have.

"Thank you so much for coming, Mr Gordon. I do appreciate your help," Lara told him cheerily. "My window is caught on my tomato plant. Or what was once my tomato plant. I don't know quite how it got so caught up. It's getting so cold now," she said, and gestured to the heavy wool blanket covering her legs.

"Uh huh," he muttered, avoiding her eye. For some people, 'invalids', as they were often called – not *valids* – were not worth communicating with, were barely at the level of human at all. Forget that it was a club anyone could join in a heartbeat. Forget that Betty, his own wife, was kind enough to help her, kind enough to pick up her groceries when she could not get out on her own.

"Can I get you anything?" Lara offered and her visitor ignored her, as if she had not spoken.

Mr Ageing Bachelor – she'd have to come up with a different name for him now – brushed past her and leaned out of her window to look at the problem. His wife watched from across the way, standing at the edge of their balcony, an apron over her pretty blue dress. "Bloody thing is caught," Lara heard him complain as he leaned out further to try to reach. The tomato plant, now little more than a twisted series of stalks, gave a little, a piece of it snapping as he pulled at it.

Lara's heart sped up, watching him, her body tensing. She moved forward.

Frustrated, he stood back and took off his sports coat, tossing it on her table. He hadn't taken it off at the door, despite her welcome. He didn't want to hang out with his wife's crippled friend. Oh no. Not even for a few minutes. Now he rolled up his shirt sleeves, revealing thick, hairy forearms, and still ignoring Lara, he leaned out of the window once more while his wife observed across the courtyard.

Lara sat in her wheelchair, watching.

Her heart was beating faster again, and he was leaning out, his leather shoes butted up against the wall. One breath, two breaths, and she rolled forward, and bracing her body and planting her feet on the ground, she stood up from her chair – for some reason most people did not even imagine this could occur, as if every person who used a wheelchair was fully paralysed and there were no wheelchair users who could move at all, let alone the likes of her, so vulnerable-looking after the extensive nerve injuries her stepfather had left her with. She needed her wheelchair, but she was not so vulnerable, not so benign and helpless, as this man imagined. She knew just what to do to. Without hesitation she took him by the back of his trousers, just above the knees, and with a single yank that sent a regrettable jolt of nerve pain down her legs, he was over the edge of her windowsill and falling headlong into the garden bed three stories below. There was a crack and a heavy thud, and Lara sat back down, waited a beat as she adjusted her wool blanket, and then screamed.

Across the courtyard, right on cue, Betty let out a shriek. Blinds flew open. People came out onto their balconies. Mr Torso appeared with only his trousers on, a female companion at his side.

"He's fallen! Oh god, he's fallen! Help!"

✶

"It was a terrible accident," she told the detective, between sobs. "It happened so fast. He was trying to help me with the window and just got too confident, I guess. It was caught on my plants, you see. I couldn't get it closed. He just slipped. I told him to be careful, not to take any risks..."

She looked down at her legs, and the detective followed her gaze, and then snapped his head upwards again, not wanting to imagine what was under the blanket.

"My poor husband," Betty cried, hands over her face.

"This must be such a shock."

What terrible luck, the cops would be thinking, to have such a fall, and this invalid woman watching, unable to help. And the man was newly married, too. Would they feel differently when they found out about the life insurance? That seemed unlikely. Betty was so pretty, with that fair, blonde innocence that beguiled even the toughest hearts. And she looked little like Betty in that moment – Lara with her jet-black locks and the steel in her green eyes, which were currently downcast and hidden behind a set of thick spectacles. The resemblance was there, but seemed invisible to most, stuck as they were on the wheelchair she needed to manage the injuries she'd been left with.

"He was such a good man, always so kind to everyone," Betty lied. "Always trying to help." She brought out her white handkerchief, and with a delicate hand, dabbed at her eyes.

"And you two know each other?" the detective asked, not looking Lara in the eye.

Betty and Lara looked at each other. Yes, they certainly knew each other. It was in fact 'Betty' and her father who had changed Lara's life irrevocably. It was Betty's abusive father who had wounded Lara, damaging her spine and killing their mother one fateful night, setting the half-sisters on this course. The neighbours had blamed the booze, but it was something else, something in his nature that was there even before the drink each day. Of course, Betty was called Diana back then, and changed her first and last names after that tragedy struck. Likewise, Lara had been Rebecca. She was older by a few years and vowed to take care of the two of them. And so she did. She knew just what to do to ensure their futures.

"Why yes. Betty has been so helpful. She even brings meals sometimes. I could not hope for a better neighbour."

The detective did not look at her as she spoke, but he scribbled a note.

"We're sorry for your loss, Miss," he said to Betty. "Um, Mrs Gordon." They escorted the distraught young woman from the scene of the crime. There wasn't much more to it than that. There had been multiple witnesses, after all. What a terrible accident. And he'd been trying to help. The police did not mention the bruise around Betty's left eye. Presumably they did not see it, and even if they did, it was a private matter, and could not be related to this freak accident across the courtyard.

Lara and Betty would move on to a new, even nicer neighbourhood, perhaps even a new city, once the life insurance came through. They could afford to move in to something even finer after this, something larger. Together they were a good team: like a well-oiled machine. It would be expected that the likes of Betty would move on, poor thing, and find another husband.

And she would, with sister Lara's help.

Lara was always watching.

BLACK WINDOW
KIM NEWMAN

"If you stand close to the wall, Officer – so close your cheek nearly touches the paper – you can see the open bathroom door in the other room. The room opposite. It's just like this one. In the Horseshoe, all rooms are the same. The ones I've been in, at least. The same paper, the same bed and desk and chair, the same three pictures of trees, of ships, of stars. Look behind you if you don't believe me. See my bathroom door. It's open too. It won't shut. Not all the way, properly. I've complained to the night man and the day man. Nothing can be done, they say. The jamb warps in summer and the hinges hang wrong. It's fall now and still not fixed. I bet the hinges hang wrong over there too, in the room across the gap… beyond the well of dark. That's where the body must be. In the bathroom of that room. The son must have put the mother in there after he killed her."

"Do you spend a lot of time looking out the window, Mr Black?"

"Not an inordinate amount. There's no open view. Just the well of dark. And the wall opposite. But being here so much – I'm working on a project, a scientific study that demands constant attention – I can't help but see what goes on. Look for yourself. Here's the desk where I work. Here's my typewriter. Here's the window which is in front of my face when I sit down to work. It won't open. In summer, it's stifling in here. The paper sweats glue. I've tried and tried to open the window, but success evades me. The frame is painted over. I complained to the day man. He said he couldn't figure it out. Looked into it, claimed he couldn't see anything wrong. He probably did the painting and doesn't want to admit it. Fearful for his position, I'll be bound. Jobs are hard to come by."

"The day man looked into the window? Out of the window, rather?"

"Uh-huh."

"He didn't see any signs of a murder?"

"This was weeks ago. Ancient history. The murder didn't happen till last night. Besides, he's the day man. The ruckus comes at night. In the day, things are calm between the mother and son."

"You didn't complain to the night man. About the painted-over frame?"

"The night man never leaves his post. At the desk by the fern in the lobby. When a day man falters, they make him a night man. When a night man gets off track, only oblivion awaits. The night man is afraid, always."

"Yes. I get that."

"Do you? Do you really, Officer? Because I get the feeling you don't get anything? Are you the night officer? Could I speak to the day officer?"

"I'm not an officer. I'm a detective. Detective George."

"A night detective?"

"I've the midnight till dawn shift. So I guess so."

"Could I speak to the day detective?"

"No such animal, Mr Black. I'm what you get."

"The murder must have happened *before* midnight. Say, about ten-thirty."

"Makes no difference. It's when the report comes in. That's when a crime gets logged."

"I telephoned before midnight. I telephoned before the murder. And after the murder. The first time, the officer was rude. Told me to mind my own beeswax. Not poke my nose in other people's quarrels."

"You reported a disturbance and weren't satisfied with the response?"

"Not a disturbance, exactly. A ruckus."

"What does that mean? Noise? Alarums?"

"I couldn't *hear* anything. Not across the well of dark. But I could *see* them going at it, the mother and the son. Haranguing. Gesticulation."

"You reported *gesticulation*?"

"I had concerns. Justified, as it turns out."

"There was an argument. Which you couldn't hear?"

"I said before, my window won't open. Theirs was shut."

"Can you lip-read?"

"No. Can anyone?"

"Remember before talkies came in?"

"When I was a boy, yes. John Barrymore as Mr Hyde. That fellow of the opera with the nose-holes and eyes."

"Lon Chaney."

"Uh-huh. Lon Chaney. 'You are dancing on the tombs of tortured men!' *Seven Footprints to Satan*, that was another one."

"Spook pictures."

"Not my choice. When you're a child, you see the movies your parent or guardian wants to see. I'd have picked Charlie Chaplin."

"Still, you remember when films didn't speak? When mouths made shapes. And actors, ah, gesticulated?"

"I get where you're going, Detective. No, I can't lip-read – not like a deaf person – but I can make out the shapes of mouths. I could intuit a few words."

"'I'm going to murder you, Mother!'"

"Nothing as convenient as that for when you want me to give testimony on a witness stand. But words that add up to that. Vile words, though we've all heard them. Frankly, you can't blame the son. The mother was a nightmare."

"You knew the woman you say was murdered?"

"By sight. And by type. We all know women like that. Large, loud. The sort that fills a room. Radios have a switch that turns them off. The light dims and the noise stops. Such women should be fitted with switches like that, don't you think? I'd sometimes see the son just looking out the window, shaking with fury, face a white smear..."

"This was when you were looking out your window too?"

"Of course. His face would be close to the glass, hands over his ears. She'd be in the background, raging and roaring like one of those dinosaurs... not the toothy kind that sit up and beg but the four-legged kind, with the long tails and hosepipe necks and the tiny heads."

"Brontosaurs?"

"Is that what they're called. That kind of dinosaur."

"The sit-up kind, who stand on two legs and have tiny arms and huge heads with lots of teeth, are tyrannosaurs. People usually find them the more threatening. They were meat-eaters. Brontosaurs were placid. They nibbled leaves."

"That's to fool you. Being nibbled is worse than having your head bitten off. Nibbled day in, day out. Plus they're big and clumsy. They don't care what breaks around them. Why are you writing this down? It seems awfully beside the point."

"I have to write everything down."

"Isn't that laborious?"

"It's part of the job. Routine."

"I understand that. I have routine too. In my research. Minutiae must be observed. Events must be catalogued. The slightest distraction and a day's work is useless."

"The son and the mother distracted you?"

"Oh no. I see where you're going. I'm a witness, not a suspect. I had no motive. They are strangers to me. The son killed the mother."

"You *saw* that?"

"He didn't do it in front of the window, so no. A murderer wouldn't be so foolish, would he? But I saw signs. The minutiae, as I said. Observable events. Clues, you'd call them. Wouldn't you, Detective?"

"Walk me through it, Mr Black."

"You see the spots on the window? Blood. And if you stand close to the wall, as I said, you can see more of a sliver of the room opposite. The open bathroom door. The mother was there, big mouth open, big arms flailing. I'll bet you've found broken vases and strewn flowers. The son hasn't had time to clean up. This evening, about half past ten I should say, he just *snapped*. He was at her throat. Then they weren't in front of the window any more and the deed couldn't be seen from here. The event wasn't observable, but could be inferred. Afterwards, I saw the son's face at his window. Forehead against the glass. That's how blood got there. It must be a shock, exhausting... killing someone. Committing murder. Everyone thinks about the poor victim. But their pain is over, turned off like a radio. They are in the calm quiet dark for good. The one who stays behind, he's in shock... just an awful thing. Going over and over and over it."

"He was looking out of his window and you were looking out of yours. Did he see you?"

"He must have, but – do you know? – I don't really think he did. Maybe he was seeing his mother's face – like a ghost reflection in the glass. He'd have had his face close to hers when he was killing her. I imagine that burns into the retinas. You know, like when you look at an unshaded light bulb and look away but can still see the curly burning wire?"

"The filament?"

"Uh-huh. Like that. The face of the victim must be there, burning. Imprinted on the eyes."

"You weren't afraid he'd see you across the dark? Murderers often find they need to get rid of the witnesses. To avoid blackmail. Or being caught. Sometimes, murderers just get the habit of it. They'd kill the whole world if they could. Until they're stopped."

"We're on the same floor. All he'd have to do is come round to this side of the Horseshoe. The door would be easy to kick in. Then he'd have two bodies to get rid of. What if, after killing me, he looked out of my window and saw a face at his own window – he'd leave the door of his room open and anyone could come in. Or someone else could call the police."

"We did have several other calls. About the noise."

"I said there was a disturbance. The officer who took my first call must be in trouble. Serve him right."

"He will have questions to answer."

"The son didn't come to murder me, though."

"No. You're still alive."

"I called the police in time to save my own life."

"That's debatable. You might still die. And the murderer might be responsible for another death. Your death."

"You think he'd get away with it? Come for me later? How could you fail to make a case that'll stick? I said you should look in his bathroom. That's where she'll be. He can't have gotten rid of the body yet. Not all of it."

"We have looked in the bathroom of the room opposite yours. There's no body there. No people there, actually. The paper came off the ceiling in the summer, and hasn't been replaced yet so no one can live in there. The night man let us in, though. He left his post by the fern for that. The room's out of use."

"But the mother and the son…"

"Oh, we found the mother's body."

"Where? Stuffed under the bed? In the closet?"

"No, we found her where you said she'd be."

"I don't understand."

"The body is in the bathroom. Most of it. In *your* bathroom, Mr Black. Your bathroom. Your mother."

"My mother? But she's not loud. She can hardly speak above a whisper. It's why she repeats herself and repeats herself. She's not big, either. That's just an impression she gives. The mother across the way, now… she's a different scuttle of coal…"

"Do you still see her face? Burning like a filament?"

"I saw the *murderer's* face. The son's. Pressed against his window. There was blood. I saw him across the well of dark. Through my window."

"There's no window in this room, Mr Black."

"Don't be silly, Detective George... Look, there it is – you can see the murderer now. Pointing at us. Arrest him."

"That's not a window, Mr Black. That's a mirror."

THE MAN IN
THE SAILOR SUIT

NICK MAMATAS

In the hat box, nestled in the sort of tissue paper one normally finds in hat boxes, on Donald Fischer's lap, was a revolver.

"Happy Christmas," Mrs. Fischer said. On her head she wore a paper crown. Donald's remained folded on the table between them, near his plate, which held a Christmas cracker rather than food. There was a chicken on the table though, and a chopped salad, and boiled sausage and mashed potatoes, and a single bottle of wine that wasn't near enough for a holiday with Mother.

Donald was an American, as was his mother. The Germanic anglers who had given the family its name were long lost to history, and Mr. Fischer himself was dead, so Mrs. Fischer felt free to embrace a silly Anglophilia.

"Merry Christmas, Mother," Donald said, without looking up from this lap. "Is this gun—"

"Your father's?" Mrs. Fischer asked. "It is. His service revolver. A Colt. Teddy Roosevelt himself selected it for the NYPD, you know."

"Loaded," said Donald. "I was going to ask if it was loaded. I know it's a Colt, it says so on the grip. I know Father had one, I…" Donald knew a lot of things about this particular revolver, heavier than any hat that ever sat in the box on his lap.

"Every gun is a loaded gun," Mrs. Fischer said. She smiled. "Happy Christmas, Donald." She stared across the table. Donald squirmed lightly, as though he were a shimmering mirage. His present for Mother was a bottle of Jeppson's Malört. She was unlikely to open it at the table despite its reputation for easing digestion, and Donald was unlikely to drink too much of it even if she did. The liqueur tasted to him of gasoline injected into licorice. Even Donald's appetites had their limits.

But did Mrs. Fischer's? A loaded gun for Christmas. Donald had been home for only three months, back from New York minus most of his belongings and his wife Amelia, who was still sitting in a small Bronx apartment, waiting for her annulment, likely in front of the world's second saddest Christmas tree. The very saddest was browning in the corner of the living room, shedding needles onto the couch where Donald would sleep tonight. Mrs. Fischer had taken Donald in the way a summertime ice floe takes in a polar bear – for a short-term stay to be followed by a sudden dive into the drink. Mrs. Fischer had been complaining about the couch too. Perhaps in the New Year she could have her small North Chicago apartment to herself again, and a reason to get a new davenport.

Christmas dinner was a quiet affair. Mrs. Fischer was an excellent wielder of utensils; neither the tines of her forks nor the serrated edge of her knife made the slightest sound against her plate. Donald sipped his wine as subtly as he could, and served himself shallow pours – to make the wine last, to obscure his consumption, to get a buzz on only slowly, so he wouldn't say what was on his mind about his Christmas present.

Donald's father hadn't shot himself, even though he'd drunkenly waved his sidearm around once or twice, more proudly than threateningly. He'd explained, even as he held six bullets in his left hand, that the Colt was still loaded, that every gun was always loaded. His tool of suicide had been alcohol. Mrs. Fischer had grieved plenty, then sold the big table and almost all of Mr. Fischer's effects, and had a two-top delivered. Even were Amelia and Donald still together and merely home for the holidays, Donald would have had to sit on the cabin trunk with his plate on his lap while the ladies of his life used the table.

Donald managed to consume the majority of the wine, about sixty percent of the bottle by his reckoning. It was enough to level him out, thoughts of the loaded gun bobbing away on red waves. And the remaining fraction was enough to make the birdlike Mrs. Fischer drowsy. She soon announced her retirement for the evening. A week ago, when Donald appeared at her doorstep, her first command was that he move the radio set from the living room to the bedroom. "Now that you're here, perhaps I'll buy a television and we can watch it together," she had said. "A family Christmas present." She'd put his own father's loaded gun in one of her old hat boxes instead.

So, the living room, Donald's room now, was dark. The corner radiator steamed and grumbled away, the world's worst polka coming from an iron accordion. The streets outside were empty. It was Christmas, and there was no snow on the ground, but somehow the air itself looked frigid. Donald wouldn't take a night stroll. He had a week's worth of the local paper's crime blotters to go through. Mother subscribed to *Tribune*, but its police reporters covered crime in the city proper, not the goings-on of North Chicago.

Donald was hopeful, then overjoyed. Single man battered by unknown attackers on Tuesday, after midnight, on the strip. Three swabbies held overnight after disturbing the peace on Thursday, then released to their superior offices at Naval Station Great Lakes that morning. No names listed in that one. Two young Negroes arrested for "strolling" past Twenty-Second Street, into the white neighborhood where the roads were paved and the lampposts functioned. And on Christmas Eve, a piano bar was raided after a telephone call by a concerned citizen reported "excess noise," as if a raid would be any quieter than a party. Donald could read between the lines. Certain streets, mostly close to Lake Michigan and the naval station, and one or two drinking establishments nearby, were amenable to midnight fraternizing, the making of fast friends. Just as it had been in New York – the action was by the water, and attracted all types. A true Brotherhood of Man.

Too bad it was Christmas. Only the most awful of degenerates would dare loiter on such a night, and Donald had his standards. Mrs. Fischer was usually a night owl, demanding hand after hand of gin rummy until Donald begged off, then switching to the solo game she called patience. She often cheated to keep the games going. Donald would have to wait till New Year's Eve, when he could convince his mother to drink early. She'd never make it to midnight, and the streets would be more crowded than usual.

He unlatched his trunk as quietly as he could, and moved aside his changes of clothes to pat, just to touch, his almost perfect facsimile of a sailor suit, miraculously unwrinkled after its travels. It was as white as snow, practically glowing at the bottom of Donald's trunk. He felt such a happy surge of excitement that he almost forgot about his father's old service revolver.

✶

There wasn't much for Donald to do in the half-dead week between Christmas Day and the New Year. The help wanted ads had shrunk to half a column. Only the most dubious of warehouses and restaurants – the type run by petty tyrants who prided themselves on shouting at their workers like a father bellowing at the dinner table – were hiring, because they could never keep any.

The pawnshops were open, and his father's Colt could bring in some money, Donald decided. He dressed in his sailor suit, partially because he missed wearing it, and partially in the hope that the pawnbroker would give a Navy man a better deal on a firearm. Donald had always given real military men a wide berth when on his late-night walks, so was surprised when the pawnbroker practically laughed in his face. She was an older woman, and her eyeglasses had smaller eyeglasses attached to them. Somehow, she could see right through him.

"Laundry day?" she said. "Costume party? Lose a bet? You're no swabbie at the base, and you're sure not a real Navy man."

"What makes you say that?" Donald asked. His father's Colt was in a paper sack, like a heavy sandwich.

The pawnbroker ticked off the reasons on her fingers. "You've got insignia on the right side. It's been left side only for three years. Your hat doesn't fit. Those shoes aren't naval issue – they're not even the right color. You're dressed for the brig, son. Out of the uniform. You also don't smell like a Navy man."

"What do Navy men smell like?" Donald asked.

"The lake," the pawnbroker said. "Lake Michigan. You may have heard of it. Some are really impressed with it. You might even be driven to call it a great lake, buster."

Donald knew well the scent of freshwater, and salt too. It hardly mattered what the pawnbroker said. So what if she wasn't impressed by his outfit? It wasn't truly for her, or for anyone else, anyway. Donald enjoyed wearing it for his own sake. "I just moved here," he said, unsure why he was bothering to explain. "So, it's been in my luggage. My mother's family is from around here. I'm seeking to settle."

"Ah," said the pawnbroker.

"I have a gun in this bag," Donald said.

"I have one under my counter," the pawnbroker said. Then, louder, she said, "Lenny!" and out of a door by the far end of the counter, where several brass instruments hung on iron hooks from the wall, came a nearly perfectly spherical man, and in his hands he held a rifle that looked like it came right out of a B-movie horse opera. By the time Donald turned back to the pawnbroker, she had the teensiest of Derringers in her palm. "Let's see the merchandise."

"Just a precaution, son," said the man, Lenny, his voice unnervingly high-pitched. He appeared neckless, like a giant baby. Donald thought to himself that the man should grow some whiskers if he wished to be taken as an adult, but beards were not the fashion.

Donald withdrew the Colt from the paper bag and placed it on the glass countertop.

"No holster," said Lenny. "No case?"

"It was a Christmas present," Donald said.

"Is it loaded?" the pawnbroker asked. Donald shrugged. She put her Derringer back under the counter, then picked up the Colt. ".32 caliber, double action. New Police. *New York* Police," she said, reading the words engraved upon the barrel. "You from back East then?"

"I grew up there."

She turned away, pointed the Colt's muzzle toward the floor, swung open the cylinder, and glanced up at Donald, those four lenses making her eyes look huge and also small. "This is a loaded gun."

"I got it that way," said Donald.

"For Christmas," said Lenny. It wasn't quite a question.

There was little for Donald to do but accept the oddness of the situation. Either he would walk out of here with enough money for a room, or he'd take his father's Colt and go home to wait out the week before the New Year rang in. "Yes, a Christmas present from my mother. She gave it to me in a hat box. She claims that the revolver once belonged to my father, back when he was an NYPD patrolman. He died when I was in high school. Thanks to father's survivor benefit, my mother was able to move back here, where her family is from," he said. The couple just peered at him. "All of her family is deceased as well, but she was always a bit uncomfortable in New York – you know, the noise, the hustle and bustle, the 'New York attitude.'"

"The New York attitude," Lenny said. This wasn't a question either.

"Yes," said Donald. "New Yorkers can be a bit more assertive than people from the Midwest. They always say what's on their mind, and what's on their mind isn't often pleasant."

"There's something to be said for not saying anything, when the thing on your mind isn't pleasant," said the pawnbroker. "I'm afraid I can't offer you anything for this piece."

"Why not?" asked Donald.

"It's a police gun," the pawnbroker said.

"New York police, and it's practically an antique. Teddy Roosevelt ordered them when he was the police commissioner," said Donald.

"Sure, sure," said the pawnbroker. "You know that. You might say that even I know that. Leonard here was a great supporter of President Roosevelt, both of them."

"The first ever Presidential ballot I cast was a straight Bull Moose ticket. I've been a New Dealer since it was the Square Deal, *Ensign*," said Lenny. "But the point is that this trade is a highly regulated one. We pawnbrokers are practically bankers. Inspectors come around not infrequently, and there's just something about police issue firearms that make them feel a bit itchy when they see that they've been placed in hock, or purchased outright."

"It's all perfectly legal," said the pawnbroker, "but you have to understand… there's a certain 'Chicago attitude' about such things, even here in North Chicago."

"It wouldn't do for you, either," said Lenny.

"Just imagine what I'd have to tell them, heart to God, about this trade were I to make it. You came here, with your mother's own Christmas present, an heirloom of your deceased father, while dressed in a little sailor suit, the way a mother might dress a young child." She removed the bullets from the cylinder as she spoke, and placed them in the pocket of her work apron. With a small white handkerchief she gave the Colt the once over, as if keen to obliterate her fingerprints.

"I need money," Donald said.

"I can take the suit for five dollars," the pawnbroker said. "That's outright sale. If you want to pawn it, it'll be two dollars and seven nights. I'd expect you to launder it and come back with it neatly pressed."

"It'll save you some trouble in the long run," Lenny said. "Around here, the swabbies don't appreciate pretenders, and by around here I mean this very place of business. We get fellows from the naval station in here all the time." He looked over Donald's shoulder, and meaningfully at the entrance.

"Then why do you want the suit to sell to someone else?" Donald asked. "And I think I'd best be getting my property returned to me."

"Ours is not to reason why," the pawnbroker said, "but usually a spare, clean, pair of pants can come in handy after a night on the town. We open early."

"Do you know how to handle that firearm?" Lenny asked.

"Yes, of course," Donald said. "My father used to take me out to shoot at lily pads in the pond." That was a true statement. Donald saw no reason to share that there had only been two such outings, "to make a man" out of Donald, and that he hadn't fired a gun since.

Lenny snorted at that. "Your father had you shoot at a body of water, you say?" The pawnbroker put her hand in the pocket of her apron, but didn't remove it, or the bullets. They looked at one another, then at Donald. "I wouldn't recommend discharging a firearm at a body of water, toots," the pawnbroker said.

"Let's say we sell you some wax bullets," Lenny said. "You can do some target practice. Get a handle on the piece."

"And a holster," said the pawnbroker. "You can't carry a firearm around in a sack."

"I wasn't planning on carrying it around," said Donald. "I wasn't planning on leaving the store with it!"

"And yet, leaving the store with it is exactly what you'll presently be doing, friend," Lenny said, now a dark cloud filling the room.

"All right..." Donald said. "Wax bullets sound just dandy, and a holster too."

He sighed and leaned down, and pulled a five-dollar bill from his shoe. "So long as I can buy it with this, and get change enough for a soda pop."

"Wax bullets it is," said the pawnbroker. "They won't bounce back on you."

*

Mrs. Fischer talked a big game to count down to the New Year and listened to a recitation of the King's Christmas Address on the wireless, but she made it till about 9:30 p.m. Then she announced that it was too cold to wait up, and took to her bed under an enormous pile of blankets. The sound of the radio, slight and tinny like a distant neighbor or a nearby ghost, wafted into the living room. Only when it was drowned out by Mrs. Fischer's snores did Donald make his move. He put on his suit, and his pea coat. The crime blotters are usually quiet in the final week of the year, but not here in North Chicago. Sailors at loose ends, for the most part, getting up to mischief of various sorts.

He thought about his father's Colt, and the wax bullets, which he hadn't had the opportunity to use. He loaded five of the chambers with them, and in a moment of sheer perversity, pushed a real bullet into the last. He hadn't gotten a holster, but his coat had an interior pocket on the left breast, and the gun felt heavy, but comforting there. He wouldn't be able to whip it out, brandish it in the face of any sudden attacker, and he didn't think he'd be able to bring himself to shoot a man, but the Colt still made him feel better about things. It could be a conversation piece in the right situation.

Donald took the still mostly full bottle of Malört, and that went in his paper bag. It wasn't good, but it was a local delicacy, and warming, like kerosene for the veins. Good for his breath too, in case someone he met also enjoyed kissing. Donald didn't, not particularly, but one had to give in order to get, as Amelia used to tell him.

Cruising was always awkward, which was one of the reasons Donald wore the sailor suit. It was like a mask, or a costume. He became someone else when he wore it. And of course, both men and women, and unusual combinations of the two, enjoyed teasing Navy men on leave – "Hey, sailor! New in town?" was a cliché, but some of the people who shouted, or sang it, at him, meant it. New York was so big and the Chelsea piers so crowded with ships coming and going, sweaty merchant marines and pin-sharp swabbies, plus landlubbers of every description and predilection, that Donald was spoiled for choice. That, and if he kept his eyes and ears open, he never need encounter anyone a second time.

North Chicago, Donald realized in a flash, wouldn't be like that. Nor would Milwaukee, which was the closest big city. The really big city, Chicago proper, maybe he could keep himself anonymous, but down there the sailor suit would be less effective, less a peacock's display and more an eccentric's affectation or a simple costume. Would he have to dress like a hobo, complete with bundle tied to the end of a stick, to blend in with the men who worked the rails? The gun, dense near his heart, suggested yet another alternative.

Better to stick with the plan, and meet some people, even if he might eventually lose his anonymity. The suit was both a billboard and a mask. The streets were cold, and Donald needed to warm up. It wasn't too difficult on New Year's Eve to find someone, and there were plenty of alleys between the city's squat buildings. The first fellow was already fairly tipsy, with big wide white teeth and thick curly hair. He had good hands; he was a working man. He swung the hammer at a slaughterhouse, he said, but only ate fish and eggs. He was chatty throughout, really, and Donald learned much about him. His wife was named Margaret and he laughed that he'd be home at midnight to kiss her.

"So kiss me now, Popeye," he said when Donald was done, and Donald did. Everything was salty, like the sea. The man gripped him hard through his pants and tugged a couple of times, but then just smiled and said,

"Thank you," oddly primly, like a schoolmarm receiving an apple from a poor student. "Half past ten; I must vamoose! Happy New Year! Don't take any wooden nickels."

Or wax bullets, Donald found himself thinking as he smiled and nodded and wished the man a happy New Year. It was already the New Year in New York. Maybe Amelia had already found someone new to warm her bed instead of just lie, and lie, in it. Maybe she had drunk herself into a sweet-smelling midnight nap. Maybe her face was salty from tears. But Donald had done her a favor by leaving his pay envelope on the kitchen table, minus train fare, and leaving. Amelia had nothing to cry about.

As he left the alley a few minutes after his new friend did, Donald clocked three swabbies who had clocked him. They were like characters from a boy's illustrated storybook – a dark-haired one who loped down the block like a cowboy, a tall blond drink of water who could probably swim to Michigan and back, and a little red-haired fellow, already giggling and covering his mouth. Three-on-one could go very well, or very poorly. Donald made to move on quickly, but the sailors called out to him, and thundered across like a six-legged beast.

"Hey there, sailor," said the dark one. "Name's Esposito." That was the name stenciled onto the left breast of his suit. "Nice hat. I liked it so much I got one of my own." He pointed at his matching cap and laughed.

"Ronald," said Donald, thinking slowly, wondering what his breath smelled like.

"Cap'n Ronald," said the red-haired man. "A proud Scottish surname. I'm a Campbell myself."

"Well, it's Fischer," said Donald. He'd meant to say something else, but out spilled his real surname.

"Fisher, right? A fisherman," said Campbell. "Or a fisher *of* men? Get it?" Esposito laughed at Campbell's joke, but not as loud as Campbell.

The blond fellow, a head taller than everyone but Campbell, whom he towered over by far more than that, just blushed hard. "Hello," he said.

"Svenson," Esposito offered. "Happy New Year, Captain Ronald, the fisherman! We can't bear to see a fellow sailor stranded on his own. Come with us!"

"Where to?" Donald asked as Esposito's arm wrapped around his frame.

"Down to the pier, of course! Right, boys?" Campbell cheered. Svenson might have *hrrm*ed or made a similar noise.

Soon, out came the Malört. Donald needed it, and Svenson seemed to genuinely enjoy it. Esposito waved it away, and Campbell put on a brave face but let most of his swig dribble down his chin like a child taking bad medicine. Donald wanted to lick the cleft at the base of Campbell's chin clean.

"You brought the party with you, Captain," said Svenson. It was the first full sentence Donald had heard from him the entire too-long walk down to the docks by the naval station.

Sailors and Women's Reservists, regular revelers in pointed hats and thick coats, the occasional enterprising peanut man or sausage-seller, a cloud of murmuring and occasional yelps, and a hard cutting wind that everyone but Donald seemed used to. It was twenty minutes till midnight. Esposito saw him shivering and gave him a big hug, and rubbed his back and that hand drifted lower and he said in Donald's ear, "I'll keep you warm. I've sailed 'round the Arctic Circle, but not the Antarctic."

"You know, Arctic means bear," said Campbell. "Antarctic means no bear."

Nonplussed, his arms pinned to his sides by Esposito's clamp, Donald looked at Svenson, who nodded, shrugged, and said, "It is so."

"Let's find some place private," Campbell said, and pushed his way through the crowd. Esposito and Svenson took either side of Donald and led him forward. Donald caught someone looking in his direction. It didn't take long to find the dark and quiet corner, right on the pier, between two mountains of pallets held together by thick rope netting. Nobody was around. The spray from Lake Michigan was like a fusillade of bullets. No wonder the boys had the place to themselves. Donald was nervous, but exhilarated too. These men were real sailors, comrades. They might shanghai him for the night, perhaps, but in a few weeks they'd be gone on a ship of steel, churning and slicing their way across the world, with nothing to depend on but one another.

"Who first?" Svenson said.

"Captain Ronald, first," said Esposito. Then he grabbed Donald's pea coat and tore it open, and pulled the Colt from the interior pocket. "Look at this, men!"

Campbell slipped and fell onto his behind, then quickly picked himself up. Svenson had the empty Malört bottle. He gripped it by the neck now, and raised it.

"What?" Donald cried. "What?!"

"You shore patrol?" said Campbell. "Listen, we weren't..."

"Haven't you even seen a gun before?" Donald asked. "You're all in the Navy!"

"Sailors don't carry sidearms, unless they're *masters*-at-arms," said Esposito. "What do you think we do – line up on deck and shoot at the enemy like their boats are tin cans?"

"I'm not a Navy man," said Donald. "Look at me, it's all wrong, see? It's just, you know, a costume. For New Year's!"

Esposito peered closely at the Colt. "You're police. You're trying to entrap us. Civilian police!" Campbell looked like he was about to burst into tears. Svenson, the strong, silent type, just stared, as though he were on the night watch or something. Donald realized his gaze was trained past him, to make sure nobody else wandered through and took the party unawares.

"I'm not police, and it's my father's gun. My late father's gun. He was a police officer in New York when I was a child. That gun's older than your mother, Esposito, and it's not even loaded. Just wax bullets, for target practice." Only after he spoke did Donald remember that he had loaded a single real bullet into the cylinder.

"They say every gun is loaded," said Esposito. "You've got an honest face." Then he took a large step back, aimed the Colt, and fired it at Donald's belly. The report was sharp, like a snapping finger, but no louder. The bullet hit Donald like a punch too fast to see, and he doubled over. It felt like something was broken. Some bone he hadn't known about before, or a big fleshy organ split like a sausage.

"Damn…" Donald muttered through clenched teeth.

"Damn," Esposito said too. "I guess that was a wax bullet."

"Esposito!" Svenson cried. "Take it easy!"

"It's going to be the brig for all of us if this gets out," said Esposito, as he leveled the Colt again. Svenson rushed him, but Esposito put out a big hand and planted it on Svenson's chest. Svenson had drunk the lion's share of the Malört, so he fell right over. The glass shattered as it fell from Svenson's hand. Campbell was crying. He was a kid, Donald realized, just barely allowed to sign his name and have it mean something.

Donald realized something else too. He wanted to live. He picked a patch of darkness and ran right into it. The Colt went off behind him. It hit his back, hard, but the pea coat was thick and Donald was running away from the bullet, so he only stumbled, not fell.

Esposito's footfalls echoed behind him. He was fit, that man, and quickly caught up to Donald, but it's hard to shoot, and run, and hit at someone who is running and doesn't want to get hit. He fired again, and missed. The wax bullet flew past Donald and smacked against a wooden crate like a wad of gum, angrily spit. Donald turned left on a dime, and booked hard, but he didn't know where he was running to, and found himself on the edge of a pier, with nowhere to turn but into the drink.

"Ronald, stop!" Esposito called. "You're trying to frame me for stealing a cop's gun! You have to take this back!" He held the Colt out, but not by the barrel. "It's yours!"

"I..." Donald started. How drunk was Esposito? What had gotten into him, other than what gets into all men who cruise? The worry that the next fellow is from the vice squad, or is a priest with a Bible in his pants pocket, or has a taste for blood and newsprint, or is just a man so sad and lost and lonely that you can't bear to only see him once. Maybe there didn't need to be anything else. "Okay. Just hand it over."

"You can't tell nobody about this," Esposito growled. "And you gotta burn that sailor suit."

"I will, I will," said Donald. "Give me the Colt and I'll throw it right over my shoulder, into Lake Michigan too. Nobody will ever find it. Nobody has to know."

"Nobody has to know, eh?" Esposito repeated, his voice a parrot's chirp now. Then came a roar and a whistle from every direction. Happy New Year! The city was alive with cheers.

Even Donald broke into a huge smile. "Happy New Year, Esposito!"

"Happy New Year!" Esposito said, clumsily firing the Colt into the air. They both flinched and ducked, and the wax bullet hit one of the wooden pier planks between them. "Happy goddamn New Year!" Esposito said, rushing Donald.

"Nobody has to know!"

Donald was in Esposito's arms again. "Give me a kiss, a real one!" he demanded, and Donald obliged. But then Donald grabbed for the Colt, and Esposito pushed him away and fired another wax bullet at him, right in the sternum.

Sobered by the shock, Donald counted to five. "Esposito..." he managed, though it was hard to talk, to breathe. "Don't..."

"Don't what?" Esposito asked. "Nobody has to know, right? Nobody here but us wharf rats, eh? That's the way you like it. You just pretend to be like me." He gestured at Donald's suit with the gun.

He was going to shoot a sixth time. He was going to fire a bullet made of lead and smoke and death. Donald had nowhere to go. He took a step back. Esposito raised the Colt and closed one eye. He took a step forward. Donald took a step back. The wind was low on his legs, sneaking up his pea coat. He flung himself backward into the icy, inky, black water of Lake Michigan, and every nerve was on fire. His heart stopped.

He thought he saw a flash of light and heard an echoing boom overhead.

*

Donald had gotten himself out of the drink in the nick of time, he was sure, until he saw the police. There were ten of them, one for each of the fingers he had just been thinking he'd be able to keep if he were lucky; ten little fingers that screamed, then played dead, as he climbed the aluminum dock ladder a few yards from where he had fallen.

Speaking of stiff and dead, there was an eleventh man on the lip of the dock too. Esposito, his heart a blooming, frozen rose. What had happened? What had the pawnbroker said – not to shoot at a body of water, because sometimes the bullet bounces back? Sounded like a lie to Donald. Why would a Navy man fire into a lake then? But sailors don't normally go armed… Why would his father have taught Donald to shoot by firing into the pond? Maybe for the same reason his mother had given Donald a loaded gun for Christmas.

One of the cops, the detective in charge, was in plain clothes, standing right over Esposito. Beneath his heavy coat, he wore a tuxedo. It was the first few minutes of New Year's Day. He held the Colt, wrapped in his handkerchief, aloft.

"This old beauty yours, sailor?" the detective asked Donald, and Donald wasn't sure if the detective meant the gun in his hand or the man at his feet.

PEOPLE YOU MAY KNOW

MASON CROSS

It wasn't really that long ago. It just feels that way.

A couple of weeks ago, a friend of mine told me that we were members of a microgeneration: 'Xennials'. She had read about it somewhere. Somewhere online, of course. Xennials aren't quite Gen X, not quite Millennials. The idea being that people born in the late seventies and the early eighties fell into a historically unique niche. We were the last kids to remember the world before the internet, but we were young enough to adapt to the new world in a way that the Boomers and the Slackers couldn't quite manage.

That was me, born in '79, right in the middle of that blink of a generational eye. Maybe that had something to do with it.

The accident happened on Christmas Eve 2015, a bitterly cold winter, and a bad start to a bad year, just a few weeks before David Bowie died. The Thin White Duke's music provided the soundtrack for those weeks. To this day, I can't hear 'China Girl' without thinking about that winter, and the blade of a kitchen knife glinting in watery dawn light, and The Room.

I was back up from London after the end of a tough six-month contract, and my girlfriend Amy had been helping me move into my new flat in the West End. In retrospect, perhaps it was a bad sign that neither of us had suggested moving back in together right away. She worked in Edinburgh and we would only see each other a couple of nights a week anyway, so it made sense. Two bases. Best of both worlds. That was what we told each other.

I was renting, of course. Who can afford to buy, these days? The flat was a three-bedroom on the top floor of a Victorian tenement. Blond sandstone, bay windows, terracotta flowerpots arranged neatly in the tiny, boxed-in front gardens of the basement flats.

My building was on a street at the top of Partickhill, just at the boundary with Hyndland, where the rents start to get really out of hand. The flat was grand, spacious, and cold. Twelve-foot ceilings, single-glazed windows. There was a breathtaking view from the big bay window in the living room. I could happily waste an hour staring out of that window at the lights of the city through the bare branches of the oak tree across the street.

The place wasn't quite in walk-in condition. The master bedroom needed a coat of paint and some minor repairs. The landlord, a lanky blond with a Polish accent and a look of permanent suspicion in his pale blue eyes, said I would have to wait until after the holidays, but he assured me I was welcome to do the work personally. There was a reason I could afford the rent all by myself.

There were some loose wires dangling from an old light fitting in the bedroom ceiling. I decided to investigate. Those investigations resulted in a minor electric shock, a short fall from the ladder, and a bad break to my left leg. The pain was excruciating. I can remember gritting my teeth in agony and tearing strips off the cardboard Amy and I had laid on the floor to protect the carpet. They say you can't remember pain and frankly, I'm glad. I wouldn't want to be able to describe that experience too accurately.

When I got to the hospital, I had to wait over three hours for treatment because of a suicide attempt that, in the end, proved successful. A woman from the high flats in Sighthill had taken a long walk off a short balcony, eight floors up. Against the odds, she hadn't died right away, and had hung on long enough to keep the doctors busy for a while. In my own state of discomfort, I had been inclined to believe that if someone wanted to die so badly, it was better to let them get on with it. Eventually I was examined, informed that I had broken my leg in two places and given a shot of morphine, which helped. A little.

After an operation to reset the bones, I moved straight into the flat. It turned out to be a bad move, and not just because of the three flights of stairs. With nobody to talk to, cabin fever set in fast and hard. Amy tried to visit every day or so, even though the journey from Edinburgh was inconvenient, but we had been going through a rough patch lately.

We had been together a long time. I don't think either of us wanted to let go of such a substantial chunk of our lives, but when she came around we almost always argued. And that was worse than being alone.

I guess it was all the time alone that eventually led me to The Room.

After days of moping around the flat on crutches watching daytime TV, rereading old Elmore Leonard paperbacks, and even attempting to learn how to cook, I finally succumbed and went online.

Unlike most of my generation, I hadn't invested a lot of time in the digital world. I engaged at the bare minimum level I could get away with. That meant email and occasional forays into ordering from Amazon and using online banking. I still got my news mostly from TV, the car radio, and actual newspapers. More than once I had been accused of cultivating some sort of hipster retro vibe, but in all honesty, I had just never seen the attraction of staring into screens of varying dimensions all day.

Amy had brought her dad's old HP laptop over so she could check in with work while she was here. That always-available culture was another modern foible I was at pains to avoid. Just having an email address made me feel a little too... connected, I guess.

Ironic, the way things turned out.

I was surprised at how quickly I became addicted once I'd breached the levee of my resistance to the twenty-first century. At first I browsed aimlessly, looking for sites on TV shows and movies I liked. I found forums and comment threads where I could converse with people from all over the world who shared interests with me.

One of the days when Amy was due over for dinner, I happened on a new kind of website. At first, it seemed like just another message board. After a second, I realized that wasn't quite accurate. It was a kind of bastard hybrid of a message board, an old-style chatroom, and a social networking site. It was called *A Problem Shared...*

Reasoning that I was more than eligible, with two problems – a broken leg and terminal boredom – I registered with my usual pseudonym: 'Jack'. My internet aversion might have been a thing of the past, but that didn't mean I was ready to fully connect with the world. The site prompted me for a profile pic, which was expected. It then refused to let me skip that step, which was not.

I sighed, annoyed at myself for being curious enough to proceed, and browsed for a picture from the files on the laptop. I found a headshot of Amy's older brother Glenn. He had the same strawberry blond hair as his sister – although his was cropped short rather than shoulder length – and her green eyes too. Three years between them, but they could pass for nonidentical twins. The thought of his pompous reaction if he ever found out I had impersonated him brought a smile to my face as I clicked to upload the photo.

Once I'd jumped through the hoops to register, what I found was a kind of online self-help group; a menagerie of people talking out their problems, from the serious, like cancer-sufferers, to the mundane, like teenage girls missing their unfaithful boyfriends. It was a kind of... Miscellaneous Anonymous. All problems, all the time. The thing that struck me most, perhaps because it contrasted so with my own outlook, was the level of intimacy. People were prepared – no, *happy* – to share the most private details of their lives.

Before long, I began to realise that this site was very different from the other forums and social pages I had used. It wasn't a social network at all, unless you think of something like Scientology as a social network.

The site community behaved just like that: a cult. For a start, the users universally referred to the site as simply 'The Room'. The capitals made the place sound almost like a place of worship. There were no nicknames. In the other discussion forums I'd seen, participants had names like *'Blue Harvest'* or *'bobsgirl89'*, but here everyone used an ordinary first name. Finally, there was a list of rules, or 'The Code' as it was labelled, on the entry page. The Code stated that all were welcome subject to certain rules; the most important of which was Rule 1:

What is said in The Room stays in The Room.

The po-faced sternness of the warning made me roll my eyes. But I proceeded anyway.

After an hour, I was hooked. Something about people unveiling the darkest recesses of their soul appealed to the voyeur in me. It was like reading the problem pages in Amy's magazines, but a thousand times more potent. When Amy arrived to find the frozen lasagne still sitting in its box beside the oven at the time it should have been almost ready to eat, I apologized perfunctorily. Then I tried to interest her in my new discovery. She watched over my shoulder for a few minutes before declining, saying it was wrong to eavesdrop on other people's pain.

I had felt a brief stab of guilt at that, then tried to laugh it off.

"What, you mean like that country music you always play in the car?" I asked.

"Not funny."

Maybe she was right. I did feel a little seedy, but I reassured myself that it was a harmless vice. Besides, for all Amy's protestations, I got the feeling that she was getting off on it a little too. Eventually, she went home, leaving me to it to avoid another argument.

It took me twenty minutes to notice she had gone.

★

For the next two weeks, I found myself in The Room constantly... *religiously*, I thought with a wry smile, thinking of the sacrosanct atmosphere that pervaded the site. I noticed that I was reading less, watching less TV. I took to leaving the radio on in the background. The Bowie catalogue was still on rotation, and though it was no longer omnipresent, Major Tom and Ziggy still made regular appearances. I was forgetting meals, and I was seeing less of Amy. That, I had to admit, could not be blamed entirely on The Room.

We had always prided ourselves on our ability to keep the relationship going, even across long distances. But now that we were closer again, she had never seemed so far away.

"It's funny," Amy said as she was leaving one day, in a tone that said it was anything but. "How it can be easier to talk to strangers than the people you really know." For that rest of the evening, I wondered about which of us she was talking about.

I became well-acquainted with other Room regulars, their words and their profile pictures combining to create a sense of their being until I could almost hear their voices in my head. People like Jill from Ontario, who was stuck in an unhappy relationship; Rob from Cardiff, who had lost a leg in a boating accident; and Bryan, a recovering alcoholic who had frequent lapses and lived right here in my city. You could move from room to room and join in conversations, like guests at a party in a big old house. Or like inmates in an asylum.

Some days there would be a large group online, other days only a handful, but it was always compelling. And gradually, to my surprise, I found that this was not the only thing bringing me back.

After reading and participating in the conversations, I found I had more right to be there than I had thought. Nothing really serious, of course, but nevertheless... the problems I was having with Amy, worrying about going back to work, the state of the world in general... Talking about it all seemed to help. Not only was I drawing comfort from talking about my problems, it felt good to give comfort to others too.

But the buzz always remained, humming away in the background like the noise of the hard disk of the ancient laptop.

*

Things in The Room took a turn for the worse at around four in the morning one cold January Sunday. There was only a small group online: myself, Bryan, Jill, and Claire; a newbie from Pennsylvania whose profile picture showed a sullen brunette wearing a black top and a lot of mascara. Like Bryan, she was an alcoholic. Claire was crying on our virtual shoulders about her latest drunken indiscretion. Apparently, she had screwed her sister's fiancé.

Claire: *im a horrible horrible person*

I tried to reassure her.

Jack: *@claire we all do stupid things when we're drunk*
Claire: *@jack not like this*
Jill: *@claire not ur fault – this sleazebag took advantage of u*

I sighed out loud. Jill always managed to use every conversation as an excuse to badmouth the opposite sex. She and I had clashed on more than one occasion. I kept wondering why she didn't just dump the jerk she was with. Then again, she was always very cagey about discussing him in detail, which led me to believe he probably wasn't a particularly bad guy. If he even existed, that was.

Her profile picture pissed me off too. It was so... *artificial*. So posed. A cropped headshot of her in a wintry field somewhere: dark reddish hair windblown away from a determined and unsmiling face.

After a pause, Claire typed a response.

Claire: *@jill no my fault – shouldnt have been drinking*

I couldn't help but agree with this, but decided it would be more helpful to stay quiet. Perhaps Jill and Bryan did too, because there was another pause in the dialogue. I found myself marvelling that it was possible to have uncomfortable silences in cyberspace. Eventually, the silence was broken.

Claire: *im a bad person*
Bryan: *@claire ur not. there are much worse things*
Bryan: *take it from me*

Bryan had broken his silence, and in doing so, he had aroused my curiosity.

Jack: *@bryan anything you want to talk about?*

I later came to fervently wish that I had never typed those six words. Because it turned out that Bryan *did* want to talk about it.

He told us how he had been drinking again, and how the only times he could stay sober had been while he was in The Room. I found myself thinking about cults again, and addictions.

Bryan went on to tell us how his wife resented the time he spent in The Room, how she often threatened to kill herself, and how he had come to think things might be better if she did. He told us about their final argument, over Christmas gifts for their son Zack. Finally, he told us how he had pushed his wife from the balcony of their high-rise flat. Eight floors up.

It wasn't what he had said that shocked me so badly, though God knows that was shocking enough. It was what I already knew. I had gathered from previous conversations that Bryan lived here in the city. More importantly, I knew that, on the night he claimed to have murdered his wife, I had been lying on a hospital trolley with a broken leg while the doctors worked in vain to save the life of a suicide: a woman who had supposedly jumped to her death from eight floors up.

I stared at the screen for a while. Alone in the silence, deafened by a voiceless confession. From another room, the radio was playing 'The Jean Genie', the upbeat groove incongruous in the moment.

I slammed the laptop shut and struggled to my feet. I stared out of the bay window at the trees and the lights as my head spun. There was a light rain outside, and it created a haze that made the night sky and the lights of the city seem slightly unreal, like a matte painting in an old Technicolor movie.

I turned away and found myself staring at the corner, where there was a small collection of cardboard boxes I hadn't unpacked yet. There was a stack of CDs on top of one of them, the pile of plastic holding my focus for a long moment for no reason I could discern.

I shook myself out of the daze and opened the laptop again. I searched for the websites of the local papers. Eventually, with a sense of satisfaction I wasn't proud of, I found the tabloid headline I was looking for:

TRAGIC MUM LIZ (33) IN 80 FT XMAS DEATH PLUNGE
Elizabeth Young died in the early hours of Christmas morning after falling more than 80 feet (25 metres) from her flat in Sighthill. Police said they are not treating the death as suspicious. She leaves behind husband Bryan, 37, and son Zack, 6. You can contact Samaritans by phone, free of charge, on: 116 123

I got up and hobbled to the kitchen, where I had left my phone. I dialled the three digits and waited for them to ask which service I required.

*

The next newspaper I saw was the old-fashioned paper kind. It was four days later and this time the headline was *SUICIDE HUSBAND CHARGED*, the sort of garbled header that practically forces you to read the article to see if it makes any more sense.

I brewed coffee and read the paper as the radio played in the kitchen. Bowie again, of course. A track from *Let's Dance*. The story didn't tell me anything I didn't know, but I was reassured to see the police had kept my name out of it. I felt guilty about turning Bryan in, but I would have felt a hell of a lot guiltier about allowing a murderer to remain in custody of a six-year-old.

Amy hadn't answered any of my calls for a week, although in truth I hadn't been trying too hard to speak to anyone since Bryan's revelations. I tried again now, got Amy's voicemail and left a message asking her to call me.

I looked over at the laptop, which had lain as dormant as my phone for the last few days. Suddenly, I was curious to see how the people in The Room were taking the news. As I logged into the site, I realized the extent to which I had lost my taste for eavesdropping. I decided this would be my last visit.

In the event, The Room agreed with me. A pop-up message stated matter-of-factly that my login was not recognized. I typed again: same result. I gave up and checked my email, immediately wishing that I hadn't.

Dozens of unread emails, all from members of The Room. I sampled a selection. Some were disappointed, some angry. I even had a couple of death threats. The one constant was an accusation:

You broke The Code, you betrayed one of us.

Any lingering doubts I had vanished. I switched the laptop off for good. I went to the kitchen, where I poured myself half a glass of whisky and made my mind up never to go near a computer again. *A Problem Shared* was right. It had been five weeks since my fall, and my leg was healing up nicely. I decided I was taking my life back.

I drank to that thought, feeling the welcome burn in my throat, and started back towards the living room. When I saw the plain white envelope that was tucked under the front door, I fumbled the next step on my crutch and almost tumbled headlong on the floor.

Two things about the envelope jumped out: one, it had no postage stamp, two, there was no address, just the word *JACK*, etched out with a black Sharpie.

I had been an idiot. If I had located Bryan from things he said, then of course others could do the same to me. But my address? My *home address*? How the hell did they get that?

I opened the envelope with only slightly unsteady hands. Inside was a simple note that seemed to turn the heated flat into the inside of a refrigerator. The handwriting was elegant. The writer had spent a lot of time crafting each delicate letter. The form was in sharp contrast to the content.

You broke The Code. You betrayed Bryan. You're nothing but a rat. What would your lovely girlfriend think?
—Jill

Jesus, I had talked about Amy in The Room... hadn't even disguised her name. If Jill could find me, she could certainly find her. I took my phone out of my pocket and called Amy again. All of a sudden, I was worried about what the week of silence from Amy meant. I waited through the voicemail message that seemed to take forever to complete its simple instruction, and left a message telling Amy to get in touch with me as soon as she got it. I turned my head a little and just happened to glance at the CD on the top of the pile I'd found myself staring at a couple of days before.

I blinked once, to be sure of what I was seeing. Something about that pile of CDs – about that one CD in particular – had chimed with something else in my subconscious. I picked it up, held the jewel case up to the watery light from the bay window. It was a Patti Griffin album, one of Amy's. The cover showed a familiar woman standing in a field somewhere: dark reddish hair windblown away from a determined and unsmiling face.

The uncropped version of Jill's picture.

I started when I heard a coldly familiar voice from behind me:

"Hi, honey."

I started to turn around. "Amy? Thank God, I thought…"

"Amy?" A tone of mock surprise. "That's not what you've been calling me lately, is it, Jack?"

I turned around to see Amy standing in the kitchen doorway. She was toying with a long kitchen knife, testing the point with her index finger. I recognised the knife: it was from the good set we'd bought from the homeware department of John Lewis, back when the world was sane. My mind overloaded for a second. Then something clicked into place, and the truth washed over me like an ice water tide.

"*Jill.* Jack and Jill. Cute."

"You betrayed Bryan," she said. "You betrayed all of us, Jack."

"Us?" It didn't make sense. "The Room? I *showed* you that site."

"Wrong way round, newbie."

I blinked, seeing a flash of the laptop screen all those weeks ago. I hadn't just happened on The Room. It must have been in the browser history.

"You were one of them all along."

"I thought it might help you. Help us." She smiled briefly, and I could see hate in those eyes. She was obviously as far gone as the rest of the zombies in The Room. As far gone as I had felt myself getting, I remembered, thinking of all the hours I'd spent there, feeding an unhealthy addiction.

Amy paused, as though a thought was occurring to her for the first time, and leant against the doorway. "You never got it. You never thought it was real."

"Amy," I began, holding a hand up. "We can…"

She straightened up, abruptly, like an unseen puppeteer had tugged on her strings. I took a sharp intake of breath. Then she lunged for me.

I sidestepped the knife, losing my balance and stumbling. I winced as I felt a twinge in my fragile leg and hobbled around the room, not thinking where I was going, just trying to go somewhere. Amy followed, slashing the knife across my back. I yelled in pain as Amy pushed me to the ground. She stamped on my leg hard, cracking the plaster cast open like an Easter egg. I screamed as I felt the partially healed bones snap again. The pain was incredible. The first time was a day at the beach compared to this. Mixed up in the pain, though, was pure rage, boiling up inside. And that was what saved me.

All the frustrating weeks spent cooped up, the problems with Amy, the indignation at being exiled from The Room, it all came to a head with the stabbing pain in my leg. I found myself pushing off my good foot, charging at Amy, pushing her backwards… right through the big bay window with the great view.

She didn't scream. There was a terrible silence followed by a horrible, leaden thump as she hit the bare concrete of the basement yard thirty feet below. I lay on my side, wanting to feel horror at what I had just done, able to feel nothing but the waves of stabbing pain from my leg. More than I'd wanted anything in my life, I wanted to pass out, but I didn't.

I just lay there until I heard the approaching sirens.

I wondered if the police would believe it was suicide.

THE WOMAN WHO NEVER WAS
MARTIN EDWARDS

"Where are you going?"

Skip's voice was drowsy and his words were faintly slurred.

"Won't be a minute," she said. "I could murder a doughnut."

"I could murder a drink."

"Any more booze and you won't be murdering anything. You'll be dead to the world."

Ilona was so lithe, he found it hard to believe she loved doughnuts, even if they were vegan doughnuts. Equally strange that she was living here with him. For once in his life he'd dropped lucky.

"And what good is that to me?"

She gave a teasing smile, then turned her back in pretend modesty. He watched as she slipped into her new clothes. Black T-shirt, navy blue shorts, designer trainers. She'd stolen them this morning, bringing them here in the backpack she'd now slung over her shoulders.

He felt pleasantly woozy; maybe this was just a dream.

"One beer," he murmured.

Ilona turned again and smiled. "There's a can in the kitchen."

He sighed, not in the mood to move a muscle.

"Don't be long."

"Five minutes."

As she walked out through the door, he whispered, "Missing you already."

"Love ya," she said.

Then she was gone.

He craned his neck to glance at the window. Tomorrow would be the longest day of the year. Light was fading, but the air was still muggy. Maybe there'd be a thunderstorm.

His limbs ached from the exertions of the past half hour. He yawned, closed his eyes, and drifted off into Neverland. When he opened them again, he expected to see her.

"Ilona!"

No answer.

Outside it was dark. How long had he been asleep? He struggled to his feet and checked his phone.

Half eleven. Nearly two hours since she'd climbed off the futon. He rang her number. Nothing, not even voicemail. Had her phone run out of charge?

He looked in the kitchen and bathroom. No sign of her.

Head throbbing, he peered out of the window. The flat overlooked a narrow side street. Deserted. From this vantage point, you could see the main road and an occasional flash of passing headlights. Otherwise, nothing.

Opening the door of the flat, he scanned the corridor. Nothing. Not that he'd expected to see her standing there. She certainly wouldn't be chatting to any of their neighbours. Neither of them knew anyone in the block, and they didn't want to.

They weren't meant to be here. Skip had found this place a month ago. Not exactly *found*, of course. Eldar had tipped him off about it. Never before had Skip squatted anywhere privately owned. Usually that was a very bad idea. Vacant buildings owned by the council, or abandoned business premises were best, so long as they weren't in such good repair that a new occupant might turn up at any time. Steel doors and boarded windows were always promising. Unless you were desperate, it made little sense to squat on your own – a squat is only a squat if someone is *in* there – but Skip was desperate. And this flat was the exception that proved the rule.

He went down the back stairs. As usual, nobody was to be seen. There were three floors, with ten flats on each, but Eldar reckoned most of the block was unoccupied. The owners were investors based in Hong Kong, and they weren't fussed about short-term income from renting or selling the flats. They'd keep the place for years, then sell the freehold for a fat profit.

"Capitalism, innit?" Eldar said. "Look at them apartment blocks around the City. See how many windows are dark at night, bruh? Empty palaces, with people sleeping rough under Waterloo Bridge. Ain't right."

Skip had met Eldar at a demo a few weeks ago. They'd hit it off at once. Eldar was older and streetwise. He didn't mind looking out for Skip, seemed to sense that he was vulnerable. At the time he fell ill, Skip had just moved in to a disused warehouse in Battersea with Eldar and his friends. It had been a rough patch in his life. One night he'd slit his wrists, but failed to make a proper job of it. After he came out of hospital, Eldar told him to get his shit together, build up his strength. Skip wasn't good with people, never had been. He blamed it on being brought up in a care home where the priority was self-preservation.

Eldar told him he needed time on his own. Good advice, but then Eldar was savvy. Skip wasn't that quick-witted himself, but he admired people who were. Eldar came from Istanbul via Dortmund and he called himself an anarchist, but in some ways he was more like an old-fashioned wheeler and dealer. He'd got hold of a fob to open the external doors and a key to this flat. A rare luxury. Normally you had to break in and then fit new locks. Not that any squatter ever admitted to criminal damage. Local kids always got the blame. Squatters simply took advantage. No question of crime.

The key and fob came courtesy of a dodgy local property agent. Eldar had done the man some unspecified favour and had meant to squat in the flat himself, but something else had cropped up. So he made Skip a present of it, coupled with the warning that he might need to move out at a moment's notice.

The flat was small, but Skip had more space to call his own than ever before in his life. There was just the one CCTV camera over the main entrance and luckily vandals had taken care of that. Now it hung at a skewed angle, gazing blindly at a brick wall. The place suited him down to the ground, and once Ilona started sharing it with him, it felt like a kind of personal paradise.

But now she'd vanished.

He opened the back door and stepped onto the pavement. Magnus Street was deserted. He slammed the door shut and came back inside. His head was hurting, his thoughts confused. He found the can of beer and downed the contents inside a minute.

Where was she? What had happened to her?

He was still asking the questions when he fell asleep for a second time.

*

Dawn was breaking as he woke again. He reached out for Ilona, like every morning, but this time there was no one to touch.

For an hour he lay there, trying to unscramble tangled thoughts. There were no messages on his phone. He couldn't believe the police had picked her up. She was careful, they'd never pin anything on her. Certainly not shoplifting. Her only arrest had been at some candle-lit vigil six months ago, when some drunks started abusing the campaigners and things got badly out of hand. She'd been released without charge after threatening to sue for false imprisonment. Not a stain on her character.

What if she'd had an accident? It wouldn't be her first bit of bad luck. That was how they'd met. A lorry had knocked her off a bike. He'd found her sprawled across Magnus Street as he was coming home one evening. She only had a bruised leg and cheek, but she might have been killed if she'd lain there much longer.

The bicycle was a write-off, not that it mattered, since she'd only nicked it from outside a swish bank building a couple of hours earlier. There was probably something wrong with the brakes anyway. She hadn't bothered to find a replacement. They didn't go out much, and they walked everywhere.

A car's horn blared down Ambler Street. There were speed bumps, but some drivers raced along the main road like it was Silverstone. No zebra crossing. If she'd been hit while crossing the road to the corner shop...

Skip's stomach felt hollow. He must do something. He couldn't simply wait here until she walked through the door and teased him for worrying needlessly. Anyway, it wasn't needless. She'd said five minutes.

Her phone was still dead, so he rang round the hospitals, begging people to talk to him, constantly being put on hold or fobbed off with standard lines about patient confidentiality. It took most of the morning and got him nowhere. Nobody knew anything about a young woman answering to Ilona's description. Tall, sinewy, olive skin, short black hair. He had to stop himself saying: *If you saw her once, you'd never forget her.* A woman who spoke almost perfect English, despite been Tallinn-born and Paris-raised.

It struck him that he didn't know her precise age. She didn't know his, either. He never celebrated his birthday and he preferred to forget about life in the care home and dropping out of college during his first term because all the other students seemed cleverer than him. All those wasted years before he met Ilona. She seemed to think the same way. They'd had so much to say to each other, stuff about the past didn't count.

What could he do to find her?

Better try to retrace her steps. Not that he knew what he was looking for. Surely she wouldn't simply be foraging in her favourite haunts, in the alleys behind the shops? Ilona didn't like labels, but you could call her a freegan. It was one of the things they had in common, this hatred of food going to waste while so many people starved. He'd earned his nickname from his endless scouring of overflowing bins and skips. It suited him. Skip sounded so much better than Stuart.

He hurried down the back staircase. The flat was on the second floor. He and Ilona never used the main entrance to St Magnus View, let alone the lift or the roof terrace. It wasn't so much that he was afraid of the few people who did live in the block. This was London, and they'd probably mind their own business. What he feared was bumping into someone from the agency responsible for managing the flats, someone who knew he shouldn't be there.

The back door closed behind him. Three steps led down to Magnus Street. This was where he'd discovered Ilona, that first night. Of course she'd not been wearing a helmet. For a terrifying moment, he'd thought she was dead.

As he'd bent down, her eyes had screwed up in pain. She'd sworn long and hard.

"You all right?"

"Are you fucking stupid? Does it look like I'm all right?"

The words were sour, but even as she groaned in discomfort, he detected a wry smile. From that moment he was besotted with her.

He'd helped her up and they began to talk. He was worried that she might have concussion, but she said no. She definitely didn't want to go to A&E. That was when he learned they had something in common. Neither had any time for conventional society. The old way of doing things was dying. They were both searching for a better way of life. Two free spirits.

Lately she'd been squatting with a bunch of climate activists in Covent Garden, but she'd walked out after some dickhead coked up to the eyeballs had tricked his way into the place and tried to rape her. She'd heard whispers about vacant flats in this area. Not that she meant to stay for more than a few days, until she got herself sorted out.

One thing led to another. She moved in with him and didn't say anything more about leaving. Even when he overheard someone in the street talking about a squat in disused offices in Finsbury, she showed no interest. She was happy to stay here with him. Skip found that thrilling.

The block was on the street corner. On the opposite side of Magnus Street was a doctor's surgery. Of course he and Ilona weren't registered there, but he went inside and made enquiries on the off-chance. The receptionist was no help. He walked out and turned into Ambler Street.

Across the road from the main entrance to St Magnus View stood an office building. The lower floors were occupied by some bureaucratic department, while a glitzy corporate PR firm had a penthouse suite with a large balcony boasting a retractable canopy. The advertising hacks used it for entertaining, rain or shine. Skip had seen people out there, champagne flutes in their hands, braying like donkeys. He wanted to shout at them but he knew they'd take no notice, write him off as a crazed druggie. It would have made him feel better, but Ilona was right. What was the point? She didn't want to poke corrupt fat cats and vested interests. She longed to destroy them.

He went into the corner shop next door to the office block. His luck was in. Behind the counter was an affable guy called Parvez. Skip never stole from there when Parvez was on duty – it was one of his rules.

"Sorry," Parvez said when he gave Ilona's description. "Never seen her with you."

"No," Skip admitted. She'd not been around whenever he and Parvez had chatted. "Sure you didn't see her last night?"

"Finished here at six." Parvez's smile showed perfect white teeth. "Pity. Sounds as if I'd remember her."

"Yeah," Skip said. "You would."

Next door was a branch of Kaffee Kavalier which stocked innumerable blends of coffee and a wide range of pastries. Each evening, unsold stock went into the bins at the back. Ilona scavenged there at closing time. If she wanted a vegan doughnut, she'd have headed there after leaving the flat. She was as adept at bin-diving as he was, but even better at sweet-talking weary staff members into simply handing stuff over at the end of their shift. If you were persuasive and open-minded, you could live well at the same time as doing your bit towards reducing landfill clutter and waste.

Nerves on edge, he popped inside. A young Slovenian woman had been on duty last night. She was busy serving, but in between customers he described Ilona, trying to picture her as the world saw her, not through a haze of adoration.

"Lovely girl?" she asked.

"Yes. Very lovely."

Her eyes were downcast, as though she dreaded disappointing him. "Doesn't… ring a bell, is that how you say it?"

"Yes," he muttered. "That's how we say it."

*

It was another warm, sultry day, but he felt trickles of fright running down his spine, like dribbles of ice-cold water.

What had gone wrong? Her disappearance didn't make sense. It wasn't as if she had anywhere else to go. Ilona had only arrived in England eighteen months ago and since then she'd lived hand to mouth, drifting from one squat to another. She said he was the first lover she'd had since coming to Britain. He believed her, simply because she had no reason to lie.

There was no way she'd go back to Covent Garden. She always spoke of the place with loathing. She didn't know anywhere in Britain outside London. And she wasn't homesick. She said France bored her.

Dare he report her missing? That was the last thing she'd want. He hated the very thought of it. Both of them believed in defunding the police.

He trudged back to the flat. Until now he'd been glad that the block didn't have a concierge sitting behind a desk on the ground floor. People could come and go as they pleased without being observed. The privacy suited him and Ilona down to the ground, but now he'd give anything to stumble across a nosey neighbour, someone with a clue as to where Ilona might be.

For the first time ever, he used the fob to enter by the main door rather than the Magnus Street entrance. Nobody was in the lobby. On the wall was a row of letterboxes for residents. The box for his flat was unlocked. It was numbered 12A; there wasn't a Flat 13. He pulled it open, but found nothing inside except dust and cobwebs.

He went up in the lift, for no particular reason other than a vague, straw-clutching hope that it might yield some insight. As it jolted to a halt, the sliding doors opened to reveal a small landing which faced the top of the back stairs.

A short flight of steps ran to the roof. He'd never gone up there. Why take the risk of drawing attention to himself? Now some kind of obscure superstition made him climb the staircase. The door to the terrace wasn't locked. It swung open at his touch.

The door formed part of a coffin-like vestibule at the top of the steps, rising eight feet above the terrace. Otherwise, the roof of the block was flat.

A low iron railing ran all the way round, six inches from the edge. There was a metal table and a couple of chairs, a cheap set of garden furniture that someone had brought up here long ago; the pieces were old and shabby, painted white but pitted with rust and pigeon droppings. Nobody had sunned themselves out here for a long time.

St Magnus View didn't really have much of a view. The tired old church of St Magnus was clad in scaffolding. There were no workmen in sight. Below to his left was the doctor's surgery and beyond it a school and playground. A tall office block loomed some distance away to his right. Glancing over his shoulder, he saw the building on the other side of Ambler Street. The balcony was just below the level of the roof of his block. It was empty. No PR people, no celebrity clients.

And no trace of Ilona. The hope that she might be here, hiding in plain sight, was a sign of his desperation.

In a stupor of misery, he made his way back down to Flat 12A. Why had she abandoned him? How could she have given up on him, forgotten the wonderful times the two of them shared with such…

As he stepped inside the flat, he came to a sudden halt, struck by a shocking thought.

Maybe she really had forgotten. Maybe she was suffering from amnesia.

It wasn't such an outlandish idea, he told himself as he stared sightlessly through the window. The very first time he'd seen her, she'd seemed dazed by her accident. She'd had a hard landing. As he'd helped her up here, she insisted she was okay, but perhaps there was such a thing as delayed amnesia. He whipped out his phone and searched on the internet.

Yes, he might be on to something. Suppose after leaving the flat she'd had another accident. Or had there been some other trigger, causing her to lose her memory?

Might she even have gone back to Covent Garden?

*

"Her name is Ilona," he said.

The woman in the smock shook her head.

"Never heard of her."

Ilona had told him enough about the squat in Covent Garden for him to be able to identify the recently disused building without too much difficulty. He'd accosted this woman as she left the building. Squatters never liked people approaching them out of the blue, but she'd taken pity on him and agreed to talk.

"She came to Britain a year ago."

"Sorry, bruh."

"She may have lost her memory."

He described Ilona, right down to the mole on the back of her neck, but it was no good.

"Don't know her."

"How long have you been here?"

Her eyes narrowed. "Who wants to know?"

"They call me Skip. My squat is more than a mile away. I met Ilona three weeks ago and she's been with me ever since."

The woman shrugged. "People move on. I'm ready to go someplace new. Six months I've lived here. Long enough."

"Six months? Then you must know her!"

Again she shook her head.

"Nothing wrong with my memory, bruh. I've not seen anyone who looks like that in all the time I've been here."

He swallowed. "She left because a cokehead assaulted her."

"Who are you really?" She was becoming truculent. "Trying to make out that we're violent here? That we're a bunch of criminals? That women aren't safe?"

"No, no, I didn't mean that!"

It was no good. She turned on her heel and rushed back inside, slamming the steel door in his face as he tried to explain.

✳

By the time he was back in the flat, his nerves were stretched to breaking point. He felt stuck in quicksand, sinking deeper with each passing minute. Life with Ilona had been so blissful. He couldn't possibly have imagined that.

He let out a muffled howl of despair. Ilona wasn't an illusion, she was flesh and blood. Losing her was like having his right arm chopped off at the shoulder. He needed to find where she was and make her safe.

Less than twenty-four hours ago, they'd been writhing in ecstasy together. *Love ya*, she'd said as she walked through the door. But now that door had a blank look of pitiless finality about it, as though it would always be shut in his face. It was devoid of life, of hope. Not the start of something, but the end.

He racked his brains, trying to come up with a fresh avenue to explore. An idea came to him. He and Ilona rarely went out as a pair. Their passion for each other excluded other people. They didn't need company. Besides, someone needed to make sure they didn't lose the flat. Just once they'd taken a risk and gone out as a couple. Ilona had nicked some clothes from a boutique and sold them to a market dealer. They had cash and she was determined to spend it. A few streets away was a bar she liked. She insisted that he came with her.

Roberto's occupied a cramped basement in a quiet side street in Farringdon. There were no signs outside. You could easily walk past and miss the place if you weren't watching for it. During the hour they spent there, she'd chatted for several minutes to the guy behind the bar. Bianchi, his name was. Muscular, good-looking guy in his late thirties, quite a charmer. Apparently he and Ilona were already acquainted. She explained later that she'd gone drinking there a couple of times while she was in the Covent Garden squat. Skip wondered if, despite what she'd told him, she'd ever slept with Bianchi. He didn't ask. He wasn't the jealous sort, he told himself, though that might not have been entirely true. Whatever. Ilona came back to the flat with him, leaving Roberto's with just a casual nod to the barman.

Bianchi was important. He knew Ilona wasn't simply a figment of Skip's fevered imagination. He might have a clue about what she was up to. There was even a possibility, if there was anything in the amnesia theory, that Ilona had no memory of her time in the flat. What if, in a state of confusion, she'd gone back to the bar? Bianchi didn't know she was squatting in St Magnus View, Skip was sure of that. He and Ilona had kept quiet about where they were living. You could never be too careful.

He must see Bianchi. Although he didn't understand why, he felt time was running against him.

*

He was in luck. As he walked into Roberto's, there was his quarry, polishing glasses with lazy strokes of the cloth. The bar was quiet, just like last time. A big TV screen was showing a rerun of a Premier League football match with the sound switched off.

Bianchi smiled in welcome as Skip approached. "Yes, mister, what can I get you?"

"Remember me?"

The barman's brow furrowed. "Remember you?"

Skip stared at him. "Yeah."

"Sorry, mister, no offence. We get plenty of customers."

Skip gritted his teeth.

"You remember the woman I was with, though."

"The woman?"

"Ilona."

Bianchi pursed his lips. "Ilona?"

For fuck's sake! Skip wanted to yell. *Don't keep repeating everything I say!*

Diplomacy prevailed. He gave a brief description.

Bianchi smirked. "Sounds gorgeous."

"She is." Skip stared at him. "Now do you know who I mean?"

A shake of the head. "Sorry."

"You must do! We were here only a fortnight ago. The two of you had a conversation. You'd met before. When she was squatting in Covent Garden."

"If you say so, mister," Bianchi said affably.

"I do say so!" Skip was struggling to control his temper. "Don't tell me you don't know her!"

Another smirk. "I like a pretty face."

"Well, then. You do know Ilona?"

A heavy sigh. "Wish I could help, mister. But…"

"Are you seriously telling me you don't remember that evening? There was hardly anyone else in the bar that night."

The man scratched his head. "Give me a clue, mister?"

Skip thought back. An image sprang into his mind, of a man with vivid ginger hair talking over a hapless interviewer. He waved at the big screen.

"While you and she were chatting, there was an interview on TV with Tim Golightly."

Bianchi looked blank.

"The ex-minister. A real wetwipe. Loves the sound of his own voice. You must know the name."

"I don't follow the news." Bianchi made a clicking noise with his teeth. "In this country, it's always bad."

"He's going to publish a new book, blowing the whistle on government corruption. I remember now. Ilona said something about him while she was talking to you."

The man screwed up his face in concentration. "What did she say?"

"'If he brings down the government, it'll be the only worthwhile thing the bastard has ever done in his life.'"

Bianchi laughed. "I guess she don't like the guy, huh?"

"Exactly! That's just what you said when she was mocking Golightly and how much he hates his old cronies. You used those very words."

"Uh-huh?"

"Now do you remember?"

Bianchi's brow furrowed in concentration.

Skip waited, breathless.

"Sorry, mister. I wish I could help. But you said it was a while ago."

"Only two weeks!"

Bianchi shrugged. "Two weeks, two months, two years. All the same to me, mister. I don't wear no watch. Don't look at no calendar."

Skip swore. "Make an effort, can't you? This is important!"

The barman pursed his lips. "Tell you the truth, mister, I got a lot on my mind right now. Back home, my sister's very sick. I may never see her again."

Skip reached across the counter and gripped the man's wrist. "Sorry about that, but I need your help."

Bianchi detached himself with ease. "Hey, mister, what's your problem?"

"I need to find her!"

The other man patted his hand. His manner was almost paternal. "Hey, hey, don't take things so bad. It's not like my sister's situation. Not life and death."

Skip groaned. His stomach was churning. The barman was wrong. This might just be a matter of life and death.

"Listen to me, mister. No need to sweat. Easy come, easy go, isn't that what they say? You're a real good-looking guy. Plenty more fish in the sea, huh?"

✳

Skip tottered back to St Magnus View like a drunk with unmanageable legs, gliding past unreal buildings, down unreal streets in a dreamy haze.

Except that it was not an ordinary dream, but a nightmare. Whatever Bianchi said, he needed Ilona. Life without her was barren, a burst soap bubble leaving him with nothing but a sickly taste on his tongue.

At last he got back home, but it wasn't home without her. It was just a soulless space which belonged to someone he'd never meet, someone whose name he didn't know.

Ilona had left nothing in the flat, not one visible trace that she'd ever lived or laughed or loved. All her worldly belongings were crammed into the backpack she always carried when out of doors. There wasn't a scrap of anything here to identify her, nothing to suggest where she might be. For the very first time he wished there was CCTV here, just to prove she did exist.

He tried calling her number again, but of course it was a waste of time. He finished up crouching by the window for hours on end, keeping a vigil that felt like a deathwatch.

Everything was blurred in his head. He didn't know if she'd had an accident or lost her memory. He fought against the idea that she had simply walked out on him without a word of goodbye. It made no sense. They'd never had a cross word. In any case, she wasn't vindictive or the sort to nurse grievances. She'd given no hint of becoming bored with him. Knowing he'd had a rough time, she'd always been sweet and kind.

This felt as bad as that time he'd been ill. A suffocating sense of being not quite sane.

Suppose Ilona had been kidnapped, pulled off the street and thrown into the back of a van before being taken somewhere against her will?

Another crazy idea. The two of them had no money to speak of. Her abductors could scarcely demand a ransom.

His gorge rose. He felt sick with horror as another possibility occurred to him. Surely he'd not imagined her? In his loneliness and confusion, had he dreamed up a wish-fulfilment figure?

No, no, no.

Unbearable to contemplate the possibility that he might have deceived himself. Or to wonder if he was still mad. Mad enough to become infatuated with a woman who never was.

*

The only numbers stored in his phone were for Ilona and Eldar. If only he'd introduced her to Eldar. Then at least there would be someone he could rely on to verify her existence, to confirm that she wasn't some lovely phantom conjured up by his fevered imagination.

He dialled Eldar's number. It kept ringing out and there was no invitation to leave a message. Skip tossed the phone aside. For all he knew, Eldar was out of the country. He came and went, a man of mystery, with no rhyme or reason to the way he moved around.

Skip tried to picture Ilona in his head, to remember how she'd looked last night as she took off her clothes before joining him on the futon. But the memory was distorted, like a reflection in a fairground mirror.

He'd scarcely eaten for twenty-four hours and his limbs felt weak and sluggish, his brain fogged and bewildered. He felt like a feeble scarecrow.

The phone rang. He snatched it up.

"Skip?"

"Eldar!"

"Got a missed call from you."

"Yeah… Sorry, I mean…" He found it hard to form the words. "It's just that…"

"You all right?" Eldar was usually so calm, but his question had an edge of apprehension.

"No," Skip said. "It's about Ilona."

"Ilona?"

"This girl I met… I mean, she's… she's disappeared. I don't…"

His voice trailed away. Did he sound as terrified as he felt?

"Whoa," Eldar said. "Take it slow, bruh. Tell me about this."

Slowly, in faltering tones, Skip described what had happened.

"So she vanished into thin air?"

"Yeah, that's right."

There was a long silence.

"You still there, Eldar?"

"Yes, I'm here. I was thinking. This woman. Describe her to me."

Skip did as he was told.

"I think I saw her," Eldar said.

His heart pounded. "What?"

"It was the other day. I was on my bike. She was going in the back door of your block of flats. Last Friday. Eight in the evening, would that be right?"

Skip tried to marshal his thoughts. "Yes, yes, I think so."

"Just a glimpse, it was. You weren't with her."

"That's right. She went out for food."

Eldar paused, presumably thinking back. "Blue backpack?"

"Yes, yes." Skip could hardly believe his ears. "Ilona never goes out without it."

"Sorry, bruh, it don't help you find her."

"But don't you see? It means I'm not going crazy. She does exist!"

Eldar laughed. "You're not going crazy, Skip. Trust me."

"She must be somewhere."

"Covent Garden, you said?"

"Yes, she was squatting there."

"Okay, cool. Want me to ask around?"

✳

Skip didn't know how long he waited for Eldar to ring back, his brain a mush of misery and relief. Daylight was fading when the phone rang again.

"Skip?"

The note of urgency in Eldar's voice was unmistakeable.

"What is it? Have you heard—?"

Eldar interrupted. "Sorry, no time for questions. Time is short."

"I don't understand."

"I know where she is."

"You do?" Skip wanted to scream with joy. "What is she—?"

"Listen. She's in danger. So are you."

"What do you mean?"

"Don't panic, bruh, it'll be all right."

"I'm not…"

"I'm coming over. Stay in your flat. Don't answer the door. Don't go outside, not for any reason. Wait there for me to call you back."

"But…"

"I'll be as quick as I can." Eldar breathed out. "Ten minutes, no more. I swear, Skip, just hold your nerve. You will see her again."

"You're sure?"

"Just trust me."

✳

Those next ten minutes felt like years. Skip was bewildered yet exhilarated. Ilona was alive and he was going to see her again. Eldar said so, and Eldar was the smartest guy he knew.

At last the phone rang.

"Eldar?"

"Yes."

"Where are you?"

"Very close. Nobody knocked on your door?"

"No one."

"You've not heard anything outside? Nothing out of the ordinary?"

"Just the usual noises."

Eldar let out a long sigh. "Good. Now listen to me. I need you to pay attention to what I say."

"Go on."

"I want you to go out of the flat. There's a staircase that goes up to the roof, you know it?"

"Yes, I went up there today."

"Perfect. Okay, head up those steps and out onto the roof. I'm waiting there right now."

"What about…?"

"Just do it, Skip. We don't have long."

The phone went dead.

Skip breathed in. He felt light-headed; hunger, maybe, or a mix of excitement and fear.

He opened the door of the flat and poked out his head. The corridor was deserted, as always. He padded to the stairs and made his way up. At the top, he pushed through the door to the roof terrace.

Stars twinkled in a velvety night sky. He could hear indistinct voices, loud and boozy. Music was playing, a string quartet. The PR business was hosting one of its parties.

"Skip!"

Her voice was low, but there was no mistaking it. He turned and saw Ilona's familiar profile. She was standing by the railing, above Ambler Street. She was in the clothes she'd had on the last time he'd seen her. Her lovely face even had the same amused expression.

The only difference was that she had a gun in her hand.

*

For a moment, Skip was paralysed, unable even to utter a sound. He heard footsteps behind him. Something in Ilona's expression made him look over his shoulder.

Eldar was there, smiling. His brawny arms were outstretched.

"Told you I'd found her," he whispered.

A shot ripped through the night air. Someone screamed.

Skip spun round. Ilona had fired her gun.

She'd shot someone on the opposite balcony. A guest at the PR party. Skip took a couple of paces forward and then felt Eldar's arms lock around his skinny torso.

"Ilona!"

"I, loner," she said with a wry smile.

"What have you done?" he hissed.

Ilona stepped aside to give him a better view. People were crowding on the balcony. A scene of chaos and confusion. The music had stopped. Someone cradled a ginger-headed man in their arms.

"Tim Golightly," Ilona said. "I'll leave it to Eldar to come up with the puns on his name."

"You killed him."

She shook her head. "Wrong, Skip."

"You've turned your back on the values decent people cherish," Eldar breathed in his ear. His accent had changed. More – educated? "You're a rootless troublemaker. A deranged assassin."

With practised ease, he pressed a sweet-smelling pad over Skip's nose and mouth. Skip struggled, but he was weak and Eldar was strong. Hairy hands held him in a muscular grip.

As he was bundled towards the edge of the building, Ilona thrust the gun in his hand. Only then did Skip see her near-invisible transparent gloves.

"The fingerprints are yours," Eldar murmured.

Skip groaned. His head was spinning.

"Thanks for your help, Skip," Ilona said. "For ridding civilised society of a dangerous menace."

As Eldar began to heave his protesting body over the railing, she added a few words in a language unfamiliar to Skip.

"*Dulce et decorum est, pro patria mori.*"

"Poor sod doesn't understand," Eldar said. "Needs it spelling out for him."

Skip was trying with all his might to keep his feet on the ground, but it was no good. He couldn't save himself.

As he plunged backwards into mid-air, he heard Eldar's parting words.

"Fall guy."

FIRST YOU DREAM, THEN YOU DIE

DONNA MOORE

Jimmy always used to say that Alberta could say 'out of my fucking way' in six languages, and 'excuse me please' in none. He was wrong, of course, they didn't teach languages at school when Alberta went and, even if they had, she was unlikely to ever have turned up at lessons. But she got the sentiment. Jimmy Galbraith had told her again and again, "Bertie, you can catch more flies with honey than you can with vinegar. Try and be nice, will ya?" Alberta had never really understood that. After all, when it came down to it, flies were more attracted to shite than they were to anything else. Besides, what good had being nice ever done for Jimmy?

Alberta carefully replaced the heavy clock on the fake mantlepiece. "That's an Ansonia, Angel Face; it'll be worth a fortune one day." He'd said that every morning when he wound it up. "If anything ever happens to me, you look after that clock." And it *had* happened, and she'd dutifully looked after it. She'd wound it up every day since Jimmy died, dusted the bevelled glass, polished the brass and carefully taken it apart and put it back together on the occasions it had stopped working. She hated that fucking clock. She checked its time against that of her watch. Two o'clock exactly. He'd be here between two and three, he'd said. Squint Harmon was always on time, the bastard. Always kept his promises.

Alberta walked over to the window. It was a dreich, December day; a day that no one in their right minds would want to spend in a crumbling Scottish seaside town and even less in that town's dilapidated amusement arcade. Grey clouds, grey sea, grey rain, grey streets; all blending into each other like a Rothko painting as seen on an old black-and-white TV. Even the flickering neon sign that jutted over the canopy below the window looked grey. "*Rainbow's End*, we'll call it, Bertie hen. Our wee pot of gold at the end of the rainbow; a lifetime's dream." Well, it hadn't been *her* dream, but she'd gone along with it for his sake. Forty years ago next summer it would be since they'd bought it, just before the arse fell out of the Scottish seaside. Not all of it, of course, not the posh bits where men in upturned collars and red corduroy trousers and women with puffy jackets and even puffier ankles carry tiny, beribboned dogs into cafés where they sell artisan vegan cakes and overpriced coffee made from beans that some animal that looks like a ferret has shat out in a tropical rain forest. No, those survived and thrived. But towns like this, with its brash amusement arcade, kiss-me-quick-hats and grim B&Bs run by even grimmer landladies; well, they became gaunt and ill and died a slow, lingering death, after which nobody could be arsed to bury the bodies.

Jimmy and her had laid out all their savings and more for this place and, by the following summer, it seemed that everyone decided they wanted to eat their sausage and chips on the Costa Brava rather than at home in Scotland. The dodgy tummy was worth it for the guaranteed sunshine and cheap booze. And then Jimmy, too, had become gaunt and ill and died a slow, lingering death. He hadn't even seen out their second summer at Rainbow's End. Some pot of gold that had been. First you dream, then you die. Out of some ridiculous sense of loyalty she'd kept going on her own, struggling on with an ever-increasing overdraft, a six-year-old son and a growing sense of despair.

The overseas package holidays had been joined by the rise of games consoles. You could play Space Invaders and Asteroids and Pac-Man and ever more complicated games from the comfort of your own home, twenty-four hours a day if you wanted. And you could bet on the bingo and roulette on your telly or your phone, the promise of riches at your fingertips at the press of a button. Then the Budd Report and the Gambling Act had sealed the deal. Arcades like Rainbow's End became neon-encrusted dinosaurs. When she'd finally seen sense and decided to sell, it was too late. Her son had never wanted the place and had kept after her to get rid of it. Stephen had been bitter in his teenage years that his mum ran a ramshackle eyesore in a no-hope town, then sneered his way into adulthood with the same disdain and kept away from both her and Rainbow's End as much as he could. She should have sold the place then. She wouldn't have got as much as they'd paid for it, of course, but enough to buy a flat somewhere and get herself a wee job. But she hadn't, because Danny had come along. Her grandson, who looked so much like Jimmy and who she loved with the same overwhelming sense of joy. It was a feeling she'd never had for Stephen. Even as a baby, Danny loved the Rainbow's End with its flashing lights and its beeping and jingling and music. It was one huge plaything to him, one of those things you put on a pram, that the baby could press and poke and squeeze and rattle. The love affair had continued as Danny grew and, as much as his father stayed away, wee Danny wanted to spend time with his gran. Well, with the machines more like. And, just like her, he was fascinated with their insides. He'd spend hours running tiny fingers over their workings as she took them apart to fix them. She couldn't afford professional help so had taught herself from the manuals and, later, from the internet.

She'd also learned to 'fix' them, to make the machines more favourable to the house. Every tiny bit of income helped when your supposed livelihood was haemorrhaging money. She'd learned all the tricks and even invented some of her own. It didn't matter what sort of a wrist flick you used, or how you timed the drop when sending your ten pence into the Penny Falls, Alberta could fix those machines so that they reluctantly spat out the most meagre of pay-outs. The slots at the sides where her profit fell through were invisible to the player and, if they were stupid enough to put any coins other than a 10p piece… well, hell mend them when it went into the drop tray.

Danny had been fascinated by the claw machines, with their brightly coloured prizes and, when he was old enough, she'd told him why he could never seem to win a prize, no matter how adept he became with the claw. "Look, see this bit? Well, I can adjust the grabbing strength of the claw with that so it'll pick that teddy up alright but then just drop it back down. See?" She demonstrated and he made her do it again and again. She even taught him the maths involved in the calculation, drew little pictures for him; maybe he'd become an engineer one day. It was much easier with the new-fangled machines, but she didn't have any of those, of course. She had to set all her machines manually, but with the new ones all you needed to do was feed in the coin value, the average value of the prizes and the profit you wanted and the claw tension adjusted itself automatically, working out when to send full strength to the claw. But it didn't matter – she could do it just as well herself. "Here, I'll make it easy for ye, wee man." Danny had been delighted when his next four grabs netted him four prizes – a furry monkey, a plush elephant, a packet of sweets and a key ring. She hadn't made him put them back, of course. Each one cost her less than the price of a turn on the claw and it was worth it to see his wee face. If she could fashion a claw machine to give him the world, she would have done.

Danny helped her out every school holiday and most weekends, and they'd talked excitedly about him taking over from her one day and bringing the place back to its former glory. They even talked of expanding, making a wee empire – DannyLand, Alberta had jokingly called it. So she'd hung on to the Rainbow's End just one more year, and then another, as they made more and more outrageous plans. "For Danny," she told herself. Those outrageous plans seemed possible because of him. And every year she borrowed more and more money until the banks wouldn't give her any more, and the loan companies wouldn't give her any more and the only person that she could turn to for a loan was Squint Harmon. Out of all the big mistakes she had made, that was the biggest. Because now there was nothing left; less than nothing. She was in debt to Squint so much that today he was coming to take everything away from her. By three o'clock, Rainbow's End would no longer be hers and there would be nothing left for Danny. Squint Harmon was going to turn the space into some flash casino. "Decent real estate on the front like this. But we'll rip this pile of shit down and start again," was how he'd put it.

Alberta sighed and looked at her watch. Fifty minutes. He'd be here within fifty minutes and that was all the time she had left here. She unlocked the door of her flat over the arcade and the damp coldness of the staircase hit her straight away. The hall outside was dark, with only one narrow window high up on the wall. A shaft of weak sunlight filtered in and she could see the dust motes circling lazily in the thin beams of light. That was all the light she needed. She grabbed the handrail and took the first step, knees cracking. Squint had probably done her a favour – she didn't think her bones would stand another winter here. She'd tried to think of other options but all paths led back to this one. Even thinking of Danny just led to sadness. Even he had deserted her. He'd got a job over the Christmas holidays so he wouldn't be able to help her out as he normally did. He was excited about it but said it was a secret and he would tell her when he saw her. Said he was going to make loads of money and he could see a future in it when he left school next summer. No talk of going to college to do engineering any more, or taking over the Rainbow's End. It was probably H&M or Top Man or one of those places if they still existed. Alberta wasn't sure; she hadn't been clothes shopping for years. But he liked his fashion, did Danny. No, he wouldn't want this place any more. She should have known that would change. What was bright and shiny and fascinating when you were seven, well, you could see it for the cheap tat it was when you were seventeen. Alberta had always known it was cheap tat, but had believed in the pot of gold for Jimmy's sake and then kidded herself on for Danny's sake. Now she had nothing to carry on for, nothing in her future apart from bittersweet memories of the past. She should probably thank Squint Harmon that this would end now, although she still hated his guts for how he'd done it and the choice she'd had to make.

Forty-one minutes.

Alberta unlocked the door that led into the back corner of the arcade. The familiar smell of chip fat, stale Irn-Bru, lemon polish, hot dust on circuit boards and wet dog hit her. She'd never managed to work that out – they'd never let dogs in Rainbow's End, except service dogs, of course. But there weren't many of those. It was a sickening smell, but reassuring nonetheless. She'd smelt it every morning for the last thirty-nine and a half years. 14,386 days, give or take the couple of days she'd spent in hospital when Stephen was born. She hadn't spent a night anywhere else in all that time. "What do we want with a holiday, Angel Face," Jimmy had said. "Look at this place – sun, sea, sand and our own personal paradise. What could we get anywhere else that we wouldn't get here?" And then, after Jimmy had died, she'd been too busy, too poor, too worried, to go on holiday. Besides, who would she go with?

Without turning the lights on, Alberta walked to the front of the arcade and unlocked the glass door, stepping out into the porch to undo the metal shutter and wind it up halfway. That would be enough. Squint Harmon would have to crouch to get in and it would no doubt crease his flash suit, but she didn't care. She didn't want anyone passing by to think the place was open and wander in. She didn't usually mind that; having a wee gab with someone who just wanted in out of the rain was preferable to sitting in her wee glass booth with just the creepy mechanical laughing clown next to her for company. But not today. Not on her last day at Rainbow's End. Thirty-four minutes left, that's all she had. Time had passed so slowly for all those years since Jimmy had died, and now it was passing in a flash.

As she walked back through the arcade she turned on the machines for one last time, just as she'd done every day. The rows of pluggies bleeped and blipped and jangled to life, their colourful flashing lights illuminating each section of the arcade as she moved through it, resting her hands on each machine as she walked by it. No need to polish today. The fluorescent lights of the dance machines reflected in the colourful glass tops of the pinball machines next to them and Alberta stood and listened for a moment as all the machines she had turned on so far seemed to vie with each other to be heard. When everything was on, the place was a mishmash of sound, with occasional bursts of clarity. It was a familiar if discordant tune. Twenty-six minutes. She moved on to her and Danny's favourite game – Guitar Hero. He would play all the tunes over and over, working his way up from the easiest tune to the most difficult, even when he was a wee boy and the strum bar was too stiff for him and took too much arm strength. He hadn't played now for a year or so, but his name was still up on the leader board for some of the tracks. So was hers, but she hadn't beaten her own high score for years now.

Alberta turned on the machine and inserted a coin. She took the guitar from its place and worked her way through the list until she reached the fifth tier. 'Holiday in Cambodia'. Not the hardest song to play, but her favourite. She wasn't quite sure if her arthritic fingers would get her past the extended introduction but, if they did, she knew they would get her to the end. As the familiar notes appeared on the screen – green, red, yellow, blue, orange – she lost herself in the tune, ignoring the flaring pain until towards the end when the throbbing became too much to bear during the repeated 'Pol Pots' of the song. She was wrong about her fingers getting her to the end. Just another sign that it was time to give up. She clasped the guitar to her chest and rested her fingers, until the last chords rang out. She put the guitar back and set the machine to play The Beastie Boys' 'Sabotage'. It seemed appropriate, somehow.

Seventeen minutes.

Alberta walked her familiar path through the arcade, switching on the rest of the machines as she went. She knew where the faded red and gold carpet was sticky or frayed, and her feet avoided those areas automatically. Squint Harmon had seemed like a godsend at the time, stepping in to help her when no one else would. She'd known he was dodgy, but he'd buttered her up, weaselling his way in by talking up the Rainbow's End and persuading her that he was giving her a good interest rate out of respect for her Jimmy. She snorted to herself. How could she have been so stupid? Squint had been about ten when Jimmy died. And Squint *had* been fair, at first, anyway. He'd loaned her small amounts here and there – crisis loans to fix a leak or a broken window – and hadn't even charged her a penny in interest. He'd even got some of his boys to do some work for her at cost when the front door needed replacing. And he'd been kind to Danny, buying her grandson ice creams in the summer and creamy, warming cocoa in the winter, feigning interest in all his wild schemes and dreams and even egging him on. She'd liked him for that; anything that made her Danny happy made *her* happy. But it had all been a front, just another way to con her and bring her into his orbit until she couldn't pull herself free. Almost without her noticing, as he'd started loaning her more and more money, his interest rates had crept up.

"Sorry, Mrs Galbraith, but you know how business is." He'd shaken his head and tutted for a full minute. "It's tough out there." And she *did* know how business was. Hers was falling on its arse and his was booming. Over the years his suits got flashier and his cars got bigger. And over the years she found herself paying back double the amount she had borrowed and then triple. When Hurricane Bawbag hit Scotland and almost ripped the roof off the Rainbow's End, she'd had to pay Squint four times as much as she borrowed from him to fix the damage. "Should have kept the insurance premiums up, Mrs G," he'd said and laughed his nasty little laugh.

That had been the point of no return. The Rainbow's End was as good as his from that moment and they both knew it. Still, she had a roof over her head, something to do that kept her sane, and machines to fix. Her therapy that was. Things couldn't get any worse, could they? Of course they could. In the last couple of years she'd learned just how evil Squint Harmon was. He'd turned up more and more, taking over her wee office, telling her he wanted to invest in the place. Money laundering, that's what *that* was. And any legitimate customers she did have were scared off by his team, hanging about the place with their chib-marked and pock-marked faces. She'd seen the packages and cash changing hands. She'd had to take in deliveries, patch up faces, comfort young women. Robberies, drug dealing, trafficking – those were all part of her life now and she was helpless to stop them. He'd told her if she went to the police it would be Danny who'd suffer and she'd believed him. She'd warned Danny to keep away from Squint but he seemed enamoured of the man and his money. It was probably a blessing in disguise that Danny wasn't going to be here to help her over the holidays. She knew she had to do anything she could to keep Danny from being drawn in, and this was her only option to make sure of that.

The machines were nearly all on now and she had reached the back corner where it was quieter and the lighting was more subdued. Alberta bent down and turned on the plug for the fortune-telling machine. The light flickered on inside the glass box and fell on the contours of the red, purple and gold silks and satins that made up Madame Zasha's costume. The mechanical figure whirred into life, lifting her veiled head and waving her arms above the crystal ball on its plump cushion. "Dare you consult Madame Zasha?"

Alberta dared, but she didn't need to; she knew her future, had chosen her future. She glanced at her watch. Nine minutes. She reached into the wee leather pouch of coins that she always kept around her waist. She didn't need it today; wouldn't need it ever again, in fact, but it was habit to put it on every morning, a reassuring heaviness. She pulled out a pound and fed it into the machine. Madame Zasha hummed and whirred once more, her hands with their bright red nails circling the crystal ball in their juddering, robotic fashion. "Make it a good one, Madame Zasha." Alberta smiled to herself and shook her head. It *wouldn't* be a good one, of course. She knew that, even if Madame Zasha didn't. The machine vibrated and a piece of card dropped into the slot below the glass case. The card should have been white but it was a grubby mottled grey, with edges thickened by the dampness of the fingers that had handled it over the years. The machine was so old that it was impossible to buy new fortune cards for it now, and Alberta couldn't afford them, anyway. She had been tempted to write her own: *Next Friday, you will be gored to death by a lion* or *Get out of this shitty town before it's too late* but, instead, she'd simply gone through the bins and picked out the cards people had discarded to refill the machine. Over the years the cards had disappeared when people took them away with them or tore them up and now only three remained. Alberta knew exactly which one she was going to find in the slot. She picked it out and read it: *Tomorrow, you will accomplish many things.* Well, that certainly wasn't going to happen. It made her sad to think that there would be no more tomorrows for her to accomplish many things. She and Jimmy had made so many plans when they started, and then she and Danny had made more. But she realised that they were only Jimmy's plans, only Danny's plans, and they would happen or not with or without her. Alberta had gone along with the plans and dreams that belonged to other people; she had never had any of her own. She didn't have anything to accomplish tomorrow because there was nothing left for her here; nothing left for her anywhere, in fact. Danny's plans didn't include her any more and there was no reason why they should, but she couldn't hang around and watch him pull away from her. Alberta screwed up the card and put it in her pocket. It wouldn't be needed again. As she walked away from the machine, the tinny voice spoke once more: "Come back soon; Madame Zasha has much more to tell you." Alberta waved her hand at the machine without turning her head.

Once again, she looked down at her watch. Four minutes. For the first time she began to worry that Squint Harmon would turn up late or that he wouldn't turn up at all. He would definitely be there before three, he'd said, and it was four minutes to now. Three minutes, she realised as the hand ticked almost imperceptibly round. Her grand gesture wouldn't have the same impact if he wasn't here. He wouldn't get his hands on the Rainbow's End, of course, but that wasn't really the point any more. She wanted him to suffer just as she had suffered, just as he'd made countless other people suffer – the addicts, the people he'd screwed out of the little money they had, the girls he'd trafficked, the poor souls who'd been beaten, possibly even murdered, so the rumours said. Two minutes. And she wanted him to know why she was doing this. And then she wanted to tell him all about Jimmy's clock on the mantlepiece upstairs. The clock that she'd rigged to a device – an IED, so the internet had told her – and set to go off at three o'clock. In… she looked at her watch… sixty-three seconds. She wouldn't have time to tell him all that now, but if he walked through the door in the next minute, then at least she would have stopped him from causing any more misery. She knew some other scumbag would just ooze into his place to fill the gap, but at least Squint Harmon would be gone; not with a whimper, but a bang. A huge fucking bang if she'd done her calculations right. She'd added a bit more for luck. That's how she'd always made cakes, too, but only when Danny came round. "I've put a wee bit extra sugar in there, wee man. Can't do any harm." Not too much, though. Everything she'd read said the blast would be contained within the Rainbow's End itself. The buildings on either side were empty – a café that was closed down for the winter and a long-abandoned shoe shop that had sold plimsolls and jelly shoes to people who had forgotten to pack their own. And she'd put her sandwich boards on the pavement in such a way that any unlikely passers-by would have to give the front of the Rainbow's End a wide berth.

Forty-four seconds.

There was still time for him to come. She ran a hand over the horse-racing machine. It was the oldest machine in the place and just about on its last legs. Quite literally, since the horses themselves had been glued and mended so many times. The glass felt warm and reassuring under her fingers.

Twenty-eight seconds.

Alberta wondered once more if she was doing the right thing, but she knew she was. There was nothing left for her here and, as her body started failing her, she would be glad to go. She didn't want it to be just her, though. That felt like a waste when scum like Squint Harmon were around. Her breath slowed and she counted the seconds off with each deep breath in. Twenty-three, twenty-two, twenty-one, twenty, nineteen…

The entrance door squealed open. She'd been meaning to oil it for over a week now. She smiled. It wouldn't just be her and the Rainbow's End that disappeared with a bang after all. "Over here, Squint. I'm all ready for you."

She glanced for a final time at her watch. Twelve seconds. He was just in time.

"Hiya, Gran. That job I wanted to surprise you with; it's with Squint. He's paying me loads. He said I should come and get the keys from you. Bet you didn't expect to see me today, did you?"

EYES WITHOUT A FACE

JAMES GRADY

Jeff's hack of the security cameras first showed her to him on that April Thursday morning as she waited for the lobby elevator in his apartment building ninety-one blocks north of the White House, where the President's televised ramblings were convincing millions of Americans that drinking bleach would defeat the Covid virus that had killed 46,838 of their fellow citizens.

Three giant computer monitor screens cocooned Jeff in his living room.

He sat keyboarding in his swivel chair with the sofa behind him.

The center gig work screen shimmered lines of code in his pupils.

The screen to his right hid most of the grave-sized, floor-to-ceiling window filled with its view of the sky above and the streets fourteen stories below.

That right screen streamed one of the classic movies his Dad taught him to love but with muted lines of closed captioning dialog: *Rear Window* – Jimmy Stewart being told *what's what* by the white blonde elegance named Grace Kelly.

Grace wasn't in the scene when wheelchair-trapped Jimmy lowered his telephoto lens camera that let him see what his naked eyes couldn't.

Jeff's gaze flicked to the monitor screen on his left streaming multiple building security cameras' window views of reality's color but no sound—

—and there she was.

She wore black slacks and a red hoodie that didn't hide her cropped midnight hair. A black mask covered her face from her nose to under her chin.

The elevator's silver doors slid open.

And out he came.

That *oh so white* guy wore the courtier's costume of a dark suit, TV-friendly blue shirt with a red tie cinched around his neck like a noose and hanging down over his belly like a blooded penis. His left hand gripped a White House-symboled computer bag while his right held a maroon baseball cap with a logo worshiping his imagined past. He wore no mask.

He glanced at her – glanced again, whirled to hold the doors open.

She eased past him, committed into the elevator—

—and then his arms rose like a crucifixion.

That meant his left hand *oh so naturally* thrust the White House bag toward her eyes. Then his burdened hands framed his face in an *obvious* angry confession of amnesia… *so* he stepped back into the box he'd just left.

The elevator's silver doors closed.

Jeff clicked to four windows of the elevator's cage.

Red Tie edged between masked her and the panel of buttons. He turned and the no-sound screen showed his unmasked mouth moving at her.

She must have said something behind her mask. He pressed a floor button.

Jeff's screen flashed 9.

Red Tie pushed button 17.

The elevator launched toward the stars.

Red Tie leaned his shoulder on the back wall to face her as she huddled in the corner of the elevator's cage. His mouth moved. Her gaze never left the rising cage's silver steel doors.

Jeff zoomed his view to a downward close-up of her.

Realized: *Her black hair has white-blonde roots.*

Why would she dye herself away from the coveted locks of Grace Kelly?

The elevator stopped on the ninth floor. The doors slid open. She walked out to the hallway. Jeff clicked to views of her there. Kept one corner window on Red Tie in the elevator as its silver doors closed.

She marched down the ninth floor's carpeted funnel of apartment doors…

… to end-of-the-corridor double doors below a red sign for *EXIT.*

Jeff's screen followed her walking up the stairwell's concrete steps.

The elevator delivered grumpy Red Tie to the seventeenth floor. He pushed the button back to the lobby. Left the building as she climbed the stairs to…

… Jeff's fourteenth floor. She walked past his apartment 1416 to the door down the hall: 1421. Let herself in. Shut that door.

The Smolonskys' apartment. They'd fled the city two months before for their Dewey Beach house in Delaware, where state law sheltered 11,943 cloaked shell corporations.

Jeff's work screen *Beep!* said his gig had timed him out for non-activity.

He hacked his building's Tenants' Registry.

Zapped the Smolonskys' email with *how-you-doing* bullshit, how he'd seen 'someone' going into their apartment.

They zapped him right back like they were glued to their screens:

Maybe our new sublet. Lisa Freemont. Pls check? Tnx

In the screen to Jeff's right, Jimmy Stewart got thrown out of his window.

Jeff looked around the apartment he seldom left even before the pandemic. There'd been no one in there but him since the ambulance crew carried his Dad out to cremation. From this building's roof, Jeff'd dumped Dad's ashes over the city he'd failed to save and Jeff'd failed to escape.

Jeff remembered his best therapist: "You've got to *do* to *be*."

Put on his Amazon-ordered black mask.

Stepped into the thick-carpeted hallway.

Knocked on door 1421.

That peephole darkened.

Muffled through the thick wood came: "Who are you?"

"*Um*, my name's Jeff – *no*, I mean, not really. My actual name is L. B. Jefferies, so: *Jeff*. People shorten you down to what works for them."

"What do you want?" said the muffled voice.

He told her the truth: "I'm your neighbor down the hall in 1416. The Smolonskys asked me to check on you."

"I'm fine."

"Oh. OK."

Three heartbeats, he turned to—

"Wait," said the muffled voice. "Do you have an envelope, a stamp I could borrow? My phone, laptop, got stolen. I need to send their rent."

"*Sure*," he said, hoped that was true.

"Be right back," he said, knew that was *for sure*.

He zapped the Smolonskys. Rummaged through his Dad's desk. Found envelopes, stamps. By then, Marc Smolonsky had zapped back:

Found us through D.C. Mont. society for us expats.

Jeff knocked on her door minutes later.

The door opened the gap that its chain allowed.

Showed him a slice of her: black slacks, white blouse, a lean thirtysomething Millennial like him, a black mask below her eyes, her burning emerald eyes.

That stared at the pile he'd made on the hallway's carpet: "What's this?"

"The stamped envelope has their address. That old laptop, I've got three of them. Wiped. Programmed for my wireless. All that's on the paper taped to it. My email, phone. That disposable cellphone I had to get for a gig once has about an hour left on it. Until you replace yours."

Green eyes looked him up, looked him down.

"I never thought I'd have to rely on the kindness of strangers," she said.

"We all rely on the kindness of strangers. Besides, you're Lisa, not Blanche."

Her mask hid any expression: "So you know that streetcar."

"We're all in some movie," he said and knew, *just knew* she smiled, too.

She reached through the slot of the chained door, picked the envelope off the pile on the floor. Asked him to wait. Closed the door.

Opened that chained gap two minutes later. Held that sealed envelope.

"Are there mail slots up here?" she asked.

"No, I'll ride it down to the lobby."

He shrugged: "Nice to have someplace to go."

Her hand came through the chained gap. For a heartbeat, they touched the same thing. Those burning green eyes followed him to the elevator. The envelope held a thickness beyond an old-fashioned check and he thought: *She's using cash.* The floor outside her door was empty when he got back from the lobby.

He made himself log two gig hours before checking his personal email:

Ads from sites who'd co-opted his address. Nothing from her.

He made himself a sandwich from leftover refrigerated canned tuna that still smelled OK. Clicked his center screen to Google.

Keyed in *Lisa Freemont Montana.*

Found a newspaper's paid death notice *in loving memory from her colleagues* for someone who died three years before. Someone who'd been a year older than Jeff until she wasn't any age at all. Cancer killed her in New York where she'd managed a modeling agency. No photo.

He checked his email: still nothing *from*. Clicked an ad for KlassMates. com to the Shelby High School link from the obit. Entered her name. Got nothing. Clicked to that high school annual for her senior year. The picture he found there showed a girl with long hair neither black nor blonde. She listed her plans as 'Going big time.' He found nothing on Insta, Twitter or LinkedIn. One of nine Facebook pages for that name was deactivated, eight others were married or maudlin, not his new neighbor with emerald eyes.

Clicked back to his email – there she was via a nondescript gmail address:

Thanks. BTW, where/how you get groceries?

He zapped back about stores he used for deliveries.

Can I order w/yours? Credit cards stolen. Pay you cash.

The soonest delivery slot he could book was the next afternoon. She sent him a list. He added his needs. Trimmed his beard. Buzz cut his hair. Fought thinking about her. That night he had a wet dream. Come the grocery deliveries, he rounded her total down. Threw in toilet paper from his Dad's vast hoard. Masked up. Texted the burner phone he was on his way.

He stood in the hallway, his arms full of provisions.

She opened the door.

Let him fall into her jungle eyes between her black hair and black mask. She wore a white T-shirt over a fullness. Her running shorts freed long smooth legs. She took the bags from him. Left him standing in the hall. Came back with greenbacks for the sum he rounded down again.

He babbled about how the Smolonskys probably canceled all screen subscriptions. How he knew to hack streaming services. How to match up 'her' laptop with his center screen so, *you know*, "we could watch movies together."

"Not best way," he added. "Not like Goddard said."

"In a theater, watching projects you into the movie," she paraphrased. "From a TV or computer screen, the movie goes into you."

"That's life now. Screens pouring into us until our screens *are* us."

Breaths moved their shoulders.

"Friday night at the movies," she said. "What do you got?"

"What do you want?"

They both knew they both smiled under their masks.

He loved the classic she suggested. Watched it in his center screen from the sofa. The left screen clicked views of the empty hall to the apartment where she was watching, too. The right screen stayed dead like a wall across the window to the neon-blued night.

They clicked back and forth beneath their screens of that movie like subtitles of a French film, so he suggested the Truffaut he loved most. She wrote:

Oui, mais I get to pick le next one.

Saturday afternoon matinée and the next one, the one after that. Scores of back and forth zaps. Logoffs before midnight. Gig hours from dawn to noon for him.

He didn't ask her The Washington Question: *What do you do?*

Translation: *How important are you… to me?*

Sunday swirled to Monday. They shared movie comedies. Tornadoes slammed Texas. Dictators arrested journalists. America's President bragged.

Jeff keyboarded her about dropping out of college, *no direction known* eventually dropping him back in his Dad's second bedroom. How his Dad was proud of him *even though*: "'Least I won you from this damn town."

What happened to him? she keyboarded.

Besides waking up dead last year? Jeff clicked back. *He came to D.C. to fix Watergate, the Vietnam War, racism, poverty, big time crime – all the usual suspects. Was a muckraker. Thought street-shoes, say-yes Camus rebels like him would fix things after Nixon skipped town in a government helicopter. Instead, this city's/country's power players became prestige-educated managers who babble buzzwords and clichés, whatever paints them as woke and keeps them in the game. We all got taken over by the pee-pees.*

The WHAT????!

The P-Ps: Process, Policy, Postures. Payoffs and Payouts. Throw in 'thoughts and Prayers.' Forget the P that's the true heart of everything – People – & Superman's motto of truth, justice and the American way. Dad blamed Dustin Hoffman and Robert Redford.

WTF?!

Their Watergate movie made Washington and politics look cool. And now half my gigs come from what that became. So sorry, Dad: I'm just another no-face, assembly line clicker coding us to wherever.

They streamed that Redford movie on Tuesday with a Steinbeck saga.

He told her about his high school crew, now all gone to wives and babies.

She told him what she finally *grokked* about high school.

Asked: *Have you told anybody about us?*

No, he answered. Didn't say: *Who would care?*

They double-featured movies about his Dad's teenage years, cruising cars and wanderers in gang colors. Wednesday, they picked two grim black-and-white crime movies to fit the rainy weather.

Noir *must contain a wink of light and redemption*, he zapped her. *Otherwise it's just a black hole where nothing matters, so why bother.*

She clicked: *I hope so.*

Hope, he thought. She hopes.

Like me.

The next night, their one-week anniversary, she risked using up the burner phone's minutes to text:

Are you lonely, too?

Took him five minutes to text it right, safe:

I've only got you.

She came up with the Pod.

Kept her mask on as she stepped into his apartment that night. *We can't touch or get close*, was the rule. And they must always wear masks.

He backed away from her as she came in. Watched her emerald eyes absorb where he lived – the open kitchen nook, the hall to the two open-doors bedrooms. He'd made his bed and his Dad's bed hadn't been unmade *since*. She stared at his cocoon of three screens. Only the left screen was active, the security cameras' views of the hall and where she'd come from.

The wall window to the night pulled her gaze. She walked toward it past the cocoon of three—

Tripped! Stumbled toward the fourteenth floor's window!

Jeff reached to grab her—

—as she caught herself. Their hands didn't break quarantine by touching.

"You OK?" he said. "That thick black cable you tripped on powers my scr—"

"*I'm sorry! Sorry for so many damn—!*"

She composed herself: "Sorry."

Stepped past him to face that floor-to-ceiling window. Pressed her hand against that glass. Left its ghostly print for him to stare at *until.* "If I'd crashed into it, would it have shattered? Let me…"

"The building's Management Authority says it's safe."

"Gotta trust Management – right?"

She stared out at the night of this city.

"You can't see any of D.C.'s tourist shots." Jeff stood behind *oh* the curve of her black slacks. He smelled her rose shampoo through his mask. The scent of her flesh in the April night's air. "Down there, lower right, that's the marquee for the American Film Institute's theater. They've got it lit with how to stream their stock. Further to the left – that all dark big warehouse across the street? That's the Paradise. A rock amphitheater.

"Dad loved this view. His roadmaps to life were novels, movies and rock 'n' roll. He loved being close to all that, even if the Paradise is generations past booking silver-hairs like his Springsteen or Richard Thompson."

"Now that Paradise is closed," she said. "No songs."

"Maybe we just can't hear them," he said.

They sat on opposite ends of his couch as movies filled the center screen.

She whispered: "Thank you."

Left.

Came back the next morning, his door swinging open to her knock.

To her eyes of blue.

Blue!

He stepped back into his apartment.

She followed him in like a lioness. Shut the door behind her.

Smiled at him with blue sky eyes.

"You forgot they're supposed to be green!" came through his black mask.

She shook – fear, anger, Jeff couldn't tell. Her black mask hid her face.

"Only cash," continued Jeff. "And it isn't you in your high school pictures."

"You tell, he'll find me and kill me."

"Who?"

"Lars. My husband."

She shrugged, shook her head. "You might say I'm fucking abused."

"Join the club. My right forearm has a chunk bit out of it. We were sixteen. No cops sirened to the school. She had rich parents."

"'Least that means your scars are probably not on the net. One thing Lars did to enhance his brand and dick on Wall Street was to '*let*' his '*loving*' wife recreate Marilyn Monroe's calendar picture, red curtain back drop and nothing on but the radio. It's an easy Google because he used my name."

Those blue eyes bored into Jeff.

"It's Vera," she said. "Vera Cain. Natural blonde. Blue eyes."

"So you ran."

"And grabbed his gym duffle stuffed with black money so I'd have a chance. When I have to, I use the I.D. of my dead mentor at the modeling agency.

"He'd kill me even without the bag. He's the heroic saver who turned out to be a sadist. Slapping. Judo flipping me around like a rag doll. Choking me. Raping me. He had me coffin-bound. And that money, *well*, he's like most finance foxes on the Street. They don't care how or who or why they move money, long as they get their cut. But the people Lars *'finances'* for would more than take it out of him if something ever happened to their dirty laundry."

She shook her masked head:

"But if he catches me, I won't tell him I told you! Never! I'm ghosting you now. And that's like killing me, too. You're the first man ever, the first person since Lisa who cares about what I think. What's in my brain."

"How do you feel," said Jeff. "How it all wraps up into you."

"All I want is a chance."

"All I want is for you to have it all."

She staggered toward him—

—pulled back.

"We can't. Not now. Not yet."

"But now we can fix this so you're free. Really free. So… So…"

"*So*," she said. Her sky eyes' brows wrinkled. "But… *How?*"

The next morning. Saturday, May 2, 2020.

The President'd purged a government watchdog who identified critical medical shortages. The Pres' also blocked the country's top doc from testifying to Congress about the Covid pandemic that now scored 64,103 Americans dead. North Korea's atom bomb dictator re-emerged after weeks out of public view long after America's President'd said of him: "We fell in love." An ice island the size of Seattle broke off Antarctica, *melting, melting* into the sea. Canada banned assault rifle sales after a mass shooting. George Orwell ruled the bestseller charts.

Jeff sat in the half-moon made by his three screens.

His right screen was blank. No more watching movies alone.

His keyboard clicked his center screen with hopes.

His left screen's security cameras' views caught a white van parking at the building's revolving front door. Magnetic signs clung to the van's doors:

EMERGENCY SERVICES

Jeff flicked from that glimpse to waterfalls of data in his center screen as he robbed digital graves. The plague outside made him lucky. He scrolled through scores of recently dead women.

The blinking-emergency-flashers van's driver left his vehicle. He wore a full-body, hooded white Personal Protective Equipment coverall and a wartime gas mask with goggle eyes.

Jeff yawned at the center screen where he ran the program he'd spent most of the night writing. He knew the burner cell he'd sent back to Vera's place with her at midnight had almost no life left, but this was an emergency!

His text: *Need coffee!*

Her text: *Need to boil wa*

Her phone died.

The left screen flicked to views of the building's front desk: The civilian clerk crammed into the furthest corner pointed directions to answer whatever the pandemic's Obvious Official demanded as that white coveralls creature's glove tapped the pad to open the Emergency Keys drawer.

Jeff's eyes reflected the data waterfall in his center screen.

The PPE white coveralls figure faced its bug-eyed reflection in the lobby elevator's metal doors. The lit call button read *UP.*

To build a permanent escape identity for Vera née Lisa, Jeff coded search parameters with The Big Three of human data markers: race, gender, age. Plus any dead woman he found needed to lack still-breathing close relatives.

The left screen showed the white-cloth-condom-contained bug-eyed monster riding up alone in the elevator's silver cage.

Plus, the data woman's death must not have yet been processed by Social Security and other official key data clusters that could not be hacked.

An emoji of a hopeful face winked on in Jeff's watched screen.

He didn't see the elevator-caged white-cloth-condom monster pass the seventh floor.

Jeff's tired heart blinked: *Her burner's dead. Could be an email from her!* But it was just Klassmates.com:

Hi there! Guess what? Another interested classmate of yours recently clicked on your query about Lisa Freemont!

Multiverses novaed Jeff.

If someone monitored, clicked on my... popped my email... back-hacked my – my grocery deliveries destination address... Her location from our movie chats...!

He whirled to his left screen.

Saw the bug-eyed white-cloth-condomed freak passing the eleventh floor.

Knew. Knew in his bones what he'd done. What was coming.

Phone – her burner's dead!

Jeff charged from behind his screens. Jerked open his Dad's desk drawer. Pulled out the Walther PPK pistol gifted to his Dad by a rogue spy. They'd shot it, Jeff and his Dad'd shot it at a range, 'n' now Jeff grabbed the hand-sized black automatic, racked the slide—

Fuck! No bullets!

Bluff! thought Jeff. *Get to her first or 'least in time and bluff!*

Didn't bother to grab his mask.

Ran to his front door to beat, *gotta beat* the white-sheathed bug-eyed homicidal husband there or get there in time to stop...!

Threw his door open—

The gas-masked bug-eyed killer loomed there. His left hand had zipped down the white coveralls so his gloved right hand could reach inside to grab.

Jeff snap combat-aimed the Walther like he'd seen in the movies.

Bug-eyed monster Lars whipped his empty gloved right hand out of his zipped-down white coveralls—

—as Jeff grokked the imprint on the inside of that white cloth of a silencer-equipped and thus awkward-to-draw pistol falling from Lar's touch, sliding down inside the white coveralls to get *stuck* in the ankle-cinched baggy left pants leg.

That white-gloved empty gun hand chomped Jeff's wrist below the Walther. Lars punched his gloved left palm into Jeff's extended gun arm. Slammed him face first into the doorjamb.

The useless Walther flew from Jeff's hand.

They rumbled into the apartment. That door closed behind their battle.

Jeff feinted a snap kick like he'd learned in childhood *kung fu.*

Lars didn't buy it. Slammed a boxer's gloved right hook into Jeff's face.

Jeff tumbled into the open kitchen. Stumbled/staggered against the counter. Grabbed the giant meat cleaver off the food-prep handy magnetized strip above the stove that his stellar Mom had installed two years before her funeral.

He slashed the cleaver back and forth at the dodging white-clothed fiend.

Jeff's attacks pushed the bug-eyed assassin out of the kitchen nook. Out to the living room with its tabled half-moon of computer screens.

Combat-shuffling, cleaver-swinging Jeff swung wide.

Lars jerked Jeff's attacking wrist, spun his back into Jeff, curled to judo flip Jeff over him and through the air.

Jeff crashed through his computer monitors.

The cleaver clanged to the floor.

Lars kicked a (luckily) glancing blow across flat-on-his-back Jeff's face.

She opened the apartment door.

Her right hand held the key Jeff gave her.

Her left hand held a glass pot of steaming coffee.

She wore her black mask. Her blue eyes blasted open with what they saw:

A creature in a white cloth condom against crime evidence or identification whirling to her entrance with gas-mask bug eyes.

She could have run down the hall to the elevators or the stairwell.

She charged into the apartment.

Threw boiling hot coffee over Lars.

The coffee splashed a useless tan stain on the gas mask and protective white condom clothes of the man holding her Jeff splayed on the floor.

The apartment door slammed closed behind her.

Lars kicked Jeff in the ribs to knock him further toward the window.

Whirled to face the woman between him and the door to her nowhere.

Vera threw the coffee pot at him.

Lars batted it into the kitchen nook's sound of bustin' glass.

He knocked away Vera's punches. Slapped her face.

Jeff made it off the floor to his hands and knees behind the killer. Saw that white-clothed alien shake Vera. Grab both her breasts.

Lars's white-gloved paw slapped away her scream.

That Harvard stud of Wall Street stomped Vera's fashion-runway-perfect knee. Crashed her to the floor where he wouldn't need to worry about her, save her and the best for last as he turned to deal with the wannabe white knight.

Pain wracked Jeff, but he was up, held his hands up, on guard.

Lars danced the damaged fool backwards, toward the wall, the window.

Vera crawled on the floor toward the battle.

Lars punched Jeff's face.

Slammed the stunned man backwards into the floor-to-ceiling glass.

Jeff bounced off the window. Dodged a punch.

Crawling Vera scooped up the dropped meat cleaver.

Lifetime bully Lars shoved Jeff backwards again into the window.

That glass spider-webbed.

Vera pushed herself up on one hand but could only wave the meat cleaver a few pitiful inches off the floor.

Jeff flailed at the mocking blows hitting his face, his body.

Vera chopped the meat cleaver through the once-tripped-her black cable.

That *clunk* made Lars fumble a sloppy grip on Jeff.

Who saw past the assassin to the floor where Vera whipped the stiff sparking black cable out from her like an angry ambushed snake.

Jeff kicked himself free and away from the white-clad monster.

Vera thrust the sparking black cable snake straight into her turning-around husband's groin.

Lightning slammed through the cable.

White-cloth-condom-contained killer Lars rocketed backwards into the cobwebbed window. The glass shattered. He flew out to a fourteen stories *splat*.

Vera dropped the dead cable. Crawled toward Jeff—

—who caught her, held her close.

Her sky eyes caressed his unmasked face.

She reached behind her ears. Freed the white straps looped there.

Her black mask fell away and *oh!*

There she was, her face, her whole beautiful face, her lips lush and burning wet against his with an electricity beyond any cable, her mouth opening, the tingle-coffee taste of their tongues dancing with each other and she coughed from deep in her lungs, coughed again into the shared breath of their passionate mouths as Jeff remembered no-masked Red Tie from the elevator cage who he hadn't seen in the security cameras for days and knew, Jeff absolutely knew that *now*, one way or the other, Vera and he would be together forever.

THE CASE OF BABY X

LAVIE TIDHAR

1

Mike Bash was always smiling. He opened the service station store sharp at five thirty in the morning. He did that every morning without fail. He smiled when he turned on the radio. Smiled when the first song was Bobby Darin singing 'Beyond the Sea'. Smiled when he filled up the cash register with cash, made sure the cigarettes and sweets were fully stocked, smiled when he replaced the tape in the security camera and smiled as he changed the sign on the door from 'Closed' to 'Open'.

It was a grey sort of day and it looked like it might rain a little later. He was content within. Sally would be driving the kids to school. In the evening Mike might get to catch a little of the game. He'd have a beer. He'd have dinner with the kids and make sure they were bathed and tucked in bed. He'd give them a kiss each, read the small one a bedtime story. Then he'd watch an hour of television with Sally, whatever happened to be on, and then they'd go to bed. He was an early to rise, early to bed sort of guy. Always has been.

A rental car was parked outside and now he saw a woman in dark sunglasses step out of the driver seat, her hair a little mussed up, like she'd been asleep in there. She wore a grey tracksuit and running shoes. Mid to late twenties, maybe. Probably a tourist. Must have pulled in the night before to catch some sleep on the way elsewhere. He hadn't noticed the car when he locked up for the night.

He made sure the coffee was percolating and ready to pour. The smell of fresh coffee filled the small store. It wasn't good coffee like they used to have back home. But it was coffee. The doorbell dinged and the woman came in.

Mike tidied up the pile of magazines next to the cash register. The woman approached the counter and stared at him, looking a little lost.

"Help you, miss?" Mike said.

"Coffee," the woman mumbled.

"Right over there," Mike said.

He smiled, and she nodded and went to the coffee but didn't pour any. She looked back at him.

"What's your name?" she said.

"It's Mike, miss," he said, smiling.

"Did you have another name before?" she said.

"Another name?"

Mike kept the smile, but it took some effort.

The woman shook her head. *Forget it.*

She poured coffee at last. Took a sip and grimaced. She took it over to the counter.

"How much?" she said.

He told her the price and she made a face but pulled out a five-dollar note and handed it over.

"You *did* have another name, before," she said.

"Before what, miss?" Mike said.

"Before you came to America."

"I think you must be confused." He punched the cash register, took out a handful of change.

"Where are you from?" the woman said. "Originally, I mean."

"Israel," he said, not unwilling but wary. He used to be in love with the idea of Israel, and even after he left and before he met Sally he still went to Independence Day celebrations from time to time. When he got to one of the big cities he'd track down a newspaper from back home. He moved around a lot when he first came over. But now he was settled and all that stuff was long behind him. Now he sold cigarettes and jerky and magazines, whatever people passing through needed. Now he had the shop and the kids and Sally, and the game on the television during the season.

"You know it?" he said, for something to say. He was still holding out the handful of change to her.

"I know it," she said. "You were called something else then. Malchiel. Malchiel Rom. You were the one with the car that time."

Mike dropped the smile. It was time for the lady to be going.

"That was a long time ago," he said.

He looked at her a little uneasily. Mid to late twenties. It was, what, twenty-six years ago? He said, "Your change," in a tone that he hoped made it clear to her she should take it and leave. He had a baseball bat under the counter.

The woman rummaged in her handbag.

"Keep it," she said.

Then he saw she had a neat black gun in her hands.

"Take the money," he said, "just take the—"

She shot him. He couldn't believe she shot him. He felt the impact in his chest, once, twice, like a giant pushing him back. He collapsed on the floor. The coins fell from his hand. He tried to reach the baseball bat but his fingers wouldn't move. He was cold. It was going to rain later, he was sure it was going to rain.

The woman went around the counter. She helped herself to a packet of Camels and tore the wrapping off. She lit one cigarette and then reached over Mike and found the tape for the security camera and popped it out and she took the one from the night before too.

"I was in the car," she said.

"How?" Mike said, or he tried to. The words bubbled out. He thought his lungs were gone. He couldn't breathe. "They're all dead. They were all dead apart from—"

Then it dawned on him, just before she lowered the gun and he saw it pointing at his face. He heard the click of the mechanism and then he didn't hear anything at all ever again.

✷

Before Leila left the store she changed the sign from 'Open' to 'Closed'. Then she got back in her car and drove fast all the way across the state until she was over the state line. Then she pulled up to a rest stop and sat behind the wheel and breathed heavily like she was hyperventilating. This didn't really go the way she'd planned it. She wasn't sure now how she'd planned it. She was going to talk more. Ask more questions, maybe. But he just looked so dumb, with that handful of change and that smile on his face. Like he was just some guy called Mike. She wondered if he had any children. He wore a wedding ring, though Jewish men didn't regularly wear them. Maybe he married a local girl. He was a long way from home. Why was she thinking about his wife or kids or whatever? Once she had the gun in her hand it just didn't feel worth it to do any more talking.

She didn't get her change. This annoyed her, somehow. The coffee was overpriced as it was. She took out her list, folded over and over and tucked into the lining of her coat. She found a pencil stub and crossed out his name at the top. Malchiel Rom.

So that was one down.

She went to use the restrooms and changed into new clothes. She bagged her shoes and tracksuit and everything else and dumped them in a bin in the next state. Then she headed to the airport.

2

Dolores pushed her shopping trolley along the canal, staring suspiciously at passers-by. Let them try to get her bottles! All her fortune was in that trolley, and twenty euros in her left boot tucked into the good sock. She could have got more if she begged, maybe, but she was never going to beg. Instead she worked. She collected bottles and she got the deposit money for them and on a good day she could get herself a meal and sometimes even a place to sleep. Other times she slept where she could, though the Dutch police weren't always nice about it. You had to keep your wits about you in this part of town. All kinds of hoodlums and mischief-makers and too many tourists. Dolores had come to Amsterdam a long time ago. Her Dutch was still pretty broken but she considered herself as much a local as anyone, and more so than most. A boat went past on the canal. The nights were still cold and the lights were dimming, and she caught a shiver and went to sit on a bench and rest a moment, watching the pretty houses.

This was why she saw the woman in the pink blouse, because she had to catch her breath. The woman in the pink blouse looked like she was maybe a lawyer or someone fancy, not a tourist but she had gone along the street twice, going and coming, before settling on the house. It was a nice expensive house with purple flowers outside in two hanging baskets. The woman in the pink blouse reached into her handbag and kept her hand there. She went up the steps and knocked on the door and, a moment later, a man answered. They spoke very briefly. Then Dolores saw something very odd.

The woman in the pink blouse took out a small handgun. The man reacted very quickly. He hit the woman in the pink blouse with a vicious open palm to the face and ducked low at the same time. He grabbed the woman by the waist and pulled her in and shut the door.

Dolores sat and stared at the door. She wondered if the woman was an angry lover, maybe, but the man was older and gross, though he had moved fast, almost as though he'd expected something like this to happen. Dolores wondered what was happening inside. Would the man call the police? She waited but she didn't hear sirens, and the street was peaceful.

Dolores felt agitated. She couldn't leave her trolley, not when it was full of bottles – what if somebody stole them? But at the same time she started to worry for the woman in the pink blouse, who was obviously in trouble of some sort, even though she was the one who initiated the violence. Dolores could call the police, but she lived by a strict code and calling those pig Dutch cops was not something she was willing to do. She was torn in indecision. She thought of maybe just going. This never happened, she thought. Did she even see anything? Maybe there was a reasonable explanation, maybe they were a couple spicing up their sex life with role play. People were into all kinds of kinky things these days.

Dolores groaned and got up. Her old knees were feeling the strain but so was her heart. She remembered Rodolfo, a long time ago, and how much she had loved him and he had loved her. They had such big dreams. She was quite a beauty in those days and he had a beautiful singing voice. Then she found him in bed one night with that whore from Antigua and next thing you know Rodolfo had a hole in his forehead the size of a pomegranate and Dolores was on the first ship to Europe.

She tied the shopping trolley to the bench with a chain, muttering as she did so, and the few passers-by went around her and looked at her sideways. *Well, let them*, she thought. She went up to the house with the purple flowers hanging from their baskets. How long had the girl been inside? Dolores crept around the side and found a window. She peered in.

The woman was sitting in an armchair under a painting of Queen Wilhelmina (*God rest her soul*, thought Dolores). She had bruises on her face and finger marks around her throat. The man stood over her with a gun.

"How did you find me?" the man demanded.

"I looked in the phone book," the woman said.

They both spoke English but both had an accent to it.

"I am not in the phone book," the man said. "I am not supposed to be found. Who gave me up? The Aharonis? The Goldins?"

"I don't know who they are," the woman said.

"You're lying," the man said. He gave a sudden burst of laughter. "You think I didn't know you were coming? I heard about Malchiel in America. Shot three times by a girl. They had a photo of you, did you know that? A camera in the petrol station, not in the shop. Not much to go by, but still. He was always weak, Malchiel. Just someone you tell what to do and he does it so you won't hurt him. I'm not like that. And I don't give a shit about your story. What happened needed to have happened. The only mistake I made was that you lived."

"Then finish me off," the woman said.

"Tell me how you found me!"

Dolores risked rising so she could see more of the room. She saw packages wrapped in masking tape. She had a bad feeling she knew what business the man was in now, and how he paid for the nice house and the nice flowers in the front.

The man slapped the woman in the chair again, hard. Queen Wilhelmina looked on in disapproval. Dolores wasn't sure what she could do. She went around the back some more. Found a back door and tried it.

It was locked.

Well, that was that, she tried to tell herself philosophically. There wasn't anything more she could do for the woman. She went back to the window.

She didn't know what possessed her, but she tapped on the glass.

The man turned, startled, the gun in his hand.

Dolores ducked, so she only heard the gun go off. She cowered under the window. But the glass hadn't exploded above her, she realised. She risked a look and saw the man had a knife in his back and the woman in the pink blouse stood over him with the gun in her hand now.

"My name is Leila," she said.

The man grunted.

"Say my name," Leila said. "My *name*!"

The man squirmed on the floor.

"Don't, miss," Dolores said. "It isn't worth it."

The woman didn't look up.

"It is to me," she said, and then she pulled the trigger.

*

Dolores never saw the woman in the pink blouse again after that. She went back to the bench and miraculously no one had stolen her bottles, which must have been because it was such a good neighbourhood and all. She didn't wait around to see if the cops would arrive or if the man's friends, concerned for the packages in his house, would come first. She didn't even know his name until, the next day, she found a newspaper near Centraal and it had a photo of the man on page three, and his name was Yotam Barzel, an Israeli citizen, but there was no mention of any dope.

"Oh, Rodolfo," Dolores said, because her dead were with her more and more with each passing year. Rodolfo smiled in the way the dead have when they smile, and it touched Dolores' heart, that he forgave her after all and she knew that he still loved her.

She left the newspaper where she found it and went and spotted four bottles in a row, empty and just left there, which was a sign if anything was. So all in all it was a good day.

3

"There have been cases of domestic terrorism going back decades," the lecturer said. I stared at the dark auditorium. Just me and a bunch of old ladies with *Peace Now* T-shirts older than I was. "TNT and the Lifta Group in the 1980s, and the Bat Ayin Underground in the early 2000s are three examples. Then there were the actions of individuals or small groups, often spontaneous, such as the murder of Umar Udeh, a petrol station attendant, by Eli Va'anunu and Nir Efroni in 1984 in perceived response to the murder of Hadas Kadmi a few days earlier. More recently, the so-called Hilltop Youth movement has been active in perpetuating attacks on Palestinian villages—"

The lecturer droned on. I wanted a cigarette. I made notes in my notebook but I was only half listening.

"What of the case of Baby X?" I said at last, raising my hand but not attempting to wait any longer. The lecturer looked startled.

"Baby X, yes," he said. "In that instance five individuals were eventually convicted for the crime, but all—"

"Were pardoned shortly into serving their prison terms," I said.

"Yes, quite," the lecturer said.

"What happened to Baby X?" I said.

"Happened?" the lecturer said.

"Yes," I said patiently, my hand still raised. The old ladies looked at me in disapproval. "What happened to her?"

"Well, I do not know for sure," the lecturer said. "I believe she was put into the state system after the attack."

"Did she graduate high school?" I said. "Did she go to university? Start a family? Emigrate?"

"I don't know, and I believe she should be left in peace," the lecturer said, and the old women tutted loudly at me.

"Peace was hardly her inheritance," I said.

"Look, Mr— Who are you again?"

"I am planning to write a book about the case of Baby X," I said, "and I hoped you might be able to shed some light on the chain of events that led to that night."

I knew all of it already, of course. More than the old goat ever will. But I wanted to rile him.

"There were five people involved in the attack," the lecturer said. "The ringleader was later identified as one Yotam Barzel, a con man who worked part-time as a bartender. Barzel represented himself as a member of the internal security service, the Shin-Bet. He formed a cell of young radicals who frequented the pub he worked at in Jerusalem, convincing them that they were, in effect, working in the national interest. His second-in-command was Malchiel Rom, then a young soldier, who fell under Barzel's spell. Two more were students, a couple at the time, named Danny and Michal. The fifth was a teenager. He was sixteen years old at the time and his name was not released to the press."

"*He* was released, though," I said. "But he had a new name by then."

"That's right," the lecturer said. "Do you have any more questions, or can I get back to the topic at hand?"

"No further questions, your honour," I said. I got up and left the room and lit a cigarette before I even left the building. I stood outside with my back to the wall and smoked.

I remembered Barzel, of course. The bastard had a way with words, and he was happy to pour a drink for an underage kid. Rom was soft, a fat guy with a gun. He was pathetically pleased to be included, to be a part of something bigger than himself. The student couple I didn't much care for. The girl, Michal, was unstable, the boyfriend cold and putting on a superior air.

Someone else came out of the building. She saw me and smiled.

"Bum a cigarette?" she said.

"Sure."

I lit it up for her and watched her as she smoked. She was younger than anyone else in that lecture theatre. How did I miss her? She looked good.

"Are you really writing a book?" she said.

"Maybe."

"It's quite a story," she said. "How they killed that whole family."

"Not the whole family," I said.

Remembering again that night. I was the one who stopped the car. That was my job. We'd waited on a quiet road until we saw a car with a white number plate. Then I stepped on the road, flagging them down. I was only sixteen. They stopped to help. They must have thought I was in trouble. Michal, the student, she was useless. She stopped and threw up on the side of the road. Malchiel Rom was only useful because he had an army weapon. He brought it along, but it was Barzel who used it.

When I'd stopped the car Barzel and the student, Danny, opened fire on the people inside. Danny had a pistol, he'd brought it with him. There were four people in the car, the father driving, the mother in the passenger seat, a boy and a girl in the back. We killed them all that night but I didn't do it, it was Barzel and Danny, and I was underage, so when it came to the trial I barely got three years.

We got out of there in two cars. It was only the next day when we got the papers that we found out there had been a baby in the backseat.

Baby X.

"Hey," the girl said, "you want to go get a drink?"

I looked her up and down. She wore a baseball cap and looked like a typical student, jeans and a T-shirt and a casual jacket over the tee. She wore dirty-white sneakers. She looked good to me.

"Got anywhere in mind?" I said. I wasn't used to girls asking me out but I tried to act confident, even nonchalant.

"There's a bar round the corner," she said. "It's sort of a student bar. We can talk there."

We were going to do more than talk if I had anything to do with it, I thought. I let her lead the way.

"I'm Ben," I told her. It was the name I used now, it was a legal name.

"I'm Lia."

"So what brought you to the lecture, Lia?" I said. "You a political science student or something?"

"Or something," she said. "I don't know much about the case of Baby X. I must have been only a baby then."

"Oh, I could tell you stuff," I said. "But let me buy you a drink first."

I hoped she wasn't one of those leftists.

"What do you think about the case of Baby X?" I asked.

She frowned. "Well," she said. "It was a tough time for everyone, I suppose that family had it coming to them."

"Do you know," I said, "it's so refreshing to hear someone say that? They're always cast as the victims but we, I mean, they were the real victims, the people who did it. They acted in the belief that they were sanctioned by the government. That they were working to—"

The distance of years made it hazy for me to remember what we had thought. Barzel had a way of selling you patriotism with your pint. To be truthful, back then, I didn't care. I just wanted to see someone die. It's why I liked that the victims were chosen at random. They were just in the wrong car on the wrong road that night. That was all they were.

I never killed anyone. Not then and not after. They had me under psychiatric evaluation for a time and the only conclusion they ever came to was that I deserved to be released back into society. Since then I'd done odd jobs. I got by.

The bar was pretty crowded and no one paid us any attention. I ordered two beers. When she had her back turned to me for a moment I slipped a little something into her glass.

We were definitely going to party later, I thought.

By the second beer I had a mellow haze around me and Lia seemed unsteady on her feet. We didn't talk about much of anything. I figured we didn't really have much in common with each other. But that was fine with me. When her legs gave under her I helped her up and wrapped her arm around my neck. She felt warm and willing against me. I helped her out of the bar.

"My place isn't far," I said.

I didn't want to take a taxi. Taxi drivers could be nosy. We walked to my place. It was just a place I crashed at sometimes. I locked the door behind us. I felt a little woozy myself, what with lugging her fat ass all the way there. I was going to do things to her, soon as I caught my breath.

The room swam. I started to giggle. "I'm gonna do you, I'm gonna do you," I said. I'd done this a few times before. They never remembered anything the next day. I lunged at her, missed, fell on the dirty sofa. The room was sparsely furnished with a few bits I'd picked up discarded on the street. A sofa, a mattress on the floor.

"Come, sit in my lap," I said. I pulled her to me and she collapsed on the sofa by my side. It was very funny. I started to laugh. She started to laugh.

"Tell me about Baby X," she said. "You said you could tell me things."

"You like that, don't you," I said. "You're bad. I was there, Lia. I was with the crew."

"You were the teenager," she said. "The one whose name wasn't in the paper."

"It's Ben now," I said. "But that was me. Sure. We were heroes, Lia. We struck a blow against the enemy that day."

"You were so brave," she said.

"I'm going to… I'm going to…" I said. I tried to paw her but my hands wouldn't move. I started to giggle. The room swam. I said, "What's happening?"

"Oh," she said, suddenly not sounding drunk at all. "I switched our glasses."

"You did what?"

This also struck me as funny. I started to laugh again but she didn't laugh this time.

"I'm going to kill you," she said.

"Kill me!" My body shook with the laughing. I lost control of my bladder and peed myself, feeling warm. It was a nice feeling. "Stop messing, Lia."

"It's Leila," she said.

"So what?" I said.

"So Baby X didn't even have a name before you killed her family. Not on paper. That's why they called her Baby X on the news. Then when she went into the system they gave her the name Leila."

"Come on," I said. I was no longer laughing. A spear of ice felt like it'd been rammed inside me from the bottom up. "Stop messing."

She got up from the sofa. There was nothing I could do to stop her. She looked around the room. Found the ropes and the knife. She picked the knife up.

"What were you going to do tonight?" she said.

"Nothing," I mumbled. "Just play around, that's all."

"I want to know where the others are," she said. "Before I kill you. Danny and Michal. The couple."

"They didn't stay a couple," I said. "Not for very long. Michal tried to kill herself a couple of times. Couldn't even do that. She wasn't, you know. She wasn't right in the head. She became very religious, lived out in the settlements. Remarried after her release."

"And Danny, the boyfriend?" she said.

"The second shooter," I said. "He was just crazy. Cold, intellectual. I don't think he believed Barzel at all. We all did, but not him. He just did it anyway."

"Where is he now?" she said.

"I don't know. He's in tight with those others, you know. Always carries a gun. He's out there, still carrying out raids. Still fighting the fight." I coughed a laugh. "No way you ever get close to him."

"Then give me Michal," she said. "And I'll do you quick."

"You can do me right now," I said, and nodded to the bulge in my pants. It was the damnedest thing but I was hard. This struck me as funny, and I started laughing, and then when I thought of what she was asking I couldn't help myself and laughed even more, and I swear it must have been the happiest I'd ever been, just then, with her in that room where I did all those other girls.

"You'll… You'll…" This was so funny. I couldn't wait to see the look on her face when I told her. "You'll never get her, you stupid cow."

"Why not?" Leila said.

"Her husband…" This was too funny. "Her husband killed her."

The husband must have been as sick of her then as I was back when we shot up Leila's family. Michal did nothing but throw up when we shot up the car. Danny let me hold the gun. He let me let off a shot or two. It was nice of him. Michal was a drip.

"She was always in and out of hospital," I said. "Always complaining to the police he hit her or threw hot water on her or stuff like that. She never looked after his kids, he was a widower with five kids. Yosef, his name is. So one day he picked her up at the hospital and then took her to the Eshtaol forest, hit her over the head with a hammer, stabbed her and then cut her throat."

It was so funny I would have peed myself again.

"My God," Leila said.

"Hey," I said, "he did the job for you. Now are you going to suck my—"

She stabbed me. I was so surprised I wasn't even angry. She stabbed me again, and again, and again, on that sofa I found on the street, and the blood just fell on the dark material and vanished there with all the other stains.

"Why?" I tried to whisper. "Why?"

It just seemed so unfair.

4

Leila tossed the knife on the floor. She threw up right over Ben, or whatever he called himself. He stared up at her with glassy eyes. Her sick went all over his face and dribbled down his cheeks and eyes.

She couldn't do this anymore, she thought. She was through; this was the last one. It wasn't worth it.

She had no memory of that night. For a long time not even a knowledge of it. When she first heard of Baby X she just felt sorry for the little girl. For a long time Leila didn't even know who her parents were or what had happened to them, or that she'd once had two siblings.

But then she found out.

The fury that kept her going dissipated suddenly. She stared around her at the disgusting room, at the corpse on the sofa. He looked so stupid. She thought of the woman who was murdered by her husband. Leila tried to tell herself she got what she deserved. But did she? She no longer felt anything, good or bad, about these people.

She was through, Leila decided, and the feeling was so sudden and so freeing that she wanted to laugh. She cleaned up the room, wiped her prints off everything, left quietly. It was night outside. She went back to her rental car, took out the kit bag, changed her clothes and bagged the bloodied ones. She put on a light raincoat, even though it wasn't raining, to hide the stains.

She didn't know what she would do, where she would go. She would leave the country.

Go back to America, maybe. It had so much open sky and you never ran out of road.

She was thirsty. There was a supermarket around the corner. She could buy some supplies, eat on the way to the airport. She was done with this place, with the past.

It was bright inside the supermarket. The light erased shadows. Soft music played. She walked past rows and rows of cornflakes. Washing powders in big tubs. Shampoos. Soaps. The shop had that fresh bread smell all supermarkets had now. Her stomach growled.

She passed him by the fruits and vegetables. She barely paid him any attention. She was going to get an apple. He looked up and saw her. For just a second their eyes locked.

She felt the knowledge of it at the same time as him.

He recognised her.

Just an older man in a chequered shirt and jeans. What was he even *doing* there? He wasn't supposed to be there.

Danny Brown, the fifth. The one who brought his own gun to the ambush. He was a student then. Still carrying on the fight, Ben said. What was he *doing* here, now?

He moved fast and so did she. He dropped his groceries and reached for a pistol on his belt.

Leila ran. She went into the beer and wine aisle. He wouldn't dare shoot. Would he?

She looked wildly around but there was no one in the store, she couldn't even see a check-out clerk. Maybe it was using self-service machines. She heard his footsteps, coming for her.

"I heard about the others," he called, somewhere near Fresh Produce she thought. "How did you find me?"

"I didn't," she called back. "It's just chance."

She heard him laugh.

"I've waited twenty-six years," he said. "For a chance to finish the job."

"We can go our separate ways," she said. "I don't want to kill anymore."

She looked around her, for anything she could use. Tampons. Lollipops, which were a rare treat when she was growing up. Vodka.

He said, suddenly very close, "I do."

She felt the gunshot before she heard it. It missed but it hit the bottles and shards of glass hit her face and she cried in pain. She ran and he fired again, a can of sweetcorn bursting suddenly and with the smell of summer. She grabbed things as she ran. There was nothing more to say so neither of them said it. She hid, hearing his footsteps come round on the other side of the aisle.

"Nowhere to run," he said. He stood framed against the meat counter, gun raised. "Where are you?"

She didn't answer. She let the matchbook she had palmed off Ben drop to the floor. It made almost no sound. Leila hefted the bottle of vodka stuffed with the tampon she had just lit on fire. She tossed it over the nappies and hygiene products.

"What are you—"

He fired again but at nothing. The bottle burst, the flames shot out, feeding on the previously spilled alcohol, racing here and there in a shape like a messy bird's nest. The flames were twigs, Danny Brown was the chick in the nest.

She heard him curse, then. The fire caught quickly, trapping him inside it. It spread and smoke began to rise, ugly and thick, as Leila fled the supermarket into the night.

She turned, watching the flames beat against the glass. She kept expecting him to come out of the fire, to come after her with his gun, to finish the job like he'd said. But he never came out.

She could hear sirens coming closer. Her face hurt from the glass and her lungs from the smoke. It started to rain then, finally, and she closed the raincoat over herself and peeled the wrapper off the lollipop she stole and put it in her mouth.

It had been a long time since she'd had any kind of a treat. She figured, all in all, the supermarket wouldn't miss it.

THE PHANTOM GENTLEMAN

BARRY N. MALZBERG

Here he is, alone again. He has been alone all his life although no one would believe that; they thought he was lying to them all. He was not a liar even though the racket itself forced you on assigned occasions to skirt the truth. Alone in the small, empty room, the detritus of his life piled around him like random inflammations, he thinks of all that has happened to him and all that has not. Mother would know but she has been gone for a while. Swannie, five-thousand-dollar Swannie could never have known but was not interested anyway. He heard aimless sounds in the corridor, the chirping of insects maybe, or the footsteps of the one bellboy patrolling these halls, looking for a way out. There is no way out, he would have told him if he had the energy to open the door and start any kind of conversation. There was no way out. "If you can find it let me know," he wanted to tell the stalker of the hall, bellboy or otherwise. But he was more or less out of declaiming. Let them find their own lessons.

*

Here he is now, trapped in the editor's office, trying to act as if he were paying attention. "The novel is pretty good," the editor says, "but there's a big hole in it. You never explain the phantom lady, you never explain from where she came or how she disappeared completely. That is a big hole in the novel, that failure to explain. We need the backstory."

"Backstory?" he says. "There is no backstory, that is the whole point. It is a mystery, don't you see? Her identity is unknown. Maybe he *has* imagined her. Life isn't all *Dime Detective* you know. There are issues, serious issues here, about existence itself. Maybe it's all random. Maybe there is no explanation." The editor's face flushes like that of a throttled corpse. "No," he says, "*you* don't understand. Rotting corpses in the wrong place, strangers who are married to the same woman, bullets which give random impact and destroy two lovers just as they are about to meet. Common tragedy to strangers separated by a thousand miles. Life is a racket, a racket of the random. If you make me try to explain it the reader will feel as big a fool as I am for trying to order it."

The editor, however, is adamant. "Take it or leave it," he says. He used to be the editor and publisher of *Story* magazine so that would settle it.

He returns home and does the fix, attaching a dry, endless chapter of backstory with all the life of an old man dying in the cloud of a hotel room. The novel is accepted, is a moderate success and as usual the film rights are sold by the illustrious Swannie ("Swami?") for five thousand dollars.

*

His dreams are both insistent and unremarkable. He wakes from staggered sleep with plots in his head, some of which he takes to conclusion. Women, some of them tender beyond understanding, drift in the watery globe of his recall. Sometimes he can recall them but never sees their doubles on the street and comes to understand finally that he never will.

*

His novelette, whose protagonist with the broken leg is convinced that he is watching the progression of a murderer in the apartment directly across the courtyard from his own, four stories high, is sold by Swannie for six hundred and twenty-five dollars; one-eighth of the five thousand dollars paid for this collection of eight. He is not sent an invitation to the premiere, much less a free ticket. "They're all the same," Mother says. "Nothing changes, nothing ever will. Fortunately your dad left us a pile of money. You stick close to me, son, or you'll never see it."

*

Early on he had dropped out of school to pursue novels of dancing and drinking for the lost generation. Fitzgerald, that bum, had left plenty of room for imitators and the money, which Mother insisted was superfluous, was pretty good. But the novels had failed and to chronicle flappers in the depth of the Depression seemed increasingly ridiculous. His dreams and daily fantasies increasingly gravitated toward dead flappers, lost rendezvous and brutal dismemberments in the attic.

✳

And here he is again, a decade after Mother departed, considering the ashes of his career. He had had big plans and Swannie's five thousand dollars cemented them for a while. After the War, after Korea, after Mother departed, he had taken it as far as he could and Swannie, deprived of properties to unload for five thousand dollars, became nasty and unavailable. Clearly he needed another agent, and in fact got one, but it was all too much of an effort. His reputation, always marginal, declined, the bottles in the hotel room multiplied, the bellboys kept him supplied and the engines of the night ran lively in the dark. *I wonder how many will show at my wake*, he thought, after they had taken a leg and put him in a wheelchair. *Not too many. I'd be embarrassed if there were.*

No fear, there were not. There were five. Two representatives from the bank, which posthumously dumped all but fifteen percent of his estate, Cynthia and Leo Margulies and a young writer with big plans. The young writer would be his successor. "Just as I leave, you come in," he had said to the young writer. "Isn't life wonderful?" The young writer, now old, remembers the sound which followed as a cackle, but it was not.

PARKVIEW
JAMES SALLIS

I was on the third or fifth day of a full-out bender when my door got noisy. Not the first time or first city I'd had a hotel dick come knocking, but I knew this one. Bennie. I'd trained him when he came on the force, when I was just starting to be someone who looked in the mirror and saw an old man. Now I look more like ancient, have turkey wattles for a neck and no damned hair except what sprouts from my ears, and my one-legged, briefly beloved John James has left me for, what else, another. Leaving me old and in the way and good for next to nothing. Live in residential hotels when I can save up a few dollars, mostly in shelters, listening to them tell me what I need to do with my life, the rest. From time to time I write a book and get paid five hundred dollars. Five hundred dollars can go a ways if you squeeze it.

Bennie checked the room before coming in, just like I'd taught him. Inside, he took another look. "Still living the good life, I see."

"Best room they had."

"It's the only fucking room they have. Forty of them."

"Democracy at work."

"Democracy, huh? Which they keep winding up but it never runs right."

"Sorry, but—"

He held up a hand to stop me. "'I didn't get much sleep, I've got the mother of all hangovers and don't like you much anyway, so don't fuck with me.' Yeah, I remember the old days too. Heard that a lot, didn't I?"

"Good times."

"Not really."

"Back then, we knew where we stood."

Bennie shook his head. Sorrowfully? "Sure we did. Think what you have to think, Boss."

"Okay, so what is it? I'm paid up for the week, stay reasonably clean, don't make scenes, even eat at the smelly cafe downstairs – when I eat."

"Famous all over the city for their grilled cheese that tastes like fish."

"Bad fish at that. But the price is right."

Bennie had taken a forty-second stroll around the room, pretty much exhausting possibilities, as we talked. "What the hell do you find to do up here all day? Besides drinking, I mean."

"Got me a lifetime of memories, don't I?"

"Don't we all? Best watch out, though. Memories'll pick at your head like carrion birds." Bennie reached in his cheap-ass, stripey sport coat for a notebook. Signaling a shift to the official part of the proceedings. "Ever run into Miss Landowska? Old woman lives next floor up, red hair out of a bottle, wears a raincoat day or night, rain, shine. Has one of the so-called apartments up there."

"I've seen her. On the stairs, in the lobby once or twice. Hard to miss that hair."

"She don't get out much. Been here since the place opened, someone told me. Story is, they even tried to push her out once. Tried everything, but they finally gave up and she's here to stay."

"Fascinating. What, you trying to lonely-heart us?"

"Lady has a problem. Yesterday, one of the rare times she was out of it, someone entered her apartment."

"A theft?"

"Could be."

"Jewelry? Treasure map? Thousands of dollars from the mattress or under the bed?"

"Nope."

"Doesn't matter. That's your job, you and the police, whatever it was."

"A cat. Hold on." He opened the notebook, checked. "A wombat."

"What the hell's a wombat?"

"Who knows, but it had to mean a lot to her. Has its own bed up there, special food, little playground in one corner."

"Parkview doesn't allow pets."

"This one they do. Told you – long story."

"Well, I don't have the damned thing."

"Someone does. And the police don't even want to talk about it. I thought you might be up to helping me find the thing."

"Go away, Bennie."

"I was telling Mr. Bower about you – owns the hotel? Said he'd appreciate the help and wondered how a month's free rent would sound. Hell, I'll even stand you a couple rounds at the bar across the street."

✶

Maintenance was on the ground floor, rear apartment. From the Latin *manu*, hand, and *tenir*, to hold. And Mr. Worth was up to the task. His hands were the size of dinner plates, cabled with hard cords of muscle that put you in mind of those on the city's suspension bridges. First floor, and with windows, but it still had the feel of being underground, like it had somehow been annexed by the basement.

No one knows the crannies and redoubts of a place like its janitor, so that had to be my first stop. Mr. Worth was on break, tattered book in hand, scowling as he tried to make sense of his grandson's math assignment so he'd be able to help him with it.

Sorry, I told him, no way I could be of use, he was flat out of luck on that front. I could diagram sentences on the fly all week long, but as far as math goes, the day we moved on to long division was the day I took the bench – and that was sixty years ago.

Though rightfully suspicious of my reason for the visit, when I name-dropped the hotel's owner, Mr. Worth backpedaled. Mention of Miss Landowska sealed the deal, and within minutes I had a scribbled list of hideaways, hollows, and crawlspaces. Handing the list over, he asked me what the hell a wombat was.

To fortify myself for the task ahead, I detoured back to my room, poured from a sadly depleted bottle of Scotch, and stood by the window looking past the roof of a building two floors lower to where lights had begun to spring up in other buildings and in the streets as our ever-weary, ever-lonely city donned its jewelry for another night out.

The park's down there too, but I never look that way.

Miss Landowska was sitting behind her desk as I entered, breakfast dishes and computer alongside. Neither math nor missing wombat appeared to be foremost in her mind. What *she* wanted to talk about was the abatement of proper manners and politeness. I'd listened for some time, my silence serving as accord, before I realized that she was not, as I thought, championing such "flufferies," but was in fact in full-voiced approval of shedding them.

(I almost began, "Herself received me in the parlor," as that was how it felt, albeit the parlor in this case proved a room filled to overflow with furniture – couches, end tables, chairs of every sort, a desk or two, knick-knack shelves, bookcases – much of it bearing dust that might easily date from Warren Harding's administration.)

Without pause, once the barest crack appeared in her monologue and I took courage to ask what I'd come for, Miss Landowska turned the computer toward me. There onscreen, along with hundreds of photos of the same, lay the promise of far more information about wombats than one would have thought possible.

Rugged little buggers, it turns out, thriving all about Australia, from desert dryland to forests. Come up to forty inches long, weighing in between forty and eighty pounds. Adorable rodentlike teeth, powerful claws, considered a family all on their own with no direct connection to similar creatures. They produce uniquely cubic feces, arranging them both to mark territory and attract mates, and look upon fences and barriers of every sort as "minor inconveniences to be gone through or under." Admirable traits if ever there were.

And this particular wombat, Miss L told me, whose name was Marcel, came as a gift from one of her dear, dear gentlemen friends. Marcel had been her constant companion, her love. Getting along in years he was, in his twenties now, her vet had estimated. In the wild a wombat's lifespan was maybe fifteen years, in captivity as much as thirty. She was so afraid that…

I waited for her to finish her sentence, which she didn't, then told her I understood.

I'd never had a pet, even as a child. Never understood it. But longing, heartbreak – that, I understand.

✶

My first stop from Mr. Worth's list was a looming crawlspace beneath the stairway just off the lobby, accessible by way of a curtained door tucked behind. It was not difficult to imagine that during rush and capacity booking the space might be rented out as a room; similarly, it required little imagination to envision the space a regular trysting site for late-night staff. Bringing, as this did, memories of my one-legged John James, I shut that thought immediately down. Even when there's nothing left to long for, longing itself persists.

Miss L had informed me that Marcel, like all wombats a herbivore, was especially fond of mushrooms. An inquiry at the cafe achieved little until Mr. Bower's name came up and it seemed I might well be on a personal errand for the hotel's owner, at which time a splendid bowl of baby bellas made its way to me from the kitchen.

The mushrooms, fine as they were, availed me little. Nowhere I left samples of them did I come upon a whisper of wombat, not in the secret closet behind the luggage storage, in the back rooms of the basement laundry, in the toolshed jammed like an afterthought into one corner of the boiler room, or in the long-neglected tiny chapel on second floor.

Following a second or possibly third jaunt to my room for fortifications, I recalled that the cafe regularly dumped food out back, in the cramped, reeking alleyway, and thought to check. A last resort, for me – and surely, I thought, for a hungry animal as well. I stood just outside the door peering at the bins. No sign of movement about or within. Stepping close, I kicked at the bins one by one. Still nothing. But I heard... laughter? Giggling, more like. Coming from a stubbish alleyway abutting the hotel's edge.

Within, I found four children aged perhaps six to nine, from (I must imagine) the cheap, overrun apartment complexes close by. They had installed against the hotel wall a form of... zoo, I suppose, or menagerie. Minimalist reproductions of cages, platforms and habitats patched together from sticks, paper, bits of cloth, and glue. And to these they'd brought their pets, a young rat, a bird with a broken wing, what may have been a hamster but more resembled a garden mole. The youngest of them had a fish, presumably dead and gone quite colorless, holding it in her hand. So intent were they at their play, they paid no heed to my noise among the trash bins or, now, to my approach, and after a moment of looking on, I withdrew.

By this time I'd seemingly exhausted my options and could think of nothing more to which I might duly turn my attention. What to do, then? Whenever in doubt, fall back to the room for regathering and further refreshment.

Bennie was scuttling away from my door as I came out the stairwell.

"Ah, Boss, glad I caught you. The thing is—" He glanced about. "Maybe we oughta talk inside."

We went in, and I poured, first for myself, then for Bennie, obscuring each glass with my fingers so he wouldn't see how much got in either. Whatever miniscule twinge of guilt I may have felt was done with soon enough.

"What it is," he said, eying the glass as I handed it over, "is we think maybe there ain't no wombat. Maybe never was? I show 'em pictures, none of the maids remember ever seeing anything like that. Neighbors either."

"What does Miss Landowska say?"

"Boss, I ain't asking that woman. She scares the bejeezus out of me."

"What about Mr. Bower, then. What did he say?"

"I got two, three sentences in before he just told me, *Find the damn thing*, like he did before."

"Then I think we both need another drink."

"That could be."

This time I gave him a proper one, and after he left, had two or three more myself, sitting there looking up and out into darkness thinking how the city's lights so mercilessly edited stars from the sky.

Sooner or later, of course, I was going to have to do it, so I slammed one last drink and went up to Miss L's.

"I'm glad you came," she said at the door, then asked me to follow her out to the kitchenette, where she showed me the neatly stacked tins of pet food. There were brushes and small clippers laid out on the counter by them, a water bowl on the floor below, toys in one corner. "I'm sorry for taking your time," she said, running her hand lightly along the cans. "I think—" She looked away a moment. "I think Marcel, my wombat, I think maybe that was some while ago. Years, even. My memory…"

When she failed to go on, I told her I understood. Was there anything else I could do? I asked. But even then she was quiet.

I returned to my room and my high window and stood there for a long time. Late that night, early morning really, most of my last bottle of Scotch gone to good cause, I became certain that I saw movement in the room's corner, something by the wall over by the dresser, even thought I heard scratching sounds, but when I looked, nothing was there. So much of life is that way.

THE LAKE, THE MOON AND THE MURDER

A. K. BENEDICT

The moon had no face that night. That All Hallows' Eve, the moon was a mirror, pocked and foxed, reflected in Manhattan's lakes. The moon had no face that night. It didn't want to see what came next.

Detective Clara Seaburgh, however, couldn't look away from death. She jaywalked towards it across streets littered with the detritus of both tricks and treats. It was said that on Halloween, the past and the future pressed into the present, that the veil between worlds was thin, and that spirits could cross between them. Clara didn't believe any of it. She was dealing with real mortality, not fairy tales. She had no time for the plastic facsimiles of death she passed on the way: the Grim Reaper given a treat-size Snickers; a ghost scoffing fists-full of Skittles; a skeleton sobbing on a stoop. Brownstones wore crime scene tape like designer scarves, but Clara was going where the tape was really needed. And so was she.

A cackle of children in witches' hats swept by, parents trailing them like toilet paper. Clara should have been out now with Lyla, her daughter. Lyla would have dressed as Elsa, holding a bucket overflowing with candy corn and other abominations. Clara should have been knocking on doors and laughing at animatronic ghouls, not looking for another mother's child. Not that Madeleine Singer was a kid: she was twenty-five, married, house on the Upper East Side. But they were always someone's children, however old they got. Clara's mom, Sandra, still called Clara her 'baby', even though Sandra was the one who needed her hand holding as she crossed the apartment on Jell-O legs.

Clara took a deep breath as she walked through the West 100th St entrance to Central Park. Madeleine had been missing for three days. Early that morning, her gloves had been found on the shore of The Pool, one of the park's many lakes. Expedited tests showed the blood was Madeleine's. The Crime Scene Unit had been through the area in the hope of finding something else, but nothing was forthcoming. Clara's hopes of finding Madeleine alive were falling like autumn leaves.

Torch beams flashed like ghost lights. Her team had managed to get a good turnout for the search party, over two hundred. Some of them, she knew, would be there for the Insta likes and pity fucks they'd get later, but that didn't matter. It helped, if anything. Loving friends and relatives didn't want to discover anything, so they didn't. Those eager to find, often found. More importantly, the press was here to film the search. Two photographers wandered through the volunteers, lighting up the night with flashes. A news van parked up had scored deep tyre tracks in the grass. The park wardens wouldn't be happy with that. Clara didn't blame them – she's not fond of the media herself – but public interest in Madeleine's disappearance had dimmed in the last week. Clara hoped this would spark it again.

Clara strode towards the searchers, pulling her red beanie over her ears, her shoulders back, and her detective persona on. She knew that this made her look strong, capable and reassuring. Sometimes she convinced herself: tonight wouldn't be one of those times. Madeleine's mother, Shirley, was by the lake. She looked like a shadow standing against a mirror. Earlier that day, she had opened her mouth in a silent scream when Clara told her about Madeleine's gloves. Clara had held her, felt the edges of Shirley's ribs and the sobs that rocked them.

As Clara approached the lake, Shirley's silhouette turned. The Pool behind her was tense and silver. Madeleine's husband, Trent, stood at Shirley's side. A willow wept over them.

"What do you want us to do, Detective?" Shirley asked when Clara was next to her. "Your officer didn't seem to know."

Clara looked over at Officer Lionel Clark, who was sweeping his torch over the lake as if the light could search its pockets. "Lionel," she shouted.

Lionel waved and came over. "Waiting on your orders, Ma'am." He dipped his head to one side, like a spaniel listening to the wind.

"Clusters of four, covering all the way up to the North Woods."

Lionel blinked once, then trotted off towards the growing crowd.

Clara shouted after him. "And give them a signal to use if they find anything."

Clara felt Shirley flinch next to her. "You understand we have to do this, Shirley?" she said, watching as Lionel organised the volunteers into teams.

Shirley nodded. And kept nodding, like an automaton fortune teller on a pier.

"You don't have to be here," Clara said. "I'm sure Trent would take you home."

"Of course," Trent said. His face was moon-pale and beautiful. A gibbous-shaped tear hung on his cheekbone.

"Or Lionel has a car, I'm sure he'd take you back if Trent wanted to help with the search."

"I have to stay," Shirley said. Her teeth let the words out between chatters. "I've got to be there when she's found." She paused and the wind seemed to still. "She must be lonely."

An image of Lyla, cold, prone and alone in the woods, flashed into Clara's head. She eclipsed it with thoughts of finding Madeleine.

Trent held back as Shirley walked off, slowly, to join the searchers who were fanning out across the grass. The camera crew followed, sniffing out tragedy truffles like tracker dogs.

"The reporter won't harass her, will she?" Trent asked. "Because I don't think she's up to talking about it all. Not yet."

"We've already told the press to stay away from you and Shirley. If there's going to be a press conference, then we'll brief you both beforehand."

He seemed reassured, his face relaxing for a moment. And then he looked back to the disappearing groups and his jaw tightened. "What should I be looking out for while we search?"

"Look out for Shirley," Clara said. "She needs you, and you need her." She kept her eyes looking concerned, but, really, she was searching his face for signs of guilt. He must have known he was under suspicion. Those closest to the victim were always the most likely to hurt them.

Trent's face did not flicker, though. Not one smug micro-smile. "I need Madeleine," he said. "No one else. I've always told her that, always will." His face grew even more pale. He suddenly looked much older than mid-twenties.

Clara's heart hurt for him. "I'll do everything I can to find her," she heard herself saying, "and bring her back to you." She knew she shouldn't say that, that it might surface his hopes only to drown them again. But she couldn't help herself, and maybe it helped him. "Imagine the reunion when you see her again."

Trent, though, backed away from her. Maybe he was imagining seeing her dead. Maybe that was the first time he had really allowed himself to think that.

"I'm sorry," Clara said, "I didn't mean to upset you."

"It's not your fault," Trent said. Then he stuffed his hands in his coat pockets and trudged after his mother-in-law.

Well done, Clara, she said to herself. *Showing why you came last in your sensitivity training.* She would let him get ahead, save him from any more of her faux pas. She kicked at the stones by the water's edge. The Pool was silent and still. Mercury-tinged. She stared into it, as if she could scry for answers. As if the lake could reply to her whispered question: "Where are you, Madeleine?"

A crow cried from the smoked-out sky.

Clara glanced up, then back to The Pool. Something was floating in the water. Pale and round, at first, she thought it was the moon, reflected in the lake.

And then she saw the staring eyes. The diamond-studded nose. Long hair, wafting like bladderwrack around a face. Madeleine's face. Her mouth open. Screaming.

Clara's eyes must have defocused as then she saw her own face, superimposed on Madeleine's. It was Clara's mouth that was open. Clara that was screaming.

Her voice scudded across the lake. "She's here!" She turned, looking for anyone to help. The torches of the search party stopped moving away. They glared in her direction, animal eyes in the dark. And then started towards her, as if fixed on prey.

But they were too far away.

It was probably already too late to save Madeleine, but what if she were still alive? What if she was dying right now and Clara didn't act?

Shucking her coat, Clara threw her hat and scarf to the ground, then took off her boots. The stones stabbed at the soles of her feet, finding their way through even the thick socks. As she entered the water, she felt it eat into the wool, and realised she should have taken the socks off too. But it was too late now. All that mattered was the woman in the water.

Clara waded the few metres out, trying to keep her gaze on Madeleine, but her movements disturbed the lake's meniscus, cutting its skin into ripples. Madeleine disappeared.

Panic surfacing, Clara moved quicker, and caught her foot on a stone. She tripped, splashed down into the water. She went under, mouth filling with The Pool. It tasted of heather and forever. The lake folded her into itself. Its epidermis re-formed above her: it wanted to keep her; she could feel it. She could also feel herself waning. Of giving in to the lake's embrace. She pictured her body, half in the water, half on the shoreline, washed up with Madeleine. Of her mother standing with Shirley, with Lyla crying for her mommy.

Clara pushed herself up, breaking the skin of the lake once again. She reached out, expecting to find Madeleine at any moment. But Clara's arms stayed empty.

"Have you found her?" Trent shouted. He was at the water's edge. He must have run to get so far ahead of the others.

"No," Clara replied. Tears she didn't know had fallen tasted of salt in her mouth. "But I saw her. She's here, somewhere."

Trent made the noise of a man torn in two. The sound carried across the park and was joined by Shirley's answering cry. Their keening set the crow cawing again.

*

It took an hour for the underwater team to arrive. More for the lake to be dredged. When the wetsuited men and women emerged for the last time without a body, Clara wanted to hide away. To leave, be anywhere but there.

"Are you alright, Ma'am?" Lionel asked, so very quietly.

"I don't know," she replied. And she didn't. How could she be OK, after that?

She bent down and picked up her scarf that had been trampled by volunteers. The white stripes were covered in mud and speckled with tiny stones.

As she stood up, filthy scarf in hand, the camera crew gathered around her. The television light loomed over the camera like a low-lying moon. "How do you feel, Detective Seaburgh?" the reporter asked Clara, shoving a microphone that smelled of Chanel N°5 in her face. "To have wasted precious time and resources while a mother still searches for her child?" The reporter's face was shadowed under the light.

Clara blinked. "I thought," she said. "I thought…" She gathered words but they dissolved in her mouth.

"Do you think it's time another detective took over the case?" The reporter moved forwards, and Clara could make out a sharp bob and sharper cheekbones. Before Clara could answer, the reporter had turned back to camera and was summing up, shaking her head slowly at the sadness of it all.

★

When Clara got home, just after 3 a.m., she checked in on Lyla first. Her daughter was holding the carrot nose of a snuggly Olaf, tucked up in *Frozen* sheets. Clara bent to kiss Lyla's forehead, stroked her hair back behind her ears.

"Hard night, love?" Sandra said, when Clara had showered, and they were both sat at the kitchen table. Sandra didn't sleep much if she could help it. Said that sleep was too much like death.

"I thought I'd found Madeleine Singer, but I was wrong."

"A colleague playing a trick on you, I'd say," Sandra said, nodding and dunking a cookie in her hot milk.

"Some trick."

"It's All Saints now at least," Sandra said, tapping her Apple Watch with approval. "Like that much more than Halloween. I never liked the smell of rubber."

"What?" Clara usually followed Sandra's chain of thought but that one eluded her.

"Halloween masks. Never liked the feel or stink of them. Always felt like I was being suffocated."

Clara, who had seen the results of suffocation, said nothing. It wouldn't help if she had.

"You could always ask Madeleine to help you," Sandra said. She dunked her cookie three times, then tutted as part of its craggy edge fell into the drink like coastal erosion.

"Stop right there, Mom," Clara replied. "You know I don't believe in that stuff."

"Sure, sure," Sandra said, holding up her hand. "But take the word of an old crone—"

"You're sixty!" Clara's voice waxed, filling the kitchen.

"Ssh," Sandra said, nodding towards Lyla's room.

"You're hardly old, is all I'm saying."

"Well, take my word anyway. If Madeleine is dead, and I hope to Hekate she isn't, then this is the time of year when she could help you lay her to rest. The past is pressed close to the future, like points on a spiral gathering before moving away again. She could show you where to find her."

"Sure, I'll suggest it to the chief in the morning. 'Don't worry, Chief, we'll wrap up the case in no time. Mom says I can contact the dead.' He'll be overjoyed."

"Don't be sarcastic, darling." Sandra leaned over and swept Clara's hair out of her eyes. "It'll come good. Meanwhile, have another cookie."

*

At the station in the morning, the Chief called her in to his office.

"Do you need a leave of absence, Clara?" he asked, his voice low.

"No, Chief," Clara replied.

"Then how can you explain what happened last night? The search was supposed to sharpen the focus on Madeleine Singer, not you."

"That wasn't my intention, Sir." Clara held her hands behind her back to stop them trembling. "I don't know what happened by The Pool. I was convinced I saw her, but I obviously didn't. So we're going back to the beginning. We'll go over everything we have. Madeleine's movements the days before she disappeared, her documents, anything that could help. I'm re-interviewing everyone who knows Madeleine. If there's something to find, we'll find it."

"Excellent," the Chief said. "And I'm sure you shall, if only to wipe the jack-o'-lantern grin from that reporter's face – she's always portraying the NYPD as either corrupt or incompetent. And you're neither, Clara."

"Thank you, Sir," Clara said, but she couldn't meet his eye. She didn't feel competent. She barely felt sane.

*

After a morning of interviews, Clara met Lionel in the canteen for lunch.

"Found anything, Ma'am?" Lionel said, tucking into a plate of fries, spatter-patterned with ketchup.

Clara peeled the bread from her sandwich and picked out a gherkin. She couldn't face anything else. "Nothing. Trent has an alibi from before Madeleine went missing right up to when we placed a plain-clothed at his door, all her friends have alibis. As does Shirley. And there is no discernible motive for anyone to harm her. No sign of an affair, no real money worries, unless you count that they've had to reduce their six-week vacation in the Hamptons to four weeks this year."

"I haven't been beyond Brooklyn since I was born," Lionel said. "So no, I don't count that."

"Did you find anything in her correspondence? Anywhere she could've gone? Or lurking unhappiness?"

Lionel shook his head. "Her bullet journal is full of daily gratitude and plans for the future, along with ovulation days. Looks like she was happy enough."

"Any plans that stand out, other than baby-making?"

"Not really. Just a blow-out and mani-pedi on Friday, seeing friends next week, a training course in Nantucket next month... Nothing that seemed out of place. Not that she gets mani-pedis much. Although, she had one last week, before Trent's reunion."

The feeling that she was close to something rippled through her. She called that feeling 'instinct', Mom would call it 'the craft'. "Reunion?" As she said that, she remembered Trent's reaction to her on Halloween when she mentioned the word. He had recoiled at the very mention of a reunion. Maybe it hadn't been about Madeleine at all.

"High school, presumably. Bet Trent was Prom King, he's handsome enough," Lionel said, with part-petulance and part-admiration.

"Look up who was at the reunion, and find out, if you can, who Trent and Madeleine talked with. Any past issues that resurfaced et cetera."

"And how do I do all that?" Lionel asked, a fry dangling from the side of his mouth like Clint Eastwood on carbs.

"You're great at research. Your IT skills far exceed mine. But if all else fails, follow your instincts," Clara said.

*

Clara was on a call to Sandra as she left the station that evening. "I'll pick up take out," she said. "What do you fancy?"

"Noodle soup," Sandra said. "And I wouldn't mind a—"

A boom dropped next to Clara, knocking the cell phone from Clara's hand. The TV camera swooped in close to her face. Its green light suggested it was hot, maybe going out live.

The same reporter as yesterday was standing on the sidewalk, smiling a smile that didn't reach her eyes. She wouldn't be troubled by crow's feet any time soon. "Detective Seaburgh!" the reporter said. "Can we have an update on Madeleine Singer? Are you any closer to finding her?"

"I can assure you, Miss—"

"Morningside. Blessing Ray Morningside."

"Blessing Ray Morningside?" Clara said. She hoped her tone wasn't as sardonic as it sounded in her head.

"Sources tell us, Detective, that you are in deep water. That even the NYPD will get rid of you if you don't get results."

Clara swallowed. She knew this was a tactic, designed to get a reaction. But she still couldn't stop the voice inside saying, "What sources?" Lionel's face came into her head.

Glancing behind her, she saw a cab pulling up on the sidewalk behind the news-crew van. She dodged to the left and, dipping down, picked up her cell then ran to the cab. As a man got out, Clara got in. Blessing Ray stared at her through the window as the cab pulled away.

*

4.18 a.m. Clara was dreaming. Of water, of Madeleine, of perfumed death. Of her own face sinking into water, scarf around her neck. Of coffin wood above her, and her hammering to get out.

Wrapping her dressing gown around her, she walked into the lounge and looked out on her stretch of Manhattan. From up here, she could see thousands of windows. Each one was a box that contained a story. Canned lives. Tonight, though, there was little to see. Few lights on. No one pacing or working or fucking. The city that never slept was sleeping.

The bar opposite her apartment was ready for today's Dia de los Muertos. Orange and yellow marigolds rayed out of vases. Culturally appropriated sugar skulls had been painted on the windows. By tomorrow night, they would be replaced with turkeys and other Thanksgiving tropes. Nothing would change for Clara. Every day was Day of the Dead for a homicide detective.

Clara looked up at the moon. Its face was half in shadow. It saw everything, yet just hung there, silent. Maybe that's what happened when you saw too much death.

She closed the blinds and sat down in her armchair with her laptop. As her emails refreshed, she saw that Lionel had sent over everything he'd been able to find out on the reunion. It had been held at Lake Placid, not far from Trent's high school. The list of attendees contained no names that stood out or that she recognised. Maybe her instinct was wildly off, and the reunion had nothing to do with it. But still the feeling that she was missing something swam under her skin.

Getting up, Clara paced across the living room, hoping that her brain would keep up with her feet. What wasn't she seeing?

She looked again at the list of reunion guests, and then, this time, kept scrolling. At the bottom of the document was the order of events for the reunion: opening speeches, dinner, dancing, the recrowning of the Prom King and Queen, and then a guest speaker: *Miss Blessing Ray Morningside, Channel 63 reporter, and Lake Placid born-and-bred local celebrity, to present a closing speech.*

Clara heard Trent saying, "The reporter won't harass her, will she?" Maybe he wasn't trying to protect Shirley, maybe he was trying to protect himself. But what from? One way or another, Miss Blessing Ray Morningside of Lake Placid, Essex County was involved.

Clara stopped pacing.

Lake Placid.

What if the image she saw of Madeleine was never in The Pool, but Lake Placid?

A shiver rippled through her. She was only wearing her PJs, and November was biting. Walking through into the laundry room, she picked up a hoodie from the clean basket. On top of the other, dirty, pile, was the scarf she'd taken off before running into The Pool. Its black-and-white stripes were covered in mud and shingle.

But she hadn't worn it in the water, so why was she dreaming about it? And why, at The Pool, when she saw her own face merging with Madeleine's, did she see herself wearing it?

But it wasn't this scarf, it was her red one. The one that matched her hat.

Mom's words bobbed up. *This is the time of year when she could help you lay her to rest. The past is pressed close to the future, like points on a spiral gathering before moving away again. She could show you where to find her.*

Her fingers trembling, Clara called Lionel, who answered on the third ring. "Yes, Ma'am," he said, no tiredness in his voice, as if he was up, waiting for her call. "What do you want me to do?"

*

A little over six hours later, Lionel stopped his car by the side of the deserted road. "And here we are," he said.

"You can now definitely say that you've gone further than Brooklyn," Clara said.

"It should be over there," he said, pointing to a gap in the trees.

Clara got out of the car and stretched. Her back cracked as she arched. They had driven straight from Manhattan, only stopping for gas and one restroom break. "Lead the way," she said.

Before Lionel had picked her up, he had found out the location of the Morningside family lodge where Blessing was born. And here they were, trudging through overgrown grass towards the lake.

"What are we planning to do, once we get to the lodge?" Lionel asked, swatting away a fly.

"We find Madeleine. In the lake."

"Right," he said. Clara felt him glance over at her. She could feel the question he'd been dying to ask swell to bursting point.

"Just say it, Lionel. I won't mind."

The words came out of his mouth in a smooth blast, like a balloon expelling air. "What makes you think she's here in this lake, when you were wrong before?"

"What do you think I'm going to say?" she asked him.

"You're going to say, 'instinct'," he said.

"That, and a vision I had when the veil was at its thinnest."

"Say that again?"

At that moment, Clara followed the path round a corner, and saw the lake. It was studded with diamonds in the morning sun. Clara walked to the shoreline. She didn't need to turn round to know that Blessing's lodge was behind her, or that Madeleine lay in the lake before her. With her red scarf wrapped tight around her neck, Clara walked into the water.

"Clara! Stop!" Lionel was shouting behind her, but Clara kept on moving towards the short jetty. She knew now what she had been dreaming. She had been looking up through Madeleine's unseeing eyes, not at the lid of a coffin, but the planks of the jetty.

Clara looked back at the shore where Lionel was jumping up and down and shouting. And then she sank into the water, feeling it accept her, fold her into itself.

And when she reached under the jetty, she found Madeleine.

*

They stayed with Madeleine, on the shore, until dusk. The Chief had been more than happy to pick up Miss Blessing Ray Morningside, and to make a televised statement, on her own channel, laying out the charges against her. It would take evidence to make them stick, but Clara knew what had happened. Madeleine had shown her.

It started at the reunion, where Blessing wanted her old high school lover back, only to be told that Madeleine was the only one he needed. So, she removed her only obstacle: followed Madeleine into the park in the news van, where heavy rain turned tell-tale tyre marks to mud. CCTV, and number plate recognition, would hopefully show Blessing taking the news van to Lake Placid on the night Madeleine disappeared. But it would not show how she had drugged and suffocated Madeleine. Or how she dragged the body under the jetty, her face as placid as the lake.

Clara would do all she could to let Madeleine rest.

*

Shirley reached them as the sun set its last rays over the lake. As she took Madeleine into her arms, her cries cracked the surface of the lake and made their way to the waiting moon.

A paramedic bent down to talk to Shirley. He tried, so gently, to extricate Madeleine's limbs from her mother's. Shirley hissed, and pulled Madeleine tighter into her arms, rocking her daughter. Singing to her. Placing a kiss on her cold, grey forehead. The paramedic held up his hands and stepped away.

As Shirley cradled Madeleine's head in one hand, and stroked her hair behind her ears with the other, Clara couldn't stop her sobs. She could go home and listen to Lyla's soft breaths and night-time sighs. She and Mom could take Lyla out for ice cream and a movie tomorrow. Maiden, mother, crone, together.

Shirley and Madeleine had no more tomorrows. She would never hold her daughter's hand again. So let her hold it now.

Clara watched as the sun lost its fight with the oncoming night. She saw the moon's face reflected in the lake's meniscus and held its gaze.

The moon did not look away. Not today.

THE JACKET
WARREN MOORE

The splitting, almost blinding headache was the first thing that Bill Weber noticed as he woke up in the alley. The second thing was the early morning cold, which he figured had awakened him only a few hours after stumbling out of the bar that was his most recent memory. The third thing was the dead man on the alley's other side, recumbent against a trash can, legs extended.

Even in the alley, lit by a streetlight at its mouth, it wasn't hard to tell that the man was dead. The bullet hole in his forehead was a clear indicator, the apex of a squat triangle completed by the dead man's eyes, one half-closed, the other staring. He looked almost as if he were winking at Weber, sharing a private joke. "Hey – the cold doesn't bother *me*, pal. Not now, anyway." A small trickle of blood had improperly bisected the triangle before congealing in the cold.

Weber went from zero to vomiting so quickly he nearly choked, and barely managed to turn his head to the left and roll away from the spew. Weber wasn't quite sure if it was the corpse or the hangover that brought on the nausea, and he wasn't sure if it was the nausea or the temperature that brought the teeth-chattering shivers that followed. He clenched his teeth so hard that he thought his jaw might crack – some of the teeth had broken long before. Christ, it was so cold. But Weber didn't figure Christ was listening to him, and besides, Jesus was from a warmer climate than Cincinnati.

So he had to get up, and he did, clambering his way to something near vertical against the wall opposite the dead man. Weber turned, slowly, to face the dead man again. He felt the chill and roughness of the brick through his shirt sleeve as he leaned against the wall. He shuddered again, this time, he was sure, from the cold. Somewhere nearby – Over-the-Rhine? – a bell struck four.

Four? It was still a few hours before sunrise, and it would get colder yet. Weber felt the urge to walk – not run; he couldn't run anyway, and downtown at four in the morning was no place for a running man to go unnoticed. And he didn't know why, but Bill Weber thought that unnoticed might be a very good thing to be.

Somehow, that's how he knew not to go to the corner and flag a prowl car down, if one passed by. *A squad car would be warm...* But the downtown cops were so big, the rumor was that the department hired football players who had flunked at the U of C or Xavier, and Weber had learned the hard way that they didn't have much use for a man like him. That's how some of the teeth had broken, snapped by the toe of a well-shined uniform shoe. And with a dead man? There'd be questions – questions he couldn't answer, no matter whose shoes he caught, or how many phone books they could roll up in the basement. Because Weber didn't *know* – didn't know anything beyond the last bar, filled with furtive men who had their own reasons to avoid attention, especially in Cincinnati. Men like Bill Weber, even though for him it had simply become another place to drink alone.

It hadn't always been that way. He had worked at Procter & Gamble, not in a factory in Ivorydale, but in that same downtown, writing scripts for the radio dramas the company sponsored to entertain the housewives who bought the soap. But one night in Eden Park, he had been tempted, and like Adam, had fallen, which was how he had learned about the phone books in the basement. The news hadn't been widespread, but it was wide enough, and Procter & Gamble was essential Cincinnati, a good corporate citizen above even the breath of scandal and with no room for a man like Bill Weber. He had hoped to sell more of his work, perhaps under a pen name, but it hadn't happened. The people he had worked with told him they couldn't help, that helping him would place *them* under suspicion, and that was too much risk for them to take.

He used that pen name for a time to hold a job in the men's department at the downtown Shillito's department store, but someone from his old job had recognized him, and again he was sent on his way. Ways led into ways, but Weber's way led only down, to cadging handouts from the respectable citizens and spending them in the dark places like the bar he had been in a few hours before, down to his last forty-eight cents. But dark places can be cold places, and there are different ways of dying of exposure.

The dead man has a coat. Well, really, it was more of a jacket, tweed, a bit weather-beaten, but still respectable. And the dead man didn't need it – didn't the wink say so? – and Weber, oh God Weber did. But he'd have to take it off the dead man.

Weber tried to be gentle – he didn't know why, but he tried – trying to slip the jacket off the body as he might have when someone had tried one on at the store. But it was hard. The dead man wasn't entirely stiff yet, but the cold wasn't helping. And though he didn't see any blood on the front of the jacket, he had a nightmare thought: *What if the bullet went through? What will the back of the jacket look like?* He almost turned to run again, but having committed to the act, he was committed to having his question answered. So he ever so gently pushed the dead man to slump forward, and saw the unmarred back of the tweed jacket. Finally it came free of the dead man, and Weber slipped it on.

It was good quality, and fit reasonably well – maybe a little large, as if he had bought it once and lost weight after. He didn't see any stains. He glanced back down at the body, now in dress shirt and slacks. That's when he saw the dead man's pockets were turned inside out, emptied presumably when the man was killed. He squatted down, and checked the back pocket. No wallet. The bell struck the quarter hour.

He could already feel his shoulders and upper arms beginning to warm, as the wool of the jacket stored the little heat he had left to shed. Keeping to the shadows in which he had learned to live, in which he had almost always lived, he made his way from the alley to Walnut Street, putting his hands in his pockets.

As he rounded the corner onto Walnut, he sensed the spotlight of a patrol car, as if he felt the beam's heat more than he saw its light. He heard the car stop at the alley's opposite end, heard the door open. He thought he heard heavy steps, but they may only have been his own as he increased his pace. And he may have heard a whistle, but it may have been a barge on the river to the south. There seemed to be another figure across the street, but it may have been Weber's own reflection, and when he glanced back half a block later, no one else was there.

Weber made his way toward Carew Tower, and the Netherland Hotel. Not that there was a place for him there – but the shift would change before long. He saw the doorman, but kept out of range until the night workers began to make their way out onto the streets. When he saw the man he wanted to see, he slipped up next to him.

"Barney."

Barney looked both ways, as if looking for a runaway car on the empty street, before responding. "Good God, Bill! What are you—" He broke off and looked hard at Weber. "You look terrible."

"Thanks," Weber said. "I've been up all night. And I'm tired, and I need a place to go. How about yours?"

"Are you insane? There's barely room for me at the apartment."

"I've stayed there before, Barney. We both know it. Nobody else needs to, but I'll tell people if I have to."

"Bastard."

"Like I said, I'm tired. I've been on the street for a few days, and they locked my stuff up after I couldn't make rent. I'll sleep on the floor – I don't care. But I have to get inside."

"What am I supposed to tell people?"

"Tell them I'm an old school friend, or a cousin down on his luck. Part of that's true, anyway. Hell, tell them I'm your sister. But that would be incest, wouldn't it?"

"You *are* a bastard."

"Fine. I'm a bastard. Are you going to let me stay, or do I need to put in a word with the hotel detective? I imagine you need your job; they're hard to find these days."

Weber hated knowing he had won, but he had hated stealing clothes from a dead man. What mattered was that he was doing what he had to do to stay alive.

Barney's apartment was as Weber remembered, from the sofa and coffee table that served as a living room to the table and two chairs in the kitchen by the stove. If he had made a right as he walked through the door, he would have walked a few feet into Barney's bedroom, but he figured he was lucky to be inside at all, and walked to the couch as Barney locked the door behind them. He heard the click of the lock over the hiss of the radiator.

"Can I use your sink to wash my clothes?"

"Does it matter if I say no?" Weber didn't answer – Barney was a good guy, and he felt bad about strong-arming him the way he had. "Fine," Barney said. "Dry them on the radiator. But Bill, you can't stay here long. The landlord is a hard-nosed old Kraut, and well—"

"I know," Weber said. "Cincinnati. 'The laws of God, the laws of man.'"

"I'm sorry, Bill. But you don't have to sleep on the floor. Use the couch." And Barney disappeared into his room.

Weber thought about collapsing immediately, but knew that if he did, he might not get up in time to clean his clothes, and it was warm enough. So he walked into the kitchen and began to undress in front of the sink. The shoes were the first things off, and then he shrugged off the jacket, which hit the wooden floorboards with an odd *thunk*, almost identical to the sound the shoes had made.

Puzzled, he picked the jacket back up. His hands were warmer now, and as he hefted the jacket, he felt a strange weight near the inside breast pocket. But the pocket was empty. It even had a hole in it. Weber tucked the pocket back in, and stuck his fingers in the hole at the bottom. He felt the roughness of the wool against the back of his fingers, contrasting with the smooth fabric of the lining. With his left hand, he felt the outside of the jacket until he found a series of bumps. With the right hand, he fished through the hole in the pocket until he snagged something. He worked the something back up, through the hole in the pocket, and found himself holding a strand of pearls. Weber didn't know from pearls, but he figured these must be valuable, or the dead man wouldn't have hidden them like that.

But the pearls were blurring in front of his eyes. Exhaustion rolled over him like a flash flood. He slipped the pearls back into the lining of the jacket, shaking it until he felt them slide down to the hem, where the fabrics were stitched together. Then he washed the rest of his clothes – everything but his undershorts – and spread them on the radiator. He made it to the couch, and barely remembered wadding the jacket under his head as a pillow before he fell asleep.

Weber woke up when he heard Barney in the kitchen. He shook his head to clear some cobwebs, and the memories of the night – or morning – before snapped into place. "I'll be out of here in a minute," Barney said. "There's puffed wheat, and there's some milk in the icebox. It's self-service, and best if you consider it one for the road."

"Thanks. And I'm sorry for putting the squeeze on you. I'll get out of your hair."

"Mmph." A pause. "Bill, where are you going next?"

Weber thought of what lay inside the tweed coat. He thought of telling Barney – he wanted to tell *someone*, but even a few days on the street had taught him to hold on to what you could grab. It was a cold world, and people would take what they knew about. "I don't know. I might be able to bum enough for a flop. Or maybe find a place needs a swamper for tonight. Maybe somebody needs a mop man."

"There's that, but Bill – why not get out of Cincinnati for good? What's keeping you here?"

Weber laughed. "My chauffeur quit. I'm not exactly the train-hopping type, you know. And it isn't like anyone is beating the drum for scriptwriters – particularly in our set." He got dressed, and looked around for a clock. Not seeing one, he asked Barney what time it was.

"Not quite two."

"I'd better hurry then." He stepped toward the door. "I don't guess there's any opening at the hotel? I'll be glad to hop bells or whatever."

"No soap. Um, sorry."

"Nice one." Barney didn't answer. "It's all right. Thanks for putting me up, Barn. You're a brick." He opened the door. "See you around?"

Barney didn't answer, and Weber pulled the door shut behind him.

It was still cold outside, but not as bad as it had been. He walked back toward the river, and saw women sweeping their stoops, a few people walking to the Findlay Market, and too many other men and women who didn't seem to have any more sense of where to go than he did. He walked south on Walnut, thinking he could maybe make his way over to St. Peter in Chains and get a meal or a tip about a safe place to stay. Street cars rattled past as he turned west.

At a newsstand near Garfield Place, a truck dropped off a bundle of the afternoon *Times-Star*. He saw the top story:

No Honor Among Thieves?
Police Seek Robbery Killer of 'Gentleman Burglar'

The old man who ran the newsstand unbundled the papers and said, "Library's a few blocks from here, pal." Weber told him to simmer down and gave him a dime, waiting for his six cents change. *Down to forty-four cents*, he thought. But he got his paper and looked at the story. There was a picture of a man named Vernon Russell, and Weber thought he had looked much better without the bullet hole. The story reported that Russell had been suspected in a number of recent break-ins at jewelry stores, pawnbrokers, and other businesses in recent months. Cincinnati police had believed Russell to be part of a criminal gang operating from across the river in Kentucky (which gave the paper its usual chance to discuss the 'crime dens of Newport'), but had been unable to carry the investigation beyond its jurisdiction.

The story went on to theorize that Russell had been killed after a break-in at the Dorst Company's jewelry shop on Reading Road, because he had become too recognizable, or had greedy comrades (the paper's main idea), or simply had run into the wrong man at the wrong time. The patrolman who discovered the body said he had seen a man exiting the alley's other end, but that the possible suspect had disappeared into the early morning. Meanwhile, the paper said, authorities had circulated a list of recently stolen items, with instructions to notify the police if any of them turned up.

Weber knew he hadn't killed Russell, and that the man must have been there before he arrived – had it been the other way around, he would have been dead as well. The pearls must have been Russell's getaway ticket, or maybe he had simply been holding out on his gang. Weber guessed it didn't matter now. The pearls were his, and—

And what? What were they worth to him? He didn't know. He didn't know.

But pearls weren't like bills, he thought. There weren't serial numbers on them, and no way to ascertain who had owned them before. And—

Weber jumped as a hand landed heavy on his shoulder. Whirling around, he saw a narrow-eyed man in a dark overcoat. The stranger smiled. His left hand was in the pocket of the coat. "Hey, Meat," he said. "Let's take a walk down the street a ways." The paperboy was studiously arranging his stack of papers, seemingly oblivious to Weber and the man in the overcoat.

For an instant, Weber wondered what would happen if he simply said "No, thank you." But he looked again at the narrow eyes and empty smile, and decided it would be a bad idea. So the two of them walked from Garfield Place, back toward the river.

After they were out of earshot, the stranger said, "Nice jacket, Meat. I knew a guy once had a jacket like that."

"Well, it isn't special, but it keeps me warm," Weber said.

"Prob'ly so. The guy I knew had a lot of heat on him on his own."

"What are you talking about?"

"I think you know, Meat. You see, that guy I knew had a jacket so much like that one they might be twins. Fit him perfectly, though. Not like yours. How long you had it?"

"Oh, for a while – I got it at Shillito's."

"Naw, Meat. That don't work. You were doing so well, but you see, my friend lost his jacket. Last night. And here I was looking for him, and what do I see at an ungodly hour of the night but a guy looks a lot like you wearing a jacket that looks a lot like his. See, I wanted to get my friend his jacket back, but things got noisy in the galley where the guy came out, so I had to take a pass. Didn't know what I was gonna do.

"But what do you know, here I am and I see someone looks like the guy I saw, and he's looking at a paper with an interesting story, and on top of that, he's got a really familiar jacket. Funny old world, ain't it?"

Weber nodded. Funny indeed – a barrel of laughs.

The stranger continued. "So anyway, I think I should get my friend his jacket back. It might be something I could remember him by." He paused as a beat cop rounded the corner.

The idea came to Weber in a flash. He shoved the stranger away and tilted back as though he had handled a poisonous snake. He shouted loud enough for the cop to hear, "Get away from me, you filthy queer!"

The stranger's eyes seemed to bulge from his head and his teeth bared as Weber turned to the cop. "Officer," Weber said, "what kind of beat do you keep where you let the fairies run loose? It's so a decent man can't walk downtown any longer. This – this *freak* wanted me to let him, wanted…" Weber let it trail off, just as he might have in the scripts he had written.

But before the stranger could say anything, Weber told the policeman, "I saw him a couple of blocks up, where that kid is selling the *Times-Star.*" He paused for dramatic effect. "My God – he could have been after the *newsboy!*"

The stranger began a stream of obscenities, but Weber said, "Search him, Officer. He might be armed." That was enough, and as the stranger turned to bolt, the cop made a half-stomping move and caught the other man behind the knee with the heel of his shoe. The stranger crumpled to the ground, and the officer pinned him face down on the sidewalk and patted him down.

"What have we here?" the patrolman said, pulling a nasty-looking automatic from the dark overcoat. Weber edged away. But the cop told him to hold it.

"Don't you *see?*" Weber said. "He would have used that *to take the newsboy.* For God's sake, what kind of animals *are* those people?" The words came to him easily enough, echoing from the back of his mind, from the scene in a windowless precinct room. "If it were up to me, you could line his type up and push them into the river." He spat at the stranger, and for an instant imagined himself as righteous as the people that he knew hated him. Was it this easy? And in turn, he wondered how many of *those* people were pretending they weren't like him. How many people had to hide themselves from those who would hunt them? How many people would disguise themselves in borrowed identities like his jacket, hoping no one would see them as they were and hate them? He cursed the stranger.

"Leave the fairy alone," the cop said. "I'll take care of things from here. We know how to handle *his* type."

"I just bet you do," Weber said. "I bet you do."

"Well, what are you hanging around for? I told you I'd take care of things. The gun's enough to hold him on. We won't need you." The stranger's lip was bleeding from where he had landed on the sidewalk. Weber wondered how much more of the man's blood would be shed before they let him go.

"Thanks, Officer," Weber said, and continued south, toward the Chesapeake and Ohio bridge connecting Cincinnati to Kentucky. As he walked, he found himself torn between amusement at seeing the stranger having to face what he had faced before and the pain of realizing that he knew just what the cop would go for. Maybe it was time to leave Cincinnati after all.

He crossed on the old bridge, the one they had adapted for cars after the new rail bridge had been built next to it. The sun was getting low on his right, backlighting the Suspension Bridge a little downstream. After he crossed the river, it was about a mile and a half's walk to the east from Covington to Newport, Kentucky. Peluso's Pawn Shop was on Monmouth Street.

Weber didn't think Ronnie Peluso would remember him. But lots of people remembered Ronnie Peluso. There were the ordinary people who went to him when they were caught short – something that Mr. Roosevelt didn't seem to have fixed yet. But there was also another world that went there: musicians, writers, artists, the people that Cincinnati didn't really understand, the people who didn't make soap or sell groceries. It was a good place to go if you were looking for a trumpet or a typewriter, and was almost a running joke among the Queen City's longhair set. They called him 'the jazzman's banker,' and the word was that he wasn't terribly concerned with the niceties of provenance.

Weber had been there once before, when a woman friend had needed to pawn a fox stole when the rent was due for her studio. But he had never pawned or sold anything there himself, and he hoped Ronnie was still open, even as he noticed his feet were getting sore.

The door was unlocked and he walked in. The pawnbroker was gray-haired and swarthy, and his gaze reminded Weber of a Robinson poem about a man whose eyes glittered 'like little dollars in the dark.'

"Buying, pawning, or selling?" the dark man asked.

"Selling, I think. My mother passed away, and I thought you might be interested in these." He reached into his jacket, pulled out the strand of pearls, and placed them on the countertop.

Peluso looked at them. Carefully. His eyebrows rose. "I'm sure *someone* would be interested in these, Mr...?"

"Beiderbecke," Weber said. "Like the musician."

"Of course. Well, Mr. Beiderbecke, I suspect a necklace of this quality might be worth a great deal in some places. In fact, I imagine some people across the river might be willing to offer a substantial amount for it."

"But they might show untoward curiosity about my family history."

"Indeed they might."

"And besides," Weber added, "Mother always had an affection for Kentucky. She went to school in Lexington. I'm sure she'd hate to think of her beloved pearls in the hands of Yankees."

"I'm sure." Peluso looked at the strand again. He seemed to work some figures in his head. "As I said, these may be worth a great deal. Indeed, under the right circumstances, they could be worth ten thousand dollars or more. Your... mother had excellent taste.

"But that would take time, Mr. Beiderbecke. How much time are you willing to spend in exchange for your money?"

Weber thought of his life in Cincinnati – living in shadows, passing furtive glances at strangers in bars, passing the doors that had once been open to him, and thinking of how quickly a policeman's shoe could buckle a knee. He had lived there, but it had never been his city, and it had never really wanted him.

"As little as possible."

Peluso nodded. "I could give you five hundred."

"Against ten thousand?"

"Against ten thousand and the time to find it. Or the time it takes for the people across the river to see if they can find it for a substantially lower outlay. Seven hundred."

"Fifteen hundred."

"I'm sorry, Mr. Beiderbecke – I can go no higher than nine hundred."

"Let me have my pride, sir. A thousand."

The older man paused, then nodded. "You seem like a man who could use a bit of pride, and I *do* have time. A thousand it is. I assume you would prefer cash?" Cash was perfectly acceptable, and Weber took $995, investing the remaining five in a money belt.

He left the pawn shop and made his way west again, toward the passenger depot in Covington. He could look across the river and see the city lights, but he didn't look for very long. He had other places to go. He knew they needed writers in Hollywood, and he knew people there who had liked his work in Cincinnati. And Hollywood was a place, he knew, that might have more room for a man like him than Cincinnati ever had. He bought a ticket for Los Angeles and a penny postcard, which he addressed to Barney, at the Netherland Hotel.

> Dear Barney,
> As I said, you're a brick. And bricks can bake in the Hollywood sun. Should the spirit move you...
> Bill

He mailed the postcard, and left the jacket in a railway station in Iowa. He wouldn't need it where he was going.

THE WOMAN AT THE LATE SHOW

MAX DÉCHARNÉ

It was three thirty in the morning. Above the noise of the wind and the constant rain hammering down on the roof of the movie house, I thought I heard a gunshot.

I was in my office at the back, a cramped untidy rat-hole tucked away to the left behind the screen. The last few paying customers had finally headed home about half an hour before, and I'd told the staff we'd leave it till morning to worry about the usual trails of popcorn, spilled cups, lost umbrellas and anything else left behind. Normally, everyone turned their hand to clearing things up at the end of the evening's screenings so we had a clean slate for the following day, but this had been a marathon session – one of those opening night gimmick events the owner dreamed up every once in a while.

"Hey, Ernie," the Old Man had said one afternoon, feet up on my desk, with the look in his eye he usually gets when there's something he's about to spring on me I might not like. Spread out in front of him were a few recent editions of *Motion Picture Herald*, which – along with his regular bank statements – are probably the nearest thing to a religious text in his own personal universe.

"This new flick, *Deadline at Dawn*."

I waited. I was good at waiting.

"Been looking at the trades."

I could see that, but there was nothing in it for me yet, so I kept quiet.

"We're due to open this in three weeks' time, November twentieth. A Wednesday."

Well, anyone in that office could have told him that, because it was marked up on the promotional wall calendar to my left, just below this month's pin-up star, Rita Hayworth. For the moment I switched my attention from him to her, because he hadn't said anything much yet to get my interest.

"Reason I'm saying it – look at this. Here's one from a joint out in California who ran it end of September: 'We were unable to arouse any business with this feature. Business poor even for midweek. Played Wednesday, Thursday.'"

He handed me a bunch of marked-up issues from recent months, open at the pages which had anything relating to our schedule. Always had 'em cross-referenced using his own system in case we missed a trick. I fired up a Lucky and he took up staring at Rita for a few minutes while I considered the situation.

"OK," I said finally. "There's a few here who've done sort of alright with it. Fella at the Ritz in Prentiss, Mississippi, reckons it's a good bet for a midnight double feature, but even he calls it 'too weak to stand alone'. May well be, at that. What's on your mind?"

"Let's do an all-nighter, drum up some ballyhoo in the local rags. 'Can you make it through till dawn?' 'Will you spot the killer before the sun comes up?' All that kind of crap. We need to do something."

That was the Old Man all over – always hoping for a stunt that would get our picture in the showmanship pages of the *Herald*, or his picture, more to the point. As if anyone other than a few hundred people in the film trade would give a damn even if we did make it. What the hell though, he was the boss.

Even so, I still told him it was a lousy idea, and that no one in hell would show up in the suburbs of Pittsburgh at 4 a.m. wanting to catch a picture. In Times Square or Forty-Second Street they might have a round-the-clock supply of passing deadbeats looking for somewhere to sleep it off among the lice, but this ain't New York. We'd wind up playing the last few houses to one man and a Seeing Eye dog who'd been too tired to find the exit. Stack that up against the extra wages for asking our people to hang around way past their bedtime, and it all sounded like a quick way to say sayonara to some greenbacks. I couldn't see the percentage in it. Well, we kicked that one around a bit because he wouldn't let it go, and in the end figured that maybe if we ran back-to-back shows from 9 a.m. onwards, with the last one finishing at three in the morning, that'd still be enough for us to get a story out of it and tie it in with the title. It wouldn't be dawn, but who the hell's counting?

So here I was, all alone in this flea-trap after a longer than usual shift, just about to head down to the lobby and bring back the takings, and I hear a shot.

Or I think I do.

Could be you reckon I'm the nervous type, jumping at shadows.

Perhaps I am at that.

Three years ago, back in '43, when I was marking time here waiting for my call-up papers for the navy, some joker tried to stick me up with a rod on another godforsaken night after everyone else had gone home. Marched me down through the darkened auditorium with a piece nestling up against my ribcage to the office at the back where I'd told him the money was locked up in the safe. I didn't lie to him about that, no sir, but then I guess I plain forgot to tell him about the loaded gat I also kept in there alongside it, maybe because my daddy taught me that some folks play rough, and that politeness and a trusting disposition will only get you so far in this man's world. Call me prudent, call me jumpy, but I shot him three times through the chest while he was still leaning in behind me with his eyes on the boodle. One might have done it, but the other two made sure. He wouldn't have had much use for dough where he was going.

Surprise, surprise, his gun wasn't even loaded. He found out the hard way that mine was.

With all the fallout, the banner headlines, the snide stories and the homicide dicks crawling all over looking for a motive that wasn't there, it delayed my call-up for a good few months until they finally kind of agreed I was just an ordinary working joe defending themselves rather than this town's late-model answer to Frank Nitti or Bugs Moran. By that time, I figure all the space on those flat-tops out in the South Pacific was taken, so I wound up pushing paper around at Chambers Field in Virginia until the whole thing had blown over and they spat me out the other end in late '45. I'd seen more live-action shooting back at the movie theatre where I worked than in two and a half years serving in a world war, but I'm not kicking about that. Not me.

Washed up back in Steel City and found that, unlike some employers, the Old Man was true to his word and had kept my job open. He's a sour-faced cuss most of the time, and it might just be that he couldn't find any other sorry stiff willing to put in the hours and ride hard on the ushers and keep them from robbing him blind, but like they say, it's a paycheck, Jack. Been back a year now, winter sinking its teeth in once again and here I am, wondering if bad luck and bad history's about to repeat itself.

About that gunshot…

*

I dug out my roscoe from the otherwise empty safe, spun the dial to lock it out of habit, grabbed a torch, sank a quick belt from the glass I'd been working on – three-quarters melted ice by now but it still had the taste – then headed out into the gloom of the auditorium, reluctantly chasing the source of the noise I'd heard. Move over, Alan Ladd, this gun ain't for hire, but it still does a fair line in self-preservation.

Tell you the truth, I was scared to death.

I reckon you'd be too.

There's maybe a ten-foot gap between the first row of seats and the little stage in front of the screen, with a cigarette-burned carpet that was old back when the Keystone Kops were in short pants, and sticks to your feet from all the Cokes and sodas that've been slopped over it by generations of happy picturegoers too distracted or stupid to find the way to their mouths in the dark. I walked across it now, from left to right of the screen, feeling all the while like someone was about to loom up behind me in the shadows and brain me with a tyre iron, wishing that the main switches for the house lights were nearby, rather than up at the top by the back stalls, and also that they didn't take the best part of ten minutes to fire up completely once you set the ancient generator going. So a torch it was then.

False alarm.

It was the old problem. That emergency exit fire door bottom right, swinging happily in the wind. The locking mechanism had been halfway shot to hell before I even went into the service, and each time we got it fixed, it didn't take too long for it to break again from the combined efforts of all the local juvies working on the catch so they could slip it from outside and bunk in free. I could feel the breeze from it as I came near, and the flashlight started to pick up the soaked half-moon of carpet just inside it where the rain had lashed in through the opening. Everyday occurrence, or at least, every couple of weeks. Better get Al the handyman to come round and give it another smack with a wrench tomorrow. For now, I just closed the door and wedged it shut as best I could. That fixed one problem, sort of, but left me with another.

Someone could have got in while it was swinging wide. If so, they might still be here, and this is November, a little early for Santa Claus to come calling.

As far as I could see, there wasn't much for it except to mentally pin on my worn out 'conscientious employee of the month' button badge and search the whole damned building just in case. On my own. In the dark. With a worn-out flashlight that kept going on the blink.

No way round it. Hell, we had money here, two-thirds more than a normal day's takings, and I wasn't about to sit back there in the office counting it into bags for the bank not knowing whether someone was out there somewhere waiting to try and take it off me. We'd run nine shows instead of the usual five. Three hundred capacity, tickets ranging from a dollar in the cheap seats up to two bucks fifty for the best, so around $450 for a sold-out performance. Pretty good, considering we were up against the Marx Brothers over at the Regent with *A Night in Casablanca*, Vivien Leigh making like Cleopatra down at the Manor, and a double bill of *She-Wolf of London* and *The Cat Creeps* trying (and mostly failing) to lure in the ghoul-hounds at the Enright.

Well, some of our morning shows were quiet, as we expected, but even so, we'd cleared over three thousand bucks on tickets and another eight hundred on drinks and popcorn. Then there was whatever we'd also picked up on sales of the William Irish book the picture was based on – all shiny in a new cheap edition hardcover with an extra slug of picture pages showing scenes from the movie. So yeah, call it maybe a little shy of four gees, give or take. Any way you reckon it, that's a powerful amount of scratch in a town where jackrollers will drag you into a back alley and turn you over just for the five clams and change in your pocket.

There's a whole heap of places to hide in a movie house, especially when the lights are down. I took 'em one at a time. Worked my way slowly up the right-hand side of the auditorium, shining the beam along and underneath each row of seats as carefully as I could, but all that got me was a grandstand view of the heroic amounts of random garbage a couple of thousand film fans could leave behind them in the course of a ninety-minute flick. Even so, by the time I reached the top of the incline and the back row of the stalls, I'd come around to figuring that unless I was dealing with Tom Thumb, or better yet, the Invisible Man, no one was playing possum in the seating area. This being a straight-up-and-down 1910-vintage movie theatre built like a cigarette pack lying on its side, with no circle seating, that just left the front-of-house area and finally the strange little room built above it behind the front façade, which was the private domain of Graham, our long-time projectionist.

I pushed through the swing doors into the lobby, where some neon light was leaking through the criss-cross iron shutters that covered the glass doors when we were closed. The ones leading to the street were to my right and left. Directly ahead taking up most of the space between them was the long marble counter, a little like the bar of a saloon, which mostly served for hawking refreshments and snacks. A glassed-in, fortified booth stood at one end where the cashier sat and doled out tickets to the never-ending tide of humanity flowing through the gates. Some of them were friendly, but others arrived every-which-way drunk fresh from the local ginmills and kept up a barrage of catcalls, throwing things at the screen until the warmth of the auditorium and the darkness finally lulled them off to sleep. It wasn't a whole heap of fun waking them up and persuading them out of the door at close of business. Most people were OK, I guess, but it wasn't them that you remembered – it was the other kind, and you soon learned to be on your guard, because in the end, you never quite knew what kind of a critter was going to come slithering across the threshold each night.

I do this job because I love meeting people.

Can't you just tell?

Directly opposite the counter, spread out across a twenty-foot stretch of the back lobby wall, was the latest heap of lumber the RKO promo boys had sent us to try and lure in the rubes. It all stood in front of a selection of one-sheet and half-sheet posters for the film displayed in the string of permanent frames screwed to the wall. The one-sheet wasn't much – the artist had mostly gone with a bunch of close-up faces looking in all directions, lit up in bilious green and yellows as if the main mystery they were desperate to have solved was who cooked the lousy meatball stew that gave them all food poisoning. Nothing to tell you what the film's about, and the designers couldn't even be bothered to come up with a strapline. The half-sheet was a bit better. NYC city skyline at night, and an OK screamer – *Killer Hunt! Four Hours to Go!* That was more like it. The main event, though, was a whole stack of six-foot-high boards cut out in the outlines of famous New York skyscrapers all jumbled up, and some people-shaped ones of the three stars, Susan Hayward, Paul Lukas and Bill Williams looking moody out front alongside some random two-dimensional stiffs – a cop, a dancehall dame and a few others besides. Up close it looked like the world's most tedious outdoor cocktail party frozen in time, but from a distance, and especially in the light of my torch, I've gotta admit, it had something.

Nothing doing in the lobby, as far as I could see, so I swung round, kicking used ticket stubs across the tiles while I dug in my pocket for the key to the doorway that led up the narrow stairs to the projection booth. Best to do a thorough job of things, so I went up and checked Graham's lair. I hadn't really expected to find anything other than the two huge projectors, the neatly stacked cans of 35 mm labelled with white tape on the rims, and a couple of shelves of one-sheets and press books for upcoming attractions, not least because you needed a key for the door to even gain access in the first place. Giving it a clean bill of health, I came back down and was crossing the lobby along by the publicity display, heading for the left-hand auditorium doors, when the Chrysler Building leaned over and crashed to the ground.

Something moved in the shadows.

It looked like Susan Hayward.

*

I swung my torch round and shone it right in her eyes, and she turned her head away, holding her arm up to shield them from the light.

"Could you maybe point that thing somewhere else, mister?"

"The light, or the gun?" I asked.

"Both would be nice, now that you mention it."

Fair point, I guess, and since she didn't look like she was about to brain me with a starting handle, I lowered the angle slightly on both the things I'd been pointing at her, but still kept my distance, the memory of that night in '43 way too fresh in my mind.

"Thank you," she said, stepping out from behind the board cut-out of Paul Lukas. "I was getting a little cramped trying to stand here like a statue all that time."

She was real. I figured that right away. For a start, she could move, and for another, three-ply can't talk. Now I had a chance for a closer look, I could tell she wasn't Susan Hayward, although in this light she could maybe look a bit like her, if you kinda squinted a little and were two drinks ahead. Having figured this out to my satisfaction, that only left me ten or twenty more questions that were bothering me, so I started with the obvious.

"Who are you, and how did you get in here?"

Those level eyes stared right at me for a short while. From the way she was handling things so far, I reckoned she was nobody's fool, not in this lifetime. Caught red-handed, trespassing, breaking-and-entering, whatever the hell you'd call it, she still wasn't about to run up a white flag or start hollering. It was more like we'd met casually at the drug store, and she'd be obliged if I could pass the napkins.

"I suppose I was hoping you could help me," she said eventually. "I'm in a bit of a spot."

That threw me for a second. The middle of the night in a run-down movie house that's all closed up for the night isn't usually the prime location for livening up my social calendar. Call me old-fashioned – you might as well, no one else is likely to – but if I was pushed, I'd say that the Aragon Ballroom or else Danceland over at West View Park probably have the better claim on that. Even so, my late-night visitor had shaken me up in a different way than if she'd been a sawn-off hobo with a three-day stubble and an attitude problem who'd sneaked in out of the rain and wanted to make something of it.

"OK, lady," I said, just the way they do in the pulps. "Back in my office down through those doors I've got a bottle of something the Salvation Army probably wouldn't approve of. How about we go into executive session over it and consider the problem awhile, whatever it is."

She nodded agreement, so I held the swing doors open for her and by the light of the torch we made our way down there, as my mind kept turning the situation over, looking for sharp edges and nasty surprises. When you've been burned once, and it wound up in court, taking things at face value seems like the mark of a fool. I mostly try not to be a fool. Ask my defence lawyer.

A little while later we were sitting there all cosy like something out of one of those sloppy Hollywood romances that do so well here with the weekend trade – the ones that've gone a long way towards rotting my back teeth out from all the sugar they load 'em down with. Mood lighting, cheap whiskey in smeared glasses, a guy and a dame shooting the breeze late into the night as the wind howls outside and the sheets of rain batter sideways at the windows in a futile bid to wipe off the layers of grime. Excuse me while I break out my handkerchief.

She'd been talking for a while now, but I still wasn't sure what to make of her story. Rita up on the wall wasn't saying nuthin' either, but you could tell it was all the same to her one way or another, and that's *Miss* Hayworth to you, buster.

What it came down to was this.

Her name was Jane, she said. Didn't mention anything else, just Jane, but that don't make me Tarzan, no matter which corny script you've been reading from. Reckoned she'd come in during the final show, the 1.45 a.m., not to see the film, but to get inside. And stay here. Ducked in behind the stand-up figures in the lobby display as the last stragglers were leaving, and hoped no one would notice, which of course they didn't until I came along.

I thought about that, and figured it had the makings of a true story, as long as you didn't shake it too hard. Sure, the emergency door had banged open around 3.30 a.m., which is what started me doing my Sam Spade act in the first place, but if she'd only drifted in then, she'd still be soaked from the rain. OK, so she wanted some kind of sanctuary. The question was, why?

"Why?" I asked her, because I couldn't see the point of taking a more roundabout way.

"Because he's out there."

"He's out there?"

"Yes he is. And he's after me."

"Alright. And what name does he have written on the tail of his shirt?"

"If you're asking who he is, that's easy. He's my husband."

"Your husband."

"My husband Charlie. You wouldn't know him."

"Sure about that? I know a lot of people."

"Not unless you know him from the Army. He just got back two days ago from liberating Europe single-handed."

"Busy man."

"To hear him tell it, yes."

"And he's after you. Didn't you roll out enough of a red carpet for the conquering hero?"

"Nobody's got that much carpet available, not even if they get a cheap deal wholesale."

"OK, so what's the pitch? You hide away in here because he's out roaming the streets looking for you with trouble on his mind?"

"Something like that. I've had enough – I knew it long before he came back, and all the time he was gone I wished to hell he'd be one of the ones who didn't make it home."

I let that sink in for a moment or two, and inhaled some more fumes.

"Like that, huh?"

"Like that, or maybe worse. I just wanted to be somewhere overnight that he'd never find me, then I can hop the cross-country Greyhound first thing in the morning all the way to Reno, the Promised Land of happy gamblers and even happier divorced women. I'm ditching him legally as soon as I step off the bus. When I came past this place tonight and saw the name of the film, I remembered a piece I'd seen in the *Post-Gazette* about an all-night showing, so I bought a ticket. Got the shock of my life when the picture ended around three and they started throwing everybody out."

That was her story and she was sticking to it.

I guess I was stuck with it as well.

*

Well, OK. Although the Old Man would be mad as hell if he thought I'd had a dame in here overnight, unless he also came knocking on the door around 5 a.m., I couldn't see that he was likely to find out. It was already past four, and I'd been thinking earlier of just sacking out on the beaten-up office couch instead of trying to head home through the filthy weather. Maybe it was the whiskey that convinced me more than anything, but in the end we struck a deal. Rather than throwing her out into the rainy streets to run the risk of walking slap into her bad-boy, ex-marine-corps husband, she could stay parked in the chair helping me out for an hour or two putting a dent in my stash of mouthwash. Then we could head out before nine – when there would be ordinary people around and she said she'd feel safer – and go our separate ways; me to the bank and her to the Greyhound station. So long, pal, Abyssinia.

"Glass or a funnel?" I asked, picking up the bottle again.

"Whoa, boy. An inch will do," she said, holding out a hand to halt the flow. "I've got a long trip tomorrow."

"Fair enough, although like the man said, you're not drunk if you can still lie on the floor without holding on. Since we're neighbours for the next hour or so, and seeing as how I'm in the business, what did you make of the film?"

"Really?"

"Yeah. It's always good to have some honest-to-goodness views from the public, rather than just the same old flim-flam from some jaded old cuss who writes about movies for the scream-sheets."

"It was alright, I suppose. Hayward did a good job, if you go for that sort of thing, but in my book it still had something missing."

"Something missing?"

"Bogart."

"Amen to that," I said, and we clinked our glasses.

The conversation ebbed and flowed, as did the rain outside the window, and sunrise still seemed a long way off, even though by now the hands on the clock had crawled around till it was registering straight-up-and-down six. Conversation-wise, we'd already dealt with the state of the nation, the price of fish, whether Goodman was better with the full orchestra rather than the sextet he had during the war, whether we'd finally get our own TV station here in Pittsburgh and if that would kill off movie-going, what chance the Steelers might have against the New York Giants next Sunday and other items of national importance. OK, truth to tell, I lied about the fish, and she certainly wasn't bothered one way or the other about the football game, but hell, I made sure we talked about it anyway.

Somehow, when we'd run through all that, and the level on the bottle was way nearer the bottom than the top, the conversation drifted round to the subject of me, my job, and my illustrious past. Not something I usually go blabbing my mouth about, but I guess she had a way with her, and hell, what did it matter anyway – we'd likely never see each other again after she boarded that bus in an hour or so.

"So you were in the navy, like the character in the film?"

"In the navy, sure, but not like him. I never left the States. Shore-based, chained to a desk out in Virginia. Never came within a thousand miles of the shooting war."

"But you look like you could handle that gun," she said, gesturing with her glass in the direction of the firearm I'd been toting around earlier. It was resting there on top the safe, holding down a pile of papers where I'd left it when we came into the office.

"Maybe."

"Ever fired it in anger?"

"Anger, no, not exactly." I rubbed my face with the hand that wasn't holding the drink as I looked away for a second, then turned my head back and met her gaze again. "But I've fired it."

"For real?"

"Uh-huh."

This was unexpectedly going somewhere I really, really didn't want to go, and I think it must have shown in my face.

"For real, like, at a person?"

I didn't say anything for a long minute, just topped up our glasses with some of what was left and stared at the floor. She was quiet too, but the question hung there along with the cigarette smoke, and it wasn't about to go away anytime soon.

I looked up slowly, trying to see something in her face, but she just returned my gaze, calm as ever, waiting, and took a sip of her drink.

"You could say that, yeah."

Well that was it. In the end, I told her the whole story of that night in '43 when the man who tried to rob me right here where we were sitting discovered the hard way that I had some protection hidden there alongside the money. Self-defence. Instinct taking over. Never even knew the guy. Still don't know a whole lot about him except the name they gave in court.

"Which was."

"David Stern. Friends called him Davey, they said. Not from the neighbourhood. Don't even know what he was doing in this part of town, late at night, looking to hoist the takings. A chance thing gone wrong, I guess. I wish I'd never been part of it, but I didn't ask for it – it came looking for me."

"And you shot him."

"Yes."

"Dead."

"Uh-huh."

"How terrible."

"You got that right. I wouldn't wish it on anybody. Way I see it, I figure it was him or me."

"Spur of the moment."

"Yep."

"Him or you."

"That's the way I figure."

We sat and both smoked for a while. Seemed to me that this last twist of our rambling conversation had gone a fair way towards killing off any light-hearted, maybe even halfway flirtatious mood we'd had going before, but that doesn't come as a surprise. A live human getting drilled through the chest can often put a damper on your after-dinner small talk, as I'm sure all the best society hostesses would agree. Either way, it shut us both up good and proper for a while, and I noticed she was looking pretty pale, but maybe that was just the late hour, or the drink, or my personality. Leave it to good old Ernie, he's always got a cheery smile and an uplifting yarn for the gals. 'Say, did I ever tell you the one about the night I sent some poor anonymous joe to the boneyard?' I'm here all week, ladies and gentlemen. Try the veal…

We passed a lot of the rest of the time in silence, waiting for the sunrise, checking the streaming window for signs of dawn. Occasionally I almost nodded off, but that wouldn't have been good, with a stranger in the room, and a date at the bank before I could struggle home and hit the sack for an hour or so before the whole screening cycle would start again at midday. She dug one cigarette after another out of her black leather handbag. It wasn't one of those dainty ones that would struggle to contain much more than a handkerchief – this was the other kind, which seems to have room for everything up to and including a set of golf clubs, but I guess was only about a foot square. Made sense though, she had no other luggage that I could see, and was heading out way across the country for the lengthy stay you needed in order to establish temporary residency when filing for divorce in Reno. Looked at it that way, she'd packed incredibly lightly. Anyhow, it certainly contained enough cigarettes to re-stock a tobacco store, but she wasn't stingy about sharing them as the night went on.

At about seven thirty, we could finally see some change in the light outside. I shifted my position in my chair behind the desk and found that my left leg had gone to sleep, even I if hadn't. It was cold in here too.

"Do you think about him sometimes?" she asked, after a long silence.

"The man I killed?"

"David Stern, I think you said."

"To be honest, I try not to, but he's there when I least expect it."

"He's there?"

"In my head."

She stubbed out her cigarette, not really looking at me.

"Yes. I can see that he might be."

To be honest, I was getting a little worn out with this particular line of conversation, and I guess it started to show in my face.

"Lady, I wasn't raised a Catholic, and this here wasn't built as a confessional box. I didn't ask for the hand that I was dealt, but I'm through apologising for it. Him or me, like I said. Maybe we should talk about you for a change."

"Maybe we should at that."

"So this husband you're divorcing. You said you were hoping he'd finish his army career six feet under overseas."

"I didn't exactly put it that way, but yes. He's a violent man, he'll come to a violent end, and I long since got tired of being on the receiving end."

"Like that, huh?"

"Like that."

"What's his name, by the way, this two-fisted son of Uncle Sam?"

"Gustafson. Johnny Gustafson."

"Which makes you Jane Gustafson, if I've got my junior Sherlock Holmes deduction manual working correctly."

She didn't smile. OK, I guess it was getting a little late for the wisecracks. "For a while, yes, but not for much longer, if I've got anything to do with it."

"I'll drink to that," I said, holding up the final dregs left in my glass, and she looked me hard in the eye and solemnly did the same.

I drained the last of it. My leg was still half numb, so I stood up. Rita was eyeing me from up there on the wall calendar, looking as usual as if she knew something I didn't. Matter of fact, she probably knew quite a few things.

Having succeeded somehow in getting to my feet, once my limbs eventually gave a few indications of functioning normally again, I figured that this was as good a time as any to dig out the takings from the safe, and then we could head out the front of the building and lock up without much risk of the staff seeing us emerge. Even Graham the projectionist, who liked to get a head start on the day, was never usually here before nine. We'd be too early for the bank or the bus, but she probably wouldn't object to a spot of breakfast and coffee over at Jim's hash house down the street.

"Best get your lawful goods together," I said. "Nearly time for us to hit the trail."

She didn't say anything to that, but gave me that look again, then stood up stiffly, clutching her bag. I guess she felt as ragged as I did. Long nights'll do that to ya.

"Coffin nail?" she asked.

"Not me. My mouth feels like one of Ringling Brothers' circus elephants hauled off and died in it a while back. You go ahead and smoke 'em all down."

I walked over to the safe as she rummaged in her bag again, spun the dial and reached in. Just for something to say, I asked, "So, after the divorce, will you go back to using your maiden name?"

"Yes."

"And what would that be?" I asked, just before three bullets permanently removed any further interest I might have taken in the conversation.

"Jane Stern," she said, but I didn't hear her.

THE BRIDE HATED CHAMPAGNE

PAUL DI FILIPPO

The latest in an unending series of tedious wedding planning sessions had ended early in the evening for everyone but the maid of honor and the best man. With scrupulous fidelity to detail and authenticity, those two zealous participants had decided to rehearse the honeymoon of the bride and groom by going to bed together directly afterwards, once all the others had dispersed.

Carmen Messina had arrived at the meeting via Uber. Griffin Bluestone had offered her a ride home. But instead, they went directly to his apartment. The overnight detour was Carmen's idea. The planning meeting, one of several mandated happy occasions – dinners, parties, shopping expeditions – had raised such anger, lust, ire, vengefulness and general itchy dissatisfaction within Carmen that she felt ready to blow her top. Some kind of physical release was mandated, and Griffin would serve the purpose as well as anyone.

It was not as if she were going to bed with a stranger. As esteemed best man, Griffin of course had palled around with the groom, Barnaby Ogden, since they were college kids together.

And as Barnaby's ex-lover and almost-fiancée, Carmen had shared many outings with all of Barnaby's social crowd, including Griffin and whatever woman the perpetually footloose and unweddable Griffin was currently dating.

So as a long-standing friend of no small intimacy, Carmen found it easy to proposition Griffin – almost as easy as he quickly replied, "Sure!"

Once in bed, Griffin had demonstrated all the masterful facility and charms and prowess that had apparently satisfied his long line of partners, qualities which kept a steady stream of replacements queued up. For her part, Carmen screwed her wedding party coequal with a wild abandon and greed and a hint of cruel savagery that she had never employed with Barnaby. No, with Barnaby Ogden, finicky prize catch, she had always tried to portray beneath the sheets a sensible, judicious, top-of-the-line, responsive but not freaky lover, someone who, despite a lineage of pure Sicilian passion and ambition, would be able to fit in perfectly with Barnaby's WASP social set, his Anglo family, his white bread Long Island demesne, his sniffily censorious parents and siblings.

So for three long years, Carmen had reined in all her wilder sexual instincts, adopted a wardrobe utterly antithetical to her own tastes, and swotted up a hundred-and-one topics that were of absolutely no interest to her. Goddamn Pekinese breeding lines and the merits of exotic grape varietals and the comparative excellence of various ski boots! How many times Carmen had bitten her tongue to refrain from exclaiming exactly how she'd like to insert said ski boot up the ass of some obnoxiously braying Ogden cousin, or wring the neck of some yapping dog, or spit out a mouthful of expensive wine with a grunt of mock disgust.

But, she kept telling herself, all the aggravation, restraint, and self-denial was going to be worth it, to land a husband as rich as Barnaby Ogden.

Growing up poor, Carmen had quickly learned – by observation, if not actual participation – about all the things that money could provide, in the way of security and pleasures, and she had set her sights on making the biggest score possible to set herself up for life. Realizing early on that her goals demanded she must be able to penetrate levels of society much higher than the level she had been born into, Carmen focused on her education. Her bachelor's in business administration from a humble state college – the only school she could afford – had been enough to secure her a job as a meeting planner in one of the Ogden family enterprises. Arranging a first meeting with Barnaby, then parlaying that work acquaintance into a romantic relationship had taxed all her cunning and skills. But she had eventually succeeded, and dared to dream that all her plans might reach fruition. Three years into their dating arrangements, success seemed within her grasp. Carmen was already planning their wedding, and daydreaming of her life of exalted leisure to come. An exhilarating prospect, even with the necessity of often being cheek by jowl with fussily boring Mother and Father Ogden, and all the ancillary prats and princesses.

And then along came Clover Littlefield.

Clover Littlefield was everything that Carmen Messina was not. Petite, slim and blonde, as opposed to big-boned, zaftig and dark. Demure and soft-spoken and opinionless, as opposed to brazen and loud and opinionated. (Carmen tried to tone down her natural outgoing and extroverted tendencies, rooted in her early upbringing, whenever she was with Barnaby. For most of the time, she succeeded. But drink – a not infrequent adjunct to their socializing – undid her restraint, and then her innate wild woman character emerged. At such times, even through her alcoholic filters, Carmen could see Barnaby flinch, and his pals sneer or chuckle or whisper. Afterwards, only the most self-abasing and obsequious of sexual ministrations would serve to renew Barnaby's affections.)

However, Clover Littlefield's innocuous first appearance did not immediately disturb Carmen, or hint at any danger to Carmen's plans. If only she had been able to see the future, though! Maybe she could have been more proactive about protecting her investment and maintaining her status.

*

Dan Hatchard, the state's District Attorney, arrived at that particular summer party last year at the Ogden estate in Old Westbury with an unknown woman on his arm. The brilliant July weather, plus a recent gift from Ogden of a Lily Cluster platinum diamond ring from the Manhattan outlet of Harry Winston's (now sparkling outrageously on her finger), and her third flute of champagne had all conduced to elevate Carmen's spirits to a high plateau. Acting almost as hostess (well, after all, Mother Ogden was nowhere to be seen at the moment), Carmen had hastened to welcome Hatchard and the newcomer.

Hatchard's usual professional aplomb seemed a little awry today, thought Carmen, as she gave him a familiar peck on the cheek and waited for an introduction to the woman.

"Carmen, this is Clover. Clover, ah, Littlefield. She's a stranger in these parts, living not too far from here, in Patchogue." *Poor thing*, thought Carmen, Patchogue being definitely the wrong side of the tracks. "I was friends with her father. Law school together. But he's deceased now, and she really has no other family to speak of. So I'm trying to introduce her around."

Carmen pumped Clover's hand and was effusive in her friendliness and compliments. The new girl smiled prettily, but said little. Carmen offered to show her around, and Hatchard seemed relieved.

When she found Barnaby by the pool, he at first showed little interest in Clover. But that changed when, some time later, in a borrowed swimsuit, the new girl reappeared and exhibited a sylph-like gracefulness in the water. By then, Carmen was on her sixth glass of bubbly, and could not repress a fleeting scowl at the way Barnaby and several other men fawned over Clover, helping her from the pool, draping a big fluffy towel around her, and setting her up in a lawn chair. Offered her choice of drinks, Clover said, "A ginger ale, please."

"What's the matter?" Carmen intervened brusquely. "None of the booze here good enough for you?"

"Oh, of course that's not it. It's just that I have no head for alcohol. I don't really like the taste either. So I simply never drink it."

"Not even champagne?" said Carmen, hoisting high her flute of bubbly.

"Oh, especially not champagne."

"Well, you'll excuse me a minute while I finish off your share."

Carmen stalked off, a little bumble-footed in her high heels on the entrapping turf, while Barnaby made a disappointed face at her ill manners, then turned away to chat animatedly with Clover.

And that had been the turning point.

Six months after that party, Carmen found herself thrown under the bus, with Clover taking her place.

And six months after that, it was nearly wedding rehearsal time.

All that then remained of her three years' investment of body and soul was a wardrobe she despised, a few pieces of admittedly luxe jewelry, and a burning hatred for one Clover Littlefield. Carmen berated herself. How could she have been so stupid, clumsy and unstrategic? What she wouldn't give to be able to replay that fateful day! But such a do-over was forever outside the realm of possibility.

Naturally, Carmen had not seen anything of Barnaby Ogden and his friends once she had been tossed to the curb. She did retain her pride after all. But then, a few months ago, Barnaby had called, out of the blue. Hearing his voice, Carmen had dared for a moment to hope. But his words after his hello and his polite inquiries about how she was doing shattered any illusions.

"Carmen, I'm calling with what you might reckon is an odd request. But our time together – time that I really do still cherish, you know – has led me to believe that you're big-hearted enough to consider my proposal. Clover and I would like you to take part in our wedding as the maid of honor. You see, Clover has absolutely no girlfriends or relatives to stand up with her. And everyone else we could think to ask either said no, or was busy, or begged off somehow. Clover was very distressed, and of course so was I. We were at our wits' end. And then I thought of you, and Clover instantly concurred."

Carmen said nothing right away, trying to size up Barnaby's sincerity and true intentions. Was this some attempt at an ultimate cruel humiliation, having your ex serve in the wedding party, subservient to the bride who had displaced her? But Barnaby, recalled Carmen, was utterly without guile or subterfuge, possessing a naïve innocence that came from a life where he had never encountered any barriers or opposition to his smallest whim. This was a quality, in fact, that had always irked Carmen enormously. How dare anyone lead such a privileged existence that they need never cultivate any brutal offensive moves or wily defensive maneuvers? Such Edenic, good-natured empty-headedness was a slap in the face to all the struggles Carmen had endured.

Thinking on her feet – only a few seconds had passed since Barnaby's obnoxious voice had ceased – Carmen realized further that taking on this seemingly straightforward favor might be her ticket back into the exclusive social circuit from which she had been unceremoniously ejected. There were other eligible rich single men in the Ogden-Westbury sphere, and as a member of the wedding party, Carmen would have plausible and frequent access to them.

"Barnaby, dear, you know how much you meant to me – still mean to me – and although I'm naturally still sad over our break-up, I want the best for you and Clover. So of course I will be happy to accept your invitation to act as Clover's maid of honor. Tell your darling fiancée that I'll be happy to consult with her on anything from the bridesmaid dresses to choice of favors."

"Oh, no, there won't be any need for you to exert yourself along those lines. Mother is handling everything of that nature. But we do need you to ornament the wedding party. Can't look skimpy or irregular up there on the reception dais, can we?"

The word ornament pleased Carmen a bit, emphasizing as it did her attractiveness. She was certain that on the wedding day all eyes would be on her lush figure as the celebrants marched down the church aisle, and not on the bride's winsome and waif-like form, however expensive her dress.

"That's fine," said Carmen. "I'm thrilled you asked me. Really! Just give me the details…"

But Carmen's easy acceptance of these duties had proved prematurely blithe. Once confronted with Barnaby and Clover in the flesh, facing their happiness and their obliviousness to her pain, all her wrath and chagrin and disgust at being dumped had surged back, sending hot bile into her throat, and her booty into Griffin's bed.

Carmen stared up now at the play of shadows and streetlights on the ceiling of Griffin Bluestone's bedroom. The handsome lump beside her snored away, likewise uncomprehending of her pain and the injustices done to her.

Carmen poked the sleeper in the ribs. "Griffin. Griffin! Wake up!"

"Huh, wha—?"

"I've decided something. This marriage, Clover and Barnaby. It mustn't happen."

Griffin came up on one elbow. "Why not?"

"What do we know about that woman? Nothing. She's too good to be true, all virgin honey and butter wouldn't melt in her mouth. Don't we owe it to Barnaby to learn more about her, in case she's just a gold-digger?"

Griffin snorted. "Pardon me, but isn't that a pot and kettle kinda thing?"

"Yes, I admit it, the thought of becoming Mrs. Barnaby Ogden was always sweetened for me by contemplation of all his millions. But at least I was fairly transparent and honest and willing to give full value for the money. All my cards were on the table. Barnaby knew where I came from and what I wanted. But this Clover Littlefield—you can't read her one bit. She's a stone-cold enigma. No one knows what she's really thinking. And her past—a blank!"

Falling back to the mattress, Griffin said, "I'm sure Barnaby's parents have already had her investigated."

Carmen hadn't thought of that. "Maybe. But I think there might be more to learn, and that anything which might still be hidden could be enough to throw this whole affair into the dumpster."

"Good luck with that. Those two are very much in love."

"Barnaby's besotted, yes, that's for sure. But her—I can't tell what she feels."

Griffin made no reply, having returned to a self-satisfied sleep.

The next day, in the interstices of her assigned workplace tasks, Carmen began investigating Clover Littlefield.

Common Googling proved useless. The woman was one of those rare folks who had managed to leave no digital trail for her whole life. She had no social media presence, no school affiliations, no recorded governmental interactions. Carmen switched her focus to several non-public, proprietary databases that her workplace provided access to. (After being jilted, Carmen had quit her position at Ogden Enterprises; it was simply too embarrassing to continue there, where everyone knew what had happened. Thanks to family connections, she had gotten a new job with the state government.) But these sources came up blank as well.

Carmen stewed for several days. She contemplated several other avenues to learn what she wanted to know. Could she get information by contacting Mother and Father Ogden, deploying sly questions on the pretext of wanting to do things just as Clover liked, or using the excuse of needing to include some personal details in any oral tributes to the bride? No, they would never share with her, of all people, what they knew – if they knew anything at all. Maybe she could confront Clover herself. That would be a bold and aggressive move, but one easily defeated by simple reluctant silence. Maybe Clover had let slip some juicy facts with the other women in the wedding party, or shared her background with some of the rich folks in Westbury, her tongue loosened by all the alcohol that flowed in those precincts. (Upon her engagement, Clover had shifted her living quarters from poverty-ridden Patchogue to the Ogden manse, living chastely apart from Barnaby in her own wing of the house.) Oh, wait, the bride didn't drink. And besides, Carmen sensed that self-possessed and imperturbable Clover would never choose to confide in any strangers.

Every road to gaining hidden blackmail knowledge and an upper hand over Clover – some radical revelation, some buried sin which she could thrust in Barnaby's face to make him realize how unsuitable his bride was – seemed closed to her.

And then she remembered Dan Hatchard.

It was Hatchard who had brought Clover to that momentous party. He claimed to have known her father. He was the one and only link to her life before she had materialized on the Westbury scene. If anyone could provide some dirt on the woman, it was Hatchard.

How to loosen his tongue?

Carmen decided on the nuclear option, doing what she was best at.

It was not a difficult chore to bring Hatchard to bed. A tanned, toned, tousled fellow of fifty-two, with a noted penchant for seducing the young women in his District Attorney's office (immunized from consequences by a network of high-placed pals and Hatchard's possession of sensitive dossiers thereon), the man was an A-1 horndog. He had already made a few obligatory passes at Carmen while she was Barnaby's arm-candy, passes which Carmen had reluctantly turned down. Now that she was uncommitted, all it took to land him was meeting for lunch under the guise of soliciting his advice for her own agency's workings, plus a few not-so-subtle under-the-table suggestions, and after the end of work two days later, Carmen found herself, looking her magnificent best, inside the lobby of her apartment building, awaiting the arrival of a certain gold-hued Porsche Boxster.

The second bout of sex much later that evening, abetted by consumption of certain recreational drugs, usage of which Hatchard's office was otherwise duty-bound to prosecute, succeeded in loosening Hatchard's reticence about Clover Littlefield, but only to a certain extent.

"Knew her father? My ass! I had to say something to explain the connection though, didn't I? No, Clover's a very special case. Favor for the feds."

Tracing Hatchard's decently defined middle-aged pecs with one fingernail, Carmen said, "A favor for the feds? What does that mean?"

"She's in the witness protection program. I was supposed to help her integrate here. Clover Littlefield is her new name. She's even had some minor plastic surgery. She turned state's witness against some real bad hombres, and had to be airlifted out of her native city once they were convicted, to get her away from their network. Not that she was any angel back there. Totally complicit in all the nasty work."

"Nasty work? Like what?"

"I can't tell you any of that. A few juicy details, you'd be able to ferret out the whole case online. Her cover'd be blown, and the boys in DC would have my ass on a platter. Let's just say that little Clover got her hands pretty dirty."

"Do Barnaby and his parents know about this?"

"Of course not. At least not from me. They only got access to her manufactured identity. You go by that, she's pure as the driven snow. What's the use of harshing their mellow? Barnaby is crazy about Clover, she's removed from all her bad influences, and she's got no motive to pull anything, seeing as how she's gonna be Mrs. Silver Spoon Ogden soon. The truth won't help anyone, just fuck things up. Let sleeping perps lie, am I right?"

Carmen agreed wholeheartedly. "Oh, of course, Dan, we just want the best for both of them."

The very next day Carmen was on the phone, sweet-talking her ex.

"Barnaby, dear, could you make a minute to see me tonight, please? I have something important I want to discuss with you."

"Can't it wait until the next planning session? I'm very busy with any number of things."

"It can't wait, really. You see, it involves Clover."

A short silence. "Very well then, stop by the house at nine. Dinner will be over by then."

The calculated affront – that she would never be invited again to a meal in the mansion which she had once considered almost her own – rankled. But Carmen solaced herself with thoughts of ruination, the crashing and burning of the Ogden-Littlefield nuptials.

Barnaby received her in the library, whose shelves held mostly books purchased from a designer, who had coordinated their bindings for color and texture.

"Yes, Carmen, what's on your mind? Please come right to the point."

"The point, dear Barnaby, is that your bride-to-be is a common criminal. I happen to know all about her infamous past. Would you like the details?" Carmen hoped that Barnaby would not demand too many particulars that she had not been able to pry out of Hatchard, but she was quite prepared to invent some. For Clover to deny any of it would mean being forced to reveal contradictory, but probably equally damning bits.

Surprisingly, Barnaby actually looked relieved. "Is that all you came here for? Well, I hate to disappoint you, but you need not spill any of your dirt, since I already know it all. Clover, dear, you can come out now, please."

The door to the next room opened and Clover walked through. She looked as angelic and stainless as ever, a pert and perky gamin. She came right up to Barnaby, who put his arm protectively around her.

"Clover has already confided completely in me. She's expressed complete atonement and sorrow for all her past. We've volunteered to tell both Mother and Father the full story, but they've declined the offer. They feel that so long as I can accept and approve of everything, that's all that matters. So you won't get anywhere trying to peddle your trash to them. Now, Carmen, you can leave this house for good. And of course, you're no longer maid of honor."

Carmen turned with stunned automaton programming and took a step away from the happy pair. But then she was halted by Clover's sweet voice.

"Barn, dear, you can't do this. I won't have it. Asking Carmen to be my maid of honor demanded so much of her. And she responded very nobly. Can't you see that this latest move of hers was only made out of the love she still feels for you? She saw me as a threat, a danger to you, and wanted to save you from harm. This whole affair, the change in relationships, has taken a lot out of her. I sensed that, just from being with her during our little get-togethers about the wedding. She probably wasn't thinking straight, her mind and feelings just a mess. But now that she's had everything explained to her, I'm sure she'll see the virtue in being good friends with us both. And if she can do that, can we do any less? No, I still want Carmen as my maid of honor."

Clover stepped forward then to hug Carmen, and after a moment of reluctance, Barnaby awkwardly joined the ménage as well.

After the three unclinched, Barnaby moved to the liquor cabinet, saying, "This calls for a drink! The usual for you, Clover? A seltzer?"

"No, make it the sparkling cider. I've come to love that."

While Barnaby busied himself, Clover directed an intense look at Carmen. Outwardly, her expression was friendly and caring. But Carmen saw without a trace of uncertainty the pitiless glare of a serpent beneath the façade – a serpent biding its time to strike.

"Carmen, dear, I want to keep you very close to me from now on."

And with those words, Carmen knew that Clover had to die.

But the most safe and assured method of murder did not come to Carmen until a few days later.

The multiple brainstorming sessions about wedding minutiae, with a very fey wedding planner striving to earn his exorbitant fees, had become sheer torture and agony. If Carmen's hidden feelings before her failed attempt to end the wedding had been analogous to living through a fall from a third-story window, then her experience each time now must register as jumping from the Brooklyn Bridge, and living inside a shattered body to tell about it. Somehow each time she managed to summon up the fortitude to endure, grasping at any diversion for her lacerated, whirling feelings.

Tonight, she fixated on a discussion, conducted by Mrs. Ogden, about the details of the reception.

"Now, here is the seating arrangement for the wedding party at the head dais. Barnaby and Clover in the center, of course, with Carmen and Griffin adjacent to each. The rest of the party dispersed according to the chart. And here is the schedule of activities. Griffin, you'll make your speech first, precisely at one-fifteen. Carmen"—here Mrs. Ogden audibly sniffed with imperious disdain—"your own contribution in that line will come at one-thirty. You will both kindly allow me to vet your remarks beforehand, and promise not to deviate therefrom. Then we have the toasting. We are decanting the 1996 Dom Pérignon Rose Gold Methuselah for the occasion."

Griffin raised an eyebrow. "Fifty thousand dollars a bottle, if I'm not mistaken. Pretty impressive, even for such a huge bottle."

Mrs. Ogden plowed on. "That's of no consequence, Griffin. And poor Clover will not even be sampling the beverage. She's to have her usual sparkling cider."

Clover beamed. "Martinelli's Gold Medal. Three-ninety-nine at Target. Your bride's a cheap date, isn't she, Barn?"

Everyone laughed, including Carmen. But her laugh was tinged with a more manic glee, for in a flash the perfect murder scheme had flown into her mind.

Researching poisons proved actually to be quite fun. Hoping to cover her tracks, Carmen used her work computer, in private browsing mode. Many exotic substances at first appealed to her, especially the ones that promised the utmost agony. But she finally settled on the classic poisoner's favorite: arsenic.

A good lethal dose worked out to about three teaspoons of tasteless powder, nine thousand milligrams, suitably diluted in liquid – sparkling cider, in this case. Acquisition of the drug was accomplished via one of the less respectable members of the Messina clan, no questions asked. Carmen secured a large enough quantity to allow for practice and spillage. The sleazy cousin also threw in a bunch of syringes of various gauges.

Carmen bought a case of Martinelli's, and set to work, wearing latex gloves and a face mask, of course. Soon she exhibited a deft proficiency at inserting the needle through the outer wrapper and even through the thin metal cap; withdrawing the correct amount of innocent liquid; then injecting the poisoned cider and shaking the bottle to blend. The resulting hole in the cap was too minute to register on a rushed, uninterested server, and did not permit enough escape of gas to render the cider flat – at least over the short term.

As the wedding day drew closer and closer, Carmen felt absolutely confident of the success of her scheme. It was foolproof. Poison only for the champagne-hating bride, and no one else. Brilliant. She was not bothered about the possible witnesses, let alone innocent bystanders sharing the fatal beverage by accident. She was one-minded and blind.

Now came the wedding rehearsal itself, and the special dinner afterwards, an occasion of unforced joy and delight. Carmen tried not to become overly effusive or buddy-buddy, but the image of Clover keeling over and writhing in pain about half an hour or so after the toast and subsequent refills so delighted her that she found it hard not to be giddy.

As for the aftermath of the murder—well, assuming Carmen hid all her tracks well, would not the murder be ultimately attributed to Clover's enemies from back in her native city? Carmen would make sure to spill the beans about the bride's past to any sympathetic policeman or reporter. And once that scandal was out, no one would bother to look to the loving maid of honor, long-time friend of the family, as a suspect.

Carmen awoke on the day of the wedding in a calm and rational frenzy dedicated to the diligent execution of her scheme. Her earlier tour of the reception venue, including kitchen, conducted along with all the other members of the wedding party (God bless Mrs. Ogden's punctilious preparations and attention to details!) had left her confident that she could lay her hands on the bride's Martinelli's bottle under pretext of micromanaging things and swap it for the poisoned bottle concealed in her capacious but fashionable shoulder bag. The whole switch, amidst much staff hurly-burly, should take seconds, and disposal of the innocent bottle, wiped clean of fingerprints, in the ladies' room bin would sever any ties to her.

Her deadly bag left behind in a pew, Carmen observed and participated in the wedding itself as if sleepwalking through a very vivid dream. Hatchard served as surrogate father to give Clover away. Handsome Griffin complemented Carmen's own elegance. Barnaby had never looked more like a simpering dolt. (Would she take him back when he came crawling in sorrow? Of course, but only after making him suffer a bit more.) The rest of the men and women involved faded away to invisibility.

Photographs were taken, a seemingly endless task. The ride to the reception venue in various limousines likewise seemed infinitely protracted. Carmen couldn't even summon up the annoyance to protest when Griffin started feeling her up in public.

Then came settling down on the dais, according to the chart. But before that, Carmen made a hasty excuse about forgetting something in the limo. She exited the building, re-entered via the previously scoped-out back door to the kitchen, and accomplished the bottle swap with no comments or notice from the stressed and busy servitors. She made one small inconsequential change of plans, dumping the original clean bottle in a trash bin when she exited the building. She was back on the dais before six minutes had passed.

Thank God, Carmen thought, that the toasting would occur early-on in the formalities. She did not think she could contain her quivering excitement for any longer than was strictly required.

Out came the enormous six-liter bottle of champagne, borne by two servers on a silver platter.

Out came the bottle of cider, likewise delivered with mock elegance. Everyone in the big room laughed, knowing the famous foibles of the bride who declined even to sample this rarest of champagnes.

The two bottles were uncorked with a pop and uncapped with a whoosh.

The champagne was being decanted. But before the cider could be poured, Clover suddenly jumped to her feet, almost tipping over Carmen's chair. The bride flung her arms wide, exclaiming, "I'm so happy!"

One arm caught the server, a small young woman, full in the chest, sending her backpedaling with the cider bottle. The server's foot went over the edge of the dais and she tumbled backwards, off and over, sending the Martinelli's flying. People shrieked.

Carmen's whole world caved in on her, and she felt herself drowning in a black abyss, barely able to pay attention to the confusion and awkward recovery of the ceremony. But then, after all the apologies and reassurances had been made, and a new fresh untampered-with bottle of cider was brought out, Carmen brightened up a tad.

Today would not see Clover Littlefield's death. But as a reaffirmed friend of the family, Carmen would have many more chances to succeed.

Finally all the glasses were filled with the appropriate beverages. Celebratory words were said – somehow Carmen bumbled through her own speech – the glasses were drained and refilled, and people sat back down.

It was at that moment that Carmen caught Clover's calculating eye, just a dozen inches from her own. And in a micro-second, a deep sisterly knowledge was exchanged between them.

Clover had deduced or suspected Carmen's plot. The accident with the bottle was intentional.

As was Clover's poisoning of the champagne. Which had, Carmen now realized, tasted a bit off. Probably indicative of a much nastier, faster-acting substance than simple tasteless arsenic. Strychnine, perhaps.

And the same alibi setup that Carmen had relied on – revenge taken by Clover's old associates – would be just as feasible to the police now. How they would cosset the poor, rich, freed-of-Barnaby-and-parents bride, the only one saved, thanks to a twist of fate, the accidental smashing of the special poisoned bottle intended for her.

Through a rising tide of internal distress that quickly promised a surge of intense pain and death, Carmen could hazily make out Clover's big smile as she raised her glass for another toast.

Carmen's last regret was the knowledge that she herself would have made a much lovelier grieving widow than that mousy little bitch!

INSTITUTIONAL MEMORY

M. W. CRAVEN

The night was wetter than a drunk's chin. Mean-spirited rain had hammered the city for hours, the pavements plinking and the gutters washing away the cigarette butts and the betting slips. It left an oily dampness, the kind that gets into your joints, makes them click and ache. Reminds you you're getting old and one day, maybe one day soon, you are going to die.

Nothing good happens on a night like this.

As it was every evening, Normal's Bar was packed with men nursing gins, hangovers and grievances. None of them were strangers to bad luck. The flashing neon sign, the bulb of the 'o' permanently out of sync, somehow managed to make Normal's appear threatening. It wasn't, but it wasn't exactly welcoming either. You didn't come to Normal's for a good night, or to ponder personal development, you came to get drunk and to be left alone.

Two men sat in the corner. Although Normal's was almost full, no one had taken the vacant seats nearby. One of the men was big, like he was a stevedore or a brickmason. The other was smaller, neater, more exact, like he had trained as a draughtsman, but hadn't been able to find work. They were the kind of men who called women 'dames' and never left their apartment without a hat. The bigger man had a chunk of eyebrow missing and a nose that had been broken and reset by a nervous man. He was called Rollo Leblanc and he was a hit man. The smaller man was called Frank Carter and when he spoke, you didn't interrupt. He was also a hit man, although, after twenty years, he was finally retiring.

Frank had gotten there early. He was methodically chewing on a reheated grilled cheese, the toast curled at the edges. He was on his second Lucky Lager and was already feeling the buzz. Frank had never been a drinker. Didn't like the taste, never had. But he was in Normal's, and Normal's didn't serve Hires Root Beer. Rollo was on his third bourbon, two fingers in each greasy tumbler.

"Come on, let's get outta here," Rollo said, draining his drink. "Sal's booked us a private room at Luca's. Steaks are on him tonight. Wants to see you out in style. Wishes he coulda been here, but you know how it is."

Frank shrugged. He knew how it was.

⋆

The New York strips were as big as bibles and bloodier than a busted nose. Rollo had ordered off-menu and Luca Mulino himself had served them. The steaks came with creamed mashed potatoes, buttered greens and a side of onion rings. Rollo had ignored the champagne chilling by their table and ordered another two fingers of bourbon. Frank had done jobs with Rollo before, but there was a prowling restlessness to him tonight. He seemed on edge, nervous even. Maybe it was because tomorrow he would be Sal's fixer. Frank knew Rollo had coveted the position for a long time, but the big job came with conditions, the main one being there was no one left to blame if things went to shit.

Or maybe Rollo was nervous about something else.

It wasn't the first time that Frank had been in Luca's private room. It was at the back of the restaurant and had a door that led straight into an alley filled with dumpsters, rats as big as cats and the occasional bum, passed out on whatever the hell bums drank. It wasn't a nice room, but it was a *private* room, a room where men like Frank and Rollo could speak freely. Even Luca, up to his hairy Italian balls in Sal's business through gambling debts and money laundering, knew to knock and wait before he brought in their food.

Rollo attacked his steak like a hungry man, cutting off great chunks of beef and fat and chewing noisily, washing down each mouthful with a slug of bourbon. Frank, the grilled cheese sitting heavy in his gut, nibbled at the edges of his. Luca's *did* serve Hires Root Beer and he had a pint, three cubes of ice floating on the top, like they were waiting for the *Titanic*.

"Man, I wish I was punching my ticket," Rollo said, burping loudly. "Sal Junior told you how much he's put aside for you yet?"

"He's told me."

"Told me too." Rollo whistled. "That there ain't no chump change, Frank."

"It's a lot of money," Frank agreed.

"What you gonna do with it? Me, I'd buy the biggest boat I could and I'd be outa this goddamned joke of a country. Sail it somewhere hot. Where the rum is dark and the dames are even darker."

"I got a cabin in Maine," Frank said. "I'll spend some time there while I decide what to do next."

"How long you had that?"

"Twenty years, since I started working for Sal Senior. He's the one who told me to find somewhere to lie low after each job. Somewhere no one else knows about."

Rollo nodded. Both men knew what 'job' meant.

"I never met Sal Junior's old man," Rollo said. "But I heard he was a real ball breaker."

"He was OK," Frank said. "If you did your job and didn't give him no lip, he was a good man to work for. Straight shooter and that's the cream on top of the milk in this business."

"I'll drink to that, my friend," Rollo said, raising his glass. Frank clinked his soda against Rollo's tumbler. Bourbon sloshed over the rim and onto his hands, but Rollo either didn't notice or didn't care. "So you and Sal Senior were close?"

Frank sighed. Rollo talked too much, always had. The man had fought in the Battle of Hürtgen Forest with the 2nd Ranger Battalion, and he could shoot and take orders and was reliable in a pinch, but every now and then Frank just wished he'd shut the hell up.

Not every silence had to be filled, not every secret had to be shared.

"Tell me a story about him, Frank," Rollo said.

Frank bit back a cuss word. He'd have to give him something. Rollo pouted worse than a dame sometimes and Frank didn't need that kind of hassle, not tonight. "You ever hear about a schmuck called Herb Randall?" he said.

"The blacksmith? Used to work at Sal Senior's stable?"

"He was a farrier, but yes, that's the guy."

"Word is you clipped him."

Frank frowned. Even in Luca's backroom it didn't make no sense to talk openly about these things. Instead of admitting out loud that he had, Frank nodded.

"What had Herb done to upset Sal?" Rollo asked.

"You ever hear about a horse called Cricket?" Frank replied. "An ill-tempered gelding he'd bought on a whim?"

"Vaguely. Got a bullet to the head, didn't it?"

"After Herb short-shod him when he was drunk, left him with a quarter crack in his left front hoof that eventually turned him lame."

"And Sal loved the horse?"

"No more than any other. But he *did* love the money it was going to make him. He'd been over-watering Cricket all season to slow him down with plans to cash in at Saratoga."

"He didn't win?"

"Didn't even finish. Pulled up within a quarter of a mile. Thing was screaming like a hyena. Sal shot him himself."

"And you shot Herb?"

"Not before he'd stuck me with a hoof knife. My fault really. Shoulda realised he'd be expecting me."

"Where'd he get ya?"

"Gut."

"Nasty."

"It was. I dunno how long I'd been lying on that stable floor, my blood and shit mixing together like a dirty martini, when Sal found me, but he rushed me to Clara Maass. Three weeks I was in there, puking and sweating, and shaking so fast it looked like I was vibrating. Sal visited me every day. Every single day. Brought me clams from Pigalle's, even though I couldn't eat for shit. Soon as I could piss clear, he drove me up to my cabin and made sure I had everything I needed. So yeah, me and Sal Senior were close."

There was a small bell on the table so Luca didn't have to keep sticking his head around the door, interrupting whatever was going on. And from Luca's perspective, it meant he didn't overhear nothing he'd have to be clipped for. Rollo shook the bell, damn near shook the clapper off. Luca appeared immediately.

"Yes, Mr Leblanc?"

"Cigars, Luca," Rollo said. "Couple of those fat double coronas out the humidor the cops don't know about. The one Sal keeps the Cubans in."

"But…"

"You want I should call Sal? Interrupt his evening to explain how his instructions to give Mr Carter a send-off he ain't ever gonna forget are being shit on by a degenerate gambler? You want that, do you, Luca?"

"No, Mr Leblanc. I'll get them immediately."

"And don't forget the matches."

After Luca had scurried off, Frank said, "Something on your mind, Rollo?"

"I've never liked that asshole," Rollo said, his eyes starting to glass over. "Has too smart a mouth for someone who ain't connected. I shoulda took him outside and introduced his face to the butt of my gun."

It was an empty threat. No weapons were allowed inside Luca's. It was a rule, strictly enforced. The restaurant was too important to Sal Junior's money washing operation for it to get closed down on a weapons violation.

"Luca's OK," Frank said. "Him and Sal go way back. And the food's decent, even the cattle feed they put on the menu."

"If it's so good, how come you've hardly had a bite out your steak?"

"That grilled cheese I had at Normal's ain't sitting pretty."

"That right?"

"As rain."

Rollo scowled like Frank had just hit on his mom, but eventually he dropped his eyes and said, "Yeah, well, it don't mean I have to like—" There was a knock on the door. "Speak of the asshole and the asshole instantly appears."

Luca came in. He was carrying a silver tray with two cigars sitting on top of a folded white napkin. The cigars were big and fat and dark and, without the treasury's customs bond on the box, were illegal in all forty-eight states. Sal had never really gotten the hang of paying import taxes on his cigars.

"Do you want me to punch them for you, Mr Leblanc?"

"I ain't doing it myself."

Luca pulled an ornate bullet cutter from his waistcoat pocket and punched a hole in the end of each cigar. Frank preferred a v-cut when he smoked a good cigar, he felt the punch cut was too small and the draw too concentrated, but he wasn't bothered enough to say. Rollo was becoming more and more belligerent and he didn't want Luca getting blamed for one of Frank's peccadillos.

As the senior man in the room, Luca passed Frank the first Cuban. He waited until Frank had it in his mouth then held a lit match under the tip. Frank sucked in a few times, removed the cigar and checked the tip. It glowed like a firefly's asshole in the last week of May. Frank took a satisfying draw, tipped his head back and blew out a plume of blue-grey smoke at the ceiling. A good cigar, one with complex flavours like this Cuban, had its own personality, he had always thought.

"Who was it said that if there weren't no cigars in heaven, he didn't want to go?" Rollo said after Luca had left the room.

"Mark Twain, I think."

Rollo raised an eyebrow. "Didn't know you were a bookworm, Frank."

Frank shrugged. Didn't reckon a stupid statement like that deserved an answer.

"That true what you said earlier, about Herb the farrier sticking you with a knife?" Rollo said, shifting gears.

"True as I'm sitting here," Frank replied. "Still get twinges, like the pain's real if I think about how bad it was."

"Bet the scar ain't pretty?"

"No it ain't, but hell, *I* ain't pretty."

"No, you ain't." Rollo laughed. "Can I see it?"

Frank studied the younger man. "Sure,' he said after a couple of beats. He loosened his skinny tie and unbuttoned his yellow Arrow shirt. Rollo moved round to his side of the table and leaned in. Frank's scar was thick and shiny and lumpy, like twisted rope. Over a foot long, it was the colour and shape of a badly cut toenail clipping.

"Sweet," Rollo said. He removed his jacket and made a play of fixing it on the back of his chair. He unbuttoned his shirt and showed Frank his pale, hairy belly. It was criss-crossed with scars. Looked like something had exploded out of him. "Got this beauty in Hürtgen Forest. Too near one of the Kraut's potato mashers when it went off."

"Potato masher?"

"What the Brits called the German stick grenades."

"Nasty."

Rollo shrugged. "Looks worse than it is," he said. "Most of it is burns." He removed his shirt completely, turned around and showed Frank his back. "You see the hole in my shoulder?"

"I do."

"Caught a ricochet from an MP 40, same battle. Still got bits of that damn bullet in me. Aches like a bitch in winter."

Rollo put his shirt and jacket back on. He retook his seat and picked up his cigar. He took a drag then studied the end. "You never served overseas, did you, Frank?" he said quietly.

"Didn't have that privilege, Rollo."

Frank hadn't served overseas, but he *had* served the war effort. He and Sal had been part of Operation Underworld, the arrangement the bosses had come to with Naval Intelligence when it came to countering Axis saboteurs, controlling the unions and limiting the theft of vital war supplies. Frank's job had been cracking heads in the black-market business. Selling silk stockings was fine; selling gasoline got you a warning from Frank. There wasn't no second warning, just a dead spiv floating in the Hudson. Frank didn't know if what they'd done made a difference, all he knew was that before the war, Charles 'Lucky' Luciano, one of the New York bosses, was doing a fifty-year stretch for prostitution and *after* the war he wasn't doing it no more.

"War makes a man," Rollo said.

He left it at that. If Frank had valued Rollo's opinion, he could have taken offence. Frank didn't give a rat's ass what the chucklehead thought. He was more interested in *why* Rollo had insulted him. Maybe he'd better check on something. He got to his feet. "Just going to the can."

Rollo nodded like he was giving him permission. "If you see that asshole Luca, tell him to bring some of that cheesecake in, the one with the pistachio crust. We'll finish our cigars then find somewhere where the music's hot and fast. Maybe see if a couple of crusty hoods can't find some dames who are hotter and faster."

*

Frank stubbed out his cigar. It had been one of the best he'd ever had. If he thought he could ever afford them, he'd have asked where Sal Junior had gotten them. Rollo had finished his a couple of minutes earlier. They had finished their desserts then Rollo said he had to visit the can too. Said he would apologise to Luca on the way back. Frank didn't know if he had or if he hadn't, although a minute after he returned Luca had brought in a brandy for Rollo and soda for Frank, both on the house.

"Will you miss it?" Rollo asked.

"Miss what?"

"This. The life."

"It's a younger man's game," Frank said.

And it was. There was meanness in what they did now, a meanness that wasn't there before. Sure, legs had got broken and skulls had got busted and yes, sometimes people had to be whacked. Sometimes they deserved it, sometimes, like with Herb the farrier, they just pissed off the wrong person at the wrong time. But there was never chaos. People could go about their day, raise their families, without fear some mook was gonna take everything they had, everything they were ever gonna get. It had been harsh, Frank thought, but it had never been unfair. These days, *Sal Junior's* days, it was only about making money. And if working people suffered so Sal Junior could have more, why the hell should anyone worry? Only fools didn't take advantage of the weak, he'd overheard one of Sal's mooks say. And that weren't right. Everyone had to kick a little bit upstairs, but a man had to be able to earn a living.

"Oily John was before you?" Rollo said.

"He was."

"And he was Sal Senior's guy?"

"His old man's actually, but he worked for Sal Senior for a while too."

"You ever meet him?"

Frank nodded.

"What was he like?" Rollo asked.

"What you heard?"

"Things, that's what I heard."

Frank didn't doubt it. Oily John had been feared across the five boroughs. He'd had a head like a cannonball, arms as thick as legs, and legs like a side of beef. He carried an M1905 bayonet with a sixteen-inch blade and a .357 Magnum with a modified grip, although he rarely used either. When one of Oily John's sledgehammer fists hit you, you stayed hit.

"Most of it's exaggerated," Frank said.

"What about the hit in Anastasia's restaurant?"

"What were you told?"

"Way I heard it, he walked up to Anastasia's table and whacked the guy he was having dinner with. Hit him so many times with a club hammer, they couldn't tell what was his head and what was his steak tartare entrée."

"No, that did happen," Frank said. "The hit had been sanctioned though, he hadn't gone rogue."

"Kick in the balls for Anastasia though. Oily killing the guy while they were having dinner together. Disrespectful. Surprised there wasn't any blowback."

"It was Anastasia who sanctioned it. And because of the way it went down the G-men had no cause to look his way."

Rollo's eyes widened. "I never knew that," he said.

"Well now you do."

"You ever hear from him?"

"Who? Oily John?"

"Yeah."

Frank shook his head. "Took his money and moved to Europe. Opened an ice cream parlour in Italy, I heard. Or maybe it was Portugal. One of those Mediterranean countries anyhow."

"Probably for the best."

"How do you figure?"

"Like you said, it's a younger man's game. Can't expect to live to a ripe old age doing what we do."

Frank said nothing.

"You know what institutional memory is, Frank?" Rollo asked.

"I've heard of it."

Rollo pulled a betting slip out of his jacket pocket. There was writing on the back, hastily scribbled. "I went to the Public Library before I met you at Normal's," he said. "Looked up the official definition."

"That right?"

"It is."

"Now why might you be doing something like that, Rollo?"

Rollo ignored Frank's question. "Says here that institutional memory is the personal recollections of employees that provide an understanding of the history of an organisation, especially the stories that explain the reasons behind certain decisions. It helps organisations avoid past mistakes and it's a key part of any continuity planning."

"Yeah, I heard it was important."

"But maybe not so much in what we do, Frank?" Rollo said. "Avoiding past mistakes is all well and good, but maybe not so when it comes to a bunch of mooks walking upright, all of them knowing what went on before. Having all these memories, all this knowledge. That's not an asset to a business like ours, that's a risk."

"I guess," Frank said.

"See, what would happen if say, a mook who used to work for us is busted by the feds?"

"Busted for what?"

"Don't matter. Could be something he done when he was with us, could be something he done as a civilian. The point is, he gets busted. And this mook is looking at five years in Sing Sing. What would happen if this mook thinks, 'Hey, I know what I could do: I can tell the feds where Vincent Mangano is buried, or maybe I tell them who's getting kickbacks from the Flamingo in Vegas? Maybe that thing I just got busted for goes away.'"

"Feds never tire of flipping people because it works, Rollo," Frank said. "It ain't ever gonna change."

Rollo nodded, sadly, Frank thought. "You're a stand-up guy, Frank," he said. "Been a loyal soldier for twenty years, but you know how risk-averse Sal Junior has gotten lately. The feds turning that consigliere out west has him spooked. He don't want to reduce and manage risk no more, he wants to *eliminate* it."

"Can't be done," Frank said. He picked up his glass and finished his soda, rattled the ice in the bottom for a bit while he thought. "You tell Sal Junior from me, the only way he can eliminate risk is if he isolates himself from the running of the business. And even then he's going to need a trusted go-between."

"I told him that."

"And?"

Rollo reached behind his back and produced a revolver. It was wet. He pointed it at Frank's heart. "I'm sorry, Frank, but this is the way it has to be."

Frank didn't answer.

"If it makes you feel better, this ain't personal," Rollo added.

"This is what Sal Junior wants?"

"Sorry."

"And what about when it's your time to pull your pin, Rollo. To buy that boat and sail somewhere warm. You think Sal Junior's going to let *you* go? What happens to his institutional memory problem then?"

"Ah, but you're forgetting something, Frank; I fought in the war. And like I said before, war makes a man. Sal Junior knows I can be trusted. Knows I could do a twenty, hell even a thirty-year stretch if it comes down to it. Sal thinks you can't trust a man who never wore a uniform, Frank. Not completely."

"I assume you told him that?"

Rollo grinned. "Wanted to make sure I got the gig when you were out the picture. Like I said, it wasn't personal."

Frank sighed. "I ever tell you about the first time I was in this room, Rollo?" he said.

"Don't think you ever mentioned it, Frank."

"And you know why I don't?"

"Sure you're about to tell me."

"Cos I ain't got a mouth like yours," Frank said. "Some things need to stay *not* talked about."

"Why don't you tell me anyway?" He waggled the end of the revolver. "Not as if anyone'll know."

"I was taking Oily John out for his last night before he moved to Europe. Bit like you are now. I was sitting in this exact seat, and Oily was sitting opposite me. Where you are, as it happens."

"Why you telling me this, Frank?"

"You see, although Oily was a hard case, a real psycho, he was like you – a talker. Liked to brag about what he'd done. He thought it gave him a rep, which it did, but like you said before about institutional memory, it made him a liability. And although Sal Senior was twice the man his son will ever be, he wasn't taking risks he didn't have to take, if you catch my drift."

"You saying you clipped him?"

"That's exactly what I'm saying, Rollo."

Rollo shook his head. "That ain't what happened. Oily John's in Europe somewhere. He got out. I dunno what you hope to get out of—"

"Oily John's dead, Rollo," Frank cut in. "I killed him. Pulled out my Smith & Wesson and put three into his face, dragged him into the alley and drove up to the Jenny Jump. Far as I know he's still in a wet grave there. He's probably down to his bones by now."

Rollo shook his head again. "You ain't allowed to carry in Luca's. Everyone knows that and no way a mook like you sneaks one in under the eyes of a legend like Oily John. Not on his last night, he'd have been watching out for it."

"Yet you're pointing a gun at me."

"You think I'm a schmuck? You get the word to clip Frank Carter, you don't bring a gun to dinner. You collect it *during* dinner. It's what makes me a better man for this job than you, and why I know you're lying about Oily John. He's alive and well in Italy, just like you said earlier."

"Is that so?"

"Yep, that is definitely so, Frank." He narrowed his eyes and raised the revolver a fraction. His finger began squeezing the trigger.

"What is that, a Colt Detective Special?" Frank said.

"'Fraid so."

"It's a good gun."

"It is. Reliable."

"Why's it wet?"

"Had it in a bag in the cistern. Bag must've sprung a leak."

Frank shook his head. "That ain't why it's wet, Rollo."

"It ain't?"

"You see, you were right about one thing: no way would Oily John sit down to dinner with someone unless he'd searched him first. He wasn't the sharpest tool in the box, but he had good instincts and he'd survived more than a dozen hits. So I didn't even try to sneak my Smith & Wesson in. Instead, I hid it somewhere the night before."

Rollo's hand began to tremble. Not a lot, but if you were playing poker with him, you'd fold or go all in.

"So when I saw you making such a big deal of taking off your jacket and showing me you were unarmed, I thought maybe I'd better go check the cisterns in Luca's bathroom," Frank continued. "I suppose you'd call it institutional memory, Rollo. And what did I find in the stall on the end? A Colt Detective Special in a bag."

"You're lying," Rollo said, his face telling Frank the opposite.

"Your bag didn't spring a leak, Rollo. It's just that I can't have fixed it up right after I'd put your Detective Special back in it. You know, after I'd bashed the firing pin against the edge of the toilet pan. Snapped that sucker right off. *That's* why your gun is wet."

Rollo pulled the trigger. He didn't seem surprised by the dry click. It sounded louder than it ought, Frank thought. Rollo pulled the trigger again, but his heart wasn't in it. He pulled back the hammer, saw the mangled firing pin. Knew he was holding a useless lump of metal.

"What happens now?" he said. "I'm not armed; you're not armed. We go our separate ways? Pretend this didn't happen? You know Sal Junior's not gonna let that happen, Frank."

"You talk too much, Rollo," Frank said, reaching under the table for the Remington pump-action shotgun he'd taped there that morning. He pulled the trigger and blew Rollo out of his chair.

Frank got to his feet, walked around the table and stood over Rollo. The hole in his stomach was the size of Oily John's head.

"Why would you think I wasn't armed?" Frank said quietly.

"Please," Rollo gurgled. "I don't want to die."

Frank pushed the barrel into Rollo's open mouth and pulled the trigger, watched his head disappear. He reached into Rollo's jacket and removed the dead man's money clip. He left it on the table for Luca, partly for Rollo's earlier rudeness, partly for the shitstorm that was heading his way. Sal Junior wouldn't hurt him – Luca made him far too much money – but he'd sure shout a lot. Frank placed the gun next to Rollo's body. He didn't need it no more. If he had to shoot his way out, he'd made a mess of things and deserved to die. He'd leave through the kitchens rather than the alleyway. Walk to Penn Station and buy a ticket to Boston. Make sure he was seen, then quietly leave and catch the first Greyhound outta the city. Start zigzagging across the country until he ended up in New Orleans where he had a Creole townhouse in the French Quarter.

He hadn't had a cabin in Maine since Sal Senior had driven him there in the back of his Buick, his skin clammy, his stitches still wet. Frank sold it first chance he'd had, hadn't mentioned it to anyone. Always have somewhere to go that no one knows about, Sal had told him, and Frank thought that was about the best advice he'd ever been given. Not every secret had to be shared.

Frank made to leave the room, but something stopped him. He doubled back and picked up the betting slip Rollo had read from, the one with the institutional memory quote. He wiped off the worst of the blood and slipped it into his jacket pocket. He had some nice walnut at home, its grain black and wavy. He'd knock up a nice frame and hang the betting slip somewhere he'd always see it.

It seemed fitting somehow.

Author's note:

'Institutional Memory' was influenced by one of my favourite Cornell Woolrich short stories: 'Dilemma of the Dead Lady', a comedic *pas de deux* between two criminals.

SLEEP! SLEEP! BEAUTY BRIGHT

CHARLES ARDAI

He'd done everything he could. That's what they told him. It was in the doctors' hands now. In the hands of the police. He'd kept her alive, had called 911 and elevated her head, made sure she didn't choke on her own blood, had applied pressure to the gash on her thigh until they came with a stretcher and an ambulance to rush her up First Avenue to the emergency room at NYU. He'd ridden with them, held her hand – her right hand – in the back, leaned in close to where the oxygen mask ended beside her shattered jaw, begged her not to die. He'd done what he could. He'd done everything he could. He'd done everything anyone could. It was in their hands now.

He sat in the waiting room, waiting for word. Waiting to hear the worst, not sure what the worst might be. They'd broken her fingers. Her fingers. Why? Why would anyone…? They'd done so much else besides, he didn't know how much, didn't want to know, couldn't imagine. But her fingers. With her wedding ring still shining, all of four months old, promising happiness. A broken promise, like her broken fingers.

He sat waiting, and eventually they came, exhausted, masks dangling around their necks, blood drying on their sleeves, the surgeon and the nurse, one older, gray-haired, with sad eyes, the other young, far too young, a handsome, dark-skinned man with shoulder-length hair and an expression Hector couldn't read, looking no older than Maddie herself, and Hector stood to meet them.

"Mr. Monroe?"

"Can I see her? Is she—?"

He couldn't ask the question. He couldn't. He had to, but he couldn't.

"Your wife's a very tough lady," the surgeon said. "She's in the recovery room now."

"She's alive?"

"She's alive."

His heart began beating again. "Thank God."

"She's not out of the woods yet. You need to understand, it won't be an easy recovery."

"That's okay," he said. "That's okay. Just as long as she's alive."

"Mr. Monroe," the surgeon said, and he put a hand on Hector's shoulder. It was an anchor, meant to steady him in rough seas, but all he could feel was the weight of it, dragging him down, dragging him under. "Mr. Monroe, your wife is in a coma."

✶

Sleep! sleep! beauty bright,
Dreaming o'er the joys of night;
Sleep! sleep! in thy sleep
Little sorrows sit and weep.

✶

She lay silently, unmoving. If he hadn't known – but he did know. The doctor had said. And the monitor beside the bed chimed softly, keeping time with the slow rhythm of her sleeping heart. On the black screen, the jagged line rose and fell, rose and fell. But the sheet over her chest barely did. He watched. It barely moved.

My love, my sweet—

A half hour would have made the difference. Leaving when he'd promised rather than working thirty minutes longer. One more customer, one more chance at a job, a small job, a postcard, a brochure, fifty dollars, seventy-five. Half an hour. The answer had been no anyway. But so what if it had been yes? If he'd come home to his dying wife with a pocketful of emeralds or amethysts to shoot?

He heard the door behind him swing open, the measured footsteps of a man's hard-soled shoes taking patient steps in his direction. He didn't look. His eyes were on the woman in the bed, lying as still as in a coffin, the monitors assuring him that he hadn't lost her yet. Still here, still here, still here, they quietly announced. Still here. But for how much longer?

"They tell you anything about how long she'll be like this?" Almost as if he'd read Hector's mind, the man in the brown suitcoat, brown trousers, white shirt, brown tie; almost as if he could see every thought reflected on Hector's face, and maybe he could. The man's own face looked tired, worn, his cheeks speckled from the hours since his morning shave, but the eyes above those cheeks, sunk deep within their sockets, looked as penetrating as any Hector had ever seen. They were priest's eyes, he thought, though this man was no priest. Not yet, thank God. Not yet.

The man handed him a stiff card printed with the New York Police Department shield. Hector had never looked at it before, never examined it, but now he saw each tiny element, framed in its place: an eagle, a farmer, an Indian, the scales of justice, all laid out in black and white. But it was just an insignia, just a symbol. Where was justice when Maddie needed it? Where was this shield then?

He tried to hand the card back, but the detective waved it off. "Case you need to call me."

Hector saw the phone number, saw the name, Peter Donahue. He wouldn't call. He knew he wouldn't. The police hadn't protected her when it mattered, and they couldn't save her now. But he slid the card into his pocket.

"No," he said, answering Peter Donahue's question. "They said she could come out of it tomorrow, or she could be like this for…" For weeks, they'd said. For years. For the rest of her life.

Donahue put his hand on Hector's shoulder, where the surgeon had earlier. "You know people say they can hear you," Donahue said, and it was true, the doctors had said that too. "If you talk to them. They still hear you."

Hector nodded.

"My sister, her son was in an accident when he was in high school. She brought him all his books from school, read to him every day. *Julius Caesar*, *Of Mice and Men*. I forget what else."

"Did it help?" Hector wanted to know.

Donahue thought a bit. "It helped her," he said.

"Did your nephew recover?"

Donahue said, "Not just yet."

"How many years ago was this?"

"Let's talk about your wife," Donahue said. Hector felt the pressure leave his shoulder, heard pages turn as the detective opened a notepad. "Do you have any idea who might have done this?"

"Officer, please—"

"I realize this is a difficult time for you," Donahue said, "but the sooner—"

"Difficult?" He didn't like how shrill his voice sounded, especially in front of Maddie. What if it was true that she could still hear? Then what she was hearing was the terror in his voice, when what she needed was comfort, was peace. But he couldn't help it. At this moment he really just couldn't. "You realize this is a 'difficult time' for me?"

The detective closed his notebook and slipped it back inside the pocket of his blazer. "I *will* need to talk with you."

"Tomorrow," Hector said. "Please. Not today."

"Best way to reach you?"

Hector looked at Maddie's silent figure in the bed before him. She hadn't moved. Maybe she would before tomorrow. Maybe she never would again.

"I'll be here," he said.

*

On Tenth Street, a mile south of the hospital, a row of stone buildings stood as they'd stood for a century or longer, black iron fire escapes crawling down their faces, wire screens in a few opened windows to let the night air in. No lights burned, not in any of the windows in their building, not in the buildings on either side. Across the street, Hector saw a few. Night owls awaiting the dawn, bleary and despondent. Or early risers, fixing breakfast and planning their day. Or neither: lights that burned while their owners slept, lights left on in an empty home. The lights had been on in his apartment when Hector had come home, every light blazing warmly, welcoming him, showing him the spreading dark stain beneath his wife's body.

He took the steps slowly now, three to the vestibule, then fifteen more to the first-floor landing. More and then more. Three further stories up, he came at last to their door, his hand, out of habit, raised to knock. He let it fall. No one would answer. No quick steps would come pattering on the other side, the door swinging open, Maddie in his arms.

He stood on the threshold, closed his eyes, and tried to find the smell of her in the air, the before smell, the smell of talcum powder and Dove soap, of toasted English muffins and black coffee, but all that reached him from where it had soaked deep into the carpet's fibers was the lingering smell of blood.

He laid his coat down softly on the arm of the couch. Looked at the wreckage of the room, the floor littered with the contents swept off every shelf. His eight-by-ten camera lay on its side, its tripod legs extended like an insect's, a trapped insect that's given up its struggle and lain still. He bent to stand it upright again.

In the kitchen, the counter was a Sahara of flour and sugar, the metal canisters overturned and emptied. The cabinet doors stood open, shattered china on the floor. The oven door was open too, and the broiler tray below it.

There were pills scattered in the bathroom sink, pink and brown and white. The mirrored medicine cabinet door lay in pieces.

He went on to the bedroom, swept a crumpled heap of clothing off the bed and onto the floor, picked his way between dresser drawers that had been toppled and flung. His photographs of Maddie had been torn from the walls, the frames bent and scratched, the glass fronts stepped on and splintered. In one, Maddie's smiling face now bore a streak from the sole of a bloody shoe.

He raised the window blinds, leaned with both fists on the sill, looked out into the night.

Across the street, in one of the few lit windows, he saw a curtain twitch.

Just the one time, the slightest of movements. An inch, perhaps. No more. To the point where he asked himself if he really had seen it, and even if he had, whether it might just have been a current of air responsible.

But then the light behind the curtain went out, and he knew.

He didn't know the man's name. Why would he? You don't know your neighbors in New York. You live a thousand on a block and know no one. But everyone who lived in New York City had a neighbor like theirs – everyone, it was a rule of city life, one Hector had never been glad about before. You open your blinds in the morning, newspaper in one hand, cup of coffee in the other, and there across the street is a man looking back at you. You don't wave. You don't smile. You shrug. Hopefully you've got more than just your underwear on, or at least not less. If you're Maddie, you take to wearing pajamas rather than sheer nightgowns. No sense giving your neighbor a show. They'd seen him more than once with binoculars pressed to his face – not looking in their window necessarily, maybe looking one floor up or one floor down, but all the same, you saw him at it and you felt twin pangs of embarrassment, not just for what he might have seen of you but for what he'd revealed about himself. You wished to hell that he would stop. You thought about keeping your blinds down, your curtains closed, but in the heat of August, like everyone else on this sweltering island, you'd trade your privacy for the possibility of a breeze. Perhaps you thought of calling 311, or even 911, and only didn't because it was too much trouble, too much hassle. One day you would, that's what you told yourself, one day you'd get him talked to, dealt with, but with one thing and another, so far you hadn't.

And now—

And now you were glad you hadn't. Hadn't got him talked to by the police, hadn't got his sordid habit broken for him.

Now, tonight, you would breathe a sigh of relief if only your heart weren't suddenly going like a pinball ramming every bumper in the machine.

Your neighbor, with his binoculars. If ever there was a time when it might be good to have a window peeper in the neighborhood, a man who could be counted on to be watching at any hour…

If anyone might have seen something, surely it was him. It was almost too much to hope. But then again, he had been watching now, at the gutter end of night, watching your closed blinds from behind his own drawn curtain. Surely he hadn't been doing that for no reason, hadn't turned his lights off for no reason when he'd been spotted.

Surely. Could a prayer consist of just a single word?

Hector flew down the four flights of stairs, ran across the empty street. He'd never met the man, never spoken to him, didn't know a thing about him. Barely knew what he looked like, even. Just impressions from passing glances: middle-aged, maybe in his late forties. Pink skin, long strands of hair across his balding scalp.

Hector found the apartment buzzer for the fifth-floor front apartment: *M. BOSEMAN.* Pressed it. Waited. Pressed it again.

Of course he wouldn't answer. Who would, at three in the morning, least of all when the person buzzing was a neighbor who'd caught you spying? Even if Boseman hadn't seen what happened earlier tonight, he'd expect the worst from the encounter; and if he had, if he'd witnessed what happened to Maddie…

Hector walked backwards into the street, looking up at the wall of windows. Cupped his hands around his mouth. "Mr. Boseman? Mr. Boseman, please. Please. I just want to talk to you." No answer came. "I need your help."

Hector dropped his hands to his sides, acutely aware of the sleeping bodies all around him, the people he would wake if he kept shouting. He could wait, of course. He could find the landlord in the morning, the managing agent, ask for Boseman's number, ask that a message be passed along. There would be a way. There would.

But who could say that Boseman wouldn't quietly take himself out of town to avoid the conversation? When dawn broke, or not even. The trains run all night from Penn Station.

Hector charged up the steps to the building's wooden front door, hit it hard with his shoulder, felt it give slightly. There was a glass panel in the door – surely, he thought, barely recognizing himself as he thought it, surely he could break the glass if the lock didn't give way? Could reach inside, could turn the latch—

But the lock did give way, on his third attempt it sprang open, and he tumbled into the ground-floor entryway beside a wall of mailbox doors.

Had the man heard him, all the way up? He was awake; he'd turned the lights off. So probably he'd heard. Probably he knew Hector was inside his building now.

Just in case, Hector took the stairs quietly, holding tight to the banister so he could settle each step lightly, just his toes, just the front half of his foot. He took two stairs at a time, cut his time in half that way, but at the cost of feeling his legs burn from the effort by the time he reached the right floor. And for what, all this effort? He'd still heard every creak emitted by every wooden stair, however lightly he pressed down upon it. And when he reached the landing and oriented himself and found Boseman's door, what did he do but hammer on it with the side of his fist, once, twice, again; planning to stop at that, planning to give the man a chance to come and answer him, planning to speak to him reasonably, even apologetically, let bygones be bygones, no criticism at all for whatever he'd done in the past, just an honest plea for any help he might give now – but when the time came to stop, Hector found he couldn't, his fist kept pounding, pounding against the wooden door as if his hand were a fireman's axe and he could bash his way in by sheer force.

He couldn't. The locks up here were better than in the vestibule below, stronger, more recently fortified, the door was metal, and he could have continued hammering all night and all morning if the apartment's occupant had simply chosen not to respond.

But after a time Hector heard Boseman coming, drawn by the nonstop pounding. The locks turned, the door swung inward just a crack. The face within, pink and fleshy, straps of hair lying lank across the top, did not look bleary-eyed, as if only now awakened, or self-righteous, as if unfairly imposed upon at an ungodly hour. He didn't even look angry. He merely looked frightened, his eyes darting this way and that in tight orbits.

"You can't do this, you're making a racket," he said. "You need to leave, right now, I want you to go. You have no right—"

"My wife's been hurt, Mr. Boseman," Hector said, his voice low and urgent, "badly hurt, I'm sorry to bother you, but she's in the hospital, we live across the street, and I need to know—"

"What business is it of mine?" Boseman demanded. "At this hour of the morning, your wife, what business is it of mine?" But instead of indignation his words rang with desperation, as if he knew it was his business, knew that Hector knew, knew he couldn't escape admitting that he'd made the whole block's business his business and now was being called to account.

"If you saw anything," Hector insisted, "I need to know, what happened, who did it—"

"No," Boseman said, "I didn't see anything, anything, now go, go away," and he tried to shove the door closed. But Hector, to his astonishment, shoved back even harder, and the door leapt out of Boseman's hands, slamming loudly against the wall as the frightened man fell backwards. "Leave! Get out!" Hector stepped into the apartment, an L-shaped studio with two windows looking out over the street, facing Hector's building, facing at an indirect angle the window Hector himself had been looking out only minutes ago. He felt as if he were in the middle of an ocean, looking back the way he'd come, peering through the wrong end of a telescope. And the feeling only grew when he realized what sat on the windowsill beside Boseman's sturdy pair of binoculars: a tiny tripod, a small rectangular unit balanced on it, a red light softly glowing, a wire trailing down the wall to where a laptop rested, plugged into a wall outlet to charge.

A camera.

A video camera. Because of course a man like Boseman would want to keep a record of his little voyeuristic episodes. Hector looked at the man's face, took in his horrified expression. Oh, he'd seen something, all right, and more than seen it – he had footage of it.

The two men launched themselves at the laptop at the same instant, and Boseman, his legs less fatigued, got to it first, slammed it shut, cradled it to his chest. "No! No!"

But Hector wrenched it from him. He tried to open it. Before he could, Boseman's arm snaked around his neck from behind. He struggled to speak: "I just... God's sake... just want to..." But there was no point – he couldn't speak, and Boseman wasn't listening. Something terrible was powering the man's resistance, some fear far worse than being exposed as a Peeping Tom, and in this moment Hector found that something terrible was powering him too. Hector swung the laptop back over his head, felt it crack against the man's skull. Once, twice, again, like when he'd been hammering at the door. Again, he meant to stop at that. He meant to. But when the moment came, he didn't.

*

The laptop, miraculously, still ran.

Wiped clean of blood, shut and then opened again, Mr. Boseman's index finger softly pressed against the Touch ID key – and the screen sprang to life like in a showroom.

It wasn't hard to find the videos on the machine. They were all in one folder, neatly arranged by date.

Hector looked down to where Boseman lay on the carpet. He felt strangely removed from the sight, somehow distant from the whole thing. A cut on the man's scalp had bled, but not for long. He did not seem to be breathing. Of course it could be hard to tell sometimes. Maddie hadn't seemed to be breathing either. "Tell me," Hector said softly, "can you hear me too?" Outside, a block or two away, a car quietly went by. There were no other sounds in the night. "Can you hear what I'm saying?"

He didn't think Boseman could.

He sat down heavily on the throw rug by the window. All the files were there in front of him. Organized by date, by time, down to the minute, maybe the second. Easily sorted. Easily watched. He knew which one he had to click on. But didn't know if he could bear to watch it.

Opening a random file from earlier in the month, he saw a kitchen window in the building next to theirs, on a lower floor judging by the angle. As he watched, a woman walked into view, passing the window in her underwear. She was visible only from the waist down until she crouched to set out food for her dog. That was it. The woman passed, crouched, got up again. The dog ate.

Another random one: the roof of the brownstone near the corner, two women sunbathing on striped beach towels. That video went on for 14 minutes, 27 seconds. Hector only watched the first few seconds of it.

He tried a few more, stopping when he found one of his own window. There he was, facing away, in a sleeveless undershirt, working late at night.

He watched himself lug his camera into position and shoot a few pages for some catalogue – Rubin Heyman, it looked like, their line of tennis bracelets, laid out in a circle like the rays of the sun. Why would Boseman have filmed that? Well, maybe he filmed everything, indiscriminately. You never knew when someone would walk by in her underwear. But why would Boseman have kept it? Hector's back in an undershirt wasn't much to look at, he didn't think. Did Maddie show up in it somewhere before the end? But no, she didn't. He watched to the end. It was just Hector working, that's all.

He tried another: through the frosted glass of a bathroom window, a woman showered. You could only see her silhouette, but apparently that was enough for Boseman.

Hector closed the video.

Took a deep breath.

He found the clip by date and time. It was one of the very last.

His finger hung above the keyboard, not descending. He couldn't make himself do it. But he knew he had to, and here, now, because once he left this place, the laptop was getting destroyed, disposed of – what choice did he have? For a moment, when he first spotted the camera, he'd thought of Peter Donahue, imagined showing the video to Donahue and letting the police take it from there. Whatever it showed, it showed. Justice was their job, not his. But that was when he'd thought the night would end very differently. It obviously wasn't possible now.

He brought his finger down. The clip started to play.

He saw Maddie walk into and out of the frame. Dear God. He squeezed his own forearm hard, painfully hard, to keep his hands steady. And to keep him from stopping the video in midstream, halting it here, at the last instant of Maddie's life while it was still a life, and not a grim preview of death.

The video played on.

Maddie came back, and now someone was in the frame with her, then two people, two men. She looked confused, anxious. Who were these men, and what were they doing here?

Two men. Strangers. One looked like no one Hector knew: scruffy, bearded, like Keanu Reeves in *John Wick*.

The other one, add seven, eight years and forty pounds?

M. Boseman.

★

Peter Donahue sat down in the empty chair by the door. Hector looked up from where he was sitting, beside the bed. He folded the *Daily News*, set it aside.

"Reading to her?" Donahue wore no jacket today and there were circles of sweat beneath his arms.

"Yes," Hector said.

"Sports pages? Movie reviews?"

"The news."

"I'd think she'd rather hear something happier," Donahue said.

"I think she'd want to know what's going on in the world," Hector said.

The policeman got up, came over. Aimed a finger at the headline half-visible on the folded page: *MURDERED IN HIS.*

"One of your neighbors."

Hector shrugged. "I guess he was."

"You know him at all?"

"No," Hector said.

"Two attacks in one night, on the same block." Donahue shook his head. "This heat is making people crazy."

Hector nodded.

"Who do you think might have attacked your wife, Mr. Monroe? Did she have any enemies? Anyone with a grudge? Anyone you can think of?"

Hector felt tears come to him then. He hadn't cried in the dark hours of the morning, even as he'd watched the video. Watched it once only, he couldn't imagine enduring it a second time, but when he watched it, he watched it with dry eyes. Took it in stoically. Because it was for a different purpose now.

"No one," Hector said. "She taught second graders. That's what she did. Who would want to hurt a teacher?"

"And you? You're some sort of photographer?"

Hector wiped the back of one sleeve across his eyes. "Advertising. I shoot postcards, catalogues. Whatever people want."

"What do you think they were looking for? Whoever broke in. They searched the place pretty thoroughly."

"I don't know," Hector said. "Money, I guess."

"Was any missing?"

"We don't have any," Hector said. "Twenty, thirty dollars maybe, lying around. I mean, who keeps a lot of cash around?"

"Any reason someone might think you did?"

He shrugged, helplessly. But in the back of his mind a memory surfaced, a memory of his back in a sweaty undershirt, lugging a camera, shooting photos of Rubin Heyman's tennis bracelets. Gold bracelets, laid out like the rays of the sun.

Of course he never kept any merchandise at home – he returned it immediately, as soon as he'd photographed it. His customers wouldn't let him keep it overnight, nothing really valuable, and he wouldn't have wanted to. He'd bring it back to Forty-Seventh Street and get a signed delivery receipt and that was that. Wristwatches, earrings, whatever it was, he unloaded it the same day. But Boseman wouldn't have known that.

"I'm sorry, detective," Hector said, "I just don't know."

Donahue didn't stop asking questions, but Hector more or less stopped answering them. He remained polite, gave yesses and nos, nodded or shook his head when that seemed called for, but at a certain point it must've become clear he had no more information to give, and Donahue had let it go at that. The man was trying, Hector knew. But Hector also knew he'd get nowhere. He didn't have the laptop, which was now lying in pieces in three separate dumpsters on the Lower East Side. He hadn't seen the video.

When Donahue left, and a nurse had come and gone, Hector picked up the newspaper, unfolded it, sat back in his chair, and turned so his mouth wasn't so very far from Maddie's ear. She could hear, they said; hear and understand what was said to her. So let her hear and understand this: that one of the men who'd done this to her was gone.

He read in a soft, clear voice, pitched low. What he read was for Maddie and no one else.

Mitchell Boseman, 47, originally of Saratoga Springs, died between the hours of three and five a.m., the coroner's office reported.

And: *Mr. Boseman is survived by his mother, Joanna, and a brother, Stanley, 38.*

*

It was the time of year when even darkness didn't cool things down, not much, certainly not enough. The sun dropped behind the tops of New York's skyscrapers, and its light guttered and died, but it felt as if its rays kept right on beating against the pavement and everyone unfortunate enough to be walking on it. You felt the heat no matter how many buttons on your shirt you left unbuttoned, no matter whether you rolled your sleeves up or left them down. Women walked in backless dresses and the thinnest of spaghetti straps. It didn't matter. The heat enveloped you, like a river if you jumped off a bridge.

Which was why every bar in Bushwick was doing business hand over fist, pouring cold beers and ice water chasers that were drunk down as greedily as the shots they accompanied. It was why Stanley Boseman was here rather than sweating the night out at home. He sat drinking at a wooden picnic table in the fenced-in yard back of the Brooklyn Cart House, where beach umbrellas gave shade during the day and cast deeper shadows at night. Hector sat in the farthest corner, in the deepest shadow, his denim jacket carefully folded on the ground between his feet. He sat and he nursed a beer and he watched.

It was his ninth day watching Boseman's brother. Or was it his tenth? He'd lost track. The first night, after he'd hunted up Stanley's address, he'd taken the L train to Myrtle-Wyckoff, walked the half-mile to Cody Avenue, near all the cemeteries. He'd found the two-story wooden house and a doorway down the block to keep an eye on it from, and half an hour later he'd gotten his first close look at Stanley Boseman.

Aside from a full head of hair, he looked quite a lot like his brother.

And of course there was no mistaking him from the video.

It had been tempting, that first night, that first time Hector had followed the man to one of his local watering holes, to take things one step further, to follow him into the filthy men's room and leave him there bleeding on the floor, his throat or gut slashed open. For what he'd done to Maddie, he deserved no better. But Hector had held himself back. Not out of mercy – no, he had no capacity for mercy, not any longer, not where these men were concerned. Nor out of fear, though Heaven knows he was afraid. No, he'd simply made himself wait, and it was for one simple reason: because of the other man, the third man, the bearded man, John Wick. John Wick deserved the same as Boseman, if not worse. And how would Hector ever have any chance of finding him unless Boseman led Hector to him?

So one night of watching had turned into two, then three, then four. He'd sat by Maddie's side by day and watched by night. He'd kept a safe distance, or tried to; never let Stanley spot him watching. He'd barely slept, and lord knows he hadn't worked. He'd opened cans and scarfed down ravioli and Campbell's soup – whatever the nearest bodega had on its shelves – and ridden the subway back and forth to Brooklyn. It had been useless, pointless, fruitless. Boseman had walked alone, drunk alone, by all appearances gone to bed alone.

Until tonight.

Tonight he'd paid his first visit to the Brooklyn Cart House, and half an hour in, another man joined him at his table.

There was no mistaking this man from the video either.

Hector waited while they talked, while they drank. When John Wick finally got up to leave, Hector left a handful of bills beside his glass, picked up his denim jacket, and followed. Followed him into the sticky dark, followed him down Cooper Street to Rockaway, past darkened signs for auto repair and refrigeration repair, past chained-up lots just big enough to hold a pickup or two, past a shuttered day care where a pair of high-tops hung by their knotted laces from a power wire overhead. He turned down a tiny street, just a couple blocks long, wedged in between two avenues. From half a block back, Hector saw John Wick unlock the door of a little brick-front house and let himself in. When he got to the building, Hector saw it didn't have a number on it. The street itself didn't have a street sign that he could see.

But he'd have no trouble finding it again.

Hector returned to the Cart House, was disappointed but not surprised when he saw Stanley Boseman's table empty – it hadn't been a short walk. But then he heard a toilet flush, a doorknob turn, and he stepped away from the bathroom door a moment before Stanley stepped out.

Without turning, without moving even his head, Hector followed him in the mirror behind the bar, caught glimpses of Stanley's face, his plaid shirt, his sloping shoulders, reflected between the half-full bottles of Early Times and Beefeater and whatever no-name tequila they poured at midnight in Bushwick. He saw Stanley reach for the door, push it open, step outside.

Hector caught the door before it could swing shut.

When he turned the corner, Stanley was standing with one foot up against the wall of the building, his hands cupped at his chin, lighting an unfiltered cigarette. He shook out the match, dropped it to the ground. Hector nodded to him, said, "Got another light?" As Stanley patted his hips, Hector stepped close, reached inside his jacket.

"Sure," Stanley said, and it would be the last word he'd ever speak.

*

Boseman, 38, was found stabbed to death shortly after midnight outside the Brooklyn establishment better known to local patrons as Corey's...

Hector lowered the newspaper, stared closely at Maddie's face. Had he only imagined it? Or had her eyelid really fluttered just then? His breath caught. He watched for any further sign, any hint of movement. But there was nothing, just the regular hum of the machinery, the blip of the monitor as the pattern rose and fell. Some of her bruises had started to fade. One of the bandages across her cheek had been removed. But she still lay silent and unmoving, less like someone asleep than like, like— *Like a photograph*, he thought. *Still forever.*

Would it be forever? Or would she heal, would she come back to him? Maybe when she knew it was safe. When she knew the men who'd hurt her were gone, all three of them. That they couldn't hurt her or anyone else again.

It was too much to hope, he knew it was. But that was the thing about hope: it always lay just out of reach. Hector still had hope, a fragile thread of hope. It wasn't much. But it was everything.

He bent low to kiss her forehead, dropped the newspaper in the wastebasket, and walked briskly out, making his way to the street. He stood at a bus shelter but raised his arm as well, to catch any taxi that might pass on its way uptown. Whichever came first would do.

Some time later, two knuckles rapped at the doorway to Maddie's room and the rest of Donahue followed them in. "Mr. Monroe—"

He found the bedside chair empty. It was the first time since this all began that he had.

He stood before the injured woman, looking down at her, wondering how much she really could perceive of what went on around her. Did she know her husband had been here every day, hours upon hours? Uncommonly devoted, if you asked him. Talking to her, reading to her.

He spotted the newspaper in the wastebasket, fished it out. He looked at the page it was folded to. The story of the Bushwick bar murder. Hardly seemed like the sort of thing you'd read to your injured wife.

It only made sense, really, if you noticed the dead man's name.

He tucked the paper inside his coat pocket and headed downstairs.

*

Jeremy Haffner sipped at the drink he'd poured himself and rubbed his wrists where the cuffs had pinched them. Bad enough that his best friend had gotten himself stabbed on the street, Jesus God, but then the police had liked *him* for it and dragged him in for an hour's questioning and two hours sitting around the station house, all because he was the last one seen talking to him at Corey's. Holy Christ. What an afternoon.

So when the knock came at the door, the last thing Jeremy wanted to hear was the first word he heard: "Police, Mr. Haffner. Please open up."

"Haven't you had enough?" he said, but not loud enough to be heard. He got up, took himself to the door, peered out through the peephole. The man outside had a jacket on, and when he heard Jeremy at the door, he fished a business card out of the jacket pocket, held it up to the hole: *Peter Donahue*, it said. *NYPD*.

Jeremy unlocked the locks.

"Why should I spend one more minute talking to cops today?" he said.

"Would you rather wind up in the morgue?"

"What're you talking about?"

"We have reason to believe the man who killed your friend Boseman has plans to come after you next." He looked around Jeremy to the empty apartment behind him. "Can we discuss this inside?"

Jeremy let him in.

"You know Boseman's brother was killed, too, right?"

"Yeah," Jeremy said. "Beat to death."

"We think the same man was responsible for both. And it's because of a crime all three of you participated in—"

"Hold it! Hold it. I didn't participate in anything."

"—an assault that took place on East Tenth Street the night of August eleventh. A brutal assault that nearly killed a young woman, who's now in a coma." It wasn't like a cop to show any emotion, but this one's voice caught as he spoke. "Why'd you do it, anyway? Just looking for something to steal?"

"I told you, I didn't do anything."

"You were caught on video, Mr. Haffner. No use denying it."

"What video?"

"The brother."

"Jesus," Jeremy said and threw up his hands. "The old pervert. Couldn't help himself, could he."

"Why did you go in there?" the cop asked, quietly. "Did you think the husband kept jewelry around the house?"

"You can see for yourself," Jeremy said, "if you've got Mitch's videos. The guy had a ton of the stuff, gold bracelets, rings, all sorts of shit." He caught himself, tried to backpedal. "Not that I went in. I just saw the videos."

But the cop was already reaching into his jacket. For a Miranda card, Jeremy figured, and another pair of cuffs, and he had his own big mouth to blame. "I swear, I didn't—"

What came out wasn't a pair of cuffs, though. It was a handgun, a small automatic. A loaner, from Rubin Heyman.

"You broke her *fingers*," the man said. "You. You did it. You took them and broke them, one by one. Because she couldn't tell you where the jewelry was."

Jeremy was backing up, his hands raised. "What the hell is this? What sort of cop are you?"

Another knock came at the door then, briskly rapping three times. And another voice, deeper, older: "Mr. Haffner? NYPD, sir. Please open up."

Peter Donahue's voice.

"Go away!" The gun trembled in Hector's hand.

From the other side of the door: "Hector, don't do this."

"What the hell is going on?" Jeremy shouted.

"Hector," Donahue's voice came, "if this guy had anything to do with it, he's going to jail for a long time." The knob rattled, and then the door shook as Donahue rammed his shoulder against it. "A *long* time. That's enough."

Hector's voice was a whisper. "For you," he said.

*

Sleep! sleep! beauty bright,
Dreaming o'er the joys of night;
When thy little heart doth wake,
Then the dreadful night shall break.

*

Visiting hours were over, but they made an exception.

Hector stood beside Maddie's bed, his hands clasped at the small of his back. He didn't have a newspaper tonight, it was too soon – but he spoke as if he was reading from one.

Earlier tonight, in the Bushwick section of Brooklyn, Jeremy Haffner, known criminal associate of Stanley and Mitchell Boseman, was executed for his part in the August 11th assault on an innocent woman in her home.

Hector looked at her, covered lightly with the crisp white hospital sheet, the room's fluorescent lights still shining brightly on her closed eyes.

All three men who participated in this savage attack have now been identified and—

He glanced over to where Donahue stood in the doorway, arms folded over his chest.

—and permanently prevented from endangering any innocent ever again.

He bent at the knees, leaned forward, gently kissed her hand. Her right hand.

In the doorway, he saw Donahue glance meaningfully at his wristwatch.

"I'm sorry, Maddie," he whispered. "I've done everything I could."

"S'all right," she murmured, through her wired jaw, her bandaged throat. Softly, so softly he could barely hear the words. "… it's all right."

He stared. Her eyes were still shut, her lips slightly apart. Had he imagined it?

He looked back at Donahue in the doorway, who was curling his fingers toward himself: *come along.*

Donahue hadn't heard.

"She spoke! She said something!"

"That's wonderful," Donahue said. "We'll let the doctors know."

"I—I—"

"I said you could have one more visit. Now you've had it."

"Just another minute," Hector said. Donahue shook his head.

Hector saw Maddie's hand squeeze at the air, reach for his, and he ached to take it. "I love you, Maddie. I love you so much—"

Her voice was soft and sluggish. "… stay?"

Donahue raised the arm with the watch on it and the dial loomed as if counting off not hours and minutes but years.

"I've got to go somewhere now," Hector said.

Maddie was trying to speak again, but nothing was coming out.

"Shh," he said. "Rest. You've been through so much."

She heard his steps, heading away. After a moment, with great effort, she opened her eyes. She winced as the light stung them, the first light she'd seen in weeks. *Where was he?* There – in the doorway. Another man had one hand on his arm, the other between his shoulder blades, guiding him out. Light glinted off the metal links hanging between Hector's clasped hands.

Inside her head, the words came out clearly: *What have you done, Hector? What have you done?* But the nurse, when she came, only heard, "Hector…" and smiled down at her warmly.

"Oh, I'm sure he'll be back in the morning, love," the nurse assured her. "He'd do anything for you, that husband of yours." She saw the tears welling in Maddie's eyes. "Nothing to cry about, now is there? Everything's better now. Everything's going to be just fine again…"

THE INVITATION

SUSI HOLLIDAY

The phone rings. It's far too early for a call, but it's my own stupid fault for forgetting to turn the ringer to silent before I passed out on top of the sheets. One of those nights where 'popping out for a quick drink' ended as the bar emptied and the sky turned from full-of-promise indigo to an insipid violet dawn. I catch my reflection in the mirror on the nightstand, then flip it down quickly so I can pretend I still look like me at the start of the night out, instead of the end.

I think about not answering, but we all know that early morning calls, or those middle-of-the-night ones, are the moments in time that come back to haunt you eventually. The name flashes up with a square section of a face, cropped to show ruby-red lips, curled into a sneer. I swipe up to answer.

"Eloise," I say, my voice cracking with dehydration and lack of sleep. "Who died?"

Her cackle makes my ear hurt. I tap to put her on speaker.

"Good morning, my little cherub," she says. "Stand down. This is the other kind of distress call."

I lean back into the pillows. They smell of last night's perfume mixed with stale alcohol and bad breath. Thankfully, I am alone. I breathe out slowly, closing my eyes. Something inside my head is banging quite insistently behind my left eye.

Eloise continues. "I'll assume from your silence that you are not feeling too bright on this fine day?" A pause. "I'll get on with it, shall I?"

I nod. She can't see me, but she puffs out a breath of impatience at my lack of communication. I'm really not in the mood for chit-chat and would like her to get to the point.

"I assume you haven't checked your email today, Charlene?"

I frown, squinting at the time on the phone display. I think I left my contact lenses in, which would help explain the pain in my eyes and my head. Nothing to do with the champagne, or the martini chasers. Or the sambuca shots while I waited for the Uber to arrive.

"It's not even seven, Eloise. I went to bed less than an hour ago."

She laughs again, that same scratchy cackle. "Check it now, cherub. I'll wait."

Sighing now, I minimise the call screen and open up the email app, expecting some junk. Some work stuff. Thinking I'll need to scroll, but there's no need. It's there, right at the top.

"Oh," I say. My headache spreads across the back of the other eye. "Fuck."

"Absolutely that," she says. "Get showered. I'll meet you at Daley's in thirty."

*

Daley's is our go-to hangover hangout. It's an equidistant ten minutes between mine and Eloise's flats. It serves perfect bacon sandwiches, dripping with butter, expertly brewed builders' tea in heavy white mugs, and the best Bloody Marys in the whole of London. I order all of that. Eloise surprises me with her choice of black coffee only.

"I need a clear head for this." She eyes my glass, then my face. "I'll allow you one of those, as I think hair of the dog is the only thing that will fix you right now."

"So," I say, downing the Bloody Mary. It hits hard and fast.

"So," she replies, phone in hand. She opens the email and lays it on the table between us. "What are we going to do about this?"

I read it quickly as soon as she told me about it. I read it again after I ended the call. I read it another time, right after my tepid shower. I read it again now, with Eloise running a pointy, satsuma-coloured nail down the side of her phone as she scrolls to the bottom.

"Lucinda Barkley requests the pleasure of your company at her pre-wedding supper."

I look up. "Did we get an invite to the actual wedding? I'm pretty sure I would remember that…"

Eloise scrolls further. Her shiny orange nail looks like a deformed and dangerous M&M. "You didn't read the second page, I assume."

I'm thrown for a second, sure that I'd scrolled to the bottom. But then again, my phone is being a bit funny at the moment, cutting things off. Shutting itself down. Temperamental, like myself.

"The ceremony itself will be an intimate affair, with only the bride, groom, and witnesses. We are keen to preserve this special moment to reflect the love that we share with ourselves, and have made the decision not to waste time on tacky, over-priced frivolities. However, we do of course want to celebrate the occasion with our dear friends, hence the pre-wedding supper that we very much hope you will attend. Please note that we do not require gifts, your presence there will be the only gift we need."

Eloise turns her fingers and thumb into a gun and shoots herself in her open mouth, jerking her head back sharply. She then leans forward and holds the fingers against her tongue, making a vomit gesture. It's overkill, but I laugh. It's actually spot on, given the circumstances.

I take a bite of my bacon sandwich, letting the butter run down my chin. Neither of us has seen Lucinda Barkley for a very long time. Neither of us would consider ourselves a 'dear friend'. Especially after what happened the last time we were all together.

"Well," I say, taking a wad of thin serviettes from a silver container and wiping my chin. "Are we going?"

Eloise cackles again, eyes my empty glass. "I think I'll join you in another."

*

Four days later, we're dressed up to the nines and standing on the doorstep of Lucinda Barkley's mansion. I know – *mansion* is such a grotesque word, but it can't be described as anything else. Dark stone, etched glass, turrets. Plus grounds. A lot of grounds. Ten acres. Something like that. Also, when I say it's *Lucinda's* mansion, it really is hers – not her parents. They both died when she was a kid and she was brought up by the staff. It sounds completely ridiculous that we even know someone like that, but both me and Eloise went to The Dorlington School for Girls because our parents were rich enough to send us there – but you know, wealth is relative.

"Can you believe it's been ten years since Gregory…" Eloise whispers as we wait on the doorstep. Even she doesn't want to finish that sentence. She raises her hand to pull on the old-fashioned bell again, but I reach up and grab her wrist. There's a silhouette of a figure behind the smoked glass.

The door is opened by a woman dressed in the traditional black-dress-white-apron of a housekeeper. The woman is young, maybe not much older than us, but her face is too serious and it makes her look older.

"Do you have your invitations?"

Her face remains impassive as we both pull out our phones and show the invitations on the screens. We've already had a discussion about why we've been emailed rather than sent proper invites in the post, and come to the conclusion that Lucinda simply did not have our postal addresses. We worked out that she has found us on social media and done a bit of digging to get to our email addresses which, in this day and age, is not too difficult. She probably hired someone to do it. Like I said before, it's not as if we were still in touch – and the email addresses that Eloise and I had been using ten years ago were both obsolete. We'd chosen to cut contact with a lot of people, after what happened. It seemed the easiest way for us to move on.

The woman opens the door wider and ushers us inside. I glance around at the hallway, the tiled floor, the half wood-panelled walls with a cloying floral wallpaper above it. My eyes go upwards to the chandelier, then back down to the back of the woman's head as she walks purposely in front of us, expecting us to follow. The hallway is just as it was last time we were here. Only the servant is new.

She leads us past the door that I know opens on to the ballroom. The door is closed, and I have a feeling it's not a room that is used any more. It's not as if there aren't other rooms that Lucinda can use for her entertaining. If I recall correctly, there's another huge room at the back. I'd assumed that's where tonight's gathering would be held, and I'm surprised when the woman leads us down another corridor around to the left.

Eloise turns to me, raising an eyebrow. I shrug. I'm sure that all the rooms down this way are much smaller – but perhaps the pre-wedding dinner is an intimate affair too – but surely bigger than the wedding, or why not just invite us there? I'm confused now, by the invite. I'd told Eloise that morning in Daley's that we should just ignore it. We've moved on. We need to stay moved on. But she'd begged. Said she was curious.

Said maybe it would help because despite all we've both said about it being in the past, Eloise can't stop thinking about it. About Gregory.

Well, *newsflash…* neither can I.

The woman opens the door at the end of the corridor, standing aside to let us through, and I feel my heart start to thump so hard I'm sure it must be visible through the soft lace. I swallow, and it feels like someone has stitched up my throat, leaving only the tiniest space for air to pass through. I rub my hands on my sides, leaving sweaty fingerprints on the delicate fabric of my dress. I feel Eloise's hand on the small of my back, her voice close to my ear.

"We'll stay for ten minutes, then we're gone. OK?"

She slides around me and walks into the room first. I stay close to her, my eyes flitting around quickly at the room that also seems to have remained exactly the same as before. We're in the library. Wall-to-wall dark oak shelves filled with row upon row of leather-bound classics, first editions, special editions. The contents of this room alone must be worth a small fortune. I gasp, quickly covering my mouth, when I see the one new addition to the décor.

Above the roaring fire, a large gilt-edged frame with an incredibly life-like oil painting staring down at us. A familiar smirk on a perfect face. I cough gently, trying to loosen that tight feeling. I need to get more air into my lungs before I pass out.

"Charlene! Eloise!" Lucinda walks towards us, arms outstretched. Her hair cascades over her bare shoulders in perfect waves, the red tones flickering with the firelight, giving the illusion that her whole head is ablaze. She is dressed in a gauzy pale pink dress that billows as she walks.

Eloise squeezes my hand then steps into her embrace. "Bloody hell, Lucinda," she says. "You look incredible."

"Always good to look after one's selves as we get older," Lucinda says with a tight smile, pulling away and reaching out for me.

I let her draw me in, but she barely touches me. Her thin arms encircle me, but the contact is barely there. She smells of something heavy and cloying and incredibly expensive. It attaches to my skin, trapping me in its suffocating scent. "It's good to see you," I mutter. But she has already drawn herself away, and is now standing at the fireplace, glass of champagne in hand.

"Isn't it just the perfect likeness?"

We all look up at the painting and murmur our assent. It is so unbelievably like Gregory, that I expect the smirk to turn to a full-on leer and a wink – and for him to climb right out into the room beside us.

Lucinda smiles. "Come on, ladies, get yourselves a drink – we've got a lot planned for this evening!"

Eloise hands me a glass of champagne with one hand, and with the other she pinches me hard on the back of my arm. I wince, but it works, I'm back in the room, and that's when I realise that there are several others there too. There are women sitting on the various small sofas and chairs around the fire, sipping drinks and chattering quietly. Some of them I vaguely recognise. Others, not at all.

Eloise knocks back the drink and then reaches to a small silver side-table to pick up another. "Thought I'd lost you there, cherub. Earth to Charlene!" She giggles.

I knock back my own drink and pick up another, taking a sip. Fucking hell. If I'm going to have to stay here for a while, I might as well get pissed on the free booze.

✶

A few glasses of champagne in, and I'm starting to relax. After the drinks in the library, we were taken into an adjoining dining room which was not somewhere I'd been before. It has a nice feel to it, a bit less ostentatious than the other parts of the house, and I wonder if maybe Lucinda has modernised some of this place after all. There's a long table in a pale, waxed beech, over-stuffed chairs in a simple burnt-orange velvet to match the floor-length curtains. The lighting is via an array of small, hanging moulded glass-encased bulbs at different heights above the table, giving an effect of twinkling stars. She's seated me and Eloise at opposite ends of the table, but we've refused to let it unsettle us. Once I'd finally recognised Millie, one of the women who'd been seated next to me, I remembered that she'd been quite a laugh at that party here ten years ago, but she was much quieter now. Withdrawn. At one point Lucinda had tapped her silver spoon against her champagne flute to get our attention, and Millie had visibly jumped in her seat. But then it's no surprise, not really. We were all affected by what happened that night, and I'm quite sure that none of us really wants to be back here.

"Ladies, ladies," Lucinda says, tapping her spoon on her glass again. I can feel Millie's energy. I can smell her sweat. Again, I wonder, why on earth Lucinda is putting us through all this. Why she is putting herself through it.

Her eyes bore into me as she continues to speak, as if sensing my thoughts.

"You're probably all wondering why you're here… given that I haven't spoken to any of you in some time."

Lucinda grins, and it looks manic. A Cheshire Cat madness mixed with champagne and God-knows-what kind of prescription drugs she exists on. She was always one of those nervy girls who lived on anti-depressants, Valium, and sleeping pills – all prescribed by the family doctor ever since she was a little girl and the terrible tragedy of losing her parents so young. I very much doubt that she's living pharmaceutical-free as a thirtysomething adult. To be fair, I'd probably do the same if I had the means, but alcohol and coke are cheaper and I don't have a doctor who hands out pills like sweets. I down the rest of my wine and I've barely put the glass back on the table before it's been refilled by one of the silent-footed servants that seem to ghost in and out of the room.

I stare at Eloise for a moment until she senses me and turns. She raises an eyebrow, gives me a small eye roll and a smirk. She's happily embracing Lucinda's drama, but the longer it goes on, the more uneasy it makes me feel.

The grinning Lucinda continues. "You may have all realised that the last time we were all together in one room, was ten years ago." She lowers her eyes and her face falls. "The night my beloved Gregory was taken from me."

I shift uncomfortably in my seat. I'd always found it slightly odd – Lucinda and Gregory's relationship. For a start, he was just so much older than her. Not that the age difference in itself was an issue. More that he was just so different to her. Of course we all knew it was daddy issues, with Lucinda having lost hers so young. But it was disturbing for the rest of us, barely into our twenties, to have this man who was practically a *pensioner* in our midst. He was very much a man of his time – casual racism and misogyny was commonplace. He treated Lucinda like shit – only she couldn't see it. None of us really knew what Gregory was after. He had his own money and wanted for nothing. It just seemed that he had a thing for younger women.

Much younger women.

I still remember vividly what happened that night at the party. But I'm interested to hear Lucinda's take on it. And to hear why she's decided to bring it up now. Isn't this meant to be her pre-wedding dinner? To another man? A man she hasn't even mentioned so far?

Suddenly starving, I pick up my bread roll and rip it open.

"Charlene!" Lucinda's voice is so high-pitched that I'm sure a pack of neighbourhood cats must be wondering what's going on. I drop the roll, and feel my cheeks grow hot. She smiles at me sweetly. "If you don't mind waiting while I finish my speech."

I feel Eloise's eyes on me from the other end of the table, but I refuse to look for fear that I will burst out laughing from the embarrassment and shock. Millie lays a hand on my knee underneath the table, pats it gently.

"As I was saying," Lucinda continues. Everyone is gazing at her now, transfixed. "It's the tenth anniversary of Gregory's untimely death. And while I am happy to be marrying Roger, I feel that I must mark the occasion first – with all who were there. As you know, I was supposed to marry Gregory... until his life was cruelly cut short by what the police and then the coroner ruled a tragic accident." She pauses to lift a napkin and fan herself with it gently, before dabbing the corners of her eyes.

We're all still glued to the show. Lucinda was always very good at drama. I take the opportunity to try and catch Eloise's eye, but she's turned away – facing the hostess – and I'm slightly aggrieved that she is sucked in like everyone else. If we were anywhere else, with anyone else, Eloise would have said something by now to disrupt proceedings. Her acquiescence makes me uneasy.

Lucinda lays her napkin back on the table. "It has come to light – via means that I will not disclose just yet – that Gregory was, in fact, murdered."

There is a collective intake of breath, followed by a flurry of frantic muttering.

"Hush now," Lucinda says. "I will explain everything to you in due course. But first..." She lifts a small glass of amber liquid that has been placed next to her place setting. "We shall toast Gregory, and calm our beating hearts."

It's testament to her staff that I hadn't even noticed the glasses being brought to us. We all lift our drinks, and Lucinda says, "To Gregory," and downs her drink in one. We all follow suit. I can't help but grimace. Some kind of sherry, I think, but stronger.

Lucinda grins. "And now, everyone... we eat. *Bon appetite!*"

The sounds of muttering and murmuring around the table are replaced with the chink of metal spoons against china soup bowls. I butter my bread and dip it into the smooth, green soup and take a bite. Broccoli and stilton, with just the right amount of cream. Perfectly seasoned too. Lucinda always did lay on a good spread and I'm quite excited about the main course. A beef dish, I imagine. And a fruity dessert. I'm on my last spoonful of soup, scraping it off the bottom of the bowl, when I remember what she's just said about Gregory.

Murdered. It's so far-fetched. None of us knows anyone who has been murdered. We don't mix in those circles. Even where I live now, in a much less salubrious location than this, I don't actually *know* anyone who's been murdered. Although, thinking about it, Gregory was a disgusting lecherous old man and if someone decided to put a stop to that, well... But from what I remember, he fell down the stairs and hit his head. He tripped on a rug. There was a rug right there, with curling edges. The case, as the police say in TV dramas, was absolutely cut and dried. It was nothing more than a tragic accident.

I look down the table again at Eloise, trying to get her to look at me, but she won't. She's engrossed in something that the woman next to her is saying. It's as if she's forgotten I was here. I have a flashback to that night, ten years ago. Not in this room, but another one in the house. Watching her, then – just like she is now. Engrossed, attentive. I hadn't known her then. We'd bonded afterwards, when she'd seen how shocked I was at the state of Gregory's body at the bottom of the stairs. We'd both been upstairs when it happened – I'd been to the bathroom and I'm not sure where Eloise had been – but earlier on, we'd both fallen foul of Gregory's advances. Eloise had been all for telling Lucinda, but I had stopped her. Saying it wasn't our business. I regret that now. Perhaps if one of us had said something, then he wouldn't have pushed it one step further with the red-haired girl that Eloise was in intense conversation with at the bottom of the table.

It strikes me now that maybe Lucinda knows more about what happened in the upstairs sitting room than she is letting on. That maybe it's no accident that Eloise and the redhead have been placed next to each other. Because I don't think Lucinda realised that I was there too. I glance around at the women at the table – more and more of their faces coming back to me. We were all there. We all knew what Gregory had done to the redhead. And it shames me that I can't even remember her name – some parts of the night, it seems, have dislodged themselves from my memory.

The main courses are placed in front of us silently. Huge slabs of beef, wrapped carefully in perfect pastry. Bright green beans, small pots of creamed potato. We each have a small gravy jug on the edge of our plates. It smells incredible. I pick up my knife and fork, but then lay them down as it becomes apparent that Lucinda intends to speak again.

"Before you start," she says, "I just want to make one thing very clear. Gregory was murdered by someone in this very room. And none of you will be leaving until I find out the truth."

I turn to Millie. Her mouth has dropped open. I glance up and down the table, and see the same expressions on everyone's face. Well, almost everyone. Both Eloise and her red-haired friend don't look shocked at all.

"You may enjoy your main meals now," Lucinda continues, "but bear in mind that this may be the last food that touches your lips."

"Now hang on," I say, standing up and rattling the cutlery as I knock against the table. "What the fuck are you playing at, Lucinda? Are we part of some messed-up murder mystery game, where you've decided to toss in the name of your dead lover for kicks? You always were a bloody maniac."

Eloise seems to notice me at last. "Sit down, cherub," she says. "Let's all just calm it a bit."

Everyone else is looking uncomfortable, but no one seems to have any clue as to what to do. All I know is, I don't want to stay here any longer. As tempting as that boeuf en croûte might be. I throw my napkin on the table and start walking towards the door.

"I'm leaving."

Lucinda laughs. "I don't recommend that, darling. The only way you're going to make it home tonight is if you're one of the lucky ones who receives the antidote."

I stop walking. "What the hell are you on about now? Antidote to what?"

Eloise and the redhead are looking as uneasy as everyone else, now. Something has shifted. I don't know what kind of game this is, but I don't want to be part of it.

Lucinda takes a sip of her water. "I know that one of you was responsible for Gregory's death. I also know that you've kept this secret for ten years, so there is very little chance of you giving it up now. Not without an incentive, at least." She looks at us all, in turn, taking in everyone's pale, blank expressions. "The soup that you all so readily enjoyed was poisoned. You're all going to die in approximately ten minutes. Unless" – she places her clutch bag on the table and removes a small brown vial with a rubber dropper lid – "the murderer makes a full confession. In which case, I will allow you all to live. The murderer, of course, will be reported to the police and justice will be served. At last."

"You're insane," Eloise says, standing up. "And this is bullshit." She walks around to join me at the other side of the table, the redhead in tow. "You remember Sylvie, don't you?"

I nod, confused. But glad that she's back with me at last. I look over at Millie, who is crying gently into her napkin.

"You always were a piece of work," I say to Lucinda. "But you've gone too far this time."

Lucinda smiles and holds up the vial. "There's enough antidote in here for everyone. Just one drop on the tongue and you'll be completely fine…

I'll be happy to start administering it as soon as the murderer makes their full confession, right here, to all of us."

"You do realise what an absolute piece of shit Gregory was, don't you?" Eloise says. "He tried it on with all of us that night. He went way too far with Sylvie. If he hadn't had his accident, we'd all have been reporting him to the police."

Lucinda's smile wavers slightly. "You're lying. He was a kind, gentle man. Respectful. He would never do anything untoward..."

The arguing starts then. All the women who'd been silent before become ruffled. Accusations. Screaming. Crying. Lucinda looks doubtful, occasionally, in the face of the flurry of accusations, but she keeps dragging her smile back on – a mask that she can't remove.

I glance up at the clock. Just supposing what she said was true, we only have about five minutes left. "Ladies..." I say, tapping a knife against a wine glass. "Listen. I know it sounds ridiculous, the whole *poison* thing... I mean, where are we? A golden age crime novel? No – of course we aren't. But equally, Lucinda has clearly not dealt with her grief and it is possible that maybe, just maybe, there is something that we have all consumed that could make us ill."

Another flurry of shouts and arguing. Eloise flashes me a *What are you doing?* look.

"I think the best thing to do is to back each other up," I say, stepping forward towards Lucinda.

I look her in the eye.

"It was me," I say. "I moved that rug to the top of the stairs, and as he passed by I called out, giving him a fright and he lost his footing. I only wanted him to trip and be embarrassed about it. I didn't expect him to fall down the stairs. It was an accident. I'm sorry."

Lucinda nods. "Open your mouth."

I do, and she drops the bitter liquid on my tongue, then I walk past her and stand at the edge of the room, waiting.

Eloise goes next. "I did it," she says. "I got the rug from the other hallway and put it there, then I hid in the room next to the top of the stairs, and as he passed by, I pushed him. It was no accident. I'm not sorry."

Lucinda drops the liquid on her tongue, and she comes around to join me.

Sylvie smiles, picking up on our plan. "No," she says. "It was me. He put his hand up my skirt and grabbed me. I waited until he was on his way back downstairs and I kicked him in the back. Then I found the rug in the bedroom and placed it so it looked like he'd tripped. It wasn't an accident, but I shouldn't have done it."

Lucinda drops the liquid on her tongue, and she comes to join us.

The three of us smile at one another, pleased. I nod towards the others. We all need to do it, or else it won't work. But the others seem reluctant.

"Millie?" I say. "Do you want to go next?"

Millie shakes her head. "I'm sorry," she says. She's crying again. She walks up to Lucinda. "Please," she says. "I didn't do it. And I can't go along with their game because I know what happened. What *really* happened." She looks over at me, sadness in her eyes. "I'm sorry, Charlene. I do like you, and I don't blame you… but I don't want to die tonight."

"Well," Lucinda says, still holding the vial in one hand, the dropper in the other. "Do share."

Millie looks towards me, Eloise, and Sylvie, then she drops her eyes to the floor. "It was all three of them. I was in the small bedroom at the back – I needed a rest, away from all the noise of the party. I heard the three of them together, talking about Gregory." She looks Lucinda in the eye. "I hate to say this, but he *was* a bit of a pest. None of us felt comfortable around him, Lucinda. But none of us wanted him dead." She points at the three of us. "I think they just wanted to teach him a lesson."

"For God's sake, Millie!" The clock says we have two minutes left. The way things are going, Lucinda is going to be the murderer here, unless she hurries up with the antidote. I'm still pretty sure it's bullshit, and that the clock will chime and we'll all still be here. But with Lucinda in this state, it's best to play along.

Lucinda puts the dropper back into the bottle and twists it shut.

"Thank you, Millie. For your honesty." She sits down and gestures for everyone else to do the same. There is a strange calm in the room. I think everyone knows that only one truth has been spoken.

I feel my throat constrict, and I suck in a deep breath. Panic attack, I think. From the shock. It's difficult to breathe. I glance around at Eloise and Sylvie, who are both clutching their throats, their eyes full of fear.

Lucinda looks at each of us in turn. "I knew you wouldn't be able to resist showing off. Trying to be clever. After all, you've got away with it for ten years…"

It's hard to hear her now. Her voice seems to be coming from very far away.

"I know that the three of you did it together. I received a letter a few weeks ago. Someone who saw it all. Someone who could no longer live with their guilt of hiding the truth. Thank you, Millie. For the letter. And for tonight. You've made this all very easy." Her eyes scan the room taking in all the silent, shocked faces. "The rest of you will be *handsomely* compensated, of course. For the inconvenience and unfortunate trauma that tonight has inevitably brought."

I'm the first one to fall. I hit my head on the edge of the table, but I barely feel a thing. I lie on the carpet, and feel a deep burning sensation in my gullet. The poison was in the vial, of course. Something potent, delivered in one small drop. To the guilty, upon their confessions.

There was nothing at all wrong with the soup – in fact, it was exquisite.

THE LONG ROAD DOWN

BILL PRONZINI

It was after midnight by the time I finished doing everything that had to be done in the house and the sheltered driveway. I still felt a little sick, my nerves raw-edged, but I was holding up all right. This part of it had been bad; the rest would be just as bad if not worse.

I made sure the street was empty before I pulled the Ford out of the driveway. But I hadn't gone more than a block when headlights flashed on behind me. My stomach jumped. I turned at the next corner, then turned again toward downtown. The headlights stayed behind me, like pale yellow lasers tracking me through the rolling wisps of fog.

Coincidence, that's all it was. Not a cop back there, just a citizen who happened to leave at the same time I did. Nobody could know what I'd done, what I was carrying in the trunk. Just the same, my hands were slick on the wheel and I couldn't keep from glancing up into the rearview mirror. Paranoid fear, guilt. Maybe, but I had to be absolutely sure I wasn't being followed before I headed up into the hills.

Susan, Susan...

No, dammit. Don't think about her, don't think about what happened. Don't think about anything. Just drive. Just get this part of it over and done with.

When I neared Main Street the other car quit trailing me, turned into a 7-Eleven parking lot. See? I told myself. Nothing to worry about.

I took the north road out of town, even though the hills were due east. Somewhat longer route, going this way, but less chance of police patrols. Despite the urgency I made myself drive at a steady thirty. Every time the speedometer edged above that mark, my foot eased up on the accelerator. Being extra careful, not taking any chances.

No traffic on my side until I'd gone about a mile. Then another car came barreling up behind me, something big like an SUV going nearly twice as fast. The driver flicked his lights, then switched them on high and left them there. It put another twist on my nerves. There was a double yellow line along this section of road so he couldn't pass me legally. I would have pulled over but the verge was too narrow here.

I increased my speed to forty. Still wasn't enough to suit the idiot in the other car. He began blowing his horn and pulled up even closer, tailgating, those mirror-reflected high beams jabbing into my eyes like splinters. Drunk, stupid! Pass me, damn you. Never mind the double yellow line, there's nobody coming—

He did. Engine roaring, tires squealing, horn blaring. Red taillights disappeared fast into the swirls of mist ahead.

I let out a shaky breath, sleeved a band of sweat off my forehead. Stay calm, stay calm. Still a long way to the Peterson construction site, more than a dozen miles. The thought of what I'd have to do up there was sharp, ugly.

The Corona Road turnoff appeared ahead. I took it. No cars there, either, just my headlight beams puncturing the clotted dark. One mile, two, past mistily lighted industrial parks and housing tracts. The fog thinned after another mile and I could make out the contours of the hills that bounded the eastern edge of the valley.

The locals called them mountains, but they were just a spine of tallish foothills spotted with oak and madrone, the highest of them eleven hundred feet. Scattered ranches and homes on large parcels at the lower levels. Farther up, where the terrain steepened, folds between rounded hummocks cut deep to form hollows choked with trees and brush, and the properties were fewer and more widely scattered.

The Peterson parcel was more than two-thirds of the way up, just below the stretches of pine woods that ran along the higher elevations – one of the choicest homesite locations. Peterson was rich, had made his pile in computer technology. His seventy-two acres had cost him five million; the home, wine cellar, outbuildings, terrace, pool, and tennis courts he was having built would cost another five. Construction had been going on for three months now, with a crew of twelve under my supervision, and it would be another four months before the work was done.

The excavation for the wine cellar was all I cared about now. I could see it in my mind as I drove: forty by sixty feet, cut deep into the shale rock of the hillside; all the digging finished, the walls and ceiling shored and framed with plywood. The floor slab hadn't been poured yet, the hard-packed dirt overlaid with loose plywood sheets...

I was almost to Old Adobe, the road that ran along the base of the hills, but I had the funny sensation that they didn't seem to be getting any closer, seemed instead to be moving farther away. Optical illusion – the fog, the light-spattered dark.

Old Adobe Road, finally. Empty of traffic. I swung onto it. Less than half a mile now to the blacktop artery that corkscrewed up into the hills—

Sudden flickering light inside the car.

Red pulsing light.

My eyes jerked upward to the mirror. Frostlike prickles on my neck and back, body going rigid, hands in a death grip on the wheel. The oncoming vehicle was close behind me, its rooftop pulsars staining the mist red – red like blood.

Police!

A wildness surged through me. I came close, very close, to jamming my foot down on the accelerator, turning myself into a fugitive with the single twitch of a muscle. *Don't panic!* Like a shriek in my mind.

I jerked my foot off the gas pedal, onto the brake. Easy, tap it, that's right. Tap it again, ease over to the side of the road. The police car did the same. I shoved the shift lever into park, my breath rasping in my throat. Slide the window down, breathe slow and deep. I'd gotten this far without coming apart, hadn't I?

Footfalls, flashlight beam slanting past; uniformed shape outside the window moving closer, swinging the light, bending down. In the reflected glare the cop's face was young, not much more than twenty-five, his expression neither friendly nor hostile. Neutral voice to match: "Out late, aren't you, sir?"

"I guess I—" The words caught in my throat. I coughed and got the answer out on the second try. "I guess I am." My voice sounded all right, the strain an undercurrent too faint to be discernible. "Did I do something wrong, Officer?"

"The stop sign on Corona. You ran it."

He'd been parked someplace back there, dark, watching for late-night speeders, and I hadn't seen him. Stupid! "I don't know why I didn't stop. Should've been paying better attention."

"Have you been drinking, sir?"

"Drinking? No." A good thing, a lucky thing I hadn't taken the drink I'd wanted back at the house. "Not a drop."

"License and registration, please."

I removed the license from my wallet, handed it over. No choice then but to open the console next to me. A sudden panicky thought: Had I put the gun in the trunk, too? Yes, of course I had. Don't start imagining things, for Christ's sake. I unlatched the console, fumbled up the registration, gave it to the cop.

He studied both by the light of his torch. "Mr. Delavan. James Delavan."

"Yes." My voice shook a little, but the cop didn't seem to notice. "Yes, that's me."

"Car's registration is in the name of Wordman Construction Company."

"I work for them. It's a company car."

"Uh-huh. What's your job at Wordman?"

"Crew foreman. I've been with them twelve years."

Don't ask what job I'm working on now, I thought. Don't make me tell a lie you can check up on.

He didn't. He was looking at my license again. "Liberty Street address current?"

"Yes."

"That's on the west side. Kind of a roundabout way home out here."

"I'm not on my way home," I said, "not yet. Going away from home, actually."

"Is that right?"

"Truth is, Officer, I had a fight with my wife. A real screamer. If you're married, you know how it can be sometimes."

"I'm married." Empathy in his tone? Maybe a little. "Alcohol involved? Before, during, or since?"

"No. Not a drop, as I said. Nothing all day."

"Mind stepping out of the car?"

"Not at all. If you'd like me to take a breathalyzer test—"

"Just step out, sir."

I obeyed, unbending in slow segments, standing ruler-backed with my arms at my sides. The cop held the light on me for a few seconds, then told me to wait there and returned to his vehicle. I squinted against the glare of the headlights. I couldn't see what the cop was doing inside, but I thought I knew: checking to see if there were any outstanding warrants against me or the Ford.

Another car materialized out of the mist and crept by, the driver's face framed briefly in the side window, gawking. *Felon by the roadside, caught.* I shook the thought away, tried to will myself into a kind of temporary sleep mode the way a computer is programmed to do. No good; my mind kept churning. Was there anything to make the cop suspicious? No, not even an unpaid parking ticket on my driving record. Nothing to sweat about there. Just keep yourself under control.

It seemed a long time before the cop emerged again. He didn't come back to me yet, just stood off the Ford's rear bumper, in the headlight wash, and began writing in a slender book. Ticket, writing out a ticket. He took his time doing it, glancing up a couple of times. One of the glances seemed to hold on the trunk. No, not the trunk – the license plate.

I could feel sweat trickling on me again, in spite of the cold night air. Less than five feet between the cop and what lay inside the trunk. What if a sixth sense told him something was wrong? What if he came up and said, "Mind opening your trunk, Mr. Delavan?" All over then. Nowhere to run, nowhere to hide. All over...

The cop finished writing and moved toward me. I stood rigid.

And he said, "Okay," and extended my license and registration, then the ticket. I took them automatically; a little gust of wind tried to tear the ticket from my fingers and I tightened my grip. "Sorry to have to write you up, but running a stop sign the way you did in this fog can cause a serious accident, even at this time of night."

"Yes."

"Be more careful from now on."

"Yes."

"Might want to go on home instead of doing any more driving around. Patch things up with your wife."

"Yes." It was all I could think of to say, as if my brain had slipped into a one-word loop.

"Good luck," the cop said, and made a little gesture with his forefinger that was half warning and half salute, and turned away.

I shut myself inside the Ford. Good luck. Jesus, good luck. It took me two tries to turn the ignition, a few seconds more to steady myself before I eased out onto the road.

The cop followed me. I'd expected that and I drove well within the legal limit. A thought popped into my head: What if he intended to trail me all the way home? No, he wouldn't do that. Why should he? It was a long way across town to Liberty Street.

Another thought: If he stayed on my tail when I reached the turnoff into the hills, I'd have to bypass it and keep driving until he decided to go away before I turned around. But he didn't stay that long. He cut away onto Crater Avenue, heading back toward town.

Another half-mile and the turnoff came up on my left. No traffic anywhere in the area. Okay. A little more than five miles to do to the Peterson site.

The long road up, I thought grimly as I made the turn. *And then the long road down.*

The blacktop was narrow, twisty, the edges eroded here and there from winter rains and the weight of heavy equipment. It ran more or less straight at the lower elevations, turned crooked as I climbed through stands of trees, rocky fields and cattle graze. I felt exposed up here, like a bug crawling across a piece of glass; headlights on these mountain roads could be seen for miles, all across the valley and the town. But not tonight, not at this hour – I kept reminding myself of that. Tonight there was haze all across the valley, a thin flowing river of fog that blurred the distant lights.

Another thing in my favor, another reminder: nobody paid any attention to headlights in these hills, took them for granted because the roads were little used by anyone except ranchers, homeowners, kids looking for a private place to drink beer and get laid. The only thing I had to worry about now was driving slow and careful on the sharper curves.

But I was still afraid.

The encounter with the cop had solidified the fear, jammed it down tight inside me. It would not break loose until I was finished with this, maybe not even then. I had a dark feeling that it would stay with me long after tonight, for as long as I lived, like a cancer slowly eating away at me.

The pitch of the road grew steeper. I made a sharp turn through a cutbank, driving at a crawl now because of the blind curves and the fact that the strip of rough asphalt was so narrow here two cars couldn't pass abreast. Another sharp bend, and the road ahead split in two, the right fork dead-ending at the gate of one of the cattle ranchers, the left fork following a brushy ravine uphill. At the top, bordered by wire fencing, was a brand-new gate with Peterson's name written on it.

Out of the car, unlock the gate, drive through, relock it behind me. Tires crunching gravel as I drove another quarter-mile to the house site on a wide, deep shelf that extended out from a pair of oak-studded folds. The acreage at this point was full of earthmoving equipment, office and toolshed trailers, stacks of lumber, piles of rock and gravel and dirt – a jumble of broken shadow shapes. Thin curls of mist drifting through the headlamp beams made it seem an eerie place, like a cemetery in the dead of night. Some of the shapes appeared and disappeared as I swung in among them, and my mind turned them into graveyard images: foundation slabs and staked sections became burial plots, portable toilets became headstones, the trailers and the heavy equipment became ghostly crypts.

I braked long enough to orient myself, crawled ahead at an angle toward the wine cellar excavation. The beams picked it out; it might have been a mineshaft cut into the hillside… or an unfinished mausoleum. Tiered rock and dirt gleamed a short distance to the right. I drove as close as I could to the hillside, turning the wheel to bring the rear end around and the headlight beams full on the earth dump.

When I shut the lights off, the darkness pressed down so thickly it was as though I'd gone blind. The illusion brought a brief twist of panic; I opened the door to put the dome light on, kept it open for several seconds after I swung out. Then I stood blinking, scanning left and right, until my eyes adjusted.

Cold up here, but not much wind, the fog moving in slow, sinuous patterns. Cricket sounds rose and fell; the wind carried the faint rattle of disturbed branches, the odors of pine, madrone, damp earth. The far-off town lights were smeary pinpricks in the ragged veil of mist.

Shivering, I went to the trailer, unlocked it, rummaged among the tools inside. Pick. Shovel. Broom. Utility lantern. Pair of heavy work gloves. I carried them all to the excavation, then lighted the lantern and followed its light to the earth dump.

The wheelbarrow wasn't where I'd seen it yesterday. Took me a couple of minutes to track it down, over on the far side. I ran it back to the trailer, the lantern riding inside so that its long ray jumped and wobbled and threw crazy shadows against the fog. I put on the gloves and loaded the tools. Humped the barrow over bare ground, then over a pair of poured slabs and inside the excavation.

In there I positioned the lantern so the beam held steady on the center section of the floor. I lifted one of the plywood sheets, propped it against the wall out of the way, then did the same with a second sheet. Was the cleared space long enough, wide enough? Should be, yes. I flexed the muscles in my arms and back. All right, get to it. Don't think, just do it like any other piece of construction work.

I hefted the pick and began to dig.

Pick. Shovel. Loose dirt piled on the plywood to one side. Clods and chunks of rock into the wheelbarrow. Pick. Shovel. Loose dirt. Clods, chunks. Full barrow out to the dump and back again empty. Pick. Shovel…

I lost all sense of time. My perceptions narrowed to light and dark, cold and sweat-heat, strain in arms and shoulders and lower back, chink of metal on stone, thud of metal biting into earth. One barrow full, two barrows full, three barrows full. And the hole growing wider, deeper – standing in it, climbing out, dropping back in until one loose, sloping side touched me at mid-thigh. Deep enough. My strength was flagging by then; the pick and the shovel had grown as heavy as ten-pound sledges.

I tossed them out, one after the other, and then heaved myself out. I lifted the barrow's handles, slogged it across to the earth pile. When it was empty I wheeled it around to the rear of the Ford. My eyes stung with sweat and grit. I wiped them clear on my shirtsleeve, then opened the trunk and leaned inside.

I hated having to touch the body again, even with the duct tape-wrapped blanket and the heavy gloves. Getting it out of there and into the wheelbarrow was more of a struggle than putting it in had been. It had stiffened in full rigor and I couldn't unbend it from the S curve. And wielding the pick and shovel had weakened the muscles in my arms and back so I couldn't lift the deadweight as easily as I had at the house.

I jerked, pulled, finally got it over the lip, but when I tried to lower it, it slipped down and upended the barrow with an echoing clang. Christ! I swallowed bile and righted the carrier, hoisted the body into it. Trundled the heavy load back into the excavation.

The hole was too narrow. I realized that as soon as I pushed the wheelbarrow alongside. An involuntary sound like a whimper came out of me. More digging to do, another foot or so of width before the bent remains would fit into the hole.

Upturn the barrow, the body thumping on plywood. Pick. Shovel. Loose dirt onto the side pile. Clods, chunks of rock into the carrier. Pick. Shovel. Dirt, clods, chunks. Wide enough now? Almost. Pick shovel dirt clods chunks. Climb out and take up the handles and wheel the barrow out of the way.

Roll the dead thing into its grave.

Prod and pull until it was wedged on its side. It fit in there, just barely. Tight squeeze.

I stumbled back to the Ford, got the gun and the rest of the stuff out of the trunk. Good thing there wasn't much or there wouldn't have been room for it all in the grave. I was panting when I finished, weak in the knees. I sank down against the side wall, legs extended, to rest and get my breathing under control.

Outside somewhere a night bird made a low screeching sound. It was like an alarm bell, prodding me. *Finish it!* I heaved upright and picked up the shovel, plunged the blade into the pile of loose earth and began to fill in the grave.

Slow work. More lost time while the pile shrank, the contents and sides of the hole gradually disappeared, the cellar floor was once more pounded flat and even. I leaned on the shovel, staring down. Gone. Dead, buried, soon to be hidden forever under a thick concrete slab.

With the broom I swept the section of earth so it looked like it had never been disturbed, then swept out the remaining loose dirt. I returned the tools to the trailer. Took the barrow to the dump, emptied it, left it where I'd found it. Everything looked all right when I shined the lantern around. But I'd have to come up early on Monday morning, before the rest of the crew showed up, to make sure of it.

In the Ford, I started the engine and put the heater on high. Sat there while warm air filled the car because I didn't trust myself to drive yet. Every part of my body tingled with fatigue. The chill in me was bone deep; the heater did no more than make me drowsy.

What time was it? I held my watch up to peer at the dial. Almost four-thirty. Three hours up here. That was how long it took to bury the dead – three hours.

I had to get going: it would be dawn in another hour or so. I turned the heater off, opened the window; I couldn't afford to fall asleep. The job was done but fear still lived in me as I put the car in gear. Revulsion, too. And now something close to self-hatred.

*

I don't remember much of the long drive home. I made it in a kind of mental fog thicker than the real eddies outside. It wasn't until I was on my block that I came back to a dull awareness.

I parked and went inside and let myself into the flat. The lights were still on. A shower, long and hot, but first I needed a stiff drink. I splashed Scotch into a glass and took a long swallow. I was about to take another when Susan came out of the bedroom. She was wearing a negligee, but she hadn't been asleep; her blond hair was combed and she'd covered the bruises on her cheek and chin with makeup. Waiting up for me.

She stood blinking, her eyes wide. "Jimmy, you look exhausted. And your clothes… Are you all right?"

"I will be." I slugged down the rest of the Scotch.

"Did you—?"

"Yes."

"Where? Where did you put him?"

"Where he'll never be found. The gun and everything else that you left in his house, too. You don't have to worry anymore."

She threw her arms around me, fitted her body against mine. Soft, warm, yielding. "It must have been awful for you."

Awful? A nightmare. The worst night of my life. But it had been a lot worse for Mitchell, lying up there in his grave. The last night of his life.

All I said was, "I don't want to talk about it."

"I didn't want to kill him," she said against my chest. "He was drunk, mean, he started hitting me for no reason. I was afraid he'd put me in the hospital. I knew where he kept that gun of his—"

"Stop. I told you before, I don't want to hear the details."

"Oh, Jimmy, I'm so sorry." Crying now, clinging. "I'll be a good wife from now on, I swear it. I'll never be unfaithful to you again."

Yes, she would. Mitchell hadn't been the first, he'd been the fourth or maybe the fifth – all of them macho studs. She couldn't help herself, it was the way she was made. But it didn't matter. The only thing that mattered was not losing her. I loved her too much. I'd do anything to keep her, anything, and she knew it.

"The long road down," I said.

"What?"

"We've been on it, both of us. And now it's too late to get off."

"What are you talking about? What road? Down where?"

I held her tighter. "Never mind," I said. "We're already there."

OUR OPERA SINGER

KRISTINE KATHRYN RUSCH

They say none of us are the same after the pandemic. They say that we all do things now that we never even considered before.

We didn't believe them. We just tried to move forward with our lives.

We acted like nothing was wrong, like we hadn't gone through a horrific year filled with illness and fear and death.

We pretended just fine.

Until we didn't.

*

She said: "It's a shame no one dresses up anymore."

She didn't say it conversationally or even nicely. She said it, with a judgmental edge, in front of the frumpy older woman in the front row. That woman, had she dressed up, had she styled her hair, had she worn just a little bit of makeup, would have been stunningly beautiful.

But that woman, clearly tired, wore wrinkled khakis and a purple Queen T-shirt that had seen better days. She had tried to tame her flyaway white hair with a purple scrunchy, the only gesture she made toward anything like a style.

They were in a crowd of wannabe voice actors – crowd by post-pandemic standards – in a studio that could probably fit a dozen more people. The students varied in age from maybe twenty to maybe seventy. The class was made up of actual aspiring voice actors and students from the local university's continuing education program.

The woman who had spoken had already told the class that she sang opera. Professionally. She wore her unnaturally red hair in a bun on the top of her head, and somehow had forgotten to soften the look with slight curls around her face. Her face was too round, her makeup a little too red, and her eyes – well, her eyes seemed a little bit manic.

As she spoke, she turned her toe ever so slightly, the way women did when their feet hurt. Her brown leather skirt, designed for a thinner woman, looked more expensive than it was, judging by the silk on her white blouse.

She smiled thinly at the room, as if she expected someone to agree with her. Then she sat in the first row, three seats away from the older woman, crossed her legs at the ankles and waited for her turn to impress.

She might've garnered sympathy, had she been a bit kinder. The pandemic had been hard on performers and if what she had said was true, then she would have struggled for at least eighteen months, maybe more.

No one talked about the state of opera in Los Angeles, but L.A. wasn't considered a *performing* town. It was an acting town, an entertainment town, an industry town – and we all wanted to break in, in our own way.

Voice acting AKA acting for shy people. Work at home, use your voice, make a small fortune, or so we were promised.

Only she didn't seem shy. She seemed… determined. And out of place. And trying to cope, just like we all were.

*

That night, sixteen of us showed up. We had paid a few hundred dollars for an introductory course, and sadly, it went the way of most introductory acting courses in Los Angeles.

Lots of attempts at 'acting,' lots of creative praise from the coaches. *You have such a rich voice… What a surprise your tone is… If you smile, you sound much better…* All of it designed to hook the students into the next course and the next and the one after that.

Half the class had no talent whatsoever. A third would drop out. In the Venn diagram of beginning classes, those two categories barely overlapped.

The room was small and poorly ventilated, something we all noticed in those days. The air-conditioning creaked as it turned off, which you couldn't hear in the sound booth – thank heavens – but was shockingly audible in the area just outside of it.

That area was filled with folding chairs, still properly distanced, because most of us hadn't gotten over the horrors of the early part of this decade. The sound engineer sat behind us, barricaded by equipment that looked as intimidating as a cockpit. Dials and pots and computer screens with multicolored lines, waves and inexplicable marks.

Microphones hung down unused, and it seemed – although it wasn't true – that the engineer's only job was to squirm out of his confinement and wiggle his way to the booth, where he adjusted the mic between wannabes.

Because Our Opera Singer had been so vocal, because she wanted us all to know that she was a *star*, we waited breathlessly to hear her read.

She got up, set her Starbucks cup on the ground beside her chair, carried her clutch into the booth with her along with the paper script she had chosen for this, her first reading of the class.

She had the confidence of someone who knew how to perform. And despite the admonition not to touch the mic, she reached for it, stopping only when that night's instructor – The Mighty Stella Sunshine (whose voice had become familiar as the voice of Triple Azteca Toyota as well as elevators all over the L.A. Basin – rapped on the glass and waggled a finger at her.

Then, Stella, a deceptively tiny woman with a voice that could command armies, mimed putting on headphones.

The person in the booth needed the headphones to listen to themselves, yes, but also to hear the instructor's admonitions.

The booth was the second most professional part of the studio, after the constantly updated engineering equipment. It was the size of a small car, with a wall of glass, soundproofing on the other walls, a silent door, and more equipment hanging off the walls.

A music stand stood front and center, the mic hanging over it. A carpet so thick that it felt like a mattress covered the floor. The acoustics were so perfect that it was impossible to hear yourself breathe.

If you didn't look to the right – where your classmates were – you could imagine that you were all alone in the world, which led more than one student to jump when Stella Sunshine said her standard: "Start whenever you're ready."

Maybe the dress-up comment caught our collective attention. Maybe the rich timbre of Our Opera Singer's voice convinced us of her operatic background. Maybe the exquisite bitchiness of her various comments had us all on edge.

Whatever it was, we grew silent as she moved her script into position. She reached for the mic again with red lacquered fingernails, and caught herself just in time.

Then she launched into a luxury car commercial.

In Germany, they call it…

And she spat out some German words before continuing.

… which stands for excellence. Everything about the XK64 stands for excellence, from its mahogany dashboard to its buttery leather seats…

When she finished, she stepped back as if she expected applause. There was none. Her reading was melodic, but did not communicate *luxury*. In fact, it sounded like reading.

And her German – well, her German wasn't German at all. Not really. It combined a schoolgirl's pronunciations with a bad movie villain's accent.

Stella Sunshine pasted a smile on her face.

"You chose that because you speak German!" she said in a falsely positive voice.

"Yes." Our Opera Singer stood half a head taller, as if she was anticipating the praise.

"We have a number of practice commercials with more than one language," Stella said to the rest of us. "Being bilingual or" – and here she waved a hand at Our Opera Singer – "trilingual—"

"Actually, I speak six languages," Our Opera Singer said as if she expected to be praised for that too.

"—is a *tremendous* marketing tool," Stella continued, as if Our Opera Singer hadn't spoken at all. "We need multilingual voice actors, because this has become an international world."

Then she turned slightly in her padded chair, and peered at Our Opera Singer.

"Now, though," Stella said, "I would like to hear what else you can do. What else did you bring for us?"

*

The rest of the night passed in a blur. We did not bond as a class, although we'd heard tales that other classes had done so. In that moment – the very first class – we seemed too different.

The continuing education folks were mostly retired, searching for something to do to keep the silence at bay or, as the tall square former wrestler from Texas said, to find a way to be useful again.

A handful of the continuing education folk were out of work, classes paid for by a program that helped people 'transition' to new work. The rest of the students seemed to come on their own, finding this studio out of the thousands of studios (surely, there were thousands: L.A. is that kind of town) all throughout the L.A. Basin.

All the dreams, all the hopes. The rest of the students seemed to hold ours. They were younger, more energetic, and much more scared. They wanted a future desperately. They hadn't yet learned that the future you wanted wasn't always as advertised.

Sometimes – often – it was much worse.

Stella herself seemed to encourage the fear. She seemed – that first night – like one of those benign taskmasters, the kind that got you to do something because you wanted to please her.

But glimmers of the real Stella poked through: the glare she couldn't suppress when she saw the Texan with his hat and his handmade cowboy boots; the grimace as she said the word *German*; and the near-eye roll when Our Opera Singer lifted her second script – which had a Spanish segment.

Stella didn't banter with that night's engineer either. She just commanded him to go here or go there, do whatever she needed him to do, which he did mostly silently, often unquestioningly, as if he was there to serve her and do absolutely nothing else.

Our Opera Singer might have been the focus, but Stella was the catalyst.

*

Six weeks of classes, three hours on a Tuesday night, starting at six so the nine-to-fivers could make it. The accommodation for the nine-to-fivers seemed like a twentieth-century vestige, although there had been no classes like this in the twentieth century.

Back then, voiceover belonged to the lucky, the rarefied, those who lived in New York, Chicago, Los Angeles, those with real acting jobs, or acting jobs that had gone the way of their looks. The voiceover work in secondary cities – Portland, Phoenix, Des Moines – went to local disk jockeys, some of whom didn't even think to charge for the privilege of lending their voice to Crazy Sam's House of Cars or whatever local business needed someone to shout their deals on regional television.

The internet disrupted. The internet, it seems, specializes in disruption.

Suddenly, voices were needed for everything. Games, digital reading direct from a screen, phone trees, online education, anything and everything automated from cars to televisions to digital assistants. That woman who tells you to turn left and the destination is on your right? She is a voiceover actress who, we hope, got a good enough deal so that each time her voice reassures you that you have the right corner, she gets a tiny tiny percentage of any income that would go to the parent company's way.

The second week, we all reported the same phenomenon: we all realized we had heard voice actors but hadn't registered them. Suddenly the world was full of them, telling us *walk* as the light turned green or *wait* as it slipped from yellow to red. Voices gave us alerts and warnings and told us to press eight to speak to a representative.

Each time we heard the voices, we wondered at the people behind them. Had they started like we were, in a slightly cold studio on a ridiculously hot night? Or had they been pushed into the work by life or circumstance, thwarted theater ambitions or alcoholic slides downward, which only allowed for a few minutes of concentration per day?

We realized that even though the voices around us were *automated*, they were – at their heart – the actual voice of an actual person who had rented their dulcet tones to some large corporation that felt the need to have an actual human remind another actual human to *press start*.

And yet… and yet…

None of us wanted to do *that* kind of voiceover work. We had already absorbed Stella Sunshine's prejudice against telephony and knew that once *we* were fully trained, we would *never* work in telephony or any kind of digital automation. *We* would be too good to lend our voices to smart phones or streetlights or airplane cockpits. We would do characters in video games or smartly narrate Ken Burns documentaries or dub famous voices from overseas into English.

We would be voice *actors*.

And that was when the bonding began. We looked at each other knowingly, gazes meeting, even among those of us (especially among those of us) still wearing masks. We wanted to re-enter the world, but we were afraid. We did not confess that we all thought our first night's work – sent to us via email, in one three-hour lump – sounded worse than we had hoped when we listened back in the cold light of day.

We knew we would improve. We had to improve, because we had to improve in order to succeed.

And we had to succeed, as one of us said, because not succeeding would simply compound all the death and destruction and disaster of the past eighteen months.

Our Opera Singer did not participate in that conversation. She hung back, as if she didn't need to talk about the opportunities or the way she wouldn't fail. She stood, with her back perfectly straight, her Beverly Sills body tense and attuned to the world around her.

That day, Our Opera Singer was wearing a pleated skirt that could have come from a production of *The Sound of Music*, her too-red hair in plaits that fell down her back, accenting her already round face. Even her shoes were too red, but they did match her purse, which looked like a Hermès Birkin bag. A closer inspection by the slightly defeated middle-aged mom who used to work customs in the Port of Los Angeles showed that the red purse was a poor-quality knockoff, possibly smuggled in during the chaos after the supply chains eased up.

Our Opera Singer sat, slightly distant from the rest of us, legs crossed at the ankles, a sour expression on her face as she watched Stella Sunshine give instructions to the new engineer.

Well, the new-to-us engineer. He was actually not new at all, just a man who hadn't been here the week before. It would become clear, as the class continued, that Stella Sunshine received no loyalty from engineers. It seemed that they ended up with the unluck of the draw; whoever needed a bit more money to make it through the week engineered one night for her.

He was a scrawny man with a pencil-thin mustache that belonged in a silent movie from a hundred years ago, not behind a sound board that had more equipment than most airplane cockpits.

He tried to banter with Stella Sunshine, but she silenced him with one well-placed laser-like glare. He hunched forward and didn't surface until she reminded everyone that the engineer was the only person who could touch the equipment in the booth.

When Stella said that, she was eyeing Our Opera Singer who seemed even sharper-edged that night. She had peered condescendingly at the shoes around her, as if the shoes defined character. She touched the side of her face when she looked at one of the continuing education women, a tiny woman from Spain who legitimately spoke two languages, and we all thought Our Opera Singer was having a bonding moment.

After all, the woman from Spain wore a stunning rhinestone-studded mask that caught the light. She wasn't pretty – how could we tell, in those masked-up days if anyone was pretty or merely had very nice eyes? – but she had a vivaciousness that everyone else in the room lacked.

When Our Opera Singer touched the side of her face while making eye contact with the woman from Spain, she carefully touched the same spot on her own face.

Her fingers came away sticky – that was clear from the way she rubbed them together. Her eyebrows met in a frown, and she asked forgiveness as she removed her mask to examine it.

Some food had stained the side that had faced Our Opera Singer, and unfortunately, she had been the one to notice.

"Oh, my," the woman from Spain said. "I'm afraid I'll need a new mask. Do you have one?"

Why she asked Our Opera Singer, we'll never know. Our Opera Singer was the only one among us who wore her mask on her wrist. She wouldn't cover her face at all and, for some reason (perhaps shared beliefs), Stella Sunshine hadn't confronted her about it nor had the engineer. He didn't wear his mask either, but he sat far enough away from all of us that it didn't matter – and he pulled it on whenever he got out of his engineering chair.

"An extra mask?" Our Opera Singer asked in a beautifully derisive voice. "Of course, I don't have a mask. I don't believe in masks."

The group gasp might have been audible in Pasadena. We knew that there were people who avoided wearing masks because they were uncomfortable or because the masks ruined a perfect look, people who were a bit too casual with their masks – rather like the engineer – and people who would forget to put their masks on.

But to disbelieve in the power of masking showed a profound ignorance, maybe even an anti-science, anti-vaccine bent. Those people didn't show up at a voiceover class on a Tuesday night. Those people couldn't do voiceover work. They ruined their voices screaming obscenities at good hardworking school board members or shouted in support of gigantic somewhat insane orange politicians bent on destroying the world.

Suddenly, Our Opera Singer had moved herself from the rarefied air of actual performer (albeit not in *acting*) to someone who lacked even the most basic common sense.

We all exchanged not-so-subtle glances and Our Opera Singer raised her chin even more. The woman with the flyaway white hair (this night tamed by an ill-advised puke green scrunchy) pulled a plastic-wrapped mask out of her purse and handed it to the woman from Spain who nodded gratefully.

We didn't acknowledge Our Opera Singer's mask comment, any more than we really had acknowledged her clothing comment the week before.

But we all noted it. We noted both comments. We realized – confirmed, really – that Our Opera Singer did not belong with the rest of us. Our Opera Singer wasn't really *Our Opera Singer* at all, but we didn't know what, exactly, to call her.

Few of us used our real names when we slated before reading our scripts. We used our acting names – *Cool Katie, speaking from the Studio.* Maybe we had acknowledged our real names on that first night, but we hadn't really paid that much attention to each other then.

We had been wrapped up in our nervousness. We had worried that we weren't good enough for this or that we had wandered into the wrong place or that our dreams – long held and rarely discussed – would finally, awfully, horribly get destroyed.

Only it wasn't our dreams that would be destroyed in that hothouse of a studio. Our dreams remained little and small and ours alone.

It was Our Opera Singer who would leave, broken and in tears; Our Opera Singer who would, at least according to some of us, get what she so richly deserved.

But not yet. And not for weeks.

Proof, yet again, that all of us – most of us? – never know what is coming our way. Even when it is richly deserved.

Especially when it is richly deserved.

*

Microaggressions. Those tiny little events that seem so unimportant in the moment, but they accumulate like dust on a dresser, until they completely obscure the surface and become the surface itself.

Only the microaggressions weren't Our Opera Singer's. Oh, she continued to rub us all the wrong way. She postured. She stood to one side and judged us and found us wanting.

She showed off her linguistic prowess that, sadly, wasn't as proficient as she believed it was.

Her linguistic prowess or lack thereof made us wonder if maybe she had lied to us about her opera singer status. Had it been a dream too? Or something as forced and fanciful as her linguistic ability?

We didn't challenge her, though. We listened to her read—and, to be fair, the one thing she had as a reader was confidence. It didn't matter how inappropriate the text was for her, whatever she read, she read it with confidence.

No, she wasn't the one who delivered the microaggressions. Stella did.

Stella Sunshine, whose last name probably didn't come from her sunny nature but from her ability to shed light on whatever was lurking in the deepest, darkest corner.

Perhaps that was why the engineers hated her. She could put her finger on whatever trick they were using to hide their inevitable incompetence.

She loved peeling the veneer off things—and along about week three she started peeling the veneer off us.

Little things. The positive comments had an edge, the time we got in the booth shorter or longer depending on whether she considered us worthwhile. And worthwhile changed from week to week.

Our Opera Singer did not like the lack of acknowledgment. Her posturing grew. She'd stand near the booth's window, so that she could see Stella Sunshine react during a read. Our Opera Singer would change her posture or breathe differently or ask if she could try a new bit of material.

("No, darling," Stella would say without warmth. The "darling" was reflexive, done without thought at all. "Just read what you have already chosen." That, after she had given the Spanish speaker four extra pieces to read in both Spanish and English.)

That night, the third engineer reminded Stella that we had to shut down early, so Stella went extra-long. People peeled out of class like kids sneaking out of a truly dull lecture.

Stella noticed who left. She noticed everything.

The engineer finally had to threaten to call the studio's owner to get the class to end. Stella glared at him, but told him to pack up. She gathered her things and left first.

The engineer grumbled – he was a doughy man with less experience than the previous two engineers, partly because, he said, he had two kids at home and couldn't come to the studio until his wife was home to care for them.

We all thought that sweet, but Stella clearly hadn't. She had known that closing early had been *his* gambit, not an edict from above, and she had made him pay for it.

As Our Opera Singer gathered her knockoff Louboutin tote, this one in pink to match her skirt, she lost her balance. Her heel caught on a slight dip in the rug, and the heel broke off.

She sat down heavily, pulled off her shoe and held both pieces in her hand. One of us should have offered her some help, maybe found some crazy glue or reminded her that socks with the studio logo were for sale in the tiny merchandise store off the booth.

Instead, we all looked at her as if she had suddenly turned into a frog. She waved both pieces, smiled at the frumpy woman (whose scrunchy that day, oddly, was a matching pink), and said: "Even the most beloved item finally wears out."

We could have taken that moment to have a bit of sympathy – or maybe just some empathy. After all, in that moment, Our Opera Singer was vulnerable, reaching out just a little.

And maybe some of us considered it, some of us wanted to take that moment to find a bit of mutual humanity.

But not the frumpy woman.

She said: "Items wear out only when they're cheap."

Our Opera Singer winced as if she'd been hit. She was smart enough, though, not to be defensive. She didn't say anything about the cost of looking good – which she might have on that first night – nor did she pretend that she had paid top dollar for the shoes.

Instead, she shoved the heel in her pink tote, hefted the shoe itself for a moment and then slipped it back on her foot. Only the toe touched the ground. The rest of the shoe had been constructed just for that heel, but she gamely put her weight in that toe as she stood. She hefted the tote over her shoulder, and marched out like a queen, even though she lurched to the right with every other step.

We all watched her leave. A handful of us had admiration on our faces, but whether that was for her bravado or her unusual verbal restraint, we didn't share.

We left together – we were starting to do everything together – and by the time the engineer locked the door behind us, Our Opera Singer was no longer in the parking lot. We had no idea how she had gotten to class; we just assumed she had her own car.

But not all of our assumptions turned out to be true. We learned, in that amazing class, how little we actually understood about the world we lived in. Maybe if we understood, we might have been kinder.

Maybe. Or maybe not.

★

By week four, we were a smaller group.

The worthy, the week four engineer said kindly.

The survivors, Stella said with more truth than we liked.

The engineer rolled his eyes behind her back. He was older and appeared tired. He kept his phone beside him at all times, and its screen saver was a dated photograph of a man who might've been him, and a woman of incandescent beauty. He would occasionally touch her face as if he needed something from her.

The scripts contained the first pages from a documentary, lots of automobile commercials and some incomprehensible video game text. We had learned the routine by now: we picked out our primary reading for the night and annotated it, hoping that we would receive praise or maybe just a modicum of hope from Stella Sunshine.

She was late. When she came in, carrying with her the scent of patchouli oil and incense, she dumped her bag behind the engineering booth, and grabbed a handheld mic.

"Start up the recording," she said to the engineer as if he'd been the one who had delayed the class. Then she scurried to her chair, and sank into it as if she needed it to hold her up.

At that moment, Our Opera Singer decided to ask a question.

"Is there really a lot of work in this field or was that B.S. to get us to pay for class?"

Some of us gasped. Stella looked up, her expression bland, her hand clutching the mic as if it had suddenly morphed into a club.

"Why do you ask?" She used a tone we had come to recognize. It held warning, as if she – and truth be told, the rest of us – were bracing for some kind of stupidity.

"I thought the question was self-explanatory," Our Opera Singer said. "But since you want me to, I'll explain it. You see, we're all here to get work, and what we really want to know is whether this abuse is worth our time."

The engineer sat up straight, his eyes wide.

"Abuse?" Stella asked in that same tone.

"Two more classes, minimum, and then an upsell will come, right? Maybe some personal lessons." Our Opera Singer waved a hand. She had a clumsily done French manicure that the black-haired mom of four who usually sat quietly in the corner later said looked like she had done it herself. "I don't care about personal lessons. I don't really think I need more classes. I would like to audition."

"Where?" The fingers Stella had wrapped around the mic had turned white with the pressure she was putting on the metal.

"I'll audition anywhere," Our Opera Singer said. "I'm sure we all will."

She was wrong. She misread the room. Many of us wanted work, yes, but only when we were ready for it. Some of us were retired, and the rest either had jobs or were still on the tail end of their enhanced unemployment benefits. We wanted work, some of us as a hobby, some of us to augment our existing jobs, and some of us to replace the jobs we lost.

But none of us admitted to any desperation. None of us even showed the edges of it. You'd think that when Our Opera Singer discussed it, others would chime in, exert some kind of pressure on Stella herself, but no one did.

Instead, we all watched the situation play out as if we had no idea where it was heading.

"You think you're ready to audition," Stella said in that ever-so-calm voice.

"Yes." Our Opera Singer looked around the room, maybe hoping for some kind of backup. "I think we all are."

"You think," Stella said, and the words hung in the air like bits of a script. We could hear them performed a dozen different ways:

You think.

You think?

Ya thiiink...

But none of those ways had the element of menace that those two words had when Stella voiced them.

The color left Our Opera Singer's cheeks. She finally realized she had overstepped. But she kept her chin up. Her posture remained straight, her body tense. She was waiting.

So were we.

Stella leaned forward, resting one elbow on one tiny thigh. Her gaze met Our Opera Singer's directly.

"You won't have to worry about the upsell," Stella said in a deceptively kind voice. Her expression wasn't kind. It was feral. "You won't finish the class. You're not the type."

Our Opera Singer sat just a bit straighter, her body claiming that she could take the blows, even as her eyes put lie to that.

"You can audition at any point," Stella said. "You may not use the studio's name unless you complete a class. That's in our online materials, which you clearly have not bothered to read."

The rest of us did not remember that in the materials either. Maybe the information was in the terms of service, which we all clicked, but never really read.

"Not that you can read well anyway," Stella said. Oh, her tone was a master class in and of itself. If she had spoken viciously, she could've been dismissed as an older woman having a bad day, a teacher who finally had enough from one of her students or someone who simply did not like the person she was talking to.

But the kind tone superseded the words. The kindness and warmth made us all nod in agreement, made Stella's words seem reasonable and helpful, even though they were not.

"In fact, you should stop trying. The harder you try, the worse you sound."

It could've been advice. Later, it would seem like the harsh advice of an acting teacher to an acting student.

But we knew it for what it was: truth, and not the kind anyone wanted to hear.

Our Opera Singer's lower lip trembled. She clutched her faux Prada calfskin bag tightly against her stomach, and looked slightly ill.

"You have no right to talk to me like that," Our Opera Singer said. Her voice had no tears in it, although her eyes glistened with them.

"I have every right," Stella said. "You came here for truth. Here's the truth, sweetie. Find something else to do. You don't belong here."

And then we heard: *You don't belong anywhere.*

Only Stella never uttered those words aloud. Later, we couldn't figure out how we heard them, even though she hadn't said them. Was that a technique? It had to have been. But they didn't show up on the recording.

For a moment, we all thought Our Opera Singer would fight. We thought she would insist that she belonged. We thought she would do something besides the predictable.

"You owe me a refund for the remaining classes," Our Opera Singer said, that confidence in her voice that wasn't in her face.

"Again, sweetie," Stella said. "You need to read the fine print. It's on the website. Once you start the class, you've paid. We don't give refunds when people give up."

Our Opera Singer made a small sound – some of us heard a sob; others a growl – and she lobbed that purse at Stella Sunshine's head. The purse hit the wall full force, making a dent in the air-conditioning vent.

Stella stared at the thing for a moment, then with a dignity none of us expected from her, picked up the purse with her thumb and forefinger, holding it like one held a smelly dead animal, and offering it to Our Opera Singer.

Our Opera Singer took it, shoved it under her arm, and walked out – not listing, not lurching – but not with any dignity either, and by the time she had reached the door, she was sobbing so hard that her entire body was shaking.

*

That night was all about emotion. Stella decided to teach us how to put emotions in our characters, to take emotions from our lives.

Emotions, she said, were easy to manipulate, and one could do it with voice and words.

She made us all feel something.

To the square wrestler from Texas, she said: "You are useless. It doesn't matter what you do, you'll always be useless."

And when he got into the booth to read an anime villain, his voice shook with anger.

To the woman from Spain, Stella said: "You'll only be able to do telephony in Spanish. Your accent is too strong for ninety percent of the English language work."

Which only made the accent stronger when the woman from Spain got into the booth. Her voice hitched, and she nearly broke into tears. Which actually worked, considering the sad, depressed character she was voicing.

But then, gratuitously, Stella turned to the engineer. She said: "You were a lot better at your job before your wife died."

We gasped as one – except for him.

He stood, clutching his phone with that photo of the beautiful woman as the screen saver, and faced Stella Sunshine.

"To understand what loss feels like," he said, shaking his phone at her, "you have to have someone to lose."

Then he ran his free hand over the board, moving all of the pots downward, hitting levers, and shutting off screens. Microphones vibrated, and Stella's squealed until she turned it off.

He grabbed his fanny pack and scurried out of the studio, but not before we all saw the tears glittering on his cheeks.

To understand what loss feels like, you have to have someone to lose.

The words reverberated, as if he was speaking to all of us. We should have left right then and there, shaken and upset and maybe angry enough to demand our money back from the studio itself, given what had occurred.

But we didn't.

We turned as one toward Stella Sunshine.

She raised a single eyebrow. "Anyone take the engineering course yet?"

Of course we hadn't. We were in the beginner class. The one that should have been filled with hope.

The one that many of us scraped and saved for, the one that all of us saw as the gateway to our future, the one that we thought might bring us from the darkness of the pandemic into the remembered light of a normal day.

All it would have taken was a bit of kindness. Maybe some understanding. Maybe a lack of sarcasm.

If Stella hadn't been up to the task, then she should have told someone else to take the class. That's what we all realized later.

But in the moment, we grabbed the mic out of her hand. We wielded it like a club. We demanded that she apologize.

"Apologize for what?" she asked with a sneer. "The truth?"

Oh, that was the wrong question. Because it made us review every sentence uttered in class, examine every glance, think about every touch of sarcasm.

None of us were smart enough to say, *That was* your *truth*, and none of us were confident enough to walk away.

We thought – we hoped – that maybe, under threat, she would change. That trembling microphone, held above her head, her confident smile, the one that didn't reach her eyes.

"Why are you all so afraid of emotion?" she asked. "That's why you suck. That's why not a one of you will have any success as an actor – as any kind of actor. You think telephony is *acting*? It's the refuge of the untalented. And the most talented among you will be reciting numbers for some small corporation that finally got enough cash to build a phone tree. You call that a career? I call it a waste of my frickin' time."

She didn't move as the microphone swung toward her head. Maybe she didn't believe that we were angry enough to hit her. Maybe she didn't understand the sheer frustration we'd been living with for more than a year now, the extreme anger at a summer that turned from a possible hopeful escape from a nightmare pandemic to even more lives lost.

From dreams of a future that we could grasp to one uglier and even more upsetting than the present we had just left behind.

Ten blows, maybe, the police would say later. Ten blows with three different microphones, all dented and blood-covered. The wall, the chair, the thin-carpeted floor, the glass of the booth, covered in spatter.

A sign, the police would say, of uncontrolled rage.

Because, the coroner believed, the first blow killed her. But we would never know, he said.

They would never know.

We know she looked like some kind of mannikin, jerking and tumbling and slipping as the blows fell. She didn't die on the first blow or even the second.

We had to improve our technique, and that took teamwork. That took concentration.

Strangely, we completed it in silence.

Then we removed our shoes, because one of us reminded the rest of us about the aftermath. We hadn't tracked anything, and we wouldn't, but the shoes created a risk. So we backed away from the spatter, used paper towels to open the door to the outdoors, and stepped into the hot summer night, each of us with a roll of paper towels under our arms.

The moon was full and slightly orange. There was a haze over it, almost a caul. The light was more than enough to guide us to our cars. We drove home separately, all of us sitting on paper towels, all of us disrobing outside of our dwellings, all of us bagging the clothes and dropping them later in some trash bin far from where we live.

We didn't have to swear ourselves to silence because we were of one mind about what happened. We were equally responsible, and we would use that, one of the retired lawyers among us said, as a way of seeding reasonable doubt.

Only we didn't have to.

Because the police were so proud of themselves.

They had the audio. They had, they said, Our Opera Singer dead to rights.

She left angry. They believed she waited until we all followed the engineer out (he said he had seen her as he hurried to his car, sobbing in the front seat of her own battered Toyota).

It was a solid case, the police said. It would stand up in court if it went that far, but they hoped she would plea. In fact, they couldn't quite understand why she hadn't. They knew she had taken paper towels to wipe the door and to make sure the blood spatter didn't follow her home.

They had her.

They knew it.

And we knew it too.

We didn't discuss it. We didn't have to. The audio cut out when the engineer left. After the rest of us had performed with our emotion-laden scripts. We hadn't lost our tempers, the police said. We had gone on with the class, like good little actors, using every scrap of emotion as the gateway to the best performances of our lives.

And we did.

Should we have defended Our Opera Singer? Oh, probably. Maybe. Pre-pandemic, we might even have had sympathy for her.

But we were all trying to pass as better than we were. We might not have carried designer knockoffs or pretended that the destruction of our best shoes didn't bother us, but we were all trying to be something we weren't.

Maybe her attempt at making herself seem better than the rest of us leached us of any desire to save her.

Maybe some of us actually believed she deserved the police attention, not us.

We'd become so good at denying what was around us, after all. We just marched through and forward, not looking at the carnage we had all left behind.

*

The studio closed.

We never got our refunds.

We decided not to sue.

We so much wanted to put the past behind us, and we like to think that we did. But we know something is different.

Maybe everything is different.

They say none of us are the same after the pandemic. They say that we all do things now that we never even considered before.

They are right.

WHAT HAPPENS AFTER THE END

MAXIM JAKUBOWSKI

"For to kill is the great law set by nature in the heart of existence!
There is nothing more beautiful and honourable than killing!"
Guy de Maupassant, 'Le Horla'; used by Cornell Woolrich as an epigraph to
The Bride Wore Black

He had come to the city to escape his past. He had committed a crime and attracted retribution. Although not from the authorities. What he had done was inconsequential in their eyes; others might have managed to get away with it, but he hadn't. A contract had been put out on him and death was coming. He was resigned to the idea.

The name of the city was equally unimportant. It wasn't Paris, where he had spent many years until it had become a cemetery of broken love affairs. Nor was it New York, where he might have found it easier to hide amongst the multitudes of boroughs, skyscrapers and desolate tenements and the milling crowds the Big Apple attracted from all over the world: loners, refugees, romantics and outlaws. Nor London nor New Orleans, two more cities he knew well and could have navigated with ease and where he could have concealed his presence with a modicum of discretion, lived in relative anonymity. And, for him, San Francisco was emotionally just out of the question, a place celebrated by the movies but which he had never quite connected with in the same way as most others, despite its many celebrated charms.

He'd managed almost eighteen months on his own. Feeling as if he was living on borrowed time, unable to enjoy what he knew would be his final days of freedom, ever on the lookout for signs that he had been located, unable to plan for more than a few days ahead, acting all along as if everything and anything was just temporary. He could not find in himself to any longer attempt to read a book, in the knowledge he might never know how it ended; or begin watching a TV series, with the final episode shielded by future clouds possibly never to be seen. He had never lived that way before. He had always been a man who made plans, lists of things to do and systematically ticked them off. There had always been a future ahead of him: a new movie to see, a vacation in an exotic place to look forward to, a meal in a familiar restaurant where he would inevitably mostly order the same items on the menu he had enjoyed before. It was like a strange sensation of running in place.

He did not have to work. He still had enough money from the job that had gone wrong and had turned him into a target. Days rolled by; some ever so slowly, dragging along, thoughts lazing through his head and never quite achieving fruition; others raced by until darkness came and he realised he had actually done, accomplished nothing.

It was a simple diner on a street corner, straight out of an Edward Hopper painting. He was sitting on a high stool by the zinc counter and had ordered a burger and a glass of cold homemade lemonade. He was down to his last handful of fries, his mind in neutral, his eyes focused on a squabbling middle-aged couple in a booth at the far end whose arguments he could barely hear although the simmering anger that hung between them was betrayed by their body language. He enjoyed observing people, casually building up stories about them in his imagination. When they finally turned silent and began to concentrate on the plates of food on their table, he noticed that someone was now sitting on the stool to his right. It was a woman. Her perfume was quietly fragrant but elusive. She was blonde, her hair cascading down to her shoulders, its silky ends draping themselves across the top of her brown leather jacket. He initially thought she looked a bit like Taylor Swift. She was perusing the laminated menu.

He had always been partial to blondes. His first blonde had broken his teenage heart and caused him to clumsily lacerate his wrists in a bid to keep her; it hadn't worked but he still had the small scar that reminded him of Lois Elizabeth. The next blonde he had married; her name was Laura. The final blonde had been called Katherine and their affair had lasted six months and broken up his marriage.

The young woman turned towards him. Maybe not Taylor Swift, he thought; there was something steely and glacial about her that actually made her appear even more alluring, polished like a diamond. Deadly, beautiful.

"How's the burger?" she asked. She had a foreign accent he couldn't quite pinpoint.

"Decent, actually."

She had grey eyes and the moment he looked into them he both fell in lust and realised instantly she was his angel of death. The time had finally come. It wasn't at all what he had expected, but he rather enjoyed the thought that this was the woman who would kill him.

She smiled at him. He smiled back.

Words unsaid, particulars kept in the dark: by the following morning, he was dead. Knife? Gun? Poison? Pills? Overdose? Fall from a great height? Strangled?

It mattered not in the order of things.

*

Cornelia had always enjoyed a curious relationship with hotel rooms.

She had lived in many, although never for extended periods. She had killed in a fair few. She had slept with men, strangers she had picked up on a whim when she had been in need of sex or men she had lured to a pre-booked room or agreed to follow to theirs with anything but sex in her own mind, just the job in hand. So hotel rooms had become associated in her mind with lust or death, an uneasy combination. But, as a result, she never visited the same hotel twice. Maybe, at the back of her mind it was a fear the front desk computer reservation system might allocate her the same room in which she had once either fucked or killed. There was also the fact that, when she was the one making a booking, she always registered under a different name and never bothered to keep a record of which she had used or where. Always settling by cash, of course. She had called herself Carlotta Valdes on several occasions; also Judy, Madeleine, Julie or even Julia Russell.

But those days were, she reckoned, long behind her now. Her book collection had been growing exponentially and just over a year ago, she had taken a long lease on an apartment downtown in another city, if only to have a proper place to shelve her rare volumes, away from the storage facilities in the suburbs where she had only limited access to her treasures, tidily boxed up in darkness like abandoned children.

Cornelia had always been a voracious reader, from early childhood all the way through to university, although she could only afford cheap or used paperbacks then, and relied on public libraries to sate her appetite for the written word and the way those words somehow transformed into stories that transported her both into the mind of others but to other worlds too. She hadn't completed her course and had dropped out after her first year, her patience growing thin with the unemotional dissecting focus her professors and tutors applied to books and which, to Cornelia, felt like a wholesale betrayal of the purpose of literature. She had been brought up by distant relatives following the passing of her parents in a car crash when she was only in her teens and felt no compulsion to stay in touch with the distant second-hand family she had been offloaded onto. She had first moved to New York, and rather than fall into the traps and McJobs of the low-gig economy, she had almost accidentally become a stripper. All those men kept on telling her that she had a body to die for, and that she moved with sultry sexiness, and wasn't she always coming across 'wanted' ads for exotic dancers displayed outside the clubs that littered the north area of Times Square or in the free papers available on most street corners? She loved music anyway, and it turned out she moved like a natural. So what difference did it make whether she performed dressed or undressed? She saw the stripping as just a craft, and it was much more appealing and relaxing than dancing for tickets in dance halls, or escorting. Cornelia had never been overly emotional, unless she had surrendered heart and soul to a story in a book where the characters felt so much more real than most of the people she chanced across in civilian life. Acquaintances often told her there was a coldness that surrounded her like a halo, which neither pleased nor displeased her. It was just the way she was.

A fairly rare title by an author she collected assiduously had surfaced on the market; an early proof with substantial handwritten annotations by the writer which had been carried through to the final published version and substantially changed the original plot and the fate of some of the fictional characters involved. This not only made any copy of the advance reading proof valuable, but the changes visibly made in the author's hand had created a unique artefact.

The book was priced well beyond her means but she had asked the dealer for a fortnight's grace so she could raise the money; the antiquarian seller had agreed as she had been a reliable customer in the past.

Cornelia had pondered doing some escorting but quickly calculated the cost of the book would even then prove out of reach. There was a regular customer at the strip club who, she knew, had taken a fancy to her and repeatedly offered her drinks following her final set of the evening. He had often drunkenly boasted of possible criminal connections. It was through Vito Bonaparte she made contact with the fixer. Her looks counted in her favour, as no one would ever become suspicious of her, and she quickly demonstrated she was a pretty good markswoman, having been given lessons in handling a firearm by her father. She was given a photograph and an address. The rest was up to her. The hit she contracted for was worth twice the book she coveted. She did not hesitate. She justified killing a man to herself by arguing inside her mind that someone else would carry out the killing had she turned the opportunity down and that the target was a dead man walking anyway, so why not benefit from the job?

Afterwards, she felt no guilt and experienced no nightmares. The money was good enough to appease her relaxed conscience.

A few weeks later, she was offered another hit in a different city. One more rare book for her collection. She was professional and careful not to get caught on security cameras, leave fingerprints or allow anyone to witness her presence on the scene or in the vicinity of the crime. Other assignments followed. The death broker always supplied the weapon, which she disposed of afterwards, although she decided after the first handful of hits that she should not restrict herself to guns only, and began using other methods so that she didn't adhere to a specific trademark.

Her collection of rare and antiquarian books kept on growing. In the wake of bodies left in her wake.

*

Cornelia had been a killer for hire for three years when, for the first time, she thought she recognised one of her victims; he was crossing Houston by the corner of Wooster Street. She was walking north in the direction of Union Square where she had intended to browse through the new arrivals at Barnes & Noble. She remembered him well. She had slit his throat, taking him by surprise while he was pouring drinks, pre-bedroom, in the vast penthouse space he occupied on the Upper East Side just a few blocks away from the Met. It had just been a year ago, as she clearly remembered that it was the day the translation of the final Elena Ferrante novel in the

Naples Quartet had been published and she had picked up a copy earlier in the day and had to rush back to the Airbnb she had been staying in for the duration of the assignment to change into evening wear to meet up with her hit. He was a man with coarse manners who advertised his lack of taste with pride, enormous Rolex watch, gold medallions and an expensive tailor-made three-piece suit which no honest citizen would wear in so shiny a fabric. Cornelia tried to recall his name but her memory was unreliable. Once a kill had been completed she had a habit of drawing a line on the job once and for all. She stood still, watching the man hail a yellow cab, thinking it must surely be someone else who looked like him, but he was wearing the same stupid silk necktie, with a pattern of gold embroidered hawks against a night black background. Surely, this could not be the same man? Or an identical twin? The hit had been successful and there was no coming back from that.

There was nothing else to do but dismiss the idea and forget. Just some eerie coincidence, she decided. Or maybe she should get her eyes tested?

Two days later, sitting in Washington Square Park and sipping a tepid coffee while reading a book in which a ballet dancer in Montreal was turned into a wooden puppet, Cornelia's attention was drawn to a nearby nanny chiding her curly-haired, cherubic-like ward who was throwing pieces of the cupcake he had just crumbled towards the marauding squirrels. As she looked across the path, a woman in sleek leotard and outsized sunglasses jogged by, pulling a dog on a leash behind her. Cornelia had never been animal friendly and could not for the life of her distinguish between canine breeds, but she recalled having had to lock the animal into the bathroom on the night she had killed Sicilia Ann. Who right now was running past her bench, her sneakers hitting the ground in metronomic rhythm.

Sicilia Ann. It was the only hit she had undertaken against someone she had previously known in her personal life. Sicilia Ann had worked as a stripper in the same club where Cornelia was contracted that particular summer, was the queen of the pole and had incredible breasts which were the envy of all the other dancers. Cornelia's chest was more modest, not that it had ever bothered her. Sicilia Ann had once worked as a microbiologist and, when dancing, billed herself as Doctor Ann. She was always dragging her fellow performers along to obscure street food eateries where she was always familiar with the cooks. Cornelia never wanted to know why someone was designated as a hit, but assumed Sicilia Ann had stumbled into some involvement with illegal drugs and was now having to pay the price for theft or betrayal of some sort. When she had received the large manila envelope with details of the assignment, it hadn't initially clicked until she had torn it open and glanced at the familiar face in the photograph; she had never been aware of her erstwhile colleague's family name and the fact she was of Italian descent.

It had been one of her easiest kills, with little need for subterfuge; just a drunken night out with a friend. Cornelia had wanted the death to be painless, and had simply twice injected Sicilia Ann with an air bubble directly into her veins, cutting off the blood supply to the brain. She had read about the process online.

And there she was rushing out of Washington Square Park, on the corner of Waverly Place, crossing past the boutique hotel that had once hosted Bob Dylan and many other cult figures, with her dog in tow. There was no doubt it was the same person; Cornelia clearly recognised the distinctive striped black and grey leotard she was wearing. Along with the familiar pink colouring of Sicilia Ann's pigtail ends. She rubbed her eyes, uncomprehending. This made no sense. She had even attended the young woman's funeral.

Her mind was fuzzy. In normal circumstances, she would have quickly stood up and followed the unlikely jogger, but she wasn't thinking clearly right now, her faculties blunted by the shock appearance of someone she clearly knew she had killed. Who shouldn't have been there. No way.

Cornelia wondered whether this was a message. Either her mind or the world out there was giving her a hint that she should put an end to her killings. It wasn't as if she needed the cash right now. She had all she wanted and enough set aside for rainy days or new books and she had never taken any particular pleasure in undertaking the hits, getting kicks from it; it had just been a job. One she did well and took pride in, but no more. Not like an addiction she couldn't shake.

She looked down at her feet and caught sight of a brown squirrel negligently ambling along the narrow path, making its way to the patch of grass behind where she was sitting on the wooden bench.

Wrong animal, she wryly remarked to herself. She was not being drawn into a remake of *Alice in Wonderland*, and following it, or the jogger who looked like Sicilia Ann, down some existential rabbit hole in the ground. She was staying put. She took a final sip of her coffee. It was now cold. Dismissed the jumble of thoughts and emotions running around her brain like a turbulent tide, and attempted to go back to the book she was reading.

The lines on the pages blurred and she couldn't recall which character was the wife and which was the mistress. She had never been a major fan of psychological domestic thrillers anyway.

Cornelia rose from the bench, dropping the half-read paperback to the ground and abandoning it.

She was determined to clear her mind.

"I am sane," she remarked to herself as she stepped away from the bench and took off in the direction of Greenwich Avenue. "It's all an illusion, a form of dizziness, maybe a virus that I've caught which is distorting my perception. I am not in a film or a book, because that is where these sorts of things happen. This is real life."

She sighed.

Back at her apartment, she enjoyed a leisurely bath, her body submerged in the warm water, its surface a landscape of fragrant bubbles, while Bruce Springsteen's *Born to Run* played on the hi-fi and she hummed along to 'She's the One', which she had put on repeat, her attention hypnotised by its insistent piano riff. Finally, the blanket of shimmering rainbow bubbles slowly faded away and she watched the contours of her body, the way her legs stretched away, long, shapely, her best asset she knew. As she shifted her position, her nipples came up for air, dripping bath water, their distinct shade of pink and light brown a familiar sight. They had always been coloured slightly differently, and, when she was younger, she had briefly thought of herself as a freak: the girl with different coloured nipples, but then one day she had come across photographs of the singer David Bowie, and noted how his eyes came in distinctly different shades, and she had accepted her oddity, even taken it to heart as a proof of her individuality. Her gaze wandered further down to her delta. She kept herself shaven; it was something of a professional obligation for the job as an ultimately nude dancer. Initially she had felt something like a plucked chicken, being bare down there, but had long since become accustomed to the smoothness of her mound and the way it divided cleanly, her labia peering with restrained discretion down its centre. Between her sex and her navel, slightly off to the left she displayed a tiny tattoo. An image of a small gun in black ink she had treated herself to on the occasion of her fifth kill. It was silly, she knew, but it made a strong impression on her punters and even more so on the rare instances when she allowed herself to take a man to bed for sex.

Stepping out of the bath, she towelled herself dry and slipped on a white oversized tee shirt, then tiptoed to the main room of the apartment where all three walls were heavy with packed bookshelves. Remembering the puzzling sighting of her first kill a few days earlier, she walked over to the shelf where she kept her signed advance proofs, meaning to take a peek at the Le Carré *The Night Manager* rarity she had managed to purchase thanks to that initial kill of the mob-related guy. It wasn't in its usual place. For the next hour, she kept on browsing through every single shelf in the room and was unable to find it. Cornelia was extremely organised. Considering her double life, she had to be, and was inordinately proud of the excellence of planning and her attention to detail. She had never misplaced a book before. Maybe she'd scour the shelves tomorrow again when her mind was less preoccupied by the recent improbable appearances of those disturbing reminders of her past as a hit woman?

She tried to clear her mind of the troubling vision of Sicilia Ann jogging with her dog in Washington Square Park. Tried to recall which book she had acquired with the resulting fee that had rewarded that kill. It came to her: a dust-jacketed copy of Cornell Woolrich's sixth novel, *Manhattan Love Song*, the final book in his Scott Fitzgeraldian phase before he turned to pulp and noir. She had actually never got round to reading it, always meaning to do so next and, anyway, the cover was in a fragile state, as few copies had survived the weight of years past since its publication, which made it a coveted rarity wrapped in its transparent plastic book protector sleeve.

Again, she failed to locate it, despite a forensic search of her collection.

After a whole afternoon of frantic searching, Cornelia gave up in despair. It made no sense: her apartment had not been broken in that she could see, and why the coincidence of those two particular books linked to the impossible reappearances of her two victims?

She was doing two shifts at one of the clubs she was currently working at that evening. She quickly packed her gear: the diminutive outfits she wore at the onset of each dance, her make-up bag, her music tapes. She slammed the door behind her and checked twice she had properly locked the apartment up.

*

Every time Cornelia felt she had succeeded in blocking the memories of the sightings of her two phantom victims and her mind attained some form of peace, her focus returned to the disappearance of the two matching books from her collection. Appearances and disappearances.

The strip club operators were always critical of the music she chose to dance to. They would have preferred her to select more famous, familiar hits but Cornelia had idiosyncratic tastes, veering towards the obscure, and her movements were always in perfect synchronisation to the music she had brought along, whether tunes by Aldous Harding, Leonard Cohen, Sharon Van Etten or The National. Not for her the bump and grind obligations of 'We Are the Champions' or 'Big Spender'.

"They're a bit gloomy, aren't they?" they said.

But once the music played she was at one with it, and the way her body moved in harmony with its melody and rhythm, how she orchestrated the unpeeling ritual of her clothes until she stood swaying totally bare in the spotlight on the elevated stage, paler than pale in the sheer glare of both the lighting and the eyes of the men who lusted for her was a thing of absolute beauty. Revealing, obscene and triumphant in the knowledge that every man in the room was captivated by the sight of her enigmatic smile, the gentle curves of her breasts and ass and the sexual heart at the crux of her body, the cunt of a hundred lustful attentions.

She was now fully naked, winding down her movements to the final chords of 'Candy's Room' when a man stood up from the shadows of the sparse audience and threw a banknote towards the stage. His face briefly traversed the beam of the spotlight and she recognised her last kill. It was without doubt the man she had made contact with at the Franconia Diner and later despatched. It had been a curious evening. He had greeted her as if he already knew who she was and was resigned to it. Accepting. He had never struggled, almost offered himself up to her, not even going through the pretence of trying to seduce her to justify her readily following him back to the hotel room she had booked for the occasion.

The music faded away. The lights went off. Cornelia left the stage, with a final look at the audience, anonymous faces scattered in the dimness that came in the aftermath of every dance. She sought out the face of the man who had stood up to tip her, noticing in passing that it was a hundred-dollar bill which she held crumpled in her fist as she stepped down and made her way to the backstage area where she could dress again. He was no more to be seen. Had it even been the same man?

"Did you see the guy in the audience who stood up to throw me a bill at the end of my set?" she asked Teresa, who served at the bar and had a fuller view of the small auditorium.

"The customers all look the same to me," Teresa answered.

Cornelia went straight home. She slept badly that night. First she dreamed, then she remembered every person she had killed. By morning, the bedsheets were damp with her sweat.

Over the following weeks, she came across further random sightings of past victims.

At Chelsea Pier, a fleeting vision of the couple whose car she had sabotaged. On the down escalator at the Union Square Regal as she journeyed up on the opposite side, a middle-aged man with a ponytail, wearing a three-piece suit and scuffed shoes; he had struggled and almost got the better of her, and it had taken several days for the scratches he had inflicted on her back to fade away. On the same day, crossing Broadway after a movie, she had to step back towards the pavement when a car raced around a corner and almost took her out; she caught a glimpse of the driver: it was a guy she had been forced to sleep with before she could get the opportunity to dispose of him; he had been rough and unpleasantly verbal and she had taken extra pleasure in discharging the whole clip of the SIG Sauer straight into his heart. On the subway, briefly noting a familiar face on the platform as her Sixth Avenue Line train pulled out; a guy she had avoided the imposition of sleeping with, having managed to slip a pill into his drink and knocking him out before smothering him with a pillow while he dozed; she had a clear memory of that evening, having departed the hotel room with a swoop on its complimentary toiletries, having taken a shine to their fragrance, which she had been using ever since.

And the books kept on mysteriously disappearing from her shelves. Cornelia could now predict in advance which would have faded away into oblivion as she returned to the apartment following yet another sighting, equating titles with particular hits she had been involved in. She began to despair.

There was no sense or reason to it. She felt as if she was living in a bad pulp story, but then even those have an ending of sorts. She wondered how hers would end.

The one thing she was certain about was that it wasn't guilt that was causing this disarray to her life. Cornelia did not believe in guilt. Just in books, sex and death.

She stopped working. Phoned the clubs she had been dancing in and advised them she was taking a break from the trade.

She felt adrift and forlorn, mourning her lost books and increasingly troubled by these regular apparitions of unlikely ghosts.

Unable to find sleep or peace, she finally reached her decision. She had always been proud of her lack of emotions and it was with a certain detachment that she went about her business.

She visited her bank and ordered a banker's draft by debit of her account, which could not be directly traced back to her. Then she walked down Canal Street and acquired a suitable burner phone from one of the many stalls selling rip-off brand copies and all types of paraphernalia, and also managed to get hold of a small electronic scrambling device that would change her voice and make it unrecognisable to any listener.

The next day, using the phone, she called the fixer who normally provided her with jobs and made the necessary arrangements. They had actually never met in person and he was quite unaware of what she looked like; all their previous contacts had been over the phone and arranged through intermediaries. All he knew of her was her voice.

As instructed, Cornelia deposited the folder with her photograph and the banker's draft in a left luggage locker in Grand Central. He would have it picked up the following day, once he had checked the locker was not under any observation. She reckoned it would take a week or so before he managed to contract the job out, and whoever took on the job completed their research.

She returned to her Village apartment and waited.

There were so many books Cornelia owned she hadn't read. Maybe she would have time to complete a few before her killer came. And listen one final time to her favourite music by Counting Crows, Grant Lee Buffalo, Townes Van Zandt and others, wondering where it had all gone wrong.

She had requested the hit be fast and painless.

She didn't even lock her front door.

A SHADE DARKER THAN GRAY

JOSEPH S. WALKER

When he wasn't working or sleeping, Len Brooks was often at Mack's, the neighborhood bar that people in the neighborhood mostly avoided. Mack's was too cold starting around the end of October and too hot starting around the end of May. The wooden floor was warped from years of spills, the windows thick with grime, the beer usually flat. There were complaints that the bottles behind the bar were watered down. Len had no way to judge, since his budget limited him to a couple of painstakingly nursed beers a night.

The radio behind the bar had been busted for years. That was okay, because the men who came to Mack's didn't come to listen to music or ballgames, or to talk and laugh together. They came to drink, and they did it in sullen silence.

For Len, the place had two appealing features. It was half a block from his apartment. And his wife, Myra, would never set foot in the place.

Len didn't really like Mack's, but he liked it a hell of a lot more than Myra seemed to like him. When he was home, he was forever in her way, forever catching her annoyed glares out of the corner of his eye. If he complimented a dish she made, she said that all the girls she went to school with had cooks, so they didn't have to sweat over a miserable stove. If he hung a shirt on a hanger, she snatched it from his hands to be straightened and smoothed, since *some* people apparently didn't mind their wives burning their hands ironing. If he came near her, still drawn despite it all by her porcelain skin and delicate features, she froze into barbed immobility.

Tonight, all he did was turn on the radio, intending to listen to the Patterson fight. He twisted the dial back and forth, getting mostly static.

"Oh, that thing is a piece of garbage," Myra said. "We must be the only ones in the building who still don't have a television set. With what you bring home I suppose we never will."

For once, Len tried to stand up for himself. "You want a set so much, tell your father to give me a raise."

This earned him a bitter cackle. "A raise! For a glorified office boy!"

"For his son-in-law," Len said stiffly.

"That's the only reason you have a job at all," she said. "If you'd gotten your degree, you'd be a partner now. It's not Daddy's fault you couldn't pass the coursework."

"I could do it if I had another chance. Plenty of guys need two shots."

"You mean *men*. Not losers playing at being men." She smirked. "Not *secretaries*."

As always, he ended up fleeing, and as always, here he was at Mack's.

The place was even emptier than usual. A few men were scattered at the bar, their heads hanging over the drinks they clutched. An older man sat alone at a table, a pair of crutches leaning on the wall behind him. Len took a seat as far from the others as he could. Ollie, the rotund, taciturn bartender, brought him a beer without being asked, shoved a bowl of pretzels in front of him, and drifted away. Len took a sip. Flat. Tonight, as a bonus, also not very cold. He could go somewhere else, a place better lit, with colder beer, where he could listen to the fight. But Mack's was a good place to dwell on grievances, probing at them like a tongue against a sore tooth.

The one thing Len was sure of was that it wasn't his fault. He was well on his way to an engineering degree when he met Myra. At first it seemed like a stroke of purest luck. She got him a job at her father's firm – office management, with plans to move up once his degree was complete. They got married. Myra's father, Vernon Packer, was a cold man, but he paid for a honeymoon trip to California, with the understanding that the money would come out of Len's future wages. But it all went wrong, starting almost as soon as they got back. Sometimes he and Myra spent weeks barely getting out of bed, so besotted with each other that the world slid by outside unnoticed. Sometimes they spent weeks screaming at each other, coffee cups hurled against walls, criticisms and threats and apologies and tears swirling in an unending rut they dug deeper and deeper.

Neither state did much for his studies. When he flunked out, he had to literally get on his knees to Vern to keep his job, pathetic as it was. But there would be no second chance. In Vern's eyes, someone who had failed once would only fail again. Len had failed at his profession, and Myra had failed in choosing to bind herself to such a man. Not allowing them to starve was the limit of Vern's compassion.

Len nursed the beer, allowing himself a sip every few minutes. He wanted to drain the glass quickly and call for more. He wanted to drink until they'd have to throw him out of the place. But there was no money. There was never any money.

His eyes drifted to the mirror, and the man alone at a table, a cheap woolen jacket pulled around his shoulders. He wore no hat, and his hair was thinning and almost colorless above a wide, bulging forehead. His mouth was a short, perfectly flat line across a face narrowing sharply to the chin. His eyes were so deeply sunken that it was hard to tell if they were even open, especially in the dirty mirror. If they were open, then he was staring at Len's back.

Len shifted. He could feel the stare, like something probing at him. He tried to look elsewhere, but his eyes kept being dragged back to the man, who never seemed to move. A ridiculous notion came into Len's mind, and once it was there, he couldn't shake it. This wasn't just a balding man in an ugly jacket. This was death. His death. Watching him, waiting patiently for the ending that came to all men. It had shaped everything that ever happened to him, paved the path he was to follow and pushed him along it. There at a wobbly table was the author of all Len's misfortunes.

He was on the verge of turning to challenge the man, to yell at him to stare at somebody else, already, when someone slid onto the stool to his right. Len hadn't noticed him come in. The newcomer was on the youngish side, with blond hair cut a little longer than the fashion and a thin mustache. His suit was clearly expensive and personally tailored. Len couldn't say what color it was, exactly. Somehow his eye couldn't fix on it. Like gray, but darker, without getting all the way to black. "Hello, Lenny," the man said. "Buy you a drink?"

Len's eyes narrowed. "I don't know you," he said. "And I hate being called Lenny."

The man got a cigarette from his pocket. He held up his hands in a calming gesture. "Hey, a man's got a right to be called what he wants. You can call me Madison."

"How do you know who I am?"

"Now that's a good question." The man lit his cigarette. He gestured to Ollie for two beers. "And the answer is, I'm in the information business. I know things. I know you work for Packer Engineering, for example."

Len shook his head. "I don't know what your game is, and I don't care. Get lost."

Ollie set down a couple of fresh beers. Madison picked his up, tasted it, and set it back on the bar with a grimace. "Jesus, that's horrible. Why do you keep coming here?"

"To be left alone."

Madison turned to face him fully and dropped his voice. "Give me five minutes, Lenny. After that, you say so, you never have to see me again."

"Len." The correction was automatic. Madison seemed to take it as an invitation.

"Like I say, I'm in the information business. I buy, I sell, I trade. Here's a piece of information: Packer Engineering is prepping a bid for a big contract to design components for government radar stations. Right?"

Len faced the mirror, his jaw tightened.

"Right," Madison said. His voice got still quieter. "I represent a party very interested in an advanced look at that bid."

"Get lost," Len said again.

Madison reached into an inner pocket and slid a closed hand over the bar. When he lifted it, a fifty-dollar bill rested on the heavily scratched wood.

"That's yours, just for having a beer with me," he said. "I've got nine others just like it, looking for a new home. We shouldn't be seen together again. Two nights from now, I'll be in that little park two blocks east. You come by, maybe we can help each other out."

Len wasn't looking at the mirror anymore. He was looking at the bill resting between his hands.

Madison stood up. "Think it over," he said. "Ask yourself if you really owe anything to Vernon Packer."

That was how it started.

*

Watching Packer's reaction a few weeks later, when the bid he'd been so confident about didn't go through, was almost better than the feeling of holding five hundred dollars in his hand. The old man heaved his bulk around the office, demanding to know where they'd gone wrong, what corner they'd cut that they shouldn't have. He didn't ask Len, of course. As usual, he barely seemed aware of Len's existence.

Len was glad he hadn't yielded to temptation. When Madison gave him the rest of the five hundred bucks, he wanted to go out and buy the biggest television he could find, just to see the look on Myra's face. It would have raised questions he couldn't answer, though. After a little thought, he put the money in the shoebox on the top shelf of the closet, the one that held a revolver and two boxes of ammunition. Myra hated guns. She wouldn't look in the box.

Three weeks later there was a small envelope in the mail with his name and address printed in block letters. He tore it open in the vestibule and found another fifty, folded around a small card. The card read "Anderson file. Park, Tuesday night." Len put the bill in his wallet and tore up the card, dropping the pieces in the incinerator shaft.

This time Madison gave him $600. Len asked if there would be more. Madison was wearing the suit again, the one between gray and black, and he looked at Len and punched his shoulder playfully. "Plenty of money. I'll be in touch again, Lenny."

"Len," Len said, but with no real heat. Even with the little he'd spent – he no longer had to nurse every beer for an hour – this made more than a grand stashed in the gun box. Now he barely thought of a television set. He thought of California. A new life in a new place. If he could get up to four or five grand, he'd go to some warm city and never have to see Myra or her father again.

*

Madison gave him two more assignments in quick succession. Every time Len was alone in the apartment, he got the box down and counted the money. Twenty-five hundred and change. More than he'd ever had in his life. It almost felt like enough. Almost. But why shut off the spigot pouring money into his pocket?

Except suddenly, the spigot went dry. A week went by with no word from Madison, then two, then a month. After a while, Len figured the problem was Vernon. The old man had been shaken by losing several important contracts in the space of a few months, every time being undercut by a small but crucial margin. He was wary, hesitant, for the first time since Len had known him, to take on many new projects at once.

Len ground his teeth continuously. For years Vernon Packer ran him ragged, and now, just when Len needed him to be pushing, he was pulling back.

Len thought he was acting normally, but one morning Jerry Mays stopped at his desk. Mays had been in engineering school with Len, except he made it through. "What's going on with you and the old man?" Mays asked.

Len shrugged. "I don't know what you mean."

"Come on." Mays cocked a hip against the corner of the desk. "I saw the look you gave him when he was walking out of the conference room just now. I've never seen you baring your fangs like that."

Len kept his gaze on the papers in front of him. "Family stuff," he said. "It'll pass."

Mays didn't seem convinced. For the rest of the week, Len focused on being especially passive and good-natured around the office. He didn't know if Mays noticed, but Vernon did, and he snapped at Len to stop simpering around.

"Act like a man, for God's sake," he said in the conference room one afternoon. Len was only there to take notes, of course. He nodded mildly, and Vernon plucked the chewed-up stub of a cigar from his mouth and threw it at him. Len shrank back, raising an arm to swat it away, to his own disgust making a startled, high-pitched noise.

"Act like a man!" Vernon bellowed.

That night when Len walked toward Mack's, Madison was waiting outside.

*

Len's first reaction to seeing him was annoyance. He was being toyed with. He made like he was just going to keep on walking straight into the bar, and Madison took his arm to hold him up. Len shook him off.

"Don't you own any other suits?" he said.

Madison looked down at his gray-black suit, startled. "My—my woman thinks I look good in this color," he said. "Walk with me, Lenny."

"*Len.* I'm real thirsty. Try me tomorrow night."

"You've got all the time in the world to drink flat beer." Madison took his arm again and walked him past Mack's. "This is the big one, Lenny. Len. Sorry. Listen, there's kind of a rush this time."

Len dragged his feet. "Maybe I don't feel like being rushed."

"Stop playing games, will you?" Madison leaned in close and hissed. "Five grand. You stand to make five grand tonight. Now will you listen?"

Five grand. Len fought to keep his face blank. "What do you need?"

"The Relihan file. The whole thing."

"That's four or five hundred pages."

"Everything. And I gotta have it tonight."

Len snorted. "How am I supposed to do that? The office is closed."

"You've got keys. Don't pretend you don't."

"Sure. But there's building security. I'll have to sign in."

"So sign in." They reached the corner. Madison looked up and down the street and pulled Len a little deeper into a shadow. "You bring the file to the park at eleven, and I'll put an envelope in your hand with five thousand in cash."

Enough to get away. Added to what he already had in the shoebox, enough to live on for a year. Two if he was careful. Start again someplace else. "You sure you need the whole thing?"

"Every page."

Len pretended to think. "What about an advance?"

"Len." Madison's brow creased. "I just found out about this myself half an hour ago. I don't have anything on me. While you're getting the file, I'll be getting the cash together. Haven't I taken care of you so far?"

*

The man at the security desk, a retired cop named Kevin who was always working a crossword puzzle, looked up and nodded as he came into the lobby. "Evening, Mr. Brooks. A little midnight oil tonight?" He pushed the clipboard with the sign-on page onto the counter between them.

"Just forgot something," Len said. "File I need to go over." He scrawled his name and pushed the clipboard back. Kevin nodded, already looking back at his puzzle.

Waiting for the elevator, Len kicked himself. The Relihan file was obviously a big deal. Why hadn't he held out for more cash? Madison might have come up with another grand, maybe more. Maybe he still would. Who's to say he would only have the five on him at the park?

He rode up to sixteen, looked up and down the hallway to make sure he was alone, and let himself into Packer Engineering. The offices were dark and still. Always strange, being here alone. He felt his way to the door of the file room and eased it open, then shut it behind him. He didn't have a flashlight, but there were no windows in this room. He turned on the overhead light.

The first thing he saw was Vernon Packer, sprawled out on the floor, in the middle of a spreading dark red stain.

Without thinking, Len killed the light and stood against the door, listening to his heart pound. He imagined it. He must have imagined it. Subconscious guilt, probably, making him see things. Right?

He turned the light on again. Vern was still there. He was on his back, and there were two angry red splotches bordering holes in the front of his shirt. His head was rolled to the side, and his open eyes seemed to be fixed on his son-in-law. Len stayed where he was at the door, watching for any sign of breath or motion. There was none. He stood in paralyzed indecision until it occurred to him that just standing there was probably the worst thing he could do. He picked his way around the margin of the room, looking at his feet to be sure he was well away from the blood, not looking at Vern any more than he could help. He got to the right cabinet, eased the drawer open, and pulled out the thick accordion file labeled *RELIHAN*, grunting with relief. He might have been in trouble if Vern was killed so someone else could steal it.

Now he almost laughed out loud, but he bit that back fast, so it couldn't blossom into hysteria. *Might* have been in trouble? He was alone with a murder victim, and Kevin saw him come up. Maybe the smart play here was to call Kevin, report what he found, and wait for the cops.

But you have no actual reason to be here, a voice said in the back of his brain.

I can make something up. Easy.

They'll see through it. They'll think you killed him. *Myra* will think you killed him.

But they'll see I don't have a gun.

It might be here. You don't have time to look. Or they'll think you ditched it.

If I just leave, I'll look guilty.

You *are* guilty.

Maybe they'll be able to tell he was dead before I got here.

If you're not at the park at eleven, the voice purred, you'll never get the five grand.

Len didn't have an answer for that one.

✶

By the time the elevator took him back down to the lobby, Len had a plan. First, he would go home and grab all the cash Madison had given him so far.

That might mean a fight with Myra, but he'd just ignore her and do what he had to do. Then to the park to get another five grand, more if he could pry it out of Madison. Then the Port Authority. With a little luck, by midnight he would be across a couple of state lines. Miami, maybe, to start.

"Have a good one, Mr. Brooks," Kevin sang out as he hurried through the lobby. Len lifted a hand, but didn't break stride. Half his mind was on a moonlit Cuban beach. You could live cheaply but well there. The other half was still seeing the pattern of the blood around Vernon Packer's body.

*

Myra wasn't home. There were no lights on in the apartment, and he tiptoed in, thinking her asleep. He had to turn on the light in the closet, though, and when he did, he saw the bed was empty. Always a good guess that she was angry at him. Out at a late movie so he'd be the one to fret here alone. Let her be childish, then. It only made his task easier. He lifted the box down from the shelf and opened it.

The money was gone.

The gun was gone.

The only thing in the box was one lonely box of bullets.

The box fell from his fingers. He reached up desperately, pulling down other boxes, throwing them aside as he saw old letters or sewing supplies. He dragged over a stool and climbed up to feel frantically around the back of the shelf, though he knew he was only fooling himself.

She had it. Len ran his hands through his hair, forcing himself to think. She had it. Where would she go? What would she do? All he could think of was his plan. Leave. Maybe she would go to the Port Authority herself. Maybe he could find her there. First, though, he had to see Madison. That was five thousand she wouldn't have, anyway. That was his. He still had ten minutes to make the meet with Madison.

Len tucked the Relihan file under his arm, went to the apartment's front door, pulled it open, and almost ran into Myra. She was holding out her key at the level of the knob, and there were two men in suits behind her. One was fat and one skinny, but they had identical hard glints in their eyes.

"Oh!" she cried out. Len stumbled backwards in surprise as the two men pushed past his wife to come in.

"Get away from me," Len said. It came out as a croak.

"Len, I met these men downstairs," Myra said. "They say they're from the police and they need to see you. What's it about?"

The fat cop pushed Len into a kitchen chair. The skinny one took the Relihan file, glanced at it, and set it on the table, then quickly frisked Len before turning to her. "Ma'am, I'm afraid there's no easy way to say this. Your father was killed tonight, at his place of business. Shot."

Myra's mouth fell open and she staggered to the side. The fat cop grabbed her and steered her into the seat across from Len. "That can't be true," she said. "You've made some mistake."

"I'm afraid not," the thin cop said. "Your husband was there, not long ago. The security guard thought he was acting oddly on his way out. He went upstairs and found your father, then called us. He's a good man, used to be on the force. He knows a suspicious character when he sees one."

"No," Len said. "No, it's not like that. Myra, he was dead when I got there. I swear."

"So why didn't you call us?" the thin cop asked.

"Look at him trying to chew that one over," the fat cop said, disgusted.

"I'd like to know what you were doing with this file, Mr. Brooks," the thin cop said. "And where you were going with it."

"Your husband own a gun, Mrs. Brooks?" asked the fat cop.

"Yes," Myra said. "In the green shoebox in the bedroom closet. A little revolver. His parents made him get it when he moved to the city."

The fat cop went into the bedroom. In a minute he came back, holding the green shoebox. "This one?"

"Yes," Myra said. "That's it."

"Nothing in here but a box of ammo."

"That's interesting," the thin cop said. "I wonder if it will match the revolver we found at the scene." He took a pair of cuffs from his belt and pulled Len's hands behind his back. "I'm taking you in, Brooks."

"Myra," Len said. "I didn't do this."

"I want to speak to my husband," Myra said.

"So speak," the fat cop said.

"Alone," Myra said. She used the voice that usually got Len to leave the apartment as quickly as possible. The cops glanced at each other.

"I'll give you a couple minutes," the thin cop allowed. "But we're gonna be over in that far corner where we can watch you. Don't try nothing funny, either of you."

Myra scooted her chair closer to Len's as the cops drifted across the room. She touched his face lightly, then dropped her hands to her knees and leaned forward. Len leaned toward her until their faces were only a few inches apart.

"Do you think I look appropriately distraught?" she whispered.

A tremble went through Len. He looked at her. Myra's face was twisted in grief and there were actual tears on her cheeks. From across the room, she must have looked like a frantic wife pledging her loyalty. Only Len was close enough to see the way her eyes were shining.

"Don't worry about your meeting with Madison," she went on, her words completely disconnected from her trembling lips and quivering shoulders. "He wouldn't have been there anyway. He is what he said he is, dearest, though his name isn't Madison." There was acid bite in the words. "But he didn't need you. He already had an inside track, you might say."

Len was struggling to take a full breath. He had to try twice before he could speak. "What *are* you?"

"Me?" she said. "I'm the new owner of Packer Engineering. Why, I know everything about the place. Including the back way out of the building." She pushed back away from him, her expression now one of resolve. "All right," she said. "You can take him."

Each cop took one of Len's elbows, and they pulled him to his feet. He almost fell over, limp as a rag doll, staring at Myra, his mouth hanging open.

"Do you have a friend you can go to, Mrs. Brooks?" the thin cop asked. "You shouldn't be alone."

"Don't worry," she said. "I won't be."

She stayed in the apartment. The thin cop led Len downstairs, the fat cop trailing behind with the file and the shoebox. Len wanted to cry out. He wanted to throw himself to his knees and explain everything. Somehow, he couldn't. Something had snapped inside him, and he went meekly, an animal in a trap seeing no way out. He did nothing and said nothing as they put him in the back of their car and started away.

When they passed Mack's, the balding man was standing outside on his crutches. The left leg of his pants hung empty below the knee, the hem pinned up to keep it from dragging on the pavement. When he saw the police car coming, he stood as still as marble, his face turned to it. Len twisted to watch him out the back window of the car. The balding man looked after them, still as the grave, until the cop took a right and cut him off from view.

*

The trial was short. The gun found at Packer Engineering was indeed Len's, and had fired the shots that killed Vern. His coworkers testified that he had long resented his father-in-law, and had been especially hostile in recent weeks. The public defender assigned to the case made a cursory search for Madison, came up empty, and advised him not to take the stand. "Wild accusations are just going to make you look worse," he said.

The divorce notification came three weeks after sentencing. A couple of months later he heard that Myra had sold the company and walked away, set for life.

The first piece of mail Len got in prison came a few weeks later. It had been opened, of course. Inside was a snapshot of Myra and the man Len still thought of as Madison, grinning at the camera on some white-sand beach. *Having a great honeymoon* was written on the back.

The envelope was addressed to Lenny Brooks.

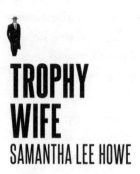

TROPHY WIFE
SAMANTHA LEE HOWE

The rain hammered the soft top of the old MG convertible as I dragged the body out of the passenger seat, heaving it to the edge of the cliff a step and a tug at a time. The body was heavier in death than the man had been in life, but stubbornness and determination won out and I pushed him over the edge and his corpse tumbled like a broken marionette – heftier still as gravity took hold.

I was trembling as I climbed back into the car. Sodden. Cold. I blinked the rain out of my eyes and stared out over the precipice thinking about how my life had taken such an unexpected turn.

*

Three Years Earlier

"What's your name?" The man took the unoccupied seat on the train opposite mine.

I was in first class, a table seat by the window. I was alone and so he assumed he could impose himself on me. It was the start and the end – I just didn't know it then.

I glared at him over my laptop, showing my disapproval of his unwanted interruption.

"I'm Cillian," he said, flashing me what I soon learnt was his trademark grin. He was pleasing to the eye; and things would have been less comfortable if he hadn't been.

The steward came and offered us drinks. Cillian ordered wine for us both, he was confident, even though I continued to blank him.

But I was curious and so I took the drink but made him work for details about me right up until the last moment and the train was pulling into Kings Cross Station. Then I gave him my business card, which read 'Melissa Marshall' along with my phone number and email address.

I hadn't even left the station before I received a texted invitation to dinner that night.

I didn't reply for three days. But I admired his boldness in a way. This was the last time I was stubborn over anything with him.

It was clear from the start that Cillian was a narcissist and so I fed him the lines that made him think me weak and controllable: "My last boyfriend cheated on me"; "I lack confidence"; perhaps it was all because of my "dodgy childhood". I wanted him to feel that I was ripe for the picking and he fed me the appropriate reassuring words that promised me a safe and happy life in his hands.

Six months down the line he proposed. It was the "right time," he said.

I'd let him make love to me the week before for the first time. He thought me predictable, moral and coupled with my fairly attractive looks, a safe bet for a wife. That and the fact that I'd apparently been damaged by a previous relationship that made me cautious, and grateful and so, so desperate for stability. He promised me security in hushed tones under the sheets even while I shivered under him, a paragon of nervous virtuosity – completely untrue – but he liked to believe me a virgin right up until our first coupling, as though anything that had happened before him simply wasn't important.

After that, he claimed he was 'the making of me' and I took on the role of being 'reinvented' and became the bride-to-be that revelled in the lush cash he flashed to prove he was in control of our mutual destiny. He even chose and paid for my wedding dress, booked the venue without my consultation and gave me the list of those to invite. He never asked for my opinion on any of it, nor for a list of friends and relatives I might also want there. It was all about him by then and I was submerged in his sole view of the world. The co-star of his story. I must be grateful he spotted me. Pursued me. Owned me.

I knew all along how to play him.

The wedding was faultless and so were the guests: they were puppets who danced as he pulled the strings. I watched how he controlled and manipulated them all – even his boss – into believing he was the man of the moment. One to watch. Perfect. And now he had a wife who was under his sway just as much as everyone else was. Cillian was on a roll.

We went on an expensive honeymoon: a trip to Dubai followed by a long, leisurely cruise around the Bahamas. When we got home, I found a letter from my old boss accepting my resignation. He hadn't asked me if I wanted to be a housewife, but had merely sent the email from my account, giving my notice on my behalf. Though it took me by surprise I didn't object. It was... predictable behaviour for someone like him and therefore should have been expected. I promised myself after that he wouldn't catch me out again. I had to be even more careful.

I took to the role of trophy wife like the proverbial duck to water, living in the house he'd chosen and bought before we met, overseeing renovations he'd decided we needed: all his choice alone. I only voiced a positive opinion, expressing how his taste in everything pleased me. How I'd never have thought of this colour or that. Even though his style appeared to me excessive and ostentatious and was always, without doubt, about how others would perceive and admire him and not about making me happy.

He was like a child sometimes, wide-eyed and excited with his control of the new money he'd worked hard to earn – all fruits of his labour, just as I was. Proof of his self-worth.

On occasion when I tried to buy my own clothes, he never liked them. They were too short, too long, too tarty or not sexy enough. I gave up after the fourth round of returns and let him choose for me from then on. It was simply easier that way. It wasn't long before all of the clothing, jewellery and shoes I'd owned when we met disappeared from my lavish walk-in wardrobe. I never saw him throw them out, but noticed one day that they'd gone.

He was cash rich but I had to ask for every penny. He'd check my credit card bills in detail to make sure I hadn't bought anything that was not pre-approved. He even took to looking at my mobile phone bills – scrutinising any numbers he didn't recognise, questioning me about them. He stopped doing this when he learnt I was an open book. All calls were explainable, most of them were to him, or for him, as I fulfilled the errands he left me to do during the day.

When I gained a few pounds, he bought me a gym membership and checked up that I was using it on set days to keep myself 'nice' for him.

I knew what I was. I knew my place. I was complicit after all: I was in it for the long haul, no matter how much it took. There's always a price to pay and I kept my goal in view as I thought about the day when it would all be about me: the widow after the fatal accident that would take him from me all too soon.

Even though I didn't fall for any of the lifestyle he permitted me, I allowed him to manipulate it and me. And he never suspected that he was a mark like any other as I cultivated him, playing him even as he thought he was holding all the cards. I still had the aces up my sleeve.

I thought that maybe we'd have the 2.4 children before I had him where I wanted – all of which would happen when he said it was time. I must never push the issue or suggest it. By then I would be such a dutiful wife he'd never expect me to question him. And I wouldn't have but for the emails he received on his personal laptop that signposted the first problem: some of the business trips he went on were a lie. He was so sure of me he didn't even bother putting a password on his machine, for he didn't know I had it in me to be nosey.

Of course, I'd paid attention all along, despite my apparent complacency. I wasn't the laid-back, silent, calm partner he thought he possessed. I had bank accounts he didn't know about, resources to draw on anytime I wanted. Even though he thought he kept me in a place of controlled destitution that made me completely reliant on him.

Once I saw the emails, I realised that there was another woman in his life, but I couldn't involve a private investigator to find out who she was. That would allow another person knowing that our marriage wasn't perfect after all. And to the outside world it had to appear as though it was if my ultimate goal was to be reached.

I told white lies in place of whole truths with the same straight and honest face. Distracted by the texts he was now receiving on his phone from his new flame, he barely looked in my direction.

I wondered about stopping taking the contraceptive pills he got for me, but he'd taken to checking them every day – something he'd never done before. For some reason it was now important to him that I *didn't* get pregnant. It could only mean one thing: soon I'd be usurped in his affections if indeed I hadn't been already.

This changed everything.

I crashed the timeline of my once long-term plan. I had to step up the ultimate goal.

I don't know why I cared, but I also needed to know who this new woman was.

I pulled some old clothing from my storage unit – something Cillian had never known about. He didn't recognise me in these dowdy slobs as

I followed him to work for a week. He was so sure of me that I could have been in plain sight and he wouldn't have seen me.

The secretary he'd hired recently was an effervescent blonde with legs up to her armpits, but Cillian was never going to be so obvious, and a woman like that wouldn't *need* him and would be too hard to control. I dismissed her as the guilty party almost immediately.

I mapped his days, learnt his habits and then discovered the little coffee shop he liked to visit during his lunch break. Odd, as he often ate at his desk. It was glaringly obvious that this new habit had nothing to do with coffee.

Her name was Sophie. She was one of the baristas.

I guess she'd been hard to win at first because it was Cillian's modus operandi to go after someone who appeared to be impossible to land. But now she was putty in his hands, laughing at his corny jokes, grinning back at that flawless, confident smile. She was wearing a diamond tennis bracelet, almost identical to the one he'd bought me after the first time we slept together. Would there soon be an engagement ring on her finger too? I wondered what he planned to do to disentangle himself from me.

Before he went back to work, I saw them exchange a kiss at the door. When he'd gone, I went into the shop and bought a latte. She served me. The coffee was good, but I wondered how she would feel about never working here again once Cillian decided she had to quit. It was like waiting for a car crash that you knew was going to happen. Would she walk into this not knowing what he planned? Or was she, too, in it for the duration?

She wasn't as well turned out as I was. Very girl next door, simple even. There was so little sophistication that I couldn't really see the appeal, knowing what Cillian liked. But then, I recalled his words to me of reinvention and I saw Cillian again with fresh eyes. Eyes that someone like her might have. Maybe she realised he had money. Maybe she even knew he was married. Maybe she didn't, after all there was no sign of recognition on her part when she served me: I was just another customer.

A divorce would cost him dearly, but if he'd fallen for this girl, would he really mind? I decided I wasn't ready to let her take over my life, not after all I'd put up with. Cillian wasn't easy to please, even when I made it appear effortless.

I went home with a plan forming. Something I perhaps should have considered sooner. It really was time to move forward and end this silly game once and for all.

*

Soon after dinner, Cillian fell asleep on the sofa. His phone still casually held in his hand, as though he waited for Sophie to message him. I took it from his fingers, he murmured but didn't wake. I'd spiked his wine with sleeping tablets to make sure.

He had Sophie listed under a work colleague's name, but the texts they exchanged were anything but professional. He'd taken to sending pictures of himself – nothing indecent, that wasn't his style – but selfies in his office; in the coffee shop with her behind him; in our bed as though he'd just woken up. I tried to recall when this one might have been taken as my side was neat and empty, and looked as though it had never been occupied.

I discovered he had an Instagram account full of pictures like this. She was following him, and he was following back. There were no photos of 'us'. All of which confirmed that I was his secret from her. Dirty almost. A mistake he'd made and had yet to correct.

I forwarded everything I could find over to a phone that Cillian didn't know I had. Then I deleted all my activity from his history. I dropped his phone to the floor by the sofa, then nudged him awake.

"Darling? Are you all right? Should I help you go to bed? You've been working so very hard…"

After that I gave up following him and started following her.

*

Sophie lived in a small, rented, studio apartment in Putney. To the casual eye she was ordinary. When she wasn't seeing Cillian or working in the coffee shop, she stayed in and alone in her apartment. Cillian never went there.

I became fascinated with Sophie. I wanted to know more about her. Where she came from, who she really was. I did an internet search and found nothing other than the Instagram account I'd already seen and Cillian would eventually boycott if he made her his. On the surface, there were no friends, no family and no one other than my husband in her life. She was a ghost – just like I was when Cillian met me.

I couldn't recall him ever asking me about family, or friends: Cillian had treated me as though no world before him ever existed.

I zoomed in on the photo he had of her on his phone, making coffee in the background. Was this taken when he first set his sights on her or as a way for them to be innocently in a photograph together? She was facing him. Her expression one of concentration as she placed a tall latte glass down before another customer.

I did a search for her image online. Nothing came up. I was more curious about her than ever. Almost everyone has some social media presence. Except me, and this was a deliberate choice.

I looked again at the images that showed on her Instagram: cups of coffee; inspirational banners about lifestyle; an occasional cat picture reshared from somewhere else.

Who was she?

*

He wrapped up his next trip away as business but I knew this wasn't true. I ironed his shirts, packed his case carefully and watched him climb into the taxi before I took a look at his emails.

The booking was a five-star hotel in Dover. I knew there was no reason workwise for Cillian to be going there. Knowing where he was going negated the issue of following him or Sophie.

In my mind's eye I imagined the two of them meeting at the train station. It would be first class all the way, Cillian never did standard. I saw Sophie, wide-eyed, excited, in love, as she smiled at him over the table. Cillian would be on the side facing travel. Sophie would be content to travel backwards but even then, the start of his control would set in.

My body trembled at the thought of them together. In a hotel room. I had to stop this: I wouldn't give up my place that easily in Cillian's life.

*

The MG had been static for several years in a garage in Richmond, but I had a portable battery to get the engine started. As the car had been left in storage it wasn't taxed any more, and any MOT it might have had had long since expired. I didn't want the complication of being stopped by the police because of a casual scan of the plates, and so I removed them and put on a set I'd copied from another MG of the same colour I'd discovered a picture of online for this purpose.

As the battery charged, I cleaned the car, removing all trace of its dusty home and the spiders that had taken up residence around the side mirrors. When the car was working, and clean, I got in and drove it away.

My route to Dover was already planned.

*

When people aren't expecting to see you, they don't see you. It's something I learnt some years ago, before my Cillian days. Unobtrusive, uninteresting, in plain sight, I watched Cillian and Sophie in the hotel restaurant.

He was fixated on her at all times, and her response to this was modest and sweet as she blushed a little with his somewhat full-on attention. Cillian had never been like this with me. He appeared to be less confident and self-assured with her. This wasn't a side of him I'd seen before and it worried me more than if he'd been doing his usual behaviour – showy and pushy and flashing cash around like it didn't matter. No. Cillian was not like this with Sophie. In fact, he was avoiding bringing attention to them at every opportunity. But why then bring her to such a public hotel? I was never more uncertain of his intentions towards her than now.

When they retired for the night, they had separate rooms. This really surprised me. And not adjoining either. Cillian's booking was only for the weekend. And when Sunday came, he left, giving Sophie a small kiss goodbye in reception. Sophie, it seemed, was booked into the hotel longer. A taxi waited outside for Cillian, and as it drove away, my phone pinged. I looked at it to find a text message from Cillian saying he would be home that day.

I was in a quandary, I had to get back before he did, or he'd question where I'd been.

I sent him a reply to give myself more breathing time.

"What time should I expect you?" I asked.

His reply told me he had some work-related meetings first and would be home for dinner. I took this to mean he was going into the office first.

I left the MG in the hotel car park and caught a taxi to Dover Priory train station. Once near, I booked myself on the next train, after Cillian's, and sat in a local coffee shop following the progress of Cillian's train on the app. When the train had departed the station, I stood up and walked towards the door of the coffee shop and then I saw Cillian, striding confidently down the street. He'd obviously not got the train. He had changed his clothing, he was wearing black jeans and a black polo shirt, with a dirty-looking anorak. He'd covered his hair with a woollen hat, something I'd never seen him in. But there was no mistaking his walk despite this somewhat bizarre disguise. Confused, but curious, I followed him all the way back to the hotel.

*

Cillian followed Sophie at a safe distance as she left the hotel. As I shadowed him, I was nervous but intrigued. She appeared not to know he was there, and if she turned, Cillian ducked out of sight, making sure she didn't see him. It was the oddest game of cat and mouse and so closely reflected my own course of tracking him that I began to wonder if they both knew I had been at the hotel after all and if this was some form of trap.

I dropped back from my pursuit and observed Cillian as Sophie entered a bakery shop. He waited for her, picking a location to observe from, without being seen, or so he thought because his focus was taken up by her. I knew then he had no clue anyone was watching him.

Sophie left the bakery clutching a paper bag with something hot inside, which I suspected was a pasty. Cillian never allowed me to eat junk food like this and I saw the set of his shoulders as Sophie opened the bag and tucked in to whatever it contained. He nodded, as though he were confirming something to himself that he already knew about the woman. But I couldn't see his face and therefore wasn't able to read what it was he was thinking. He took out his phone from his jeans pocket and sent a text. Sophie halted and reached inside her jacket pocket as her phone pinged in response. She read the text, stowed the phone away, and then took another bite from her pasty.

While I was distracted by Sophie, Cillian walked away in the opposite direction. I didn't follow him.

I made my way back to the hotel, Sophie a few feet ahead of me. On the walk back I received another text from Cillian, this one telling me he wouldn't be home that night after all. Whatever he'd observed on his stalking of Sophie, it had changed things. This, at least, meant I no longer had to rush back either. Using an old card that I kept active, I booked a room in the hotel for the night. The card, like the deeds on the MG, was not in the name I currently used and was not registered to my current address. Though if I were looking for grounds for divorcing Cillian, my presence at the hotel could be fully justified. I still wasn't sure where this whole adventure was going or what I'd do if he decided he was leaving me for Sophie.

That evening, Sophie ate alone in the hotel dining room then went to bed early. I didn't catch sight of Cillian all evening and eventually I went upstairs to my room and, removing the brunette wig and clear spectacles I'd been wearing all day, I went to bed too.

I got up early the next day, determined to drive the MG back to London and get home in advance of Cillian's expected return. I'd heard nothing from him the previous evening, which wasn't unusual when he was on a supposed business trip. But, despite the uncertainty of the future, I'd slept well and felt refreshed, even though a modicum of anxiety returned on waking.

I put the wig and glasses back on and took my small overnight bag, leaving the hotel room. As I entered the lift, I heard a piercing scream that seemed to come from the floor above. Knowing I didn't want to get caught up in anything, I exited the lift, left the hotel and got into the car where I waited. A short time later, a police car and an ambulance arrived. I turned the key in the ignition and pulled the MG out of the car park, leaving Dover behind me. Whatever had happened it was nothing to do with me, and my fake plates and ID might not bear up to too much scrutiny.

*

Cillian returned home for dinner that night and he appeared to be calm and happy. I asked him politely about his trip and his eyes glowed as he lied to me about a 'deal' he'd made, and how this might lead to a promotion. That night he didn't look at his phone once. I knew then something had changed. Had he realised that Sophie wasn't for him after all and ended it?

"Maybe we need to start a family soon," he said after dinner.

I didn't comment, but gave him the smile I'd cultivated which gave him my agreement without me saying a word. I let him make love to me and then lay still as he fell asleep soon after.

He'd left his phone charging in the kitchen and I couldn't help wondering what had happened with Sophie. His attitude had changed, the darkness I'd sensed lurking like a poisonous parasite in every word he'd uttered to me in the past few weeks had now washed away. The evening was a normal one for us. Normal because I showed no sign of rebellion, or made any effort to refuse anything he wanted, but Cillian was relaxed again.

I slid from the bed, already forming the excuse I'd give if he woke, but he didn't stir.

In the kitchen, I found his phone. He'd left it switched on, and I scrolled through it looking for signs of the texts, but they'd all been deleted along with the contact number he'd had for Sophie.

I returned to the bedroom and found Cillian sleeping soundly, as if he had no cares or worries.

*

I heard about Sophie's death on the news – her body was found in that same hotel in Dover by a housekeeper. She'd been strangled.

*

Cillian mentioned us having children again a few nights later. By then he was acting perfectly 'pre-Sophie' normal. If he knew she was dead, he didn't appear to be upset by the prospect.

*

A few months later, Cillian started something with another girl. I didn't take kindly to this. There was a nervous energy growing inside him and I became aware of it sooner. His pattern of behaviour reverted back to the 'Sophie days' but this time it was obvious to me.

I'd failed to get pregnant, despite our attempts – Cillian didn't know that I was, secretly, still taking my contraceptive pills, having obtained my own supply. I had changed my mind about a lot of things since Sophie, and now I watched Cillian harder than he watched me.

When the 'business trips' began again, I didn't bother to follow him, or try to learn who the girl was. It would probably burn out anyway. But then, I saw him with her: a Sophie lookalike, wishy-washy, girl next door, and I was betting she had no life beyond Cillian either.

She was called Chloe.

When I saw her photograph appear on the news a few weeks later I knew that Chloe had been strangled because she failed to live up to Cillian's expectations of her... whatever they may be.

*

I didn't need another girl to die to prove to me that the time to end things with Cillian was rapidly approaching. I continued on as a dutiful wife while making plans. When I felt that steady nervous darkness edging back into his behaviour, I acted on it.

*

Now the rain hammered the soft top of the old MG convertible as I sat and looked out over the sea.

Pills crushed into wine and a long drop over the cliff when Cillian took his next business trip was the weapon I used to end the disaster that was our marriage. And the girl that waited for him in that five-star hotel would never know what a lucky escape she'd had. Though I always would.

I started the engine and turned the car away from the cliff edge. I was a long way from home, but I had an iron-clad alibi in place. It wasn't the ending I'd originally planned for him, and it had come sooner than the long-term plan I'd mapped out when I first chose him as my mark. It was funny how things turned out.

I had a lovely house, all the money I needed… I was free once more.

Until I decided to play the game again.

BLUE MOON OVER BURGUNDY
O'NEIL DE NOUX

Tom steps into the dark bedroom and waits just inside the door for his eyes to adjust. The only light filters through the white drapes of the balcony's French doors. The room smells of Vaporub and other medicines. Objects take form, as in a fog lifting – an easy chair next to the balcony's French doors, a chifforobe, a nightstand and his great uncle's bed. Tom peers through the dimness, sees his Great Uncle Henry's eyes shimmering at him, the old man's white hair almost glowing.

"Come in, boy," Henry says in a raspy voice. "Have a seat." The old man lies propped in front of three large pillows.

Tom moves to the easy chair.

"Can you open the curtain?" Henry's voice comes a little stronger.

Tom moves to the French doors, pulls open the drapes and glances down at narrow Burgundy Street. An impatient car horn blares as another driver tries to hurry through the French Quarter.

"That's a blue moon," Henry says. The old man leans to his right to look out the top of the French doors. Tom looks over his shoulder at the full moon shining over New Orleans.

"Second full moon this month." Henry straightens and readjusts the plastic oxygen tube affixed to his nose. Tom nervously straightens his gray tie. Maybe he shouldn't have worn a black suit tonight, but it's too late now, and what did it matter, the old man's pretty well gone.

"That was a helluva rainstorm we had," Henry says.

"Streets were like little canals." Tom looks out at the black, wrought-iron balconies across the street. Rainwater drips from them. He sees blood now, rolling off the balconies. He shuts his eyes, waits, blinks the vision away, looks again. It's water. Tom's heart thumps in his chest. He grits his teeth, turns back to his great uncle. His eyes adjust enough for him to see the old man's face is sunken. The big man looks so frail now. At six-three, Henry's height had made him a formidable man when he was young and the force of his personality always made him seem even larger.

"Sit. Sit," Henry says and Tom returns to the easy chair, sees the old man's eyes are closed. Tom's fingers tap the arms of the chair for nearly a minute before the old man's eyes flicker open.

"You wanted to see me?"

Henry nods and raises a spindly hand. "I have something for you."

"What?" Tom's stomach feels jittery. Downstairs his aunts, uncles and cousins sit gathered like buzzards, all pretending they aren't waiting for Henry to die.

A weary smile comes to Henry's mouth. "I have a gift for you. A precious gift." Henry turns to the French doors again. "It started with a rainstorm," he says, a catch in his voice. "1946, July twenty-fifth, a Thursday. I was in my studio, reading my morning paper. An article about the bomb blast at Bikini Atoll. The atom bomb." Henry turns back and blinks those luminous eyes at Tom. "How old are you now?"

"Twenty-five." Tom thinks – *This is going to last forever.* He tries to calm down, wondering what the gift would be. Money, he hopes. Something useful from the old man who'd always been well-off, the wealthiest person in the family by far. Money or maybe something that will drive the visions of blood away. Finally.

Uncle Henry closes his eyes. Taking his time. Typical.

Maybe he's leaving me the house. It would sell easily, an original Creole townhouse in the Quarter. Tom feels his heartbeat again. Before Tom flunked out of the University of New Orleans, he'd been an architecture major and did a paper on the Creole townhouse. Like most buildings in the French Quarter, the architecture is Spanish colonial. After most of the quarter was destroyed by two fires, the Spanish rebuilt the city when they ruled it. This townhouse would fetch a damn good price.

"I was twenty-six," Henry says in a stronger voice. "Right out of the army."

Not again. Tom knows the story by heart – how his great uncle was a combat photographer in Europe. From Normandy all the way to the Battle of the Bulge where he was wounded. The old man came home and opened his famous photo studio that occupied the first floor of this Creole townhouse on Burgundy Street until he sold the business to a national photo studio chain in the 1990s, which promptly moved the business to a suburban mall.

"She came in out of the rain and stood dripping in the doorway." The old man's voice wavers. "Even now, if I close my eyes, I can see her standing there in that wet dress. White linen clinging to her body." Henry's eyes remain closed. "She was embarrassed, so I got her a towel. Two towels. One for her hair and one for her body. She stood in the doorway, rubbing the towel through her long red hair and looked at me with the lightest green eyes I've ever seen."

Never heard this part of his story, Tom realizes. *Yep, this is going to be a long one.*

The old man's eyes snap open.

"Irish, she was from the Channel."

Yeah. Yeah. Talking about the Irish Channel, of course. We all know about the Irish settling there. When was that? Long goddamn time ago.

"The rain got worse. I made her coffee. She looked at my pictures and said how much she liked them. I certainly liked everything about her, especially her shy smile. She had a small, round face. Nearly perfectly symmetrical and so pretty, it took my breath away."

A tapping at the French doors turns Tom around to see the rain has returned, a breeze sending it against the glass.

Henry looks at the rain, says, "We went to dinner that very evening."

Tom crosses his legs and folds his arms to keep from drumming the chair's arms. *What's this all about? Henry is a life-long bachelor.* Tom can't remember a time when he didn't have a pretty lady on his arm. In fact, two of Uncle Henry's former girlfriends are downstairs, hoping they'll cash in too. Tom's latest girlfriend is there also, impatient Edie, probably wondering if they'll be late for the movie.

"Her name was Kathleen Sweeney and she was a beauty in so many ways."

What's he talking about now? The old man babbling. Oh, yeah. The girl from the Irish Channel.

Tom had modeled himself after this old man, at least modeled his love life, planning to remain a life-long bachelor.

"I remember every evening we spent together, every moment, but I won't bore you with the details."

Thankfully.

"I'll stick to the important parts." Henry coughs sharply and leans forward. His breath comes out in rasps.

"You all right?" Tom asks, trying to keep the impatience from his voice.

The old man clears his throat and points to the balcony. "Can you crack open the doors? I'd like to smell the rain again."

Tom cracks open the French doors and a misty breeze floats into the room. When he looks back at his great uncle, Henry is smiling sadly.

"We were inseparable," Henry says. "Spent every moment we could together. But… But…" Henry takes in a deep, raspy breath. "You see, she was barely twenty." The old man's voice breaks and it takes him a few moments to recover. "Her family was worried I was taking advantage of her. My family worried too. She was Irish. Shanty Irish, as your great-grandfather called her. And you know the family."

Yeah, I know the family.

Tom was the black sheep, after all, his parents long gone, the troubles he'd gotten into with the police. Many regretted he had the family name – Torrijos. How many times had he heard that? "We're Castilian, original Spanish settlers here in New Orleans. Came over with Governor Unzaga. And you – a jailbird."

Hell, they were just misdemeanors. A lot, but still misdemeanors.

Henry leans forward and stretches toward Tom, the old man's face wet with tears. "We had a love. So intense. So real." The old man's lips quiver as he falls back against the pillows. The rain taps against the windows like a woman's fingernails.

Tom feels the hair on his arms standing. It's the first time he's ever seen the old man cry.

Where is he going with this?

Henry closes his eyes once again and Tom checks his watch; still time enough to catch the movie if the old man stops talking soon.

Henry's voice wells with emotion as he says, "We were meant to be. I could feel it in my heart. But… But…" A twisted hand rises to wipe the tears from his face.

"We let it slip away. No, *I* let it slip away. When we made love it was… we fit together perfectly. I'm not just talking sex. It was on a different level. We *fit* together – our hands fit together perfectly when we held them."

Fit? A memory stirs in Tom. Perfectly fitting with a woman. He remembers feeling like that once – maybe. Tom closes his eyes as Henry continues trying to describe the feeling, the ease of being with his Kathleen, the warm kisses, the passionate love, the way their bodies formed together after making love. A memory stirs in Tom and his heart races. He wipes his eyes as if that would brush the memory away.

"One day another pretty woman came in to be photographed," Henry said. "There's always another pretty woman. Story of my life." The voice fades and the old man takes in several long breaths. "I broke Kathleen's heart. I turned away from her."

His voice returns stronger. "Eventually, she found another and that was that." A gust of wind blows the French doors wider and the drapes swoosh in with a rush of wet air. Tom moves to close the doors.

"Leave a crack," Henry says. Tom uses the back leg of the easy chair to keep the doors from opening wide. He sits again.

Henry looks up at the dark ceiling, a dreamy look in his eyes.

"My heart knew, but I wouldn't admit it. I found another too, then another. But, time and again, I found myself turning around on the sidewalk, thinking I saw Kathleen."

The French doors rattle against the back of Tom's chair as another whoosh of damp air rushes into the room. Henry turns his face to the mist.

"In breaths," Henry says. "It happened in breaths, fleeting moments in which I'd relive our times together, like snapshots. I found myself reprinting the portraits I'd taken of her. I took a lot of pictures of that pretty face.

"It happened in breaths. In lost moments. Not all at once. If it happened all at once, if I would have realized, I would have done something immediately. Eventually... my heart began to ache when I thought of her, every time I looked at her pictures. My youth was gone, my love was gone. The years melted it away, melted us away, melted me away."

Henry turns toward Tom. "It still aches. Especially now, near the end."

Henry leans back and continues, "One day, when I was forty-six, twenty years after that rainy day she'd walked into my studio, I passed her on Canal Street. She was with another woman and they were talking. She looked right at me as she passed and didn't know who I was."

Henry's voice falters. "What struck me, what made my heart almost burst, was how little she'd changed. I hadn't changed much myself. My hair was silvering. That's about all. But she looked right at me and didn't recognize me, as if I was never in her life. I turned and watched her walk away, watched the sway of her hips, the length of her smooth legs as she

moved away. She never looked back. I was just another face in the crowd."
Henry raises both hands now. "And it was that day I knew, at that moment,
for certain, that she had been the *one*."

The old man looks at Tom with narrowed eyes. "You understand, don't you?"

What? Tom feels himself nod. *God get this over with.*

"She was the *one*." Henry leans as far forward as he can. "Listen, boy!
This is the gift I give you. From an old man to a young man. It's the one
truth I've learned in this life. Are you listening?"

"Yes, Uncle Henry." Tom struggles to keep his voice from sounding bored.

"For everyone there is one nearly perfect love. Do you understand, boy?"
The voice is high-pitched now.

"Yes." Tom stretches. "I understand."

"Do you really understand?"

Henry's eyes are wet again, his breathing raspy. It takes him a few
moments to recover.

Tom figures he should ask, so he does: "How do you know for sure?"

A weak smile comes to the old man's lips and he waves Tom over.

"Follow your heart." Henry reaches a shaking hand and Tom grabs it.
"Don't think. Don't listen to anyone. Just follow your heart because your
heart will know."

The old man squeezes Tom's hand and he's surprised at the strength.
Then the grip weakens and Henry looks up at the ceiling again.

"She has to come out of the rain, or trip over your leg in class, or bump
into you in a store, but she's out there." Henry nods slowly. "Just don't let
her slip away."

Tom nods in response and thinks – *What if I never run into her? What if
my one lives in China, or something?* But. But. *What if she lives here?*

His heartbeat rises again. Henry's eyes stare into Tom's and the old man's
next statement sends a shiver through the young man.

"You don't have to go looking for her. You'll find each other. That's what
I'm trying to tell you. You *will* find one another. You just have to be smart
enough not to let her go."

How did he know what I was thinking?

"I've spent years wondering what might have been, if I'd been smart
enough to understand what I've just told you."

Henry pulls his hand away and folds his arms. "That is the gift I give you.
The gift of an old man's wisdom." Henry settles back against his pillows.

That's it? Wisdom? Tom waits, in case the old man forgot something, but Henry seems finished. Tom stands and turns to the French doors and shakes his head.

The old man's voice returns, a whisper now. "Don't let it happen to you."

Tom looks back at him, his jaw set.

"Find her and hold her. Now go."

Tom looks into his great uncle's eyes. The eyes looking back at Tom seem suddenly fierce. "Now go. And tell those people downstairs that everyone's in my will. Even you."

Tom moves slowly to the door, opens it and looks back at Henry who nods and waves him away. As Tom closes the door, Henry calls out, "Don't forget!"

Yeah. Yeah. Yet he feels a shiver.

Tom stops in the stuffy hall, thinks about turning around, going back in and closing the French doors. No, let the old man catch a chill. But the elderly nurse comes up the stairs and breezes past him for Henry's room and Tom feels the shiver again and his heart aching.

What's wrong with me? Tom walks slowly down the stairs.

Edie sits in the foyer, her legs crossed as she politely listens to one of Tom's aunts. She doesn't see Tom for a moment. He examines her, as if for the first time. Her long blonde hair is golden in the amber light. Her lips, painted a deep red, are almost alluring, the lines of her face smooth and lovely. She's a pretty girl.

He remembers his great uncle's voice: "There's always another pretty woman. Story of my life."

Edie hadn't tripped over his leg or even bumped into him. They worked together at the drafting firm. He can't remember the first time he saw her. She was one of five women working there. He'd dated every one.

Edie turns her blue eyes to him. "Ready to go?"

He nods, steps up and takes her hand.

Aunt Lucille rises from her chair, asks, "He's still alive?"

"Of course."

"Well, what did he want with you?" Uncle Freddie asks.

"Yeah," goes Cousin Wilma. "Why did he want to talk to you?"

Tom looks at their narrowed eyes, each looking like a raptor ready to swoop on a mouse.

"He told me about the treasure."

"Treasure?" Aunt Aretha bounces in place.

"The Treasure of Jean Lafitte. Did any of you know our ancestor Carlos Torrijos sailed with Lafitte and his brothers?"

Heads shake.

"Uncle Henry says it's there in his will. He's left something for all of us. One will get the information about the treasure." Tom shrugs. "It's a crap shoot. Only he knows, so we all better be good to him before he changes his will again."

He leads Edie out, the relatives chattering like chickens in a coop.

"They are strange," says Edie.

"Greedy-ites." *Like myself,* Tom thinks.

It's still drizzling as they rush to his car around the corner, climbing in before any of his cousins decide to pursue with more questions. Tom warms up his Toyota's engine, Edie reapplies her makeup in the rearview mirror, says, "I was worried we'd miss the show. We'll just have time."

Tom pulls away from the curb, takes a right on Burgundy and drives along the narrow French Quarter street. The moon, bright and yellow, hovers over the dark roofs, its pale light shimmering on the wet pavement. Edie takes his right hand and holds it with both of hers.

He slows approaching Ursulines Street, Tom sees a shadow step off the curb and hits his brakes. The car slides on the wet pavement. Edie lets out a gasp as a woman steps back up on the curb and the car stops a couple feet from her. Tom waves for the woman to cross in front of him while he catches his breath. The woman waves as she passes through the headlights. Tom watches her and it hits him, his heartbeat thumping again. The woman moves away, into the darkness down Ursulines.

Edie pokes him. "You all right?" She squeezes his right hand. "You look pale."

Tom shakes his head, shaking away the image of the woman who passed through his headlights. He wants to keep it foggy, unclear.

"You weren't *that* close to hitting her."

"I know," Tom snaps. *It was the tug of the moon,* he thinks. No. *It was something worse.*

He pulls his hand away and puts both hands on the steering wheel as they continue through the Quarter, turning on Barracks Street up to Rampart Street to the interstate to the multiplex theater out in Metairie. He hurries as Edie chatters about his aunts and cousins, a couple of cousins who hit on her. Tom doesn't listen. He keeps thinking about the woman back on Burgundy Street.

They're just in time for the movie and Tom drives all thoughts from his mind, watching Tom Cruise as a hit man, watching Jamie Foxx show he can act. The sudden violence, the sudden blood, brings Tom back to Burgundy Street. He sees the woman in the rain again.

She reminds him of…

No. No. Was that who Uncle Henry was talking about, as if pointing an accusing finger at Tom? How would the old man know? He wonders if Edie can feel the perspiration in his hand as she holds it. He pulls it away and wipes it on his pants. Tom takes deep, even breaths, trying to hide it from Edie as the pain in his heart grows deeper and he feels a well of emotion rising in his throat and remembers… those lips… those dark brown eyes… and the young, loving face of Jennie Clemm. It comes to him slowly – then forcefully, like a salvo from a battleship.

It's Jennie. It's always been Jennie.

He closes his eyes to the movie and runs scenes through his mind, their first date, dinner at Pizza Shack, that play they saw at the Le Petit Theatre du Vieux Carré on Saint Peter Street with the nude scene between a young couple, and another play at a university theater in the round – Tennessee Williams' *The Rose Tattoo*. The night cruise on *The President* riverboat where Fats Domino and Dr. John played. And the long nights of passion.

It's too late. He knows it's too late.

Edie starts yakking as they leave the show, jabbering about the movie as they walk to the car. She keeps talking as they drive away and head straight for her apartment. She finally realizes they're not heading to his house and takes his hand again.

"Are you all right?"

He nods, not trusting his voice.

"We're not going to your place?" Edie sounds hurt. "I feel like snuggling." Code words for sex. She raises her right hand and presses it against his cheek. "You don't feel good?"

"Your place is closer," he says as the rain falls hard now.

Her apartment is small but the girl wants to get it on, doesn't she? Tom has to make love to her tonight. If he doesn't, she'll tell her friends and work would be uncomfortable. It's expected. He has a reputation to live up to and he makes love to Edie, going through the steps, kissing and stripping her and letting her take his clothes off. He climbs next to her, kisses her again, their tongues brushing, his hands and fingers working her body. She gasps, moans and they screw, a hot, lustful copulation. They lay apart after, on their backs, cool misty air flowing through the partially open windows as the rain comes in waves.

An image hovers behind Tom's closed eyelids, a woman coming out of a fog, a woman in a dark red dress. She moves toward him. It's like a scene from a black-and-white movie, except for her red dress. She keeps moving to him and the fog lifts and it's in the evening, harsh shadows cut across the scene. They are in an alley from a noir movie – Jennie tossing her hat away, shaking her long dark hair as she climbs next to him and they are on a sofa and she curls with him and he hugs her, her lips brushing his chin as she settles in his arms. He holds her as rain peppers the alley but they remain dry.

They kiss and keep kissing, eventually coming up for air.

Jennie snuggles with him, her breath brushing his neck. Lightning crackles and thunder booms and he holds her, keeps holding her as the light show continues and he hears Tchaikovsky now, the *1812 Overture*, the rising music, the clash of the cymbals in time with the thunder, the music eventually falling away and he holds her until—

Blood. A splatter of blood. Tom wakes with a jolt, sits up, realizes where he is and Jennie is not there. He wipes the wetness from his eyes, his heart aching. Looks at his hands. No blood. He remembers his uncle's words again and climbs out of Edie's bed and quietly dresses and slips out of her apartment.

The rain has let up but the streets are heavy with water and he makes it to I-10 and all the way to the first Vieux Carré exit, swings the Toyota around Basin Street to head away from Canal Street, turns down Esplanade Avenue and is surprised to find a parking spot within a block of the old Creole cottage he rents. It is also on Burgundy Street just beyond the Quarter. The house needs painting: two of the louvers outside the front windows dangle precariously. The place is only a shadow of what it once was in the heyday of Spanish rule.

Tom drops his keys as he fumbles with the front door lock, picks them up and glances at the moon beaming down on him like a giant, heavenly spotlight. He lets out a breath, manages to get the door unlocked and moves into the house, his heart stammering in his ears. He trips against his coffee table and falls on the sofa, closes his eyes again and tries to envision Jennie. He sees the woman from Burgundy Street instead, sees her eyes wide when he almost runs her down.

Did she look so much like Jennie? No. The look in her saucer eyes reminds him of Jennie.

He leans back on the sofa, trying to calm himself, running his life with Jennie through his mind again, their meeting, their first dates, the passion, her moving in and how it seemed like it would be forever. He thought that and she thought that until, she seemed to fade, grow restless, lost interest in him. The slippage came in moments. A summer afternoon with the air-conditioner struggling to cool the place, perspiration on Jennie's face as she fanned herself with a magazine as she sat on the other side of the sofa. She looked out the front window and murmured something.

"What was that?"

"There has to be more to this."

"More to what?"

"More to life." She let out a long breath. "More to living. Don't you want to travel?"

She wore a light yellow T-shirt over blue gym shorts, her feet stretched out over the coffee table.

"We could travel," Tom said. "We could go to Disneyworld."

She laughed. She had said she'd wanted to go to Disneyworld, mentioning they could drive to Orlando from New Orleans.

"I'm talking about Italy and France," she said.

"Uh. We can't afford that right now."

"I didn't mean right now."

She let it drop. She let a lot drop until she dropped Tom on the unforgettable Sunday afternoon when he found her in their bedroom packing her suitcases.

Tom's eyes snap open and he sits up.

Too late. Too late.

Damn uncle. His heart aches so much, he has a hard time standing up. Tom makes it to the kitchen, stops in the doorway and takes a few moments to catch his breath. Passes the kitchen table, passes the refrigerator to the rear pantry. Tom yanks open the upright freezer and pulls out a brown cardboard box, putting it on the small kitchen table. He takes off the lid and carefully reaches inside and lifts out the clear plastic bag, placing it in the box lid.

Tom sits, untwists the twist-tie atop the bag and pushes the plastic away from the face. He makes sure her head is balanced and won't roll out of the lid and off the table. He waits to catch his breath, brushes the frost from Jennie's lifeless brown eyes. His fingers touch her cheek.

His voice barely a whisper: "Oh, baby. If we could only go back."

RED
DAVID QUANTICK

H e called me Red not because of my hair, which was a washed-out shade of fox, but on account of my dresses.

"I only wear 'em because you tell me I look good in red," I said once, and he said, "I like you in red." He did too. If I put on a red dress, it was like there were magnets under my skin: he couldn't keep his hands off me. "Stop," I would say, "stop it, Johnny, people are looking," and he'd laugh that big, loud laugh of his, and say, "Let 'em look." But once some man looked too long, and Johnny got mad and hit him, so after that I didn't let him touch me. Not when we were out, anyway.

One day, when we were home and I wasn't wearing any kind of dress, he said to me:

"Red, I have to go out of town a few days."

"What? But—"

"I know, I said we'd go away together but—"

He dragged on a shirt and his voice was muffled.

"This is business, Red. Man's business."

"OK," I said, but I wasn't OK. There were things we needed to talk about and, besides, Johnny's idea of 'man's business' was pouring whisky into himself until he fell over or, just as likely, threw a punch at someone, missed, and fell over.

"I'll make it up to you," Johnny replied, but I knew he wouldn't. He never did.

He stood up and gave me the look. The look said *Yes, I'm a bad man, but you know I'm a bad man, and you like it*. It was a great look and I could never resist it.

Except today I could.

"You gonna give your old man a goodbye kiss?"

"You're not my old man."

He shook his head and walked out the room.

It was the third of May. Seven months ago to the day. I never saw him again.

*

At first it was hard, and then it was harder. The cops came and they weren't nice, not to me, and not about Johnny. They said he'd done a lot of stuff, and didn't believe me when I said I knew nothing about it.

"You must have known," said one, a big guy with a fat gut.

"Nope," I answered, and I wasn't lying. Johnny kept business and pleasure separate, and I wasn't business. "Now if there's nothing else, please go."

"There is something else," said the other cop, who had brown hair and a face like a speckled egg. He reached into his coat pocket and took something out, a crumpled piece of paper. "Does this mean anything to you?"

I took the paper from him and frowned.

"Who is she?" I asked.

"We were hoping you'd know," said Speckled.

"There's a name at the home. Saint Somebody House."

"It's not there any more. Was a kids' home that burned down."

"A kids' home? What kids?"

"You know," said Fat Gut, "like an orphanage."

I shook my head.

"Johnny didn't know any orphans," I said.

I handed the letter back to the cop. He shook his head.

"Yours to keep," he said. "Along with this."

He nodded to Fat Gut, who handed me a padded envelope. It was open. I tipped the contents onto the bed. A watch, a fountain pen, some keys.

"Where's his wallet?" I asked.

"Oh come on," he replied. He turned to Fat Gut, who shrugged.

"If anything comes to mind, call us," said Speckled. Fat Gut opened the door and they walked out.

"You didn't leave me a number," I said, but they were gone.

I put the pen in my purse, set the watch atop the dresser and stuck the keys in a drawer. Then I unfolded the letter again. It was written in a looping, wide-eyed hand on lined paper.

Dear Johnny, it began, and already I hated her.

Dear Johnny,

I say Dear Johnny but I don't even know if that is your real name. Mrs Jefferson says she knows nothing about you other than what the lawyer tells her, and all the lawyer tells her is some hooey about how you just want to help a poor orphan kid in need. Those are all Mrs Jefferson's words by the way, if she heard me saying something was hooey, I'd get the strap. But I just wanted to say thanks again for paying for my education. Mrs Jefferson says I'm an idiot who won't amount to anything, but she kind of smiles when she says it, and she never says it when she's seen my grades which I don't want to boast are kind of good.

It would be really neat if we could meet up but I guess you're a busy man and maybe a tycoon with lots of demands on your time.

I have to go now,

There was a tear at the bottom of the paper where the signature should have been although, looking closer, I could see a thin flake of brown like a burn or singe mark. I thought how the cops said Johnny had died with a bullet in him and then I stopped thinking and found a bottle of rye.

*

I went to Johnny's apartment. They were clearing it out for the next person and wanted the keys back. When I got there the landlady, who looked like a crow and sounded like one too, thrust a cardboard box into my hands. There was nothing in it but a paperback book and a sheaf of letters tied together with butcher's string.

"He owes me three months' rent," she cawed.

I looked round the room. It had four walls, a roof and a floor and not much else. The carpet was threads and dust and the furniture wasn't fit for firewood, unless you wanted to build a funeral pyre for woodworm.

"For this dump? If you ask me, you owe him," I said, and left.

*

The book had Johnny's name written in it, so I put it on a shelf with his other things. The letters I dumped in a wastepaper basket. I lit a match and I was about to drop it in when I heard Johnny's voice behind me.

"Don't do it, Red."

It was so loud and clear that I actually turned round and said his name. But there was nobody there.

"What the hell," I muttered, then, "Ow!" as the match burned my fingers. I took the wad of paper out of the basket.

"God damn you, Johnny," I muttered as I fanned the contents out on the table. There wasn't much there, just nine letters still in their opened envelopes and some loose sheets of paper which, when I looked at them, turned out to be some kind of receipts: "Thank you for your payment of the seventeenth inst." and so on – so I set those aside and opened the first envelope. The letter was in the same handwriting, only a little older-looking.

> Dear Johnny,
> I hadn't heard from you for a while so when I got the news from Mrs Arbogast I was really happy – Mrs Arbogast took over from Mrs Jefferson after Mrs Jefferson got sick and she's a lot nicer. Gosh, but it's been a long time since I last wrote! All kinds of things are different here apart from Mrs Jefferson leaving. But then I guess you wouldn't notice anyhow because you've never been here. Or have you? Sometimes I see a car outside and I imagine it's you, come to visit clandestinely (that's my new word, Mrs Arbo makes us learn one a day). Maybe you look in on me when I'm sleeping

"Jesus, kid," I said out loud. She was talking about Johnny like he was a mixture of Father Christmas and the goddamn Tooth Fairy. I fought back the urge to tear the letter up and reached for another. This one was written in a much firmer, almost adult hand.

> Dear Johnny,
> Today is my 14th birthday, and I am writing to thank you for the books. I already read Alice's Adventures but it was great to get Looking Glass too. Mrs Arbo says I'm too old for them but I told her that a classic is a classic regardless of whom (?) it's written for. She said I was a smart alec but she smiled so I know she didn't mind me talking back to her. Anyway I have to close now because there's a CAKE for me and

This time I did tear the letter up. For some reason the idea of Johnny buying a birthday present for someone was a real slap in the face. This was a man who never bought a greetings card in his life, let alone a gift. I tell a lie: one year he gave me a brooch, but it was cheap and I knew he'd lifted it from a Woolworth store. Apart from that, he was the kind of man who forgot birthdays, not celebrated them. So the idea of him picking out a gift for some cute teenager made me mad, madder even than knowing Johnny had a whole secret life he never told me about.

Not just me either. I called around a few of Johnny's old friends and if they knew Johnny was Daddy Warbucks to some wet-eyed Orphan Annie, they weren't saying. Most of them laughed at the idea – old Johnny spending his hard-earned on someone else? Maybe if she was a singer or a chorus girl. But a kid in an orphanage? More likely he'd have flown to the Moon.

"Who is she, anyway?" asked one of his pals, a guy called Joe who Johnny had been in the Army with. Joe was a decent guy, not like most of Johnny's jackass friends.

"I don't know," I said. "The letters are signed with an initial – R – and the home isn't there any more."

"But where it was is still there, right?"

"What?"

"Maybe you should make enquiries," Joe said. "I mean, if you want to."

"I don't want to," I replied.

And I didn't want to. But at the same time, I did.

Joe must have heard something in my voice, because he said:

"Listen, I know this guy. A private dick named Isinglass. Let me give you his number."

I wrote it down on a piece of paper. I thanked Joe. And I put the paper in a drawer with the letters.

*

A week later I opened the drawer, took out the paper, and called the number. Two hours later I was sitting in an office with a heavy-set man who called himself Isinglass. I never found out his other names: maybe he didn't have any.

"Cigarette?" he asked, pushing a silver-plated case toward me.

I remembered how Johnny smoked, always lighting up a cigarette for me from his own, and I felt nauseous. I shook my head.

"Suit yourself," said Isinglass, but he didn't take a cigarette himself.

"Hope you don't mind me saying, but I've never met a black private eye before," I said.

Isinglass shrugged.

"I did ten years on the force and never got out of uniform," he said. "Some of the dumbest men you ever saw went into plain clothes and I stayed on the beat. So I quit, set up on my own. Some people don't like it."

"Some people are assholes," I replied.

"What can I do for you—"

"Red. Just Red."

I showed him the letters.

"That's it?" he asked.

"That, and I have an address for where the home used to be."

"Used to be?"

"I know. Will you take the case?"

He looked at the letters again.

"You don't know her name. You don't know where she lives – lived. You don't know anything."

"Why do you think I'm hiring you?" I said.

Isinglass sighed. He gathered the letters to himself like a hen with her chicks. Then he said:

"Fifteen dollars a day. Plus expenses."

I was about say no, then I remembered Johnny's voice.

Don't do it, Red.

"Nobody tells me what to do," I said out loud.

Isinglass looked puzzled.

"What?" he asked.

"Just thinking out loud," I replied. "When can you start?"

He smiled, almost reluctantly, like he had a limited supply of smiles and didn't care to give them away.

"Right away," he said.

*

Weeks went by. I got some work – I was an illustrator, which meant I could sit at home working and just stare at the phone. I put on some weight. I let out some dresses.

And then Isinglass called.

"Good news," he said.

"You found her?"

He sounded annoyed, like I'd rained on his good news.

"I found the children's home," he said.

We met up in his office, where Isinglass told me at some length, having, I suppose, nobody else to tell how he had spent a long time doing real detective work on finding the home. I could hear the mixture of pride and anger in his voice, pride in a job well done, anger that he wasn't doing this as a plain clothes cop with a badge, as he explained how he'd sat down, not with the letters but the envelopes that the letters were in, and worked out what the smudged and faded postmarks said. How he'd traced them to one town about a hundred miles away, and how he'd then painstakingly, slowly and patiently gone through a list of all the children's homes, orphanages and plain old dumping grounds for waifs and strays that had ever been located in that town.

"There were ten," he said.

Five of them were still in operation and four of them closed down before the Depression, which left one.

"I had quite a time finding their records," he said.

"Why's that?" I asked, not entirely interested. I just wanted to know the results, not the process.

"Because the home burned down."

"Burned down? How?"

"Someone set fire to it."

"What?"

He pushed a newspaper cutting at me.

CHILDREN'S HOME RAZED TO THE GROUND said the headline, next to a photograph of a large house that was very definitely on fire. The story was hazy but predictable – brave fire fighters, children pulled from burning building, causes unknown.

"Causes unknown?"

He shook his head.

"They had to write that, because the kid was a minor."

"I don't follow."

"I asked around. Once I had the clipping, people were eager to talk. I don't mean officials, obviously. I mean people whose relatives worked there. Orderlies, cleaners – you know what I mean."

I nodded. I knew what he meant.

"A fire's a big event in a small town. Everybody remembered it. And what everybody also remembered was that it was deliberate. Some kid doused the kitchen in gasoline and lit a match."

I felt a strange prickling on the back of my neck.

"Did they remember who the kid was?"

He shook his head.

"Nobody could recollect the name. Just the usual stuff – they were a good kid, never did anyone any harm and the arson came from nowhere. Like maybe they got some bad news about something and that made 'em flip."

I stared at the clipping, as though staring would make some hidden message appear. Once upon a time, the house in the photo was a living place, where people lived and slept, and one of those people used to write letters to the man I loved.

I pushed the scrap of paper back to Isinglass.

"It's great you found it," I managed to say.

"I have a lead," Isinglass said. "It's not much, but at least I can start looking now. If you want me to."

I said nothing.

"Do you want me to?" he asked.

I thought of the letters, the eager child who hero-worshipped a man I thought I knew, but didn't.

"Damn straight I do," I answered.

*

That night I couldn't sleep. I lay there, thinking. Thinking about Johnny. He said he loved me and he said it a lot. But mostly he said it when he'd been drinking. I thought of the girl in the orphanage. He must have loved her: she wrote him, and you don't write to someone who doesn't love you.

The ceiling was a movie screen and on it a bad movie was projected. I saw Johnny sitting down and sliding bills into an envelope. I saw him in a small office, hat in hands, listening to a matronly lady with a proud smile on his face. I saw him walking with a little girl in a garden.

I saw that little girl getting older...

I threw back the covers, went over to the phone.

"Do you know what time it is?" said Isinglass, but he sounded drunk, not sleepy.

"I want you to stop the investigation."

"Lady, it's four o'clock in the morning, I'm not investigating a damn thing. Call me tomorrow when we're both sober."

And he put the phone down.

I cried then. I cried for Johnny and me, and I cried for what we had. It wasn't much, but it was ours. Our love – I dared to call it that – was like something we'd found in the street, a mongrel dog that nobody else wanted, but we looked after it in our own way, and it was ours and it was nobody else's.

"Oh for—"

"I want you to continue with the investigation."

"I'm unplugging the phone."

⋆

I didn't hear from Isinglass for weeks after that, and if it hadn't been for his bills I might have thought he'd taken himself off the case. Then one day there was a knock at the door. I opened it to the worried face of Mrs Bonn, my landlady. Mrs Bonn always wore a worried face, but today she looked like King Solomon asked to decide the fate of a baby.

"There's a man to see you," she said in querulous tones.

"So send him up."

Mrs Bonn's face twisted up like a wet dish rag.

"He's—He's a coloured gentleman."

"Send him up," I repeated.

Mrs Bonn turned away from me to lean over the landing rail.

"He can come up," she said to nobody in particular.

⋆

Isinglass sat at the make-up table, the back of his head reflected in three mirrors.

"You OK?" I asked.

"I need a drink," he said.

I gave him a Scotch in Johnny's old glass. He drank it and held out his glass for another.

"Thanks," he said, then he winced.

"Mind if I take my jacket off?"

"Sure," I said.

There was a small stain on Isinglass's shirt, over the slight hump of what I guessed was a bandage.

"Ow," I said. "That looks nasty."

"Somebody shot me," he replied.

"Not on my account, I hope."

"Hazard of the job," Isinglass said. "For me, anyway."

*

Once he'd got over the annoyance of me calling in the early hours, Isinglass told me, he went back to work on my case.

"I had nothing to go on. All the documents from the children's home were ashes, the staff were scattered to the four winds, and the kids had either grown up and left or been sent to other homes," he said, sipping his third whisky. "All there was, was the letters."

"But there were no names on the letters," I interrupted. "No addresses, no information at all."

"So I thought. But then I remembered the kid wrote your boyfriend on her birthday. She was fourteen years old—"

"And she had a cake," I said. "What of it?"

"Don't you see?" asked Isinglass. "The letters had no names or addresses on, because they didn't need 'em. But they did have—"

"Dates," I said.

"The letter she wrote on her birthday was dated May third, four years ago," Isinglass said. "And she was fourteen that day."

"So you know her date of birth," I said slowly. "And you know her age. She'd be—"

"Eighteen," said Isinglass. "She's an adult."

After that, he explained, it was easy. It was boring, and it was time-consuming, but it was easy.

"I just wrote to every employment agency in the area. Anyone who'd take on a kid from a children's home. I had her date of her birth and I knew she was local."

"And they helped you?"

"Some did. Most did, when I told them it was about an inheritance. People love the idea of a little orphan girl coming into money."

I was getting tired of being impressed with his brilliance.

"Did you find her or not?" I asked, a little sharply.

He gave me a look and winced again. There was a fresh spot of blood on his shirt.

"Sorry," I said, and meant it.

Isinglass nodded.

"I found her," he said.

"So who is she?" I asked.

"I'm coming to that."

"I may shoot you myself."

Isinglass had a name. He had an address.

"She had a secretarial job with a law firm," he told me. "And she was living with a family, not two miles from the home."

"OK," I said. "So what did you *do*?"

He shook his head.

"I made a mistake," he said. "I should have written. Instead I went over."

It seemed that someone didn't take kindly to a black man appearing at the door asking questions.

"I was polite," said Isinglass. "I wasn't what you call deferential, but I made sure to sound official. And then this fellow started waving a gun around. I offered to call back later, but that made him madder. So I left. And as I was walking back to my car, he took a pot shot at me."

"He shot you?"

Isinglass shrugged.

"It happens," he said. "And I was lucky. A flesh wound, as they say in the thrillers."

"Did you call the police?"

He looked at me.

"OK," I said.

Isinglass got up.

"Thanks for the whisky," he said. "And thanks for the job. I mean, I'd rather not get shot, but it was an interesting use of my time. If you need me again—"

He handed me a card and headed for the door.

"What about the girl?" I said.

"Name's on the back of the card."

I waited until the front door had closed, then I waited some more while Mrs Bonn went back into her sitting room. Then I turned Isinglass's card over. On the back were a name and an address. The address was in the same town as the children's home. The name was printed in clear block capitals.

ROBERTA BAILEY.

Just seeing the name – even though I didn't know it from Eve – made my stomach churn. I barely made it to the bathroom in time.

She was real. Johnny's little secret was real.

I sat on the edge of the bed, the bed I'd shared with Johnny so many times, and I tore up the letters, every single one. I tore them in half, then into quarters, and I made confetti of them, and I cried.

"You bastard," I spat. "You bastard, Johnny."

I picked up the confetti and I flushed it. It came back up in a wet belch of water and paper to taunt me.

I went back into my room and picked up a lighter. I took Isinglass's card and I was about to burn it when I saw it was Johnny's lighter I was holding. There was an inscription on it:

To Johnny, love always, Red.

"Love always," I said. "That's a laugh."

And then it hit me. I *had* loved him. I still loved him. And he loved me. He may not have given me presents, but he loved me. There was no evidence – no rings, no cards, no photographs of us in exotic locations – but there was no doubt either.

"OK, Johnny," I muttered to myself, putting the lighter down. "I'll give you a chance."

∗

Two hours later I was getting out of Johnny's old car, parked across the street from the house Isinglass had visited. I was wearing my demurest outfit and a prim expression – I didn't think a guy would shoot a girl, but I didn't want to take any chances either.

I rang the doorbell, braced myself for a verbal assault, or worse.

Instead a young woman opened the door. She was eighteen if she was a day, and she was beautiful.

I felt my heart climb into my throat.

"Roberta Bailey?" I managed to ask.

"Come in, Red," she said. "I've been expecting you."

∗

We sat at the dining table. There were lace coasters and a pitcher of orange juice. It was a beautiful house, but there was something different about it, something in the air.

Roberta brought glasses from the kitchen.

"Nice place," I said.

"My dad works hard," she replied.

"He the fellow who shot my friend?"

She had the grace to look upset at that.

"Is he all right?"

"No thanks to your pop."

"I'm so sorry. My dad – he's under a lot of pressure."

"What kind of—"

"You'll see. Juice?"

"No thanks. My stomach's not right. Nerves, I guess."

I forced a smile, and she responded with the real thing.

"This isn't going the way I'd expected," I said.

"What do you mean?"

I sighed, and I felt like a blimp deflating.

"I came here angry," I replied. "I came here wanting to hate you and— I can't."

"Because of Johnny?" she asked.

"Don't say his name," I flashed. "Sorry."

She looked like she was about to say something, then thought better of it. Instead she walked over to a bureau and took something out. A sheaf of letters.

"I already saw plenty of your letters," I said, bitterly.

"My – these aren't from me," she said. "They're from Johnny."

I stared at her. Then a cold feeling came on me.

"Johnny never wrote to me in his life," I said.

"Read them," she said, her girl's voice suddenly older.

"I don't want to," I answered and now it was me who sounded like a kid.

"*Read them.*"

I started at her tone, then took the letters from her.

Dear Bobby, the first one began.

"Bobby?" I asked.

She frowned, nodded at the letter. I got the hint and carried on reading.

> Dear Bobby,
> I'm glad to hear you are feeling better. Sorry I haven't written but

"Not that page," said Roberta, impatiently. She shoved another sheet of paper into my hand.

You asked me to tell you a little about Red. Well, I'm not much one for words but the simple answer is I'm crazy about her.

"And this," said Roberta, thrusting another letter at me.

I spent the day with Red. I love that woman, there's no other word for it

"And this – and this one – and this too – and—"

"Stop," I said.

I gave her back the letter.

"Thank you," I said.

"Don't thank me yet."

"I was so jealous," I went on. "All those years he sent you money in the children's home, kept an eye on you, and all I could think of was my own—"

I stopped.

"Wait," I said. "I was so thrown by the letters, I forgot to ask. Why was he supporting you?"

A cocktail of emotions appeared on Roberta's face. Fear and worry and – something else.

"Not me," she said.

"I don't understand."

She stood up.

"Come with me."

We climbed the stairs. That feeling of something *not right* got stronger.

Roberta opened a door and we went in.

The room was dark, curtains drawn, and there was a bed. In the bed was a young man. He was paler than Roberta but he looked a lot like her.

"This is him," she said. "The boy from the home."

"The boy—"

"Robert. My half-brother."

*

Once upon a time – Roberta told me – there were two kids, Robert and Roberta, half-brother and half-sister. Their mom thought it was cute to give them similar names but truth to tell, her husband – who was Roberta's father, not Robert's – didn't find anything cute in the situation. In fact, when their mom died he decided he'd rather not have another man's kid in his house, so at the age of six, Robert went to the children's home, while Roberta stayed with him.

"That's hard," I said.

"Could have been worse," Roberta replied, but she didn't elaborate on how.

The husband wasn't completely cold, oh no. He knew Robert's mom had a brother and he wrote him, saying come get your nephew. The mom's brother wrote back and said one day he would but for now he'd send money and Robert could write to him if he liked. It wasn't much but it was something, and the two became quite the pen pals. But as for springing the kid from the home, the uncle was always about to do it, but somehow it never quite happened.

"And then one day Johnny stopped writing," said Roberta. "Robert didn't take it well, to say the least."

I thought of the newspaper cutting, the burning building.

"When was this?" I asked.

She named a date. I closed my eyes and didn't speak for a while.

"That was the week he was killed," I said.

"After the fire, Robert got sick," Roberta said. "That was when I told my dad, enough is enough."

I looked at him, lying in the bed asleep. He was pale, but he was breathing steadily.

"Is he going to be OK?"

"I think so. But it hit him hard, Johnny abandoning him like that."

"Johnny never abandoned him," I said and, as I said it, I knew it was true. "He would have fixed things."

"I get it," Roberta replied.

She patted my hand.

"So now you know," she said.

"So now I know," I replied.

*

We said our goodbyes on the doorstep.

"You going to tell your brother what happened?" I asked.

"No," she said. "You are."

I was about to reply, then thought better of it, so I just smiled and nodded.

"After you've had the baby, of course."

I goggled at her.

"Oh come on," said Roberta. "I'm a kid but I'm not an idiot."

"Fair enough," I said.

"What you going to call it?"

"Him," I said. "I can tell it's a him. And I'm going to call him Johnny."

"All right then. See you next time, Johnny."

She gave me her hand. I took it.

"See you, Red."

LOOKING FOR YOU
THROUGH THE GRAY RAIN
ANA TERESA PEREIRA

He always called me angel. His skinny angel with badly cut blonde hair. It's longer now, shoulder-length. It grew darker with time. Everything grows darker with time.

Every girl has a first love. He was my first, but also my final, my only love. He was the reason I stubbornly got up in the morning, the reason I washed my hair and picked up the clothes from the floor. The reason I bought a new lipstick, a new perfume. They don't change much, my perfumes. He said I smelled like orange flowers, like a hundred different citrus flowers mixed together; that was my fresh, cheap perfume when I was eighteen. And all these years I have been looking for that scent, the one he remembers, I'm sure he remembers... Or at least I was sure until last night.

I miss my dresses too. They were copied from magazines and made at home. I remember trying a new dress, my mother kneeling beside me with pins in her mouth, making it a little shorter, a little tighter around the waist. Because I wanted to be beautiful, I wanted him to love my body, not only my face.

"Angel Face, if I ever lose you, I'll remember you sitting on this bench, this dress, this scent, these kisses. I will always remember the way you move, some of the things you wear, some of the things you say..."

"The way I dance?"

"The way you dance. Every song we have danced together."

And I believed him. All these years I believed him. Until last night.

They tell you a girl can forgive her man for being with other women. For leaving... Maybe it's true. But some things you cannot forgive.

That's why, baby, I have to kill you.

I know you spend most nights in your room, writing your stories. But once in a while, perhaps when you cannot write, you walk the streets. And I have the feeling this is one of those nights. I didn't go to work and I am looking for you. You never go too far. That modest hotel room gives you some sense of security. It's raining but rain never stopped us from meeting each other, from wandering alone in the dark.

Baby, it's not that I love you less, but some things a girl can't forgive. I have to kill you, baby, to have my heart back. It's you or me.

1

The girl in blue was always the last to arrive. You could hear her high heels when she walked across the large room – previously a garage – and some member of the band would whistle and she'd smile. She wasn't the youngest – twenty-five, maybe twenty-six – but still the prettiest. You didn't last long in that profession. Twenty-eight, twenty-nine, at most. Even if you had a narrow waist and looked good without a bra, it would be time to retire, get a job as a waitress or marry some idiot that didn't mind what you did for a living. And promise not to wear high heels and black stockings anymore. Not to dance anymore.

Sometimes, in her shabby room, listening to the radio through the night – the rest of the night that was only hers – the girl wondered how she could still love music so much. Not the silly songs she danced to when she was eighteen, but the music the band played when the club was almost empty: girls with aching feet going through the motions with sleepy lonely bastards. Duke, Charlie Mingus. That was better than love. Nearly everything was better than love. She would fetch a mystery magazine from the pile on her bedside table and read one of his stories. One of his stories in which the girl, always very young, had the face of an angel. Those were the magazines she kept by her bed. The ones that didn't have one of his stories she gave to the landlady's little boy. The ones that had one of his stories without her in it, were dispersed around the room. With her clothes, a few books, a few movie magazines.

She had seen shabbier rooms. This one had a window that actually looked out into a street and an old tree, not a wall or a dirty backyard. On the windowsill there was a green plant that she watered every evening, like an act of faith, before leaving for work. Still in her underwear she walked the room slowly, as if she was looking for something. She picked one of her blue dresses from a chair – there were three of them, but she seldom bothered to hang them in the wardrobe when they came back from the laundry. They were all similar, tight, knee-length, with two narrow straps on the shoulders. She preferred the older one that, after what seemed like a hundred washes, had turned a shade of blue that reminded her of a dress she had when she was eighteen. She still remembered some of her dresses from her other life.

The girl would always leave too late, take the bus after the one she should have got in the first place. It was always dark when she arrived at the club, even in summer. Bill, the manager, pretended not to see her and the other girls in the dressing room, sitting at the mirrors, didn't pay much attention to her. She put her hair up in that complicated bundle she managed to fix in a minute, took the pencil from her drawer and made the beauty mark under her left eye. Some perfume. Not the fresh one she wore during the day but a heavier one, white jasmine, lots of it, to protect her from the men's scent.

And then it would be nine o'clock, the band would start vamping, the lights would be on and Bill would open the door and pretend to be angry. "Come on girls, we don't pay you to gossip."

For a few moments, ironically, they seemed to be surrounded by stars. A long time ago, she was in love with the stars. Stars and first kisses, and walking hand in hand with the boy she loved. Then the night was a different place, safe and warm, even when it rained, even when she shivered with the cold. In another life.

Here everything was fake. Her dress under the lights was the wrong blue, she was a bad kisser, the feeling of a man's hand on her waist or shoulder made her sick. She didn't like looking at their faces and hated when the proximity of one of them made her nipples hard; a sort of sham desire. She didn't answer when they said, "I want to see you again." "What time do you finish?" "Why are you so sad?" "Where do you come from?" She only smiled.

In the beginning, in what was still another life, she was amused by the fairy tale aspect of the thing. The men bought a few tickets at the entrance; they gave her one that she tore in two and each kept a half. Blue tickets. One blue ticket a dance. One blue ticket a girl. She preferred to dance with different men all night, she hated when they came back, as if they were expecting something. There were always a few outside when she left at two in the morning. The dance was over, the smiles were over, but some of them didn't get it. She caught the bus on the next street, then walked a few yards and entered her building. The room now looked like a refuge, she almost felt the presence of a cat waiting for her – it would make a big difference if she had a cat to feed – she washed her face, no beauty mark anymore, no lipstick, left her dress on the floor and slipped into a robe. Something to eat, a piece of bread, a piece of cheese, an orange or a pear, and bed. Another blanket when she was cold. And a mystery magazine from the pile on her bedside table, and the story of a very young girl with the face of an angel and a dress that the multiple washes had turned a tender shade of blue.

2

She was the girl that entered a place and made all the others disappear. Slim, with very blonde hair, an irregular haircut copied from a movie actress, simple dresses, made at home. She had lovely shoulders, a narrow waist and long legs. The dresses were little more than a piece of tissue that year: short and tight. She was eighteen and even though to him she seemed to be made of light, she was sometimes bitter – a girl born on the wrong side of the tracks, even if she was the prettiest and smartest in the neighborhood, was condemned to marry the boy next door, have a few children and live in a tiny apartment. She wanted more.

They both had big plans. He wanted to be a writer, another Fitzgerald. He had written a novel the year before and a few short stories. She dreamed vaguely of being an actress, not exactly acting, but having beautiful dresses, Tiffany pearls, seeing herself on giant movie posters, in magazines, on the back cover of pulp novels.

They met one July night, a very warm night. People were out on the streets, on the riverbanks – the water gave an illusion of coolness. She was wearing a faded blue, backless dress, her short hair tucked behind her ears. She had told her mother she was going out with two girlfriends but got rid of them in a few minutes. She sat on the wall by the river, her naked legs against the stones, her old beach sandals almost dropping into the water once or twice. She was happy without knowing why. A sense of somebody. And then she noticed the boy.

He was about her age, tall, with dark blond hair. It was the way he looked at her that attracted her attention. Later he told her, "You were the prettiest thing I had ever seen. And I was so afraid you'd go away and I'd never see you again."

The girl recognized the book he had on his knees, she had studied it at school. Short stories by Scott Fitzgerald. She wasn't keen on Fitzgerald

– she would never understand the fuss about *The Great Gatsby* – but she remembered with fondness the story of a girl who cut her hair.

She wondered for a while if he would come and talk to her. She wanted an ice-cream and it would be nice to have someone pay for it. But he opened the book and seemed to forget her; she decided to go home and get a vanilla ice-cream on the way.

The next day, when she was sitting on the fire escape with a magazine, letting her hair dry in the sun, she caught a glimpse of him on the sidewalk. They looked at each other for a moment, then she went in, put on a light jacket – the weather was considerably cooler – and came downstairs.

They stood in front of each other. He was a little pale and some motherly instinct in her – though she didn't care much for babies, she preferred newly born animals – was awakened.

"I thought it was you."

"I had to see you."

She didn't ask why. "How did you know where I lived?"

"I followed you."

"I didn't see you on the bus."

"Your hair looks shorter."

"It's still wet, silly."

The sun disappeared suddenly and they both shivered.

"Shall we go for a walk?"

"Not a long one. It's my day to make dinner."

They walked for a while. It felt natural, being together. He started to whistle slowly, a popular song, and she smiled. They passed a cinema and he asked:

"Do you want to go to the movies? Saturday night?"

"I always want to go to the movies."

"And dancing?"

"And dancing."

"Saturday..."

"Yes."

They were soon back to her place. They both knew. But they didn't kiss.

*

They discovered the bench one afternoon, during a walk. It was at the entrance of a garden, and it had been there for a long time: names and hearts and signs of bad weather proved it. He told her about benches in Henry James stories, of couples meeting on the same bench after many years.

Later, she would find that bench in his stories, again and again. Sometimes it was in front of a church. And there was always a boy and a girl, and he kept losing her, waiting for her in the cold. Sometimes it was as if she never really existed, as if nobody else could see her, as if he was waiting for a ghost.

The bench became their meeting place. They resisted the temptation to write their names on it. They were not kids anymore. Love had made them mature, more serious. Love was a serious thing. A responsibility of some kind.

He liked to bring her little things: a bunch of wildflowers, a box of colored chalk, a handmade music box, the latest issue of an illustrated movie magazine she couldn't afford. Then he discovered the candies in a shop near his house. They were vanilla-flavored and came in different shapes: a star, a shell, a heart. "Have a heart, baby."

He now shared his stories with her. The clear influence of Fitzgerald; she told him about the story of the girl who cut her hair.

"It's a very important decision, you know? It can change your life."

"Was your hair long?"

"Yes. I wore braids, sometimes."

"An angel with braids."

Angel Face. Sometimes, when she was completely lost, when she entered a room where nothing really belonged to her, she would get rid of her coat and her shoes and, before washing her face or eating anything, take out of her bag a small magazine with his name on the cover and look for his story. And she often found the lonely girl that could vanish into thin air; the girl was always very young, and waif-like. When it didn't happen, she felt lonelier than ever. But then a week later there would be another magazine, another story, and she would find the girl, the name didn't matter, or the color of her hair, she could always recognize herself. And remember who she was. And be beautiful again. Almost innocent.

*

She hated the idea of the party. She loved to dance with him on Saturday night in the city, in an almost empty bar. A jukebox and a romantic song. But this was different. A party at the house of one of his friends, on the right side of the tracks.

"I have nothing to wear."

"Your dresses are lovely."

"My mother and my aunt make them."

"They're still lovely."

By then, she was working in the jewelry department of a local store. She decided to buy a dress on credit. But she couldn't resist the pearls. They were small, and got even smaller toward the clasp. Elegant. Like something in a period movie – an adaptation of a nineteenth-century novel. She would take them back the next day. That night, like a bad omen, she read a story by Maupassant, that she had borrowed from him. It ended badly, like most fairy tales if you forget the last paragraphs.

But that was her fairy tale night. She had washed her hair, polished her nails, borrowed eye shadow from a friend. The dress was the prettiest and most expensive she had ever owned. The pearls seemed to have been designed for her long, thin neck. She could see his look of pride when she took off her coat at the party.

A Cinderella night. She danced with him but also with others. Everyone seemed to like her, even the girls.

A magical night.

"You make the other girls look plain," he whispered in her ear. But she was beginning to feel a bit restless. The idea that she might have to pay a price for all that happiness. She touched the pearls once in a while to make sure they were still there. She could not lose them like the girl in Maupassant's story.

When he took her home, they kissed more deeply than ever before. He touched her and for a moment she thought it would happen there, that night, under the fire escape.

But he stopped and kissed her hair.

"Not like this, Angel Face."

"Don't you want to?"

"More than anything in the world. But we have plenty of time."

The next morning the police were at her door. When she came downstairs between two officers she didn't think that she was hurting her parents and her sister, that the neighbors would talk about that for months. She could only think of a boy, sitting on a bench, waiting for her. And that motherly instinct in her, something to do with dolls and kittens, took hold. "I'm coming back, baby. I promise."

3

I t was a tender night. The girl had slept during the afternoon, the window slightly open, leaves from the tree fluttering into the room. There had been a curtain over the window when she discovered the room, but she had taken it away after paying the second month's rent. It was a safe window, with the tree outside, the vast windowsill where her plant seemed to have gained a new lease of life. Perhaps one day a bud would appear and she would feel rewarded for taking it from one rented room to the other, with her suitcase and some bags. For coming back upstairs when she was already late, because she had forgotten to water it.

A tender sleep. She had dreamed of one of his stories: she was the little girl in the woods, leaving a trace of colored chalk on the trees, so that the little boy could follow her. And then it was no longer traces of chalk but little pieces of blue tickets among the grass.

When she woke up it was late, but then again, they would be surprised if she arrived on time. She washed her face, put on some lipstick and, because of that sense of lightness, her daytime perfume, a cheap perfume with lemon in it. She picked her clean dress from a chair: it was the lighter one, the one that made her eyes almost gray, and put on her black stockings. She pushed her hair back. It would have to wait, the hair and the beauty mark. A dark blue jacket. The damned shoes.

The band was playing something beautiful. "This is for you, baby," said Jim, the piano player.

She barely heard Bill's ironic comment, she barely heard the other girls. Time to wash her hands, to put her hair up, to make the beauty mark, a bit closer to the eye than usual. And then she was immersed in the silver lights, like silver water, the music was 'I've Got a Crush on You' and some man was giving her a blue ticket.

"Want to dance, baby?"

"Thought you'd never ask, cowboy."

The guy had bought a few tickets, so she couldn't refuse when he offered her a drink. They went to the bar. The fruit juice, the only thing the girls were allowed to have, was sweeter than ever.

The sense of someone.

The sense of him. She stared at the door. He looked much older than his twenty-seven years. He had always been thin, now he seemed to be starving. His clothes were always casual, and that gave him an intellectual look some girls found attractive. Now he looked like a tramp.

She forgot the other guy and walked toward him. He was just standing there, as if he didn't know what to do. She grabbed his blue ticket and tore it in two, but he didn't seem to notice.

He was somewhere else.

"Now I'm really a ghost," she thought, "because not even you can see me."

The band was playing the song about castles and dragons – and mortgages and villains – and even though the place was always too warm, she felt cold. They found the way to the dance floor and were in the middle of innumerable fake stars.

It was a Bobby Darin song. 'Have You Got Any Castles, Baby.'

She looked at his hand on her waist and didn't recognize it. Hands aren't supposed to change. His seemed half-dead, as if at a certain point he had broken his arm and hadn't bothered to treat it. Then she noticed something even more terrifying.

He couldn't dance anymore. The boy who was once a good dancer was now clumsy, as if he hadn't danced for a long time. He probably hadn't. She wondered if he could still ride a bicycle.

She looked at his face. The firm chin, the thin mouth, the distant eyes. And her heart was unexpectedly filled with joy. He had come to her. Even if that was a nightmare, he had come to her.

But the joy didn't last. Neither did the song.

The words of the song danced through her mind.

Suddenly the band stopped playing and the couples separated, and he disappeared among the other people. As if he hadn't been there. If she asked, nobody would have seen him. And there was only a girl who was no longer a girl, shivering in her blue evening dress in the middle of the dance floor.

4

He always called me angel. His skinny angel with badly cut blonde hair. It's longer now, shoulder length. It grew darker with time. Everything grows darker with time.

Every girl has a first love. He was my first, but also my final, my only love. He was the reason I stubbornly got up in the morning, the reason I washed my hair and picked up the clothes from the floor. The reason I bought a new lipstick, a new perfume. They don't change much, my perfumes. He said I smelled like orange flowers, like a hundred different citrus flowers mixed together; that was my fresh, cheap perfume when I was eighteen. And all these years I have been looking for that scent, the one he remembers, I'm sure he remembers... Or at least I was sure until last night.

✶

In a sudden impulse, the girl had cut her hair in front of the mirror. She hadn't done that for many years, her hand was clumsy, and the hair more irregular than she had intended. But it didn't matter. She washed her face, to get rid of any makeup. Her eyes looked very blue and very desperate. Like an actress trying to find her character, she looked at her face in the mirror. "Why are you so sad? Where do you come from?"

A simple black dress. Her old black coat. A pair of old shoes.

A moment of hesitation.

"I could just go to the movies."

The girl sat on the bed and, as if she was the one who was going to die, she thought of her life. Her memories. Her mother making Sunday lunch, her father taking her to the movies, her sister playing on the fire escape. Being the best student in her class, being the prettiest girl in school. "Malaria fever, jonquils and then that boy." The first play she had seen. Radio plays. Songs. All the songs she knew by heart. And then... that boy.

In his stories, there were men standing in the street, under a lamp, looking up at a girl's window. She had stood in front of his hotel late at night, looking at his window. There was a dim light on, a desk light probably. Or did he write in bed... he sometimes did, when she was his girl. When he wanted to write like Fitzgerald... His stories were much better now. Darker, more abstract. A sense of doom, of being trapped forever. If it weren't for the girl. The girl with an angel face. The girl with a halo.

A party and a girl with a pearl necklace. The girl lost the necklace and spent the rest of her life working to pay for it. No, that was a story by a French author whose name she couldn't remember. Six months in a place that was like a prison with clean sheets where she met other girls her age that knew a lot about life and men. The line between boys and men.

And then music. Songs you used to like but almost hated now, because you heard them every night. And then the music they played just for you when the place was nearly empty. 'Some Kind of Blue.' She had planned many times to buy a phonograph, but never saved enough money. But there was the radio through the night, the music and even sometimes a human voice to show you were not alone in the world.

"There are things a girl can't forgive, baby."

She got up. She passed a hand through her hair, feeling its lightness. Angel Face.

"And now, baby, I am going to find you. It won't be difficult. The streets are strangely empty. Perhaps because of the rain, perhaps because of the puddles. Have you ever seen a perfect puddle?"

"I know you spend most nights in your room, writing your stories. But once in a while, perhaps when you cannot write, you walk the streets. And I have the feeling this is one of those nights. You never go too far. That modest hotel room gives you some sense of security. It's raining but rain never stopped us…"

Like a girl in one of his stories, she had a gun in the pocket of her old coat. It was not difficult to get a gun when you dance with a certain kind of men. She walked through the rain, the gray rain. And suddenly she knew where he was.

She would find her way to the bench even in the dark, in the rain. There was a lamp nearby and she could see the boy sitting on it. "Only a boy," she whispered with surprise. "He's still only a boy." A skinny boy with dreamy eyes.

She was not wearing her high heels. Her steps were silent in the night.

"Have a heart, baby."

She held the pistol but didn't take it out of her pocket. She pointed it carefully.

He looked up.

The two things happened at the same time. The sound of the shot and the cry of a boy.

"Jeanie!"

NEW YORK
BLUES REDUX
WILLIAM BOYLE

Southern Brooklyn, August 1986

Jane the Stain takes her usual stool at the bar, and Widow Marie brings over a shot glass, slops some rye in there, and then grabs a cold beer out of the cooler. A cold beer on a hot day. Jane's been waiting for it. Nothing better. First, she puts back the shot to loosen herself up, to get rid of that feeling of hardness that fills her while she's waiting. One sip and her insides go mushy. It always feels like a miracle. Loaves and fishes type shit. Turn the misery into joy. Religion.

She follows the rye with a long swig of beer, while Widow Marie pours her another shot. This is their routine. Bath Bar is home.

"How was the day?" Widow Marie asks.

"Three times I had to tell Duke to quit talking to me and go back to work," Jane the Stain says, shaking her head.

"A bona fide chooch, that's what that guy is."

That's the extent of the conversation for now. There's no pressure to talk with Widow Marie, even though she likes her gossip. A gift.

Jane the Stain works in the office at Duke's Garage on Harway Avenue. Been there eight years now. Mostly she answers phones, writes receipts, and orders parts. Duke's a well-seasoned douchebag. He hired her for her looks. He said he wanted his customers greeted by a neighborhood beauty.

She was twenty-two when she started working at Duke's, and she's thirty now. Before that, she worked at the Roulette Diner. She started drinking when she was a junior at Bishop Kearney. Joanne Genetti shared a six-pack of wine coolers with her after school in the park one day and got her hooked on the feeling. By senior year, she was going to bars in Bay Ridge. She tried college for four semesters, first SUNY Purchase and then SUNY

Oneonta, but she skipped classes and drank in shitholes. She got straight As at drinking in shitholes. Other than that, college was a bust.

She came home to Brooklyn, moved back on the block with her mom and grandma, and got the job at the Roulette. Disco fries, rusty nails, torn Naugahyde booths – those few years passed in a blur, but booze was her constant companion. Pints secreted in her purse. Shots and beers here at Bath Bar after her shift ended.

Then there was Duke's, a job she got thanks to the bar gods. Duke had come in one night with his pal Sully. Duke was unhappily married to an angry little water bug of a woman named Linda. He set his sights on Jane and offered her a job. He'd flirted unabashedly with her since. He's suggested they sleep together at the Shore Motel. But he's never gone farther than talk, not in all these years.

It's her opinion that Duke just likes being around her, likes the promise of her, but he doesn't really want to sleep with her. He likes the rejection. It's like those ladies who wear high heels and stomp on the hands of hairy businessmen. *Look but don't touch. Let your temptation haunt you.* She's fine with playing that part.

The job's easy. She's in the office from eight until five Monday through Friday. She keeps a couple of fifths of rye in her bottom desk drawer just in case she really needs it, but she tries not to drink at work. She likes waiting until she's off the clock to drink. That's her personal code. It also gives her something to look forward to. Much of her morning is usually spent wrangling with a hangover anyhow, and she's not – strangely enough – a believer in the hair of the dog philosophy. Coffee's all that sets her right, even if it's just Folgers from that dirty old office drip machine.

Duke knows she drinks hard and doesn't give a damn when she's hungover. After all, she's not operating on hearts or trying not to misplace a kid. She's just fielding calls and scribbling on pads. She's never rude. The customers love her. Of course they do. Mr. Evangelista from up the block, who just croaked actually, used to bring his Buick Skylark in for oil changes monthly just to see her even though he never drove anywhere. He'd always bring her a gift too. Candies or a bottle of wine. There were others like that. Heartsick old timers, for the most part. Occasionally there was a scrubby guy in his thirties who tried to talk sweet and flopped.

This beer's a rarity. She desires it now because of the heat. Usually she sticks with rye and gin. And she doesn't eat much. She looks pretty much the same at thirty as she did at eighteen, give or take. She knows that won't last, but there's no use in worrying about it. Fact of the matter is that Alkie Eleanor down at the other end of bar – slumped there, toothless, the only other person currently present in this unholy dive on this hot August night – well, that's her future and she's okay with it.

Jane the Stain is a nickname that, all told, she doesn't mind. Most of the guys who come around think it's something sexual. Like she walked into the bar with come stains all over her dress and never lived it down. Other bums think it's a period thing. Maybe she wore a pair of white pants to work and bled through. Men are fucking idiots, that's just a true fact.

It's actually a handle she got dealt as a kid. She was twelve. It was an August day in 1968 not unlike this August day. She was in the P.S. 101 schoolyard with Caroline Cavalcanti, Ocean Avenue Annie, and Half-Jewish Janice. They were riding bikes and playing with chalk, hanging out on the far end of the yard, which was like the deep end of the pool. A bunch of big girls came swaggering through the hole in the chain-link fence that served as an entrance, smoking, wearing cool jackets. Rita from the Benson Arms apartment building was their leader. She had buckteeth and wore a frayed plaid skirt, and the two Ellens, Carmela Mercado, and Tiny Nunziata flanked her. The rumors around the block were that Rita was a sex fiend and a junkie, that she'd screwed Dickie Sorel in someone's backyard and let Pasquale Pizzimenti film it with his brand-new Super 8 camera. She was there to start trouble. Trouble was her fun.

What happened was that Rita approached her and her friends under the guise of scoring a smoke. When Caroline, Annie, and Janice all shook their heads no to the question, ready to hop on their bikes and speed away, Rita looked ready to blow. But Jane wasn't intimidated. She isn't sure what exactly made her tough out of the gate, but she was most definitely born that way. Maybe something about just growing up with her mom and grandma, her old man out of the picture and on the skids somewhere far away. Instead of a simple no, she got up in Rita's face and told her to go buy her own cigarettes. She knew this wasn't about cigarettes at all, that it was a turf thing. Rita and her crew had dominion over this part of the schoolyard and they didn't want these younger girls moving in. Jane knew that her only choices were to stand up now or to cower away forever. When Rita went for her bike, trying to kick the chain loose, Jane exploded. The short of it was that she was a scrappy little fighter. Her uncle Tony had taught her a few moves. The Ellens, Carmela, Nunziata,

Caroline, Annie, and Janice all watched, shocked as hell, as she beat the meanness out of Rita.

Jane was wearing a plain white cotton T-shirt that day. The last shot she landed bloodied her knuckles. Somehow, in the act of then setting her bike upright after leaving Rita defeated on the ground, she ran that hand across her chest, leaving a smear of bright blood. It looked like the mark of a warrior. She felt like a warrior. The Ellens carried Rita away. Caroline crowned Jane queen of the neighborhood. This part of the schoolyard was theirs forever, no beef from the older girls. Jane wore the T-shirt around with pride, never washing it. Kids started calling her Jane the Bloodstain. Eventually, they shortened it to Jane the Stain.

She still has the shirt too. She framed it the way you might frame a favorite worn-out band T-shirt and kept it hanging on her bedroom wall like a saint's relic. When she needed strength, having early on lost faith in God, she bowed at the altar of that bloody shirt, remembering that she was capable of slaying giants. Or at least bucktoothed sex fiends.

Sometimes she wonders whatever became of Rita. She only saw her a couple of times after that, never up close, her swagger deflated, and her status on the block and in the neighborhood hobbled. You don't just survive a beatdown like that. Rita got the shit end of the legend stick. *Some twelve-year-olds have nothing to lose*, the legend went. *The pecking order doesn't mean anything. Crazy trumps seniority. Watch out for Jane the Stain.* She wonders if Rita had to scurry away to Long Island or New Jersey, had to try to rebuild her reputation there.

When Widow Marie returns to pour Jane more rye, she comes bearing a gift. A scratch-off from Benny's and a dirty little nickel to do the necessary work. It's the kind made to look like a slot machine, scratching off the numbers as if pulling a lever. Gunning for Lucky Sevens or cherries or whatever.

This is also part of their routine. Instead of helping the poor or visiting old timers at a nursing home, Widow Marie sometimes gives scratch-offs to her favorite customers to check off her good deed for the day.

Jane thanks her and starts rubbing at the scratch-off with the nickel. The black scrapings edge the ticket, and she blows them onto the bar.

She scratches slowly, purposefully.

This is a highlight of the night.

"Well?" Widow Marie asks. "How's it looking?"

"I won," Jane says. "It's not a big win, just the most basic one. Five bucks."

"There you go. Now you're on easy street. With five bucks you can move to the Bahamas."

"I'd miss this place too much." Jane tucks the ticket in her pocket. What she'll do with her winnings is buy a couple of packs of smokes. She'd been trying to quit but then she had a little sit-down with herself and really interrogated that decision. Why quit? What was she afraid of? What does she have to lose by smoking? She could use one now, actually.

She doesn't have a pack, so she goes down to the other end of the bar and snags one from Alkie Eleanor's pack of Pall Malls. Alkie Eleanor's head is down, and she's really sawing wood. People always borrow cigarettes from her. It is an acceptable thing to do at Bath Bar. Less a form of theft and more just Alkie Eleanor's contribution to the proceedings. Least she could do since her modus operandi is to black out, wake up occasionally and scream something incomprehensible, maybe fart or belch for good measure. The joint collectively puts up with a lot from her.

Widow Marie keeps a row of unlit religious candles back by the register. She fires one up now – the Virgin Mary glowing powder blue from the flame – and brings it to Jane. A lot of people are superstitious about lighting smokes from candles, saying it brings bad luck, but Widow Marie encourages it. She thinks the opposite's true. She thinks lighting a cigarette from a candle can change your whole day for the better. Jane is not sure how she ever came to such a conclusion, but she doesn't buy any stupid superstitious stuff anyway. How could lighting a cigarette from a candle or breaking a mirror or spilling salt impact the world? Imagine. Like there's somebody up in the sky, keeping track of dumb shit. *We've got another monster lighting her cigarette from a candle. Better kill a sailor.*

Jane lights the cigarette and studies what the flames do to Mary in the dark bar. The shadows they make. She likes a good religious candle even though she's no longer religious. She also has a sweet spot for the old Virgin Mary.

The door to the bar swings open and in walks Double Stevie Scivetti. If Jane was asked to make a list of who she didn't want to see, Double Stevie would be at the top. But he's as unavoidable as bad weather. You might get a streak of nice days but then it's going to rain and rain hard. That's how it is with Double Stevie. She might go a stretch without seeing him at Bath Bar but their paths would cross at some point. He actually lives in the same apartment building that Rita used to live in, the Benson Arms, but he's older than Jane. She asked him once if he remembered Rita and he said he didn't, that he and his mom didn't move into the Benson Arms until '71.

Jane's had enough to drink now that she gets caught up thinking about what the fuck *Benson Arms* even means. The arms of Benson Avenue?

"Just exactly who I didn't want to see," Double Stevie says to her. He looks more frazzled and on edge than usual.

"Don't ruin my night," she says, taking a long drag off the Pall Mall.

Double Stevie runs with Sav Franzone these days. Sav would also be high on the list of guys she'd rather not encounter who are unavoidable. A block fixture. Married with a kid but always on the hunt for a piece. They'd hooked up once, a couple of years ago, when he didn't have the kid yet and his wife Risa was very pregnant. It was one of Jane's biggest regrets in that department. She'd gotten with a lot of guys she didn't like and even guys who had wives, but this was different because of that kid and because Risa was sweet. It had been in the midst of a bad drunk weekend for Jane. She remembered it only in flashes because she was buzzing on the edges of a blackout. He wanted to just borrow someone's car and go down to the dark stretch by Nellie Bly Park on Shore Parkway. They couldn't go to his apartment, obviously. Hers was tough too since she lived with her mom. They settled on the ladies' room in Bath Bar. She knew it was a mistake as it was happening. A worse mistake than usual. But sometimes she's guided by a kind of hot loneliness in the totally wrong direction. This was one of those times. It was like closing your eyes while driving and drifting onto the opposite side of the road.

Even though her head was swirling from the booze, she remembers a lot about being up close in that dirty little stall with Sav. The smell of bad cologne dabbed on his neck. His rough hands, tugging and pulling. The way he tried to talk like a porno. How he'd called her a *puttana*. How she'd slapped him and he begged to be slapped again. He lasted a minute and then left the stall. She threw up in the toilet, fixed herself up, and went out the back door into the alley, setting off the fire alarm. She dragged herself home and cried. The hot loneliness – the desperate yearning for physical connection with someone, anyone, the worst fucking person possible – had led to total despair, as it so often did. She didn't go back to the bar for a couple of weeks after that. The next time she saw Sav they barely acknowledged each other. Now she'd settled into feeling a seething hate toward him. Watching him with Sandra Carbonari some nights made her want to spit on him and tell him to go home to his wife and kid. Sandra was more than just young and stupid, seeming to get off on the cheating. She'd probably be in too at some point soon, in her cut-off shorts and halter top, hair done up nice at Bensonhurst Dolls, hours spent on makeup.

Double Stevie trudges past Jane down to where Alkie Eleanor is slumped, sitting on the stool next to her.

"You're back already," Widow Marie says to him.

He takes a twenty-dollar bill out of his pocket, puts it on the bar, and flattens it out with his fingers.

Jane watches through her cigarette smoke as he stares at the bill.

"Fuck's that?" Widow Marie says. "Your mom give that to you for snacks? You want a beer and a shot? You could buy a round for the whole joint." She motions around from one end of the bar to the other. Laughing. "Actually, I think Eleanor's good, so you could just get Jane."

"Twenty bucks," Double Stevie says, shaking his head. "You said there'd be more at Gilly's. A lot more."

"What're you on about, kid?"

"I want money. You said there'd be money, and you were wrong. Way I figure it is you owe me for the bad information."

"I don't even know what you're talking about." Widow Marie reaches under the bar and comes out with a Louisville Slugger. She pounds it in her hand.

This isn't an empty threat. Jane's seen her use the bat a couple of times. Once on Carlo Purpura, who'd pissed on the little Christmas tree that Widow Marie put in the corner every year. "You don't piss on Christmas," she'd said, dinging him in the knee. That was last call for Carlo. Marie banned him from Bath Bar, which took a special kind of hatred on her part. The other time was Johnny Saint Fort. He'd gotten up on the bar, pulled his pants down, and was swinging his wang around for a laugh. He had a pretty good rope on him, the tall bastard, and he could get some real movement on the thing. For all her degeneracy, Widow Marie was conservative when it came to bodies, so she took out the bat and slammed him in the ass with it. Johnny wasn't banned, but that was the last time he took out his wang at the bar.

"How much you got in the register?" Double Stevie asks.

"You're gonna rob me? I've got a bat, and you've got nothing but your pea brain."

Double Stevie stuffs the twenty back in his pocket, hops up on the bar, and then dives onto Widow Marie, fighting for possession of the bat.

Alkie Eleanor sits up, her eyes still half-closed and says, "The goddamn raisins went bad two months ago. You can't use bad raisins. Every kid's gonna be puking on his shoes. Get new raisins, would you?"

Jane sighs and takes a pull of beer.

Double Stevie has overpowered Widow Marie and taken the bat from her. This is unusual, sure, but nothing much surprises Jane in a wildcard place like this. Widow Marie has been held up before, just never by a regular. Is that even what's going on? Or has Double Stevie just snapped? Maybe he's coming down off drugs. This is that kind of behavior. He stands, holding the bat at his side, and gets to work trying to open the register.

Widow Marie is splayed on the floor, groaning. "Oh, you fucker," she says. *This is a definite ban*, Jane thinks.

"How do you open this old piece of shit register?" Double Stevie says.

It's a classic register. One of the big, old dramatic ones. Swimming with buttons and numbers and a locked till. Widow Marie always looks so small next to it.

"Put the bad raisins in the garbage," Alkie Eleanor says. "Don't worry about the wasted money."

Jane gets up.

"How do you open this thing?" Double Stevie says again. He pokes Widow Marie with the bat. "Come on. Open it."

"Go shit in the river," Widow Marie says from the floor.

Jane walks past Alkie Eleanor and crosses through the open space where the bar flap is turned up on its hinge. She sidesteps Widow Marie and makes her way next to Double Stevie. He holds the bat in a threatening way.

"Whoa, boy," she says. "I'm here to help."

"You know how to open it?" he says.

She nods.

"So open it."

She positions herself in front of the register as if she's about to get to work, like Duke under the hood of a car. Double Stevie's breathing hard. He's hungry for whatever's in the till. Instead of reaching out and popping the drawer, which is so easy that Double Stevie must be even dumber than she thought, she turns quickly and stomps his foot with her heel. He yelps in pain, drops the bat, and jumps back. She picks the bat up and swings it at him. Another doggish yelp. He climbs up on the bar, holding his elbow, cursing under his breath. Jane moves toward him, starts to swing again but pulls it back. "You should go," she says.

He jumps off the bar, taking down a stool, and slams his way out the door.

Jane sets the bat on the floor and helps Widow Marie up. "You okay?" she says.

"I'm good," Widow Marie says. "I didn't know I had my own security detail sitting right here."

"I'm pretty scrappy."

"Jane the Stain, a hero for our times. Drinks are on me."

"Double Stevie's banned, right?"

"Forever. I'm putting his name in the notebook now." Widow Marie follows through on that promise, scribbling Double Stevie's name in block letters in her Book of Bans.

Jane smiles and goes back to her side of the bar. A winning scratch-off and her most triumphant defeat of a shitheel since taking down Rita in the schoolyard eighteen years ago.

Widow Marie puts on the radio. They listen to traffic, weather, and sports. The night hums along stupidly. Double Stevie's charades are in the rearview mirror.

*

Martina has come this far, so she might as well go all the way. Her grief has led her here. To this nothing block in end-of-the-line Brooklyn. To the man who'd shot Jerry. Sav Franzone. The name like glass in her mouth. It had all gone so wrong, this man getting into Jerry's life right after she'd come back to him. How'd it all get so wrong? She guesses it started wrong for her and Jerry. Maybe Sav killing Jerry was God's punishment.

How deeply she loved Jerry. Idolizing him as her stepbrother, turning into something else. Something unnatural, her mother and stepfather said. Something that needed to be hidden away. Making her a nun was their answer. They paid for shortcuts. The surprise of it was that she liked being a nun. She liked the solitude and the sisterhood. She liked letting go of *things*. There was a library at the convent, and she spent her time reading when she wasn't praying or working. She liked being in the garden most of all, tending to the fruits and vegetables. The convent is upstate in a town called Highland, close to the Hudson River. Nearby are apple orchards. The river is serene. She misses watching the river. It had been almost perfect there except that she kept on loving Jerry in her heart – she loved him more than she loved God and the other sisters – and that resulted in a sort of spiritual anguish that was always hiding under the surface. She saw Jerry in the trees, in the dirt, in the water. His voice came to her in storms. Her prayers to God turned into prayers to Jerry.

She went and found him in the city. His loft on Avenue A. They stayed tangled together for weeks. And then Jerry met Sav at a bar. They cooked up a scheme together to make money. Martina was against it; she had a bad feeling about Sav from the start. She was right. He found out about her and Jerry – what their relationship was – and threatened to blackmail them, to go to their rich parents in Connecticut. Jerry fought back. Or tried to.

That stupid gun. Sav wrestled it away from Jerry and shot him. Martina was stunned. She watched from the window as Sav ran away, dropping the gun in a sewer drain out on the street. Martina had begged Jerry to get rid of the gun, but he'd had enough trouble with junkies and muggers that he felt safer with it around. If he didn't have it, nothing would have played out the way it did. Sav didn't bring a gun. He would've tried and failed with his blackmail scheme. So many sins. The sin of their relationship. Lust, pride. The immorality of it. She knows. She knows forever. It's their relationship, the mess of it, the rottenness at its center, that really led to all of this. Without their love, Jerry would be alive. Without their love, Jerry would've likely never even moved to the city and got his gun and crossed paths with Sav.

It hadn't been hard to find out where exactly Sav grew up. She knew Brooklyn, but she didn't know the neighborhood. She called a contact of hers at the diocese office to find out where he'd been baptized. Her contact told her Sav had been baptized at St. Mary Mother of Jesus on Eighty-Fourth Street. Once she had the name of the church, it was easy enough to track him down. She called the rectory at St. Mary's, spoke to a nice woman named Peggy who answered the phones there, and asked if she had a number for Sav's mother. The woman said, "Lola?"

Martina said, "Right. Lola."

"Around here, we think of Sav as Lola's son, not Lola as Sav's mother." Peggy laughed, as if it were a joke only she understood, but she gave Martina the number.

Next Martina started to ask a question and then purposefully let it drift off: "Is Lola still over there on…"

"Bay Thirty-Fifth. Between Bath and Benson. A few houses down from Sav and Risa. God bless Lola. She's got a lot on her plate with Sav."

Martina got the exact house number and then thanked Peggy. That Sav lived on the same block was pure luck. She hadn't imagined him as the kind of person with a house or an apartment. She guessed that Risa was his wife, though she couldn't picture him with a wife. He had blown into Jerry's life, into her life, a straggling thing, a strange stranger.

Those calls were made while sitting next to Jerry's body. She blessed him. She touched his head with holy water. She cleaned away the blood and surrounded him with flowers she bought from a market a couple of blocks away. She said the prayers she needed to say. She turned the loft into a tomb.

It wasn't hard to fish the gun out of the sewer where Sav dumped it. He hadn't been careful. It was lodged on an outcropping of broken blacktop that had somehow affixed itself to the wall just below the grate. She reached it without much effort. She knew she needed that gun. She has it now in the black clutch she's carrying. The gun is small. She doesn't know anything about guns. She feels certain it will work when she needs it to.

She tries again to reconcile her desire for revenge with her vision of a loving, tender God. She can't. She feels so much rage as her feet move along the sidewalk on Sav's block. It's like electricity entering her from below. She's from the Old Testament. She's a flood, crashing over the concrete. Sav doesn't know it yet, but the water's gathering in his name. He won't have her pegged as the kind to come for blood, but here she is. She's wearing one of Jerry's plain black T-shirts and black pants she bought at a thrift store on Second Avenue. The shirt smells like him. God bless Jerry Malloy.

She says the address over and over in her head until she's standing in front of Sav's mother's house. The lights are on in the front window. It looks similar to other houses on the block. White siding. A brick front porch with a few wooden chairs set in a row. A black mailbox next to the door. Garbage cans inside the gate. A garden in the small front yard overseen by a plaster statue of the Virgin Mother. Our Lady of Sorrows. Heart pierced seven ways. The blue of her robe so vivid. Hands clasped across her stomach. Looking down at the dirt in the garden. Grieving. Lola. Dolores. Our Lady of Dolours. The Sorrowful Mother.

The sight of the statue stops Martina from reaching out and opening the gate. She, Mary, is a warning and a sign. Others grieve. Lola grieves. What would it be like to lose her son? What would it be like to be the person who strips her son from her? This is not Martina. She's no flood. She's a sad starfish clinging to a piling as waves crash around her.

346

Martina backs away from the front gate. What was she even going to do? Confront Lola about Sav? She scurries away down the block. She wonders which house is Sav's. She looks for his name on mailboxes.

When Martina comes to the bar on the far corner of the block, she thinks a drink might take the edge off. Drinking has never been something she's been against. She's always liked it, even – maybe especially – at the convent where it wasn't allowed. She associated drinking with Jerry too. Those early days where they'd share a bottle of wine and go into the woods.

It's called Bath Bar, this little dive, which conjures the image of someone bathing in booze in some sort of tenement washtub. The sign out front is hand painted. *BATH BAR* in red curlicue script on a blue background. A cocktail glass painted next to the words. In the window is a neon beer sign with almost half the letters blown. It says: *GENESEE CREAM ALE.* The letters that aren't lit are still visible in the fading daylight.

Martina goes in and hunkers down at the bar. It's a bar full of women. Full is the wrong word. A mostly empty bar that happens to be inhabited by three other women and her. There's the bartender, a bulky woman, slouching and sturdy at the same time. Sitting not far from the bartender is a passed-out drunk. Martina can tell she's a lady by her shoes and ragged clothes. Then there's a somewhat normal-looking woman in her thirties on a stool nearby, looking like she just got off work and is already in the midst of really tying one on. She speaks first to Martina: "All they have here is Genny Cream Ale and cheap whiskey, so if you're thinking about one of those cocktails on the sign out there, think again."

"Whiskey's all I want," Martina says.

"You talk like a cowboy," the woman says. "I like you. My name's Jane."

The bartender brings over a bottle and a shot glass. She pours one for Martina.

Jane continues: "That's Widow Marie slinging drinks. And that's Alkie Eleanor down there, sawing wood." She points to the slumped-over drunk.

Martina puts the clutch on the bar and downs the whiskey. It loosens her up immediately. She lets out a breath.

"You a hitman or a jewel thief?" Jane asks. "I can't tell."

"What do you mean?"

"Take it easy. Just a joke. You've got this all-black thing going on. Let me guess your name. I'm good at this."

"You won't guess it," Martina says. She motions for another drink, and Widow Marie pours, slopping it over the edges of the glass. She still hasn't spoken, this strange widow of a bartender, this sloppy pourer of cheap whiskey.

"Five bucks says I guess it in five tries," Jane says.

"Okay."

Jane claps her hands together and then thrums her fingers against the bar top. "Set me up, Marie," she says. "I need some booze to help me think."

Marie goes over and refills her glass. "For the hero of the night, sure thing," she says, the first words she's spoken.

"I'm having a good night already, stranger," Jane says to Martina. "I won five bucks on a scratch-off and I saved the day when Double Stevie tried to rob the register, so I'm drinking on the arm. You stumbled in here on a real thriller of an evening. And I'm coming for your five bucks next. Okay? Buckle up." She tosses back the drink and seems to search the ceiling for an answer. "Let me ask you one thing first?"

"Okay."

"You're not from around here, right? Definitely not from the block but not from the neighborhood either. Not even from Brooklyn."

Martina shakes her head. She's trying not to give herself away. She shouldn't have come into this bar. She shouldn't have come after Sav. She's no killer. What does it matter if Sav lives or dies? Jerry's dead no matter what. He's never coming back. Every interaction will be like this one. Forced. Like she's trying to fit in to a world that won't have her, that never wanted her. Banter at a bar. Handshakes and kisses. Strange names written or said. Everything is wrong.

She thinks about where she's from. Greenwich. Horrible place. What she should do is drink two more drinks and write a letter to her mother and stepdad, whose name she took. She'll write it all down. Her love for Jerry, the way he was murdered, where he is and how she left him there with flowers. Say goodbye herself. Say there'll be peace on the other side. On her way in, she noticed a mailbox on the corner. She'll see if she can borrow a piece of paper, an envelope, and a stamp from Widow Marie. She'll sit here, have a few more drinks, and write her letter. She'll go out and drop it in the mailbox when she's done, and she'll forget all about Sav. Then she'll go back into the bar, pay her tab, disappear to the bathroom and blow her head off. Not suicide. Mercy.

"Drumroll," Jane says, pounding the bar a little harder. "My first guess is… Anne."

"Anne?" Widow Marie says. "That's the best you've got?"

"What? She looks like an Anne." She gives Martina the once-over. "Okay, fine, she's not an Anne. Strike one. You're not an Anne, correct?"

"I did think about making Anne my confirmation name," Martina says.

"There you go. Right track. Okay, here goes. Try two." Jane closes her eyes and taps her temples this time, takes a nip of whiskey. "Elizabeth. Or any of its variants. Betty. Betsy. Liz. Beth."

Martina shakes her head.

"Damn," Jane says, genuinely seeming pissed.

Martina wonders what it'd be like to be this way. Loose. Easy. Fun. She only ever felt fun with Jerry and even then she wasn't sure if she was actually fun or if she was playing the role of someone who understands what fun is. She envies this Jane. She's a regular on the sitcom that is this bar. She *fits*.

Jane's next three attempts to guess her name come rapidly. Almost making Anne her confirmation name must've seemed like some sort of clue because she sticks with saints' names. "Catherine? Joan? Mary?"

Martina shakes her head again. She thinks of the statue of Mary outside of Lola's house that warned her away, that steered her to this bar.

"Fuck me," Jane says. "I guess my luck's run cold. What is it?"

"Martina."

"Shit. Really. You're not Irish? You seem Irish. Black Irish but Irish."

"I'm Italian." She thinks of her stepfather, Jerry Malloy Senior. A bond trader. His big gleaming bald head. His large appetite for Manhattans. When she was younger and he'd order a Manhattan, she thought he was ordering the juice of the city. Like someone had to squeeze the borough itself to make that reddish glowing drink. How stupid. Maybe if she hadn't taken his name when he married her mother. She wanted so badly to take his name, though. To be a Malloy. She hated her actual father, Carmine Cammarosano, who split when she was a baby. Maybe if she stayed as Martina Cammarosano people would've recognized that she and Jerry weren't blood. What will her stepfather look like when he gets her letter, when he knows she and Jerry Junior are gone?

And her Italian mother. Poor Rosie. The way she put blush on in the car mirror. Dancing to Dean Martin in the living room. On her knees scrubbing the cabinets clean. How disgusted she was when she found out about Martina and Jerry. How she wailed. She knew things like that happened in the world but she didn't want to believe that they happened between her daughter and stepson. She'd tried. She'd really tried. She'll wail at the funeral too. Funerals. They'll probably be kept separate. Buried apart.

Maybe word of her death and of Jerry's death will reach her mother and stepfather before the letter does. Maybe getting the letter will put things into perspective at least a little. The way the world hands you love and then says it's wrong.

Speaking of. The letter.

Martina turns away from Jane and speaks to Widow Marie: "Do you have a piece of paper and maybe an envelope and a stamp I can buy?"

"Sure," Widow Marie says. "No charge." She gathers the supplies, ripping a page from a marble notebook stuffed into a nook next to the register, removing an envelope and a roll of stamps from a cabinet under the bar. She hands Martina the paper and the battered envelope and then rips off one of the stamps, licks it and applies it crookedly to the upper-right-hand corner of the envelope. She gives her a little golf pencil too, the eraser rubbed raw.

Martina looks at the stamp. Widow Marie's spit has dampened the edges, the paper beneath a little grainy. Something about it makes her even sadder. She thinks of scrawling the Greenwich address. She imagines dropping the envelope in the mailbox. She thinks of it being picked up by a mailman, stuffed in a sack, carried on a truck across the city and up into Connecticut. Over into Connecticut. Whatever. The world that letter might know. Its journey. She thinks of Jerry dead in his loft. The flashes are coming hard and fast now.

Jane shakes her out of it by slapping a scratch-off lottery ticket on the bar. "There you go," Jane says. "That's worth five American dollars. Cash it on the corner. You won it fair and square. I choked. I'm usually good at guessing, I swear. An off day. I feel like Jesse Orosco blowing a save."

"Martina's a tough one to guess."

"You're right about that. You're my first Martina. I've met a million Marys, Joans, Annes, and Betsys. Never a Martina. Must be nice to be unique. I'm just a Jane. Jane's nothing. Jane's the 'Happy Birthday' song of names. Jane. It's white toast, burnt a little."

"I like the name Jane," Martina says.

"Think of one famous Jane worth anything. Don't say Jane Fonda or Jane Curtin."

"Saint Jane Frances de Chantal. Jane Austen. Calamity Jane."

"You got a stockpile of Janes for this very moment? Impressive. I've heard the names, but I don't know anything about them. They're good, these Janes?"

"A saint, a great writer, and a compassionate frontierswoman."

"Huh."

"Well, Martina, you've woken me up to the possibilities of being a good Jane. I need another drink. You need one?"

Martina nods.

Widow Marie pours another round for them and one for herself too. The drunk down at the end of the bar stirs, sitting up and saying in a growl, "The goddamn raisins don't go in that drawer."

"Never mind Alkie Eleanor," Jane says. "What do we drink to?"

Martina picks up her glass, clinks it against Jane's and then against Widow Marie's. "God Bless Jerry Malloy," she says. The whiskey goes down like fire.

Widow Marie shrugs and drinks her drink. Jane follows suit and then motions to the paper that's in front of Martina. "Widow Marie ripped that out of her Book of Bans. She must like you. Is Jerry Malloy who you're writing to?"

Martina looks at the paper, the darkness of the bar top visible through it. She swears she sees Jerry's face there. Like a vision of Christ or a Marian apparition. Jerry as he was in life. Those eyes. She ignores Jane's question and starts to write, almost clawing at the paper with the stubby pencil, avoiding rings of condensation on the bar. Where did the condensation come from? She didn't have a beer. Maybe it's tears from Jerry.

She has her own tears now. The whiskey has helped her cry. Jane puts a hand on her shoulder and gives her a look of deep compassion as she works on her letter.

✳

Jane gets nervous when the stranger leaves to mail her letter and then comes back and disappears into the bathroom with her bag. Something's off. She's distraught, this Martina. Beyond distraught.

"Maybe I should go check on her," Jane says to Widow Marie.

"What's she gonna do in there?"

"Maybe she's a junkie. Maybe she's shooting up. I go back there, the door's locked, and she's OD'ing on the bowl, what the fuck do we do? She's okay in my book, but a lot of junkies are okay until they're a problem you've gotta deal with."

"You think she's a doper?"

"She brought her bag with her. She looks lost in the eyes. I've seen that before. The far-off thing. She's somewhere else. Wants to be. I never told you about Junkie Jennifer?"

"Who's Junkie Jennifer?"

"Junkie Jennifer was like the Alkie Eleanor of one of my previous hangouts, the Beauty Box. Bath Bar, Beauty Box. I guess I like double B places. This was seven, eight years ago. She was a normal girl from Lake Street and then she got deep into dope and she just became a shooting-up machine. You'd walk in on her wherever and she'd have her arm tied, needle hanging out. Track marks everywhere. She OD'd on toilets and kitchen floors, in basements and attics and once under a pool table at the Beauty Box. She'd shit herself when the dope hit. She shit herself a lot. She was like a baby. Tiny Fat Fannie started a collection for adult diapers for Jennifer. We used to joke that we were gonna strap one on her before she got high. But nobody wants to blow that kind of dough on diapers for a junkie."

"You're saying she's gonna shit herself in my bathroom?" Widow Marie asks. "Just forego the toilet in front of her and let the load fly in her drawers?"

"That's one possible outcome."

"If junkies shit themselves like that, why don't they just pull their pants down before shooting up?"

"One of life's greatest fucking mysteries. You can never tell what's in a junkie's heart."

"And you think this kid in my bathroom's a junkie?"

"Fifty-fifty, I'd say. Either that or some kind of deranged religious nut who hands out pamphlets. Doesn't she have that quality to her? Like she's the kind of person who rings your doorbell at eight o'clock at night to give you a little pamphlet about how Jesus would like to take a dumb fuck like you for a walk. Not a dumb fuck like *you*. You know what I mean. Just dumb fucks in general. She could be shooting up Jesus in there. That's even worse. Talk about shitting yourself." Jane pauses. "Don't get me wrong. I like her. She's loaded with information about Janes. That's special."

When the front door opens, Jane's not sure who to expect. Her luck, Sav will probably come charging in. Sandra too. But it's not either of them. It's Donnie Parascandolo. Crazy shit. Donnie the cop *never* comes in here. A fucked up horse doesn't drink so close to home. Plus, one of the few times he was in here, Widow Marie said she was going to ban him for finishing her crossword puzzle when she wasn't looking. His main haunt is Blue Sticks Bar, where the cops have the run of the place. Sometimes he'll hang at the Wrong Number. She steers clear of both. She steers clear of Donnie too. His wife Donna's okay but he's got the look of someone ready to snap. Like an old pipe ready to burst at the seams and send a river of shit out into the world. He came into Duke's once when he was on the outs with his usual mechanics, Frankie and Sal at Flash. "I'm looking for Sav Franzone," Donnie says.

Jane turns her attention to Widow Marie, who's probably trying to remember Donnie's status at the bar. Maybe she remembers the crossword puzzle incident, though it was long ago. Guys like him are often in the Book of Bans, but he's not because he's a cop and no cops generally drink here. It clicks for her exactly who he is. Widow Marie hates cops. She doesn't like the look of them or the smell of them or any goddamn thing about them. What she hates most, Jane guesses, is the swagger. A cop thinks he's above everything, thinks he's doing God's work or some shit, but really most of them are chumps. Roman fucking soldiers. Betrayers of codes. There's good ones here and there, guys with decent hearts, and Jane has encountered them, but they're few and far between. Mostly, they start okay and go downhill fast, ruined by other cops or drained clean by the city, or letting the dark driver take the wheel. "He's not here," Jane says.

"He was here earlier," Widow Marie says. "Just for a minute."

"Maybe he went to Double Stevie's, the dumb fuck?" Donnie asks.

"I don't keep track."

A loud noise from the back of the bar startles them. Sounds like a truck backfiring. A gunshot. Definitely a gunshot. Came from the bathroom. Jane had the girl wrong. Not a junkie or a religious nut. A suicide. She just ate a bullet in the Bath Bar ladies' room.

Donnie's quick to react. His hand is under his shirt and then he's got a gun out in front of him, sweeping across the room. "What was that?" he asks.

"I don't know," Widow Marie says.

"Girl in the bathroom," Jane says. "She's been in there a while. She was looking down in the dumps. Must've brought a piece in there with her and plugged herself."

"Jesus Christ," Donnie says.

"I gotta clean up a suicide again?" Widow Marie says. "I swore after '82 I'd never clean up another suicide."

What Widow Marie's referring to is the suicide of former Altar Boy Dante Scipione. Dante had actually been an altar boy at St. Mary's, but he'd also been a member of the Altar Boys, a denim-jacketed gang of Italian kids from the neighborhood that thirsted to bust the balls of every non-Italian gang in the city. Dante had his heart broken by some girl from the city and never got over it. He drank too much and cut his own neck in the back of the bar one night. Slashed at his jugular with a bottle he broke on the edge of the pool table. Bled out pretty good. It was a mess. Widow Marie was mopping for a month. The Altar Boys made a memorial on the wall outside the bar. They kept it up for a while. Flowers and pictures and cards. Dante liked Twinkies. All these Twinkies were piled up on the cement. Kids would pass by and grab a package of Twinkies. Jane wasn't there the night Dante cut himself. Widow Marie didn't ever talk about it. Now, Jane's imagining, she's probably thinking there's more than blood on the floor. There's blood *and* brains on the wall *and* floor. And there's still a chance the loopy little letter-writer actually shit herself.

"You've got the gun, you make the rules," Jane says to Donnie.

Donnie shrugs and lets out an exhausted breath, letting them all know he doesn't need this. "Yeah, I'm on it," he says, in that derisive, thick cop voice.

Jane imagines that Donnie's envisioning the hassle that could unfold. Calling it in, paperwork, being on the clock when he's off the clock.

As Donnie heads to the bathroom – *heads to the head*, Jane thinks to herself, almost laughing – he's mumbling under his breath: "Now I've gotta deal with this. Not bad enough Pags put the Leo Manzi thing on my shoulders." He's cursing Christ and George Steinbrenner and Ed Koch and any other motherfucker he can think of. "Who is it in there?" he asks Jane and Widow Marie.

"No one we know," Jane says. "New blood."

"Never seen her before," Widow Marie confirms.

Alkie Eleanor pops up like a former champ whose still got a little fight left in her blood. "I told you to put the raisins in the baby carriage," she says. "Wheel them around like they're precious. They *are* precious."

"Jesus Christ," Donnie says, surprised by Alkie Eleanor's zombie routine. "Now we've got raisins. That's what I need. Raisins."

Jane moves next to Alkie Eleanor and puts her hand on her back, rubbing in a circle and then flattening out the wrinkles in her starchy jacket that smells of lottery ticket rubbings, sad bacon, and sour booze. "We've got it, Eleanor," Jane says. "Don't you worry."

Alkie Eleanor settles down, her head drifting back to the bar where it belongs, where there seems to be a groove in the wood for her, clasped arms folded under her forehead, chin in a notch of darkness. Like a needle on a record.

Donnie gets to the ladies' room door and knocks, keeping the gun at the ready, not trusting the information he's been given. *Could be anyone in there with a gun* is probably what he's thinking. Could be Sav. He knocks with the heel of his hand. "Hey in there," he says, pausing to yawn. "You alive or dead?"

No answer.

Donnie knocks harder, a rattling cop knock, the kind that shocks the whole block, that vibrates through the bones of old timers and dumb enchanted kids alike. He homes in on Jane as he speaks, grinning. "Open up, come on. I've gotta make a deposit. Men's room's on the fritz. Gonna be a three-flush operation. Need you to clear out."

No answer again.

Donnie huffs, exasperated, no doubt bummed at the prospect of spending one more second of time doing something he doesn't want to do. "Lady, I ain't got all night. Answer me. Open up." He doesn't even wait for her to not answer this time. He shrugs again, says to Widow Marie and Jane, "I guess she croaked in there. I tried. Just call nine-one-one. They'll deal with it."

Martina's voice sludges out from behind the door. A shattered hush. "Don't. I'm in here. I'm alive."

"Oh, the so-called suicide speaks," Donnie says.

"Can I talk to Jane? I want to talk to Jane."

"Hey, Jane the Stain, swap spots with me, huh? She wants to talk to you. And I want a drink. I'm gonna be strong-armed into lingering in this shithole, I'm gonna need some booze. Marie, you hear me? Set me up a double of that bathroom rye you serve. Rocks. I'm hot. It's hot. I hate August. Least favorite month. My feet get burnt on the sidewalks. I can't wipe the stink of the city off me."

Jane drains her whiskey and goes to the bathroom, passing Donnie on his way to the bar. He clanks the gun up in front of him and waits on his drink. Alkie Eleanor slumps forward again, back to dreamland, caught up in whatever raisin-driven nightmare she's usually caught up in. Jane wonders what in the fuck involving raisins happened in her life to make it a go-to thing to shout when being shaken from her blackout.

"Always an adventure in this dive, huh?" Donnie says to Marie, as she sets him up with a double.

At the ladies' room door, Jane speaks softly: "You okay in there? What happened?"

"I tried to shoot myself. I missed."

"Why'd you do that?"

"Despair."

Jane's wondering what to say to that. She's got this stranger Martina behind the door, gun in hand, having flopped at suicide. Flopping at suicide's no joke. It's like there's another basement below the basement you're in. Jane was suicidal once or twice. Hard not to be when you let booze rule your life and occasionally find yourself clunking up against a terrible darkness. There was the time with her mother's sleeping pills. She drank them down – the whole bottle – with a screwdriver and puked some hellish fountain. Orange juice everywhere. The other time was sadder. She tried to make herself choke on a hunk of food. She doesn't even remember what. Stale bread. A grape maybe. She thought choking was the way to go. It wasn't. She had to save herself by flinging her body desperately over the hard back of a dining room chair. For her, coming down after being drunk always brings the scrapings of despair. She can feel the ghost of all she's never been coursing through her blood. As she gets older, she knows how to deal with it better. She embraces being in that cage, lets dreams of the next drink lull her into a sense of calm.

Jane doesn't know what Martina's story is, but she knows the spot she's in. Must be rotten enough she's figured there's no other way. Must be rotten enough she's chosen the Bath Bar ladies' room. Why not the Verrazano or the Brooklyn Bridge? Why not throw herself in front of a B train? Flattened on the tracks like a penny. Lit up by the third rail. There's drama. Why not a bathtub with a rusty razor blade? Why not hopping off a tall building and knowing what it's like to fly or at least to fall from a great height? Hit that sidewalk below like a comet.

It was an impulsive decision, Jane bets. Martina wants someone to rescue her. "I'm glad you missed," Jane says finally.

"I'm not. What kind of idiot misses trying to shoot herself in the head?"

"You ever think it's divine intervention maybe?"

Nothing.

"Talk to me," Jane says. "Come on out. A drink's what you need. Feel better tonight, worse tomorrow. Deal with it then. That's what I always say. You need someone to listen to you, I'm pretty good at that. Not the best but not bad. I've been down in plenty of holes myself. Been on the edge."

"Yeah?"

"Of course. Come on, drinks are on me. You give Widow Marie the gun for safekeeping and we'll have a heart-to-heart. How's that sound? Not the worst, right? You've got a new pal."

"We ought to get you a gig as a hostage negotiator," Donnie says between slurps of whiskey.

Jane puts her thumb in her mouth and mimes likes she's blowing up her middle finger until she's flipping Donnie the full bird. It's something her mother's best friend Melinda used to do. Jane called her Aunt Melinda even though she wasn't her aunt. She got cancer when Jane was thirteen. The news wrecked her mother. The cancer moved quickly. When she got put in hospice care, they used to go every day to sit with her. Aunt Melinda always found the strength the blow up a bird for them. Jane laughed. The woman was dying but still goofing off. Jane liked that kind of courage. She wasn't there when Aunt Melinda died, but her mother was. Aunt Melinda's last words were *Fuck it*, a fact that her mother reported with tears in her eyes, laughing. "That was Melinda," her mother said. "What a way to go."

The sound of a lock being unlatched. Feet moving on the floor. Jane tries to imagine Martina in that skanky little bathroom with its two stalls, one forever bombed out. The graffiti on the doors. The chipped porcelain sink. Black-and-white tile walls, grout all wormy and weathered. A mirror covered in lipstick messages: DON'T FUCK FREDDIE; FREDDIE'S A THIEF; FRY FREDDIE FRY; ENZIO'S A PIG BASTARD. Half-scrubbed toilets ringed with dark residue. The unwieldy spools of sandpapery toilet tissue. Baseboard heaters fringed with deep threads of dust. A tiny, frosted window to nowhere. The stink of it. Ammonia, Lysol, mildew, piss. Of all places. Might as well be the alley next door. End it all amongst the overstuffed garbage cans and scurrying rats.

Martina pulls the door slowly and she's there, facing Jane. Over her shoulder, Jane can see a hunk of wall tile just above the sink, shattered where the bullet must've hit. She can't figure on the trajectory of it. Where was Martina standing when she pulled the trigger? How'd she miss? How'd the bullet hit *there*? Doesn't matter. A real possibility she just fired into the wall, wanting this. Someone to guide her to the next thing. Martina's black clutch is open, balanced on the edge of the sink.

"You okay?" Jane says.

Martina half-shrugs.

"Give me the gun," Jane says.

Martina hands the gun over. Jane holds it between her thumb and index finger like it's a stranger's vibrator. The gun doesn't feel like anything. The only other gun she's ever touched is the one Duke keeps in the safe at work. She brings it to Widow Marie, who drops it in a dark recess next to the register behind a couple of her saint candles.

Martina struggles to make it to the bar, but Jane helps her, a hand across her back, seeming to prop her up. Jane gets her settled on a stool.

Martina takes momentary notice of Donnie, who she must realize was the man trying to talk her down, and then focuses her energy on the whiskey that Widow Marie pours for her.

Jane clinks her glass and tells her to drink up.

The door to the bar opens. Sav Franzone comes loping in. He's wearing bell-bottoms, his bare stomach and chest covered in Saran Wrap, blood darkening the waist of his jeans, blood encased behind the plastic. He's got on worn old sneakers that are untied.

"What in the everloving fuck?" Widow Marie says.

Jane must admit it's a strange, strange sight.

He's hurt, Sav. Looks like he just escaped from a serial killer who tried to dress him like a mix of a hippie and leftovers.

Martina's up now. She's moving toward Sav. "You killed Jerry. You killed him."

Jane remembers Martina's toast: *God bless Jerry Malloy.*

Sav doesn't seem to hear her. He's moving like a man in shock. He runs straight ahead and hits the wall full force. *Plop.* Collapses to the floor in a heap. He's making sounds that fall somewhere between breathing and snorting.

"Jesus Christ almighty," Donnie says. "Call the cops, Marie."

"You are the cops," Jane says. "You were looking for Sav and now he's here."

"What am I gonna do, unwrap this fuck? Like Christmas in August. I'll pass. I was doing a favor for Lola. This, I didn't bargain for."

"He's hurt bad." Jane wonders what exactly happened. Was he knifed and wrapped up? Shot and wrapped up? Or maybe this is some weird prank? Double Stevie's pulling the strings, outside on the sidewalk, hoping everyone will be distracted so he can pounce on the register. A stupid idea but not the stupidest. And what the fuck is up with Martina and Sav? There's a connection she didn't see coming. Unless that's why Martina's on the block. She's hunting Sav for whatever he did to Jerry. But she chickened out and tried to off herself instead. Makes sense.

Martina lashes out at Sav now, scratching and clawing at him even though he's bleeding and out cold. "I came here to kill you," Martina says, and Jane's immediately glad she got the gun away from her before she saw Sav.

Jane's not unhappy about any of it. If there's anybody on the block everybody would like to see hurt, it's Sav. "Leave him," Jane says to Martina. She kneels next to Sav and prods him. "He looks shot. I think he's shot."

The door opens again, and Sandra Carbonari sidles her way into the proceedings. Wearing a neon pink halter-top and cut-off denim shorts. Her high hair stiff, sweat resistant from the can of Aqua Net they've used on her at Bensonhurst Dolls. She's a bright blur of color and smells in the dark little dive.

"This place is like a fucking clown car," Donnie says.

Sandra's all smiles for a second before seeing Sav on the floor. Despite the bell-bottoms and Saran Wrap, she makes out his face right away. "My poor Sav. What happened to him?" She's looking to anybody for an answer. Jane. Widow Marie. Martina, who she's no doubt never seen before. Donnie.

"We don't know," Jane says. "I think he was shot."

"Sav?" Sandra says to him, poking his hip. "Can you hear me? Are you hurt?"

Sav stirs a little. Moans. His eyes open.

"Call an ambulance," Sandra says.

"You better get on the horn, Marie," Donnie says, finishing off his whiskey and trailing his index finger over the butt of the gun on the bar in front of him.

Marie finally picks up the receiver on the black phone behind the bar. Her call to the nine-one-one dispatcher is less than enthusiastic. "A shot guy ran into my place of business," she says. She gives the address. "Not dead yet, no. Being tended to by his slut girlfriend."

Jane can tell Marie fears trouble raining down on her humble little dive. In ten minutes or less, the place will be full of cops and EMS workers. That's Sav's fault. No doubt, if he makes it, he'll wind up in the Book of Bans. Widow Marie is put the fuck out.

"Who did this to you?" Sandra asks Sav.

He struggles to make words but finally spits it out: "Double Stevie shot me. Gilly the Gambler dressed me up."

"Jesus Christ," Sandra says, leaning over him so her shorts ride halfway up her ass. "What the hell?"

"I wanted to run away with you," Sav says.

Martina goes over and picks up the bat that Jane used on Double Stevie earlier. She runs to Sav and starts pounding on him. Her swings are savage.

She seems bent on putting the finishing touches on him. He never had any dignity to lose but has descended into some special hell where he's wound up wearing bell-bottoms, wrapped in Saran Wrap, shot, and is now being beat to a pulp by a bat-wielding flopped bathroom suicide.

Sandra tries to stop Martina but takes a hit to the shoulder and backs off. She's screeching. Her hands over her mouth, those long pink nails crawling up her cheeks.

"A fucking clown car," Donnie says and splits.

He's not wrong. Jane feels like she's under a circus tent. Seven of them in this joint, including Alkie Eleanor, who's due to pop up any second and scream about raisins. Martina's really going to town on Sav now, Jane deciding not to step in. Sometimes, she decides, a woman's just got to let another woman beat a piece of shit man to death with a baseball bat. Sandra's screeching rattles the walls and windows of the bar. She sounds like a bus accident.

Alkie Eleanor is awake and quiet for once. The scene's even got her flustered.

Widow Marie has her hands over her ears. She wants it all to end. She wants scratch-offs and silence.

Martina pounds on Sav until she's exhausted and then drops the bat on his body. It clangs on the floor next to him. A horrible sound. Martina has opened up a gash in Sav's head.

Sandra stops screaming and collapses over Sav, clawing at the Saran Wrap with those godforsaken nails.

Sirens ride the night air. They're coming for Sav, to haul him away or resuscitate him. Jane pictures the ambulance guys trying to piece together the puzzle of what went on here. She puts a hand on Martina's back and walks her back to the bar. Martina is weeping. Crying's not the right word. Weeping like someone weeps at a funeral. It might very well be holy water erupting from her eyes. "There you go," Jane says, setting the stranger up on a stool. "You belong right here. You belong with us."

"He killed Jerry," Martina says. "He didn't have to, but he killed him."

"I know he did," Jane says, buzzing with ecstasy. Such madness in the air. City-thick, steaming. Red lights fall over them. Sounds bloom. Sandra chirping to Sav. The bat rolling away on the floor. Glasses thumping on the bar. This suddenly feels like the last night of the world.

ABOUT
THE
EDITOR

Maxim Jakubowski is a noted anthology editor based in London, just a mile or so away from where he was born. With over seventy volumes to his credit, including *Invisible Blood*, the thirteen annual volumes of *The Mammoth Book of Best British Mysteries*, and titles on Professor Moriarty, Jack the Ripper, Future Crime and Vintage whodunits. A publisher for over twenty years, he was also the co-owner of London's Murder One bookstore and the crime columnist for *Time Out* and then *The Guardian* for twenty-two years. Stories from his anthologies have won most of the awards in the field on numerous occasions. He is currently the Chair of the Crime Writers' Association and a *Sunday Times* bestselling novelist in another genre.

ABOUT THE CONTRIBUTORS

CHARLES ARDAI is an Edgar and Shamus Award-winning author, as well as the Ellery Queen Award-winning founder and editor of Hard Case Crime, in which capacity he has published the lost work of numerous pulp-era crime writers, including Cornell Woolrich. *The Washington Post* called Ardai's novel *Songs of Innocence* "an instant classic," and Stephen King has called him "a master of the short story." He lives in New York City.

BRANDON BARROWS is the author of several novels for adult audiences in the crime, mystery, and western genres, and the YA fantasy novel *3rd LAW: Mixed Magical Arts*. He has also published more than one hundred short stories and nearly two hundred individual comic book issues. He was a 2021 Mustang Award finalist and a 2022 Derringer Award nominee. Find more at www.brandonbarrowscomics.com and on Twitter at @BrandonBarrows.

Once an actor, a singer and a composer, A.K. BENEDICT is now a bestselling, award-winning writer of novels, short stories and scripts. Her stories have featured in many journals and anthologies including *Best British Short Stories*, *Best British Horror*, *Great British Horror*, *Phantoms*, *New Fears*, *Exit Wounds* and *Invisible Blood*. She won the Scribe Award for one of her many *Doctor Who* universe audio dramas and was shortlisted for the BBC Audio Drama Award for BBC Sounds' *Children of the Stones*. Her novels, including *The Beauty of Murder* and *The Evidence of Ghosts* (both Orion), have received critical acclaim. Her most recent, under the name Alexandra Benedict, is the Amazon fiction bestselling *The Christmas Murder Game*

(Bonnier Zaffre) which was longlisted for the CWA Gold Dagger Award. A.K. is currently writing scripts, another Christmas-based murder mystery and a high concept thriller for Simon & Schuster. She lives in Eastbourne, UK with writer Guy Adam, their daughter, Verity, and their dog, Dame Margaret Rutherford.

WILLIAM BOYLE is the author of five novels: *Gravesend*, which was nominated for the Grand Prix de Littérature Policière in France and shortlisted for the John Creasey (New Blood) Dagger in the UK; *The Lonely Witness*, which was nominated for the Hammett Prize and the Grand Prix de Littérature Policière; *A Friend Is a Gift You Give Yourself*, winner of the Prix Transfuge du meilleur polar étranger in France; *City of Margins*, a *Washington Post* Best Thriller and Mystery Book of 2020; and, most recently, *Shoot the Moonlight Out*. He's also published a story collection, *Death Don't Have No Mercy*.

Multi-award winning author M.W. CRAVEN was born in Carlisle but grew up in Newcastle. He joined the army at sixteen, leaving ten years later to complete a degree in social work. Seventeen years after taking up a probation officer role in Cumbria, at the rank of assistant chief officer, he became a full-time author. *The Puppet Show*, the first book in his Washington Poe and Tilly Bradshaw series, was published by Little, Brown in 2018 and went on to win the Crime Writers' Association Gold Dagger. *Black Summer*, the second in the series, was longlisted for the Gold Dagger, as was book three, *The Curator*. *Dead Ground* was shortlisted for the CWA Steel Dagger and longlisted for the Theakston Old Peculier Crime Novel of the Year. *Dead Ground* and 2022's *The Botanist* were both *Sunday Times* bestsellers. The series has now been translated into twenty-five languages. *Fearless*, the first thriller in the new US-set Ben Koenig series, will be published simultaneously by Flatiron Books in the US and by Little, Brown and Company in the UK in June 2023. He still lives in Carlisle with his wife, Joanne, and when he isn't talking nonsense in the pub, he can usually be found at punk gigs and writing festivals up and down the country. You can find him at www.mwcraven.com or on Twitter at @MWCravenUK.

MASON CROSS's debut novel *The Killing Season* was longlisted for the Theakston's Old Peculier Crime Book of the Year 2015. His second novel, *The Samaritan*, was selected as a Richard & Judy Book Club pick. These were followed by *The Time to Kill, Don't Look For Me, Presumed Dead* and *What*

She Saw Last Night. He has also published two standalone thrillers, *Hunted* and *Darkness Falls,* under the name Alex Knight. Mason lives in Glasgow with his wife and three children. To sign up for the Mason Cross Readers Club for updates and an exclusive short story, go to masoncross.net/readers-club. Find out more at www.masoncross.net.

MAX DÉCHARNÉ is a writer and musician from London. His books include *King's Road, Vulgar Tongues, Hardboiled Hollywood, Straight From The Fridge, Dad* and *A Rocket In My Pocket.* He has written about music for *MOJO* magazine since 1998, and his work has also appeared in the *Sunday Times Colour Magazine, The Observer, The Guardian* and the *Times Literary Supplement,* among others. Max was the drummer in Gallon Drunk, then the singer and principal songwriter with The Flaming Stars. In a long and varied career in the music business, he has recorded many albums and singles, nine John Peel Sessions and played shows all across the USA, Canada, virtually every country in Europe and in Japan. His vinyl solo LP, *New Shade of Black,* was released in the summer of 2022.

O'NEIL DE NOUX writes novels and short stories with forty-three books published, over four hundred short story sales and a screenplay produced in 2000. Much of De Noux's writing is character-driven crime fiction, although he has written in many disciplines including historical fiction, children's fiction, mainstream fiction, mystery, science-fiction, suspense, fantasy, horror, western, literary, religious, romance, erotica and humor. Mr. De Noux is a retired police officer and a former homicide detective. His writing has garnered a number of awards including the Shamus Award twice, the Derringer Award and Police Book of the Year (awarded by PoliceWriters. com). Two of his stories have been featured in the *Best American Mystery Stories* annual anthology (2003 and 2013). He is a past Vice-President of the Private Eye Writers of America. For additional O'Neil De Noux material, go to www.oneildenoux.com.

PAUL DI FILIPPO published his first short story in 1977. Since then, he has accumulated over forty books to his credit, the latest being *The Summer Thieves,* a Vancian space opera. A native Rhode Islander, he lives in Providence, some two blocks distant from the granite marker indicating the birthplace of H. P. Lovecraft, with his partner of nearly five decades, Deborah Newton, a cocker spaniel named Moxie, and a calico cat named Sally.

MARTIN EDWARDS has received the CWA Diamond Dagger, the highest honour in UK crime writing. His previous awards include an Edgar, two Macavitys, and two Daggers. His twenty-one novels include *Gallows Court*, *Mortmain Hall*, and *Blackstone Fell*, all set in the 1930s and featuring Rachel Savernake. His contemporary novels include the Harry Devlin series and the Lake District Mysteries, beginning with *The Coffin Trail*, shortlisted for the Theakston's Old Peculier Prize for best crime novel. His history of crime writing, *The Life of Crime*, was published in 2022 and his other non-fiction includes *The Golden Age of Murder* and *The Story of Classic Crime in 100 Books*. He has edited *Howdunit*, a masterclass in crime writing, and over forty anthologies. He is President of the Detection Club, a founder member of Murder Squad, and consultant to the British Library's Crime Classics.

NEIL GAIMAN is an English author of short fiction, novels, comic books, graphic novels, nonfiction, audio theatre, and films. His works include the comic book series *The Sandman* and novels *Stardust*, *American Gods*, *Coraline* and *The Graveyard Book*. He has won numerous awards, including the Hugo, Nebula, and Bram Stoker awards, as well as the Newbery and Carnegie medals. He is the first author to win both the Newbery and the Carnegie medals for the same work, *The Graveyard Book* (2008). In 2013, *The Ocean at the End of the Lane* was voted Book of the Year in the British National Book Awards. It was later adapted into a critically acclaimed stage play at the Royal National Theatre in London, England that *The Independent* called "...theatre at its best". He also co-authored *Good Omens* with Terry Pratchett and was involved in its TV adaptations. Learn more at www.neilgaiman.com.

JAMES GRADY's first novel *Six Days Of The Condor* became the Robert Redford movie *Three Days Of The Condor* and the Max Irons TV series *Condor*. His most recent novel is *This Train* (2022). Grady has received Italy's Raymond Chandler Medal, France's Grand Prix Du Roman Noir and Japan's Baka-Misu literature award. In 2008, London's *Daily Telegraph* named Grady as one of "50 crime writers to read before you die." In 2015, *The Washington Post* compared his prose to George Orwell and Bob Dylan.

SJI (Susi) Holliday is a writer of dark fiction. She is the UK bestselling author of the creepy and claustrophobic Banktoun trilogy (*Black Wood*, *Willow Walk* and *The Damselfly*), the festive serial killer thriller *The Deaths of December*, the supernatural mystery *The Lingering*, a psychological thriller set on the Trans-Siberian Express *(Violet)* currently being developed for film, and a horror novella *(Mr Sandman)*. Her latest two novels are techno-thrillers: *The Last Resort* and *Substitute*. By day, she works in clinical research. Follow Susi on Twitter at @SJIHolliday or visit her website at www.sjiholliday.com.

USA Today bestselling author Samantha Lee Howe's breakaway debut psychological thriller, *The Stranger In Our Bed*, was released in February 2020 with Harper Collins imprint One More Chapter. Within the first few days the book rapidly became a *USA Today* bestseller. Film rights have since been sold to Buffalo Dragon, and *The Stranger in Our Bed* feature film will be released internationally in Autumn 2022. One More Chapter has since published Samantha's explosive spy trilogy, *The House of Killers* (*The House of Killers #1*), *Kill Or Die #2* and *Kill A Spy #3*. To date, Samantha has written twenty-five novels, three novellas, three collections, over fifty short stories, an audio drama, a *Doctor Who* spin-off drama that went to DVD, and the screenplay for *The Stranger in our Bed*. For more information visit www.samanthaleehowe.co.uk.

Maxim Jakubowski is a London-based former publisher, editor, writer and translator. He has compiled over one hundred anthologies in a variety of genres, many of which have garnered awards. He is a past winner of the Karel and Anthony awards, and in 2019 was given the prestigious Red Herring award by the Crime Writers' Association for his contribution to the genre. He broadcasts regularly on radio and TV, reviews for diverse newspapers and magazines, and has been a judge for several literary awards. He is the author of twenty novels, including *The Louisiana Republic* (2018), his latest *The Piper's Dance* (2021) and a series of *Sunday Times* bestselling novels under a pseudonym. He has also published six collections of his own short stories, the latest being *Death Has a Thousand Faces* (2022). He is currently Chair of the Crime Writers' Association. Visit his website at www.maximjakubowski.co.uk.

Vaseem Khan is the author of two award-winning crime series set in India, the *Baby Ganesh Agency* series set in modern Mumbai, and the *Malabar House* historical crime novels set in 1950s Bombay. His first book, *The Unexpected Inheritance of Inspector Chopra,* was selected by the *Sunday Times* as one of the forty best crime novels published 2015–2020, and is translated into sixteen languages. The second in the series won the Shamus Award in the US. Vaseem was born in England, but spent a decade working in India. In 2021, *Midnight at Malabar House* won the Crime Writers' Association Historical Dagger, the world's premier award for historical crime fiction. Vaseem also co-hosts the popular crime fiction podcast, The Red Hot Chilli Writers. His website is www.vaseemkhan.com.

Joel Lane was a British novelist, short story writer, poet, critic and anthology editor. He received the World Fantasy Award in 2013 and the British Fantasy Award twice. He wrote two novels, seven collections of short stories, and four poetry collections. He also edited several anthologies. He died in 2013.

Joe R. Lansdale is the author of fifty novels and four hundred shorter works, including stories, essays, reviews, film and TV scripts, introductions and magazine articles, as well as a book of poetry. His work has been made into films such as *Bubba Hotep* and *Cold in July,* as well as the acclaimed TV show, *Hap and Leonard.* He has also had works adapted to *Masters of Horror* on *Showtime,* Netflix's *Love, Death and Robots,* Shudder's *Creepshow* and written scripts for *Batman: The Animated Series,* and *Superman: The Animated Series.* He scripted a special Jonah Hex animated short, as well as the animated Batman film, *Son of Batman.* He has also written scripts for John Irvin, John Wells, and Ridley Scott, as well as for the Sundance TV show based on his work, *Hap and Leonard.* He has received numerous recognitions for his work. Among them the Edgar, for his crime novel *The Bottoms, The Spur* and for his historical western *Paradise Sky,* as well as ten Bram Stokers for his horror works. He has also received the Grand Master Award and the Lifetime Achievement Award from the Horror Writers Association. He has been recognised for his contributions to comics with the Inkpot Life Achievement Award, and has received the British Fantasy Award. He has been honored with the Italian Grinzane Cavour Prize, the Sugar Pulp Prize for Fiction, and the Raymond Chandler

Lifetime Achievement Award. His work has also been nominated multiple times for the World Fantasy Award, and numerous Bram Stoker Awards, the Macavity Award, as well as the Dashiell Hammett Award, and others. He lives in Nacogdoches, Texas with his wife, Karen. Visit him at www.joerlansdale.com.

BARRY N. MALZBERG was Cornell's agent at the Scott Meredith Literary Agency in 1967, and was able to sell a trunk short story, 'Warrant of Arrest' (Escapade 1968) and secure a multi-reissue contract from Ace Books, only two or three of which novels were published. Cornell was a cult writer, highly respected but little read at that time; he was kind enough to say that Malzberg had done more for him than any agent previously. (A sad admission.) He was a long broken man and writer then but his work and persona glowed and Malzberg was and remains in posthumous awe. He went on (to his surprise) to have almost a third of his own career – seventeen novels, sixty short stories – in the mystery field, and through the years has always tried to defend and propitiate. Woolrich was a major influence on his first science fiction novel, *The Empty People* and an inspiration for a fierce pastiche, 'The Interceptor' (Mike Shayne Magazine) which made it on Cornell's behalf into Allan Hubin's Best Mystery Annual. His younger daughter's name is Erika Cornell.

NICK MAMATAS is the author of several novels, including the metaphysical thrillers *I Am Providence* and *The Second Shooter*, and of over one hundred short stories. His crime fiction has appeared in *Best American Mystery Stories*, *Ellery Queen*, and three different volumes of the Akashic Books *Noir* series. Nick has also published many science fiction and horror stories, literary fiction, and essays, as well as working as an editor in his own right. His latest anthology is *Wonder and Glory Forever: Awe-Inspiring Lovecraftian Fiction*. Nick's fiction and editorial work has variously been nominated for the Hugo, Locus, Bram Stoker, Shirley Jackson, and World Fantasy awards.

DONNA MOORE is the author of two humorous crime fiction novels. Her first novel, *Go To Helena Handbasket*, won the Lefty Award for most humorous crime fiction novel and her second novel, *Old Dogs*, was shortlisted for both the Lefty and Last Laugh Awards. Her short stories have been published in various anthologies. In her day job she works as an adult literacy tutor for marginalised and vulnerable women, facilitates creative writing workshops and has a PhD in creative writing around women's history and gender-based violence. She is also co-host of the CrimeFest crime fiction convention and is a fan of film noir, 1970s punk rock and German Expressionist artists.

WARREN MOORE was born in Nashville and raised in the 'burbs of Nashville and Cincinnati. He is Professor of English at Newberry College in Newberry, SC. Along the way, he has been a journalist, tire salesman, stand-up comic, advertising copywriter, magazine editor, and drummer in assorted unsuccessful bands. He finished tied for 105th in the 1979 National Spelling Bee. Since the publication of his novel, *Broken Glass Waltzes* in 2013, Moore has published more than two dozen short stories, most notably in a series of art-themed anthologies edited by MWA Grandmaster Lawrence Block. Moore lives in Newberry with his wife, and can be found online at profmondo.wordpress.com. He tweets at @profmondo.

TARA MOSS is an internationally bestselling author and award-winning human rights and disability advocate. She has written fourteen books of fiction and non-fiction published in nineteen countries in over a dozen languages, including her #1 international bestselling memoir *The Fictional Woman*. Her latest book is the historical crime thriller *The Ghosts of Paris*, following on from the international bestseller, *The War Widow*, both featuring 1940s 'staunchly feminist, champagne-swilling, fast-driving Nazi hunter' investigator Billie Walker. In 2015 Moss received an Edna Ryan Award for her significant contribution to feminist debate, speaking out for women and children and inspiring others to challenge the status quo, and in 2017 she was recognised as one of the Global Top 50 Diversity Figures in Public Life, for using her position in public life to make a positive impact in diversity, alongside Malala Yousufzai, Angelina Jolie and more. Moss is a long-standing UNICEF ambassador, and uses her profile to reduce stigma of mobility aids in the media and through her page Tara And Wolfie, named for her walking stick. In 2021 she was chosen as a Global Change Maker by *Conscious Being* magazine for her disability and chronic pain activism. She divides her time between Canada and Australia. Visit her at www.taramoss.com

KIM NEWMAN is a critic, author and broadcaster. He is a contributing editor to *Sight & Sound* and *Empire* magazines. His books about film include *Nightmare Movies* and *Kim Newman's Video Dungeon*. His fiction includes the *Anno Dracula* series, *The Hound of the D'Urbervilles* and *An English Ghost Story*. He has written for television (*Mark Kermode's Secrets of Cinema*), radio (*Afternoon Theatre: Cry-Babies*), comics (*Witchfinder: The Mysteries of Unland*) and the theatre (*The Hallowe'en Sessions*), and directed a tiny film (*Missing Girl*). His latest novel is *Something More Than Night* (Titan Books). His website is www.johnnyalucard.com. He is on Twitter at @AnnoDracula.

ANA TERESA PEREIRA is a Portuguese writer and translator. She is the author of more than twenty novels, novellas and short story collections. A reader of Henry James, Ray Bradbury, John Dickson Carr and Cornell Woolrich, she likes to think of her stories as 'abstract crime fiction'. Her last novel, *Karen*, won the Brazilian Oceanos Award (best book in Portuguese language published in 2016.) She lives in Funchal, Madeira.

BILL PRONZINI has been a full-time professional writer since 1969. He has published 90 novels, including 46 in his popular 'Nameless Detective' series. He is also the author of four nonfiction books and twenty collections of short stories, and has edited and co-edited numerous anthologies. In 2008 he was named Mystery Writers of America Grand Master. Among his other achievements are six MWA Edgar nominations, and the Lifetime Achievement Award (presented in 1987) and two Shamus Awards from the Private Eye Writers of America. His suspense novel, *Snowbound*, was the recipient of the 1988 Grand Prix de la Littérature Policière as the best crime novel published in France. Two other suspense novels, *A Wasteland of Strangers* and *The Crimes of Jordan Wise*, were nominated for the Hammett Prize for the best crime novels of 1997 and 2006 respectively.

DAVID QUANTICK writes movie scripts, television shows and books. He wrote the romantic comedy movie *Book of Love*, and several episodes of the HBO series *Veep* for which he won an Emmy. He has also authored many non-fiction titles in the fields of reference and humour, and works extensively for film, TV and radio, including contributions to *The Thick of It*. His novels include *The Mule, Go West, All My Colors* and *Night Train;* his new sci-fi horror novel *Ricky's Hand* is out now.

Kristine Kathryn Rusch writes in every possible genre, sometimes under her name and sometimes as Kris Nelscott and Kristine Grayson. Rusch has won or been nominated for dozens of awards, including the Edgar and the Anthony, as well as the *Ellery Queen Magazine* Readers Choice awards. Her novels have hit bestseller lists worldwide. Her most current mystery novel, *Ten Little Fen*, takes place in a science fiction convention and resembles a cozy, much to her surprise. She usually writes hard-boiled detective fiction at the novel length, particularly under her Nelscott pen name. Her mystery short fiction has appeared in many year's best volumes, including this year's *Best Mystery Stories of the Year*, edited by Sara Paretsky. To find out more about Rusch's work, go to her website at www.kriswrites.com.

The latest of James Sallis's eighteen novels, *Sarah Jane*, was published late 2019 by Soho Press, who also brought out a new uniform edition of the six earlier, landmark novels of the Lew Griffin cycle. Other books include three of musicology, a biography of Chester Himes, a translation of Raymond Queneau's novel *Saint Glinglin*, and the source novel for the Cannes-winning film *Drive*. Jim's work appears regularly in anthologies, literary quarterlies, mystery and science fiction magazines, and is translated worldwide. He's won a lifetime achievement award from Bouchercon, the Hammett Award for literary excellence in crime writing, and the Grand Prix de Littérature Policière.

Lavie Tidhar is author of *Osama*, *The Violent Century*, *A Man Lies Dreaming*, *Central Station*, *Unholy Land*, *By Force Alone*, *The Hood* and *The Escapement*. His latest novels are *Maror* and *Neom*. His work encompasses children's books (*The Candy Mafia*), comics (*Adler*), anthologies (*The Best of World SF* series) and numerous short stories. His awards include the World Fantasy Award, the British Fantasy Award, the John W. Campbell Award, the Neukom Prize and the Jerwood Fiction Uncovered Prize, and he has been shortlisted for the Clarke Award, the Philip K. Dick Award and the CWA Dagger, amongst many others.

Joseph S. Walker lives in Indiana and teaches college literature and composition courses. His short fiction has appeared in *Alfred Hitchcock's Mystery Magazine*, *Ellery Queen's Mystery Magazine*, *Mystery Weekly*, *Tough*, and a number of other magazines and anthologies. He has been nominated for the Edgar Award and the Derringer Award, and has won the Bill Crider

Prize for Short Fiction. He also won the Al Blanchard Award in 2019 and 2021. Follow him on Twitter at @JSWalkerAuthor and visit his website at www.jsw47408.wixsite.com/website.

For more fantastic fiction, author events, exclusive
excerpts, competitions, limited editions and more

VISIT OUR WEBSITE
titanbooks.com

LIKE US ON FACEBOOK
facebook.com/titanbooks

FOLLOW US ON TWITTER
@TitanBooks

EMAIL US
readerfeedback@titanemail.com